SARAH MAY

# The Missing Marriage

HARPER

HARPER

An imprint of HarperCollins*Publishers*
77–85 Fulham Palace Road,
Hammersmith, London W6 8JB

www.harpercollins.co.uk

A paperback original 2011

Copyright © Sarah May 2011

Sarah May asserts the moral right to
be identified as the author of this work

This novel is entirely a work of fiction. The names,
characters and incidents portrayed in it are the work
of the author's imagination. Any resemblance to actual
persons, living or dead, events or localities
is entirely coincidental.

ISBN 978-0-00-732211-4

Set in Meridien by Palimpsest Book Production Ltd
Falkirk, Stirlingshire

Printed and bound in Great Britain by
Clays Ltd, St Ives plc

**Mixed Sources**
Product group from well-managed
forests and other controlled sources
www.fsc.org  Cert no. SW-COC-001806
© 1996 Forest Stewardship Council
FSC

This book is dedicated to George Gowans and Robert Hutchinson, who spent too long underground . . . and to the women they left behind.

# Prologue

Anna Faust saw Bryan Deane three times the day he disappeared – twice on land, and once in the sea. There was nothing remarkable about this. A lot of people saw Bryan the day he disappeared – people who knew him as Bryan Deane, and people who didn't. The fact that Anna saw him six months later near the old bandstand on South beach – newly painted in a retina jumping white – *was* remarkable. It was remarkable because only the day before the Blyth coroner had announced an open verdict on the disappearance of Bryan Deane on Saturday 11 April 2008 – Easter Saturday – age thirty-five.

Bryan Deane was officially missing presumed dead the day Anna saw him on South beach.

His brown hair, which used to have natural auburn highlights when the sun caught it, had been bleached Scandinavian blond. He'd lost about two stone in weight as well, which had the effect of making him look taller.

The man Anna saw that day – the only other person on the beach apart from herself and a bundled up woman yelling at a black Labrador standing motionless in the long rolling sea – looked nothing like Bryan Deane, but she recognised

1

him immediately despite the distance between them. She felt him in her stomach and lungs as a rising nausea, which was where she had always felt Bryan Deane ever since she first laid eyes on him in the summer of 1985 when she was eleven and he was twelve. It was how she felt him six months ago after seeing him for the first time in sixteen years, stood next to his fifteen-year-old daughter, Martha, the day he disappeared.

And when she saw him on South beach, the day after the coroner's verdict was given, it didn't surprise her; it was confirmation of what she had somehow known all along – Bryan Deane hadn't disappeared so much as failed to return . . . as Bryan Deane, anyway.

But then men – and occasionally women – have disappeared under circumstances far more infamous than those surrounding Bryan Deane; so infamous, in fact, that they have gone down in history.

Take Al-Hakim bi-Amr Allah, who mounted his donkey one night as sixth Fatimid Caliph and sixteenth Ismaili Imam, and rode into the al-Muqattan hills outside Cairo – only to dismount from the same donkey as somebody completely different. Al-Hakim bi-Amr Allah was never seen or heard of again.

Tsar Alexander I went so far as to die at Tagarog and be interred at the St Peter and Paul Cathedral of the Peter and Paul Fortress, St Petersburg – all so that he could go on living life, in one version of the story anyway, as Feodor Kuzmich in Siberia. When Soviet authorities opened Alexander's tomb in 1925, it was empty.

Who knows what prompted Ducat, Marshal and the Occasional – all three of them lighthouse keepers on Flannan Isles – to vacate their lives so suddenly one day that they left their beds unmade, the clocks stopped, a chair overturned by the kitchen table, and one set of oilskins hanging still from their peg? And who thought to ask John Stonehouse whether he preferred life as John Stonehouse, Labour MP, or – following the collapse of his companies, revelations about his extra-marital affair, and his own drowning – as a man called Joe Markham?

As Anna Faust walked into the Deanes' house – and marriage – on Easter Saturday 2008, she knew that disappearances were classified as victimless crimes. But where did that leave Bryan's stunned yet immaculate, highlighted blonde wife, Laura? Or his daughter, Martha?

Even the Spaniel, Roxy, sprawled impartially over Laura Deane's carefully positioned feet, had rolling eyes as she attempted to grapple with the notion – both instinctive and observed – that an event of such seismic significance had occurred that Laura had forgotten to feed her. Laura had also sat on her where she lay curled up and blinking in the corner of the sofa, waiting patiently for *Strictly Come Dancing* to be switched on. Not only sat on her, but become uncharacteristically furious. Laura really wasn't herself tonight, Roxy thought.

Then the police arrived.

# 1

It was almost midnight when Doreen Hamilton stepped through the front door to number seventeen Parkview and pulled it shut behind her. Holding onto the latch, she swung her body – buttoned up from throat to ankles in a quilted dressing gown that had been a Christmas gift from her daughter, Laura – away from her home of over fifty years into the night. Panting, she peered blindly through the retreating fret at the only thing she could see – the streetlight growing out of the pavement on the other side of the garden wall – and let go of the latch.

Keeping the orange streetlight to her left, she shuffled in slippers – which pre-dated the dressing gown by a year and which had a navy blue fleur de lys Doreen had never seen embroidered on them – along the front of the house, feeling her way.

When she ran out of house, she turned left – the orange light was ahead of her now – following the path until she reached the gate. It was a relief to feel its solid wood beneath her hands, and she stood there for a moment running her fingers nimbly over the edges of a sign made for them by their granddaughter, Martha, in more innocent times. She'd never seen the sign – she'd never seen the pink and yellow patio tiles paving the garden either or the stone wishing well and oak barrel planter where a relatively robust looking dwarf conifer was growing, circled by primroses – but she knew what it said: *No leaflets or junk mail.*

Her breath was quick and hissing. She could hear it – a sound close by – as she clicked up the latch and opened the gate. Out on the pavement there were other sounds – sounds that didn't belong here on the edges of the Hartford Estate where families wanting to stay afloat above the tide of social debris put in for transfers to; where vegetables were grown, laundry dried outside, and windows cleaned. The sounds came from the centre of the estate – a primitive black hole with severed amenities, boarded-up windows and bonfires burning day and night – where things had gone bad.

Feeling suddenly fretful, Doreen felt out the gate to the house next door, number nineteen, where the Fausts lived. The Fausts and the Hamiltons had been among the estate's first residents in 1954, and so proud of their new council homes that they threw parties for less fortunate friends and family still consigned to the damp, crowded miners' rows.

There was a nail on the left hand post she remembered not to snag the sleeve of her dressing gown on; she also remembered that the Fausts' gate had sunk on its hinges and needed lifting slightly. She remembered all this despite the succession of low-strung whimpering sounds she was making as she shuffled blindly – the orange streetlight was behind her now – up the garden path to number nineteen Parkview, her hands moving in slow nervous arcs.

She had no idea how long the journey between houses had taken her. Since losing her sight, things needed to be sought out, felt out . . . translated. Things took time.

She rang on the bell to number nineteen, her right palm flat against the door, overcome by the physical reverberations of relief at reaching her destination. She listened – and thought she heard the sounds of a bed giving up its sleeper; uncertain footsteps. Crouching down awkwardly, she opened the letterbox and shouted hoarsely through it – 'Mary, it's me – Doreen!'

She could smell the new gloss on the front door; she could even smell the green in it as she straightened up slowly, her left hand pulling on the collar of her dressing gown. The last time she'd knocked on Mary Faust's door at midnight – on anyone's door at midnight – was the night Laura was born. She'd been told she couldn't have children, then in 1974 – unexpectedly at the age of forty-two – she became pregnant. She never did make it to the hospital. Laura was born on the bathroom floor at number nineteen – delivered by a shaking, incredulous Mary.

The door to number nineteen opened then and the quality of light changed.

Mary Faust, in a dressing gown not dissimilar to Doreen's – the small tight curls on her head flattened by the hair net she was wearing – peered with concern, and just a shiver of hostility, at her virtually blind neighbour.

Doreen was clutching the collar of her dressing gown. Her mouth looked like broken knicker elastic and the hair on the right-hand side of her head – hair tinted with just a suggestion of purple – was flat with sleep still. Mary wanted to ask her why she wasn't wearing a hair net, but it was midnight and Doreen didn't look like she was up to having an opinion on hair nets right then.

'Doreen?' Mary patted her own hair, satisfied. Doreen was staring straight through her, panting strangely. 'Doreen, pet?' Mary prompted her. The 'pet' was condescending, but she felt that Doreen's frailty, virtual blindness and possible dementia warranted it.

'It's Bryan –' Doreen said at last.

Mary stared at her, trying to work out whether she was sleepwalking. It was difficult to tell with a blind person. 'Bryan?'

'Laura's Bryan. He's gone missing. She's just phoned. The police are there now.'

'Bryan?' Mary said again. It seemed impossible to her, given all the Deanes had achieved – Laura Hamilton had become Laura Deane when she married Bryan. Achievements such as theirs – they owned and lived in a four-bedroom detached house, and ran two cars – were meant to safeguard against tragedy. 'Missing how?'

'I don't know. Laura said he never came home.'

'From where?'

'I don't know. Something to do with a kayak. He was in the sea, and – I can't help thinking –.'

'Don't think,' Mary commanded. 'It'll give you vertigo, and you'll feel it in your joints. Where's Don?' Mary couldn't see the car where it was usually parked beneath the street light.

'He's driven over there. He took Martha with him.'

Martha was Laura and Bryan's fifteen-year-old daughter. She stayed with her grandparents most weekends.

'You'd better come in,' Mary said, taking hold of Doreen's arm and pulling her into the house.

'I didn't mean to bother you. Not with Erwin ill . . .'

'He's out cold. Morphine.'

Mary was almost cheerful now as she pushed Doreen gently into the living room, guiding her to the sofa beneath the copper engraving of the Chillingham Cattle.

Doreen poised rigidly on the edge, her left hand curled in her lap, her right hand gripping the armrest as if anticipating motion. She could smell carpet and the wood of the sideboard – as well as Lily of the Valley vapours from a bath Mary had taken earlier. She was breathless with disbelief still – even after telling Mary, who she could hear now making tea in the kitchenette.

There were other sounds – a man and woman making love – coming through the wall behind her from next door where a young family lived; a nice family, just trying to make their way in the world. Doreen felt briefly glad for them, then the panic set in again as she thought about Laura, who used to be such a happy little girl. Shocked, Doreen realised that subconsciously she must have noticed that lately Laura hadn't been happy; Laura hadn't been happy at all, but this wasn't something they ever talked about because they didn't talk about much these days.

She felt a sudden, inexplicable resentment towards Laura then, which had something to do with the dressing gown she was wearing and how much she'd always disliked it. She'd disliked it for being exactly what it was – an ugly, synthetic body bag she was meant to express senile thanks for because she was at the end of her life. It had been chosen carelessly and at the last minute – from the racks of a shop Laura would never have bought anything for herself in. When had she, Doreen, ever given the impression that silk had lost its meaning now she was over seventy? Doreen started to cry.

Mary stood in the kitchenette – her hand on the teapot; about to pour – on the phone to her granddaughter, Anna. Not only because Anna was police, but because she, Laura and Bryan had all grown up together here on the Hartford Estate.

Laura and Anna had lived next door to each other since birth, and as both of them remained only children a friendship would have been natural enough, but it had been more than friendship. They sought each other out intentionally and, growing up, they were inseparable – their own world

– until the summer after the eleven plus, which Anna passed and Laura didn't.

Mary had been telling herself for the past twenty-three years that it was the eleven plus that came between Laura and Anna, but it wasn't – that same summer, the summer of '85, the Deanes moved onto the Hartford Estate. They moved into number fifteen Parkview, next door to the Hamiltons. Bryan Deane was twelve at the time – a year older than Anna and Laura.

As she came off the phone, she heard crying on the other side of the frosted glass door separating the kitchenette from the living room.

She went through, her feet silent in the carpet's thick pile.

Doreen's skin was too loose and thin to absorb the tears whose run-off was cascading from the edge of her chin onto her dressing gown.

'I've come out without my keys and there's nobody at home. I'm locked out, Mary,' she said – as if this failing on her part far outweighed her son-in-law's disappearance. 'Stupid – stupid,' she moaned, distraught with anger, thumping her left fist into her lap.

Anna Faust slowed down, steering the yellow Ford Capri, in which she'd driven north the previous Saturday, into the small Duneside development outside Seaton Sluice where the Deanes lived. A wind was picking up, making the flags ring on their masts at the entrance to the estate while shifting the sea fret that had come in with the tide that afternoon – a dense, rolling blanket of fog this stretch of the north-east coast was famous for.

It was Easter Saturday and unnaturally quiet after London – something she hadn't got used to yet.

Marine Drive was a road of four- and five-bedroom detached homes whose uniform banality could only be described as 'executive' – a marketing ploy that explained nothing and promised everything. The houses backed onto the main road, but had sea views.

The Deanes' house – the first one, number two – was as honey-coloured as the rest of the houses on Marine Drive, which all gave the impression that they'd been tailored to suit the needs of their owners when in fact it was the owners who'd been trained – by forces far greater than themselves – to fulfil the requirements of the houses. Requirements including, but not limited to – Anna took a glance at number two and its immediate neighbours – a household income of at least eighty thousand, and a minimum of two cars to fill the double garage and drive. Preferably children – definitely pets.

After more than a decade in London 'eighty thousand' had lost its meaning, but up here it was still hard to come by – still currency.

She cast her eyes instinctively over the puddles of architectural foliage in the front garden of number two, then back up at the honey-coloured façade, aware that she was looking for signs of Bryan in all this.

Anna hadn't seen Bryan or Bryan's wife, Laura, since she and Laura were eighteen when Laura Deane had been Laura Hamilton still. But she knew all about the Deanes and their house at number two Marine Drive – Mary had described it in such breathless detail – because Mary approved of the Deanes and the way the Deanes lived their lives in a way she didn't approve of Anna.

At Friday's Methodist Church coffee morning, Mary would talk loudly and insistently about her granddaughter, Anna, and while she was talking, still loudly, still proudly, she was trying simultaneously to fathom why it was Anna lived so far away, and why it was Anna lived alone.

She'd always been ambitious for her granddaughter, but

11

Anna's achievements didn't translate into anything she – or anybody else at the Methodist Church coffee morning – understood. While Laura Deane had a four-bedroom house with a conservatory and separate utility room. She had a beautiful kitchen with an in-built microwave the size of an oven. People understood these things, and such recognisable achievements were given their due reverence by the Friday morning audience.

Unlike the Hartford Estate – where Anna, Laura, and Bryan had all grown up and where Anna's grandparents and Laura's parents still lived – Marine Drive didn't often see police squad cars, but tonight there was one parked on the drive to number two, sandwiched between two other cars. One of those Anna recognised as belonging to Laura's father, Don Hamilton, and the other one had to be Laura's.

Don – like Erwin Faust – used to work at Hartford Pit, and when that closed down Don got work at Bates and Erwin, who was near retirement, got work cleaning the buses at the Ashington Depot. He was still referred to locally as 'the German' by the older generation because he'd spent most of the war as a POW in Camp Eden, Stanton.

As she got out of her car, sensor-triggered security lighting suddenly illuminated the driveway and front garden of number two and she saw Don Hamilton walking towards his car.

'Don!'

He stared at her, not recognising her for a moment. 'Anna?'

'Nan's just phoned – about Bryan.'

As if embarrassed at this disturbance of the peace his family was responsible for, Don shook his head, which had been sporting the same Teddy boy haircut for as long as Anna had known him.

He'd put on a shirt, pressed trousers, sports jacket and loafers – with buckles that shone under the security lighting – in order to face the unexpected tragedy of his son-in-law's disappearance. It disturbed Don profoundly because he didn't think things like this happened to people who lived in four-bedroom detached houses. He thought his daughter was safe from harm inside number two Marine Drive, but here was a police car parked on the drive where Bryan's 4x4 should have been.

'You didn't have to come over.'

'Don, it's fine.'

Anna didn't tell him she'd come to give a statement because when Mary phoned just after midnight, it occurred to her – beyond the shock – that she was probably the last person to have seen Bryan, that afternoon on the beach.

'The police are in there speaking to Laura – asking questions.'

'They'll just be routine ones,' Anna reassured him. He looked like he needed reassuring. He looked, in fact, as though someone had been stamping all over his face, and he was trying hard not to bear any grudges.

'They sounded bloody weird to me – some of them.'

'It's not easy, I know, but they have to ask them.'

Don wasn't listening any more. 'They wanted to search the house as well.'

'It's just routine – standard procedure. It's what they do.'

'Well, I didn't think it was right for Martha to hear all of that. I wanted her to wait in the car with me, but she wouldn't. She said she wanted to be there when they were speaking to Laura. They asked her questions as well – Martha.'

Anna had seen the Deanes' fifteen-year-old daughter for the first time that morning – dressed in riding clothes with a brown velvet hat hooked under her arm, hitting lightly at the side of her boots with a crop. A tall, shy girl, who had stood possessively close to Bryan on the pavement outside number seventeen Parkview on the Hartford Estate.

Don stared helplessly at Anna. 'She's in her pyjamas still. I drove her over in her pyjamas. Saturdays she stays with us – I take her to Keenley's Stables.' He ran his tongue nervously round his mouth. 'Laura and Bryan have to work Saturdays, but I suppose it gives them a bit of time together afterwards – just the two of them,' he finished, uncertain.

Anna gave his elbow a squeeze, surprised to find, standing next to him, that they were the same height. She'd always thought of Don as a towering man. 'You get on home. This business with Bryan will sort itself out.'

She stood on the drive and waited for him to put the car into gear and reverse, then move off slowly up the street, obedient to the twenty miles per hour speed limit – and not because she was watching. Don was the sort of man who stuck to the rules even when there was nobody watching.

*Just the two of them.*

Anna had a sudden image of Bryan turning sharply onto the drive she was standing on, laughing, Laura leaning heavily into him. She saw them kissing and touching each other then Bryan switching off the engine and pulling Laura out of the car towards the silent house – Laura holding onto him as he fumbled with the key in the lock.

All three of them – Bryan, Laura, and Anna – knew what it was like to grow up in a mining community after the mass pit closures of the sixties through to the eighties and the Strike of '84-5. What they'd seen growing up had given them a knowledge, and this knowledge had become an appetite for escape.

The two things everybody had plenty of in Blyth by the mid-nineties were despair and heroin, but Bryan, Laura and Anna – in their different ways – clung onto their appetites and watched for a way out. Anna's appetite led her down to King's College, London. Bryan's led him to white collar work and a monthly salary, and Laura – well, Laura only had an appetite for one thing, and that was Bryan. They'd all achieved what they set out to, which was to make the unaffordable things in life affordable, and ensure that their children would never know what it was like to go hungry.

*Just the two of them.*

Anna crossed the drive to the front door, her finger pressing hard on the buzzer.

She'd been bewildered – when she first arrived a week ago – to find herself at this latitude again. It didn't feel like her country any more, although it was unreasonable of her to expect it to after so many years away. Did she even want it to? She didn't look like these people and she didn't speak like them anymore. But she had given them her childhood and she felt, pettishly, that this should have at least entitled her to a temporary sense of belonging.

Maybe the fault didn't lie with them, but with her – and anyway none of this mattered now.

With Bryan's disappearance she was no longer in their world – they were in hers.

# 2

It was Martha Deane who answered the door, in blue and yellow pyjamas that made her look younger than she had in her riding clothes that morning. It struck Anna again how similar to Laura she was – apart from the eyes; the eyes belonged to Bryan. Her hair had been scraped back hurriedly into a pony tail and her face looked uneven from all the crying she'd done. She started to cry again now and, turning away from Anna back into the brightly lit hallway, allowed herself to be held by a uniformed female constable who must have been standing close but out of sight up until then.

'I'm Anna Faust – a friend of the family,' Anna said, stepping inside number two Marine Drive.

The ceiling was punctured with high wattage halogen bulbs whose light reflected harshly off the white walls and polished wood floors so that there were no dark corners, and no shadows. The inside of the house looked like the outside had led her to expect it would. There were no surprises, and nothing that stood out as personal, which – despite the obvious space – made Anna feel claustrophobic.

'Friend of the family,' the constable announced as Anna followed her and Martha into a spacious sitting room where

16

there was another officer – male, late twenties, balding, and not in uniform – and two colossal sofas facing each other across a coffee table, fireplace, mirror, and fading white bouquet.

The constable sat down in one of the sofas, her arm round Martha's shoulders still as Martha, sniffing in an attempt to stop crying, twisted her head so that she could watch Anna.

Laura Deane was sitting in the other sofa, curled in a corner with a small chestnut Spaniel over her feet – also watching Anna, whom she hadn't seen since they were eighteen.

A faint trace of emotion crossed Laura's otherwise immaculate face – a face that had had work done to it: Botox, for sure, possibly a chin tuck, and the nose was definitely thinner than Anna remembered.

Laura wasn't sitting on the sofa so much as positioned in it, and she was positioned carefully with her legs, in loose linen trousers, pulled up under her. She was wearing a tank top the same bright white as the walls to set off her spray tan, and a loose cardigan over it that looked expensive. Light reflected off the heavy jewellery hanging from her wrists and neck and the overall effect was of somebody who either spent a lot of money on themselves or who had money spent on them – maybe a combination of both.

She was as immaculate as the house around her, and gave Anna the same impression of emptiness. It made her want to ask the woman sitting on the sofa in front of her where Laura had gone. Was she keeping her hidden in the attic? Was she up there screaming and banging on the door right now – desperate to be let out? Where had the girl with the mole on her thigh and skin that turned caramel in the real sun gone? Where had the girl with the long blonde hair that was forever getting knotted with twigs and bark and leaves from the trees she climbed gone?

Maybe Laura was thinking the same thing about her.

Maybe they'd just grown up, that was all.

Only Laura, taking in Anna – she did this by barely moving her eyes and remaining otherwise expressionless – had an air of triumph about her. As though she'd just discovered that she'd won the race after all – a race Anna wasn't even aware they'd been running.

'Why are *you* here?'

Anna turned to Martha – who'd pulled herself away from the stranger in uniform she had gone to for comfort instead of her own mother – and who was now sitting upright, her knees pulled into her chest.

'I've known your mum a long time.' Anna paused. 'And your dad as well.'

'So? I never saw you before this morning.'

'How long *has* it been?' Laura said, carefully. 'Sixteen years?'

'S-s-something like that.'

Anna exhaled with relief and opened her eyes, which shut automatically whenever she lost words. Only sporadically, and in extreme circumstances, did her childhood speech impediment come back. The moment had passed – and with it the feeling that she'd been standing, momentarily, in a precipitous place.

'I heard you'd come back. I'm sorry about Erwin.'

'And I'm sorry – about Bryan.'

The two women stared at each other, without sympathy, aware that the only reason Anna was here, inside number two Marine Drive, was because Bryan Deane wasn't.

'How did you know – about Bryan?' Laura asked calmly.

'Nan phoned. Your mum's been round to see her.'

'Well, we've got the police here already,' Laura carried on, still calm – articulating each word carefully in an ongoing attempt to eliminate any traces of accent in her voice.

'Actually I came to give a statement – I saw Bryan on the beach this afternoon.'

A sense of movement passed through Laura's body that made the Spaniel look up.

Anna swung round to the officer behind her. 'But maybe not here,' she added, taking in Martha who – distraught, tearful and enraged – was displaying all the by-products of shock Laura wasn't.

'Here's fine,' Laura said.

Martha said nothing.

Glancing at Laura, the officer hesitated before sitting down on a footstool covered in the same fabric as the sofa.

'I'm Detective Sergeant Chambers,' he said, getting out a notebook, 'and this is Constable Wade.'

He indicated the woman in uniform on the sofa with Martha, coughed and said stiffly, 'Excuse me,' then, 'which beach was that?'

'Tynemouth Longsands.'

'What time?'

Anna still wasn't sure about doing this in front of Martha. 'About half four. He was about to go out in a kayak – a P&H Quest kayak – red and black.' She paused. 'But you've probably got that already.'

She felt Martha watching her as Laura said, 'That kayak's been in our garage for months and I couldn't even have told you what colour it was.'

The officer was silent for a moment. 'Were you in a kayak?'

'I was surfing.'

'Had you arranged to meet?'

Laura's head was balanced on the Spaniel's head. The Spaniel was whimpering.

Anna wondered – briefly – what the dog was called, before turning back to DS Chambers. 'No. It was a chance encounter.'

'Did you speak to him?'

'Not in the water, no.'

'On the beach?'

'Not as such. Just about the weather.'

The first time she saw him that day, outside number seventeen Parkview with Martha, he looked and felt like somebody's husband . . . somebody's father. Standing beside her on the beach, he didn't. They'd just looked at each other; taken each other in, and here – in front of Bryan's wife and daughter – the recollection felt like a transgression.

There was a silence.

Laura didn't take her eyes off Anna, who was about to speak when the silence was broken by the front door bell ringing. Checking her watch, she saw that it had just gone one. She moved position so that she could see up the hallway as Constable Wade went to open the door and a man in a Barbour jacket, soaking wet, stepped into the house.

He flicked a quick look down the corridor and it wasn't until then that Anna became aware of Martha, standing beside her.

'Who is it?' Laura asked.

'The Inspector from before,' Martha mumbled, disappearing back onto the sofa again.

Everyone in the room became suddenly more alert – even Laura, Anna thought, turning round. No – especially Laura.

'Mrs Deane said just now that you last saw her – was it sixteen years ago?' DS Chambers, speaking loudly now, swung politely towards Laura, who nodded. 'When did you last see *Mr* Deane? Before today that is.'

'It would have been around the same time – sixteen years ago.'

DS Chambers nodded heavily and looked at her.

They were all looking at her.

'But you didn't have anything to say – as such?'

'I'd already seen him – and Martha,' Anna said, turning to the Deanes' daughter, 'this morning over on the Hartford Estate.' DS Chambers didn't comment on this. 'When I saw him on the beach we chatted about the weather conditions, which were good – until the fret came in.'

'He didn't say where he was going when you met him on the beach?'

'He didn't – no.'

'And the next time you saw him – in the water – you didn't speak?'

'No.'

Anna had called out to him when she saw him in the water – in his kayak – trying to steer a course through the surfers. In the water she'd felt much lighter and more confident than she had earlier that morning, on land.

He'd looked confused for a moment then smiled quickly, paddling out to her until his kayak was in line with her board and they were both rising and falling in the waves.

His eyes had touched her briefly as she sat with her legs straddling the board then she'd laughed suddenly and given a wet wave before moving forcibly away from him; lying down on the board and paddling hard out to sea towards the cargo ship filling up so much of the distant horizon it seemed stationary.

She took in two more waves and it was while she was paddling back out after this that the sea fret came in.

Looking around instinctively for Bryan, she'd seen him heading in a direct line north away from her towards Cullercoats and St Mary's Island – against the tide.

Then he disappeared into the fret – and some of Europe's busiest shipping lanes.

'When was the last time you saw him?'

'Like I said, just as the fret was coming in – around five. He must have been about thirty metres out from shore – heading north up the coast.'

One minute the sea had been full of mostly men and some women poised in their wetsuits, looking out to sea

– the next it was as though the sun had become suddenly thicker. She had felt inconsolably alone, hesitant and watchful, unable to make out any other black-suited figures in the water.

Glancing back to shore, the line of people at the edge of the beach and the dogs in the water were visible for a few seconds more then they too vanished – along with the beach, the cliffs behind, the building housing the Toy Museum and Balti Experience, and the spire of St George's Church. She'd tried to keep the board as still in the water as she could – if the nose swung round she knew she'd lose all sense of direction. The beach sounded further away than she knew it was – the waves slapping dully against the shore and voices carrying high one moment only to be suddenly cut off the next. The tide was still coming in, she told herself, aware that the temperature was falling and that she was uncomfortably cold – all she needed to do was take any wave that came and let it carry her in.

Other surfers had the same idea and they came at each other suddenly, figures in black manoeuvring their boards through the water, slightly irate now. Nobody wanted to come off; nobody wanted to be left in the water.

When she finally got back to shore, she stood shivering on the beach, holding the board against her. The headland shielding Cullercoats Bay to the north was lost. She waited a while – for the red and black kayak to come nosing through the fret – but it never did.

'I didn't see him again,' Anna said, 'but by then I could barely see the end of my own board.'

The Inspector was standing in the doorway to the sitting room, watching her with a blank face, the skin pockmarked across the lower cheeks as though someone had repeatedly attempted to puncture him there.

'Sir, this is Anna Faust – a friend of the family,' DS

Chambers said, starting to cough again. 'I think we've got a last sighting.'

The Inspector nodded at her – Anna wondered how long he had been standing there – introducing himself in a rapid mumble as, 'Detective Inspector Laviolette.'

His re-appearance had created a sense of expectancy, and focus.

His coat and hair were soaked with rain and Laura Deane's eyes automatically followed the drops as they ran off his coat and onto the solid oak floor. Her eyes unconsciously checked the hallway behind him as well – for footprints – because this wasn't a house that encouraged people to leave a trace.

'It's raining outside,' he said to her. Then, suddenly, 'D'you mind if we go over a few more things, Mrs Deane – in light of this new statement?'

He shuffled forward awkwardly, the soles of his shoes squeaking on the polished wood floor.

After a second's hesitation and a brief smile he sat down on the same sofa as Martha, who automatically pushed herself further back into the corner.

'Haven't we been over everything?'

Ignoring this, Laviolette said, 'When did Bryan say he'd be home by?'

Anna had the impression that he was doing this for her benefit – that he wanted to question Laura in front of her.

Laura took a while to answer, looking momentarily distracted – as if she had far more important things to attend to than her husband's disappearance.

'Around seven,' she said, pronouncing the words as carefully as she had when she spoke to Anna before. 'We had lunch in Tynemouth then I went into Newcastle and he took the kayak out.'

'And you haven't been in contact at all since lunch?'

Laura was thinking. 'He called me – around three thirty – but that's it.'

'What time did you get back from Newcastle?'

Laura shrugged. 'I can't remember – it must have been before eight because Strictly Come Dancing's on at eight, and we watched that.'

Turning to Martha, Laviolette said pleasantly, 'You like Strictly Come Dancing?'

'I think it's shit.'

'Martha!' Laura interceded sharply, losing her composure for the first time.

'When she says "we",' Martha explained, 'she's talking about the dog – Roxy. They watch it together.'

They all turned to stare at Roxy who, becoming conscious of the sudden attention, raised her head from Laura's ankles and panted expectantly.

'Did you check the garage when you got home – to see if his kayak or his wetsuit were there?'

'Not until later, no.'

'And his car wasn't on the drive?'

'No.'

'When did you first try ringing Mr Deane?' the Inspector asked after a while

'As soon I came in and realised he wasn't here.'

'And he didn't pick up?'

'I left a message. Then I rang two of his friends – ones he sometimes meets at the pub – in case he'd gone there – and they hadn't seen him.'

'You've got their names and details?'

This was directed at DS Chambers, who'd been looking at Laura.

'And the pub he sometimes goes to?'

'The Shipwrights Arms,' DS Chambers said. 'We've already been there – nothing.'

'You've got all this,' Laura said, openly hostile now.

'Sir, we've done a full open door search – this isn't a voluntary disappearance.'

Inspector Laviolette turned suddenly to Anna. 'When did you find out that Mr Deane hadn't come home?'

'Six minutes past midnight. Mrs Hamilton told my grandmother, who then phoned me. They're old friends.'

'Six minutes past midnight,' Laviolette repeated as something close to a smile crossed his face so rapidly Anna wouldn't have noticed it if she hadn't been looking. 'And then you drove over here –'

'To give a statement. I saw Bryan Deane this afternoon down on Tynemouth Longsands – as you heard.'

Laviolette turned back to Laura, without comment.

'So Bryan was meant to be home around seven, and you phoned his two friends roughly when?'

'Around eight – I was worried.'

'Around eight,' Laviolette repeated. 'He was an hour late at that point – when you phoned.' The Inspector was silent for a moment. 'Is he not usually late?'

'He's not – no.' Laura's stance was becoming increasingly defensive. 'Look, I told you – they said he was never there. His car wasn't on the drive and his kayak wasn't in the garage,' she carried on, raising her voice and looking genuinely upset. 'He's never not come home before. Why don't you *do* something?' she exploded. 'Why aren't you out there looking for him?' She collapsed back in the sofa, her hand over her face.

Anna looked quickly at Martha, who was staring at her mother with a mixture of worry and what could only be described as hatred.

'Look,' the Inspector said sounding suddenly exhausted; apologetic. 'I'm going to try and get this categorised as high risk.'

Laura, looking surprised, at last uncurled herself from the sofa and stood up, the linen falling in crumpled folds around her, the abandoned Roxy looking momentarily confused.

'DS Chambers and Constable Wade will stay here with you. There's a lot of procedure it's essential you understand.' He broke off, staring thoughtfully at Laura. 'Did your husband have a nickname?'

'A nickname?' Laura shook her head, glancing quickly at Anna.

The Inspector noted the glance then turned to DS Chambers. 'Can I have a look at what you've taken down?'

'We've covered a lot,' Chambers said.

Laviolette nodded absently and read through the investigation notes. 'No distinguishing marks?' he said, looking first at Chambers then Laura Deane. 'No scars? Tattoos? Nothing?'

'No,' Chambers confirmed, sullen.

Laura said nothing.

Anna was watching her, her face momentarily tense with conflict. 'What about the appendicitis scar?' she said at last, appealing not to the Inspector – but Laura.

'He never had an appendicitis,' Laura said, her eyes on Anna again.

Feeling Martha's eyes on her as well, Anna smiled quickly at her before turning back to Laura. 'It happened before we knew him,' she responded, uncertain, 'but it was always there. Unless it's faded or – I don't know, do scars like that fade?' This time, she appealed to the Inspector, who was staring at her.

'Can I have a few words – my car?' he said at last.

Anna and Laviolette left the room, making their way up the hallway followed slowly by Laura – who made no attempt to speak to Anna.

They stood outside, the rain that had started since Anna's arrival banging on the porch roof.

Laura remained in the doorway, dry and distant, watching as the Inspector and her childhood friend headed out into the night.

'It'll be okay,' Anna shouted back, through the rain. It sounded like a promise, she thought.

'Wait!'

Anna and the Inspector turned round.

Martha Deane had appeared suddenly in the doorway. She pushed past Laura, running barefoot through the rain towards them.

'Martha!' Laura yelled, but she didn't follow her daughter out into the rain.

The next moment Martha slammed into Anna, who almost lost her balance.

She braced herself thinking Martha might start hitting her, but then she felt the girl's narrow arms tighten round her waist, and understood.

She hugged her back – for no reason – just as hard. Martha's thin pyjamas were already soaked through at the shoulders, as was her hair, pressed into Anna's red sweater. The girl's earlier hostility had been replaced by a sudden clinging need.

'You were right – about dad's scar. I know the one you're talking about. She was right,' she said, excited, to Laviolette, before turning to Anna again. 'You'll come back, won't you? You'll come back tomorrow?'

Anna smiled down through the rain at her, although Martha was only a head shorter – aware that the Inspector hadn't moved.

'Martha!' Laura yelled again from the front door.

Martha turned and ran back towards the house on tiptoe, her shoulders hunched. She stood in the doorway for a moment, next to Laura, but not touching her, until Laura pulled her back in order to shut the door.

A few seconds later, Anna saw Martha's face at one of the front windows, framed by curtain. Then the face vanished and the curtains fell back into place.

She hesitated for a moment before following the Inspector to an outdated burgundy Vauxhall, the rain loud on the car's roof.

# 3

The Vauxhall had been taken for a valet service recently – very recently. It smelt of cleaning chemicals and the strawberry tree, hanging from the rear view mirror. When the Inspector turned on the car engine in order to get the heating working, music he must have been listening to earlier – some sort of church music – came on automatically and the strawberry fumes from the air freshener intensified, making Anna nauseous. She wondered, briefly, if the car was even his.

'That's not a coat,' he said with a heavy accent, turning off the music and giving her a sideways glance. 'Not for up here anyways.'

She looked down at herself. The jumper had got soaked between the Deanes' house and the Inspector's car.

'What brings you this far north?'

Anna turned to stare at him. 'I was born here,' she said defensively.

He put the windscreen wipers on and for no particular reason it immediately felt less claustrophobic in the car.

'Lung cancer,' she added.

'Not you,' he said, genuinely shocked.

'No – my grandfather. Advanced small cell lung cancer.

The specialist refers to it as "metastatic", which is specialist-speak for cancer that's behaving aggressively.' She stopped speaking, aware that she felt tearful. 'It means there's no hope.'

'I'm sorry to hear that.' Laviolette closed his mouth, and looked away. 'Who's your grandfather?' he asked after a while.

Anna had forgotten that these were the kind of questions people asked up here – questions that sought connections because everybody belonged to somebody. It was difficult to stand alone.

'Erwin – Erwin Faust.'

Laviolette nodded slowly to himself. 'The German.'

'That's him,' Anna said, unsurprised. 'I'm on compassionate leave.'

'How long for?'

'A month.'

'A month?' he said, surprised.

'Unpaid.'

'Where are you on leave from?'

She hesitated. 'The Met.'

Now he was staring at her again. 'Rank?'

'Detective Sergeant.'

'Why didn't you say anything earlier?'

'It didn't seem necessary. I came here tonight as a friend of the family and because I saw Bryan in the sea this afternoon, which could well be a last sighting.'

'A friend of the family – and yet you haven't seen Laura Deane or Bryan Deane for that matter, in over sixteen years.'

They paused, staring through the windscreen at the curve of houses, which looked strangely desolate in the rain – as though they'd been suddenly vacated for some catastrophic reason.

'Was it sudden – your grandfather?'

'Very.'

Anna wondered if Laura could hear the car engine from inside number two, and if she could, would she want to know what they were doing out here still, parked at the end of her drive? As soon as she had this thought, she realised that the Inspector was doing it on purpose. She didn't know how she knew this; she just did.

'D'you want to tell me what you told DS Chambers?'

'You want me to go over my statement again?'

'If you don't mind.'

She didn't answer immediately then when she did, she said, 'DS Chambers didn't like me very much.'

'DS Chambers doesn't like anybody very much at the moment. He's got a newborn baby and he's sleeping on average two hours out of every twenty-four. I think he's got post-natal depression.'

'He liked Laura Deane.' When the Inspector didn't comment on this, she added, 'But you didn't, did you?'

He smiled. 'You're happy for me to correlate what you're about to say with CCTV footage?'

'Of course,' she said, without hesitation. 'I saw Bryan Deane this afternoon. I was surfing on Tynemouth Longsands.'

'Were the waves good?'

'I only go out when they're good.'

He nodded and carried on staring through the windscreen.

'We saw each other on the beach first – I was just about to go in.'

'So you had your surfboard – he had his kayak – who saw who first? Who was at the water's edge first?'

She thought about this, and the obtuseness of the question. 'Me – I guess.' She saw herself toeing the line, the water freezing cold, staring out to sea, waiting. Then Bryan had appeared suddenly to her left. He must have come up behind her, but she didn't want to tell the Inspector this.

'So – he saw you on the beach – came up to you. Did he say anything?'

No – he hadn't. He'd stood beside her, not saying anything.

'We chatted about the weather, sea conditions and stuff – like I said,' she finished flatly, repeating what she'd said earlier – in front of Laura and Martha – to DS Chambers.

After a while, sounding almost regretful, Inspector Laviolette said, 'It was a beautiful day today.'

'It was.'

'The last time you saw Bryan – heading north up the shoreline – presumably you saw him from behind?'

'Yes.'

'It was definitely him?'

'Yes.'

'After sixteen years, you see him from behind in the water as a fret's coming in, and it was definitely him?'

Through the windscreen, Anna saw a fox appear beneath a street lamp before sliding across the garden onto number four's drive – momentarily illuminated by the same security lights that the Deanes had at number two; that all the houses on Marine Drive probably had.

The Inspector sighed, looking at her. 'What happened sixteen years ago?'

'Nothing happened,' she said smoothly, almost believing it herself.

'But you and Laura Deane were close up until then?'

'We grew up together.'

'And Bryan Deane?'

'We all lived next door to each other. Me – Laura – Bryan.'

'So Laura and Bryan Deane were childhood sweethearts?'

'Something like that.' She turned away from him.

'Then what happened?'

'We grew apart. They stayed. I left.'

32

'You didn't keep in touch?'

Anna shook her head. 'Like I said – I l-l-left.'

It took a while to get the word out, but the Inspector didn't look away. He kept his eyes on her – she felt them.

'Only nobody ever does, do they? Not completely, I mean. Childhood's a place you can never go back to, but you never fully escape from it either. Where did you go – when you left?'

'King's College, London.'

'You didn't have to answer that.'

'I know.'

It was warm inside the car now, and the clock said 01:22.

'What did you study? You don't have to answer that either.'

'Criminology and French.'

He smiled suddenly at her.

'What?'

'Nothing. Have you ever seen Martha Deane before?'

'Only in photographs.'

'Only in photographs,' he repeated, quietly.

They were both thinking about the way Martha had come running through the rain towards her.

'We had a call earlier from a security guard at the international ferry terminal on the south side of the Tyne – he thought he saw a body in the water.' Laviolette was watching Anna as he said it. 'You put a call out and people start taking every bit of driftwood they see for a body. Coastguard got a call earlier from a woman at Cullercoats who claimed she saw a body in the water – turned out to be a log.'

Anna was aware that she was holding her breath.

'Well, the security guard *did* see a body – but not our body.'

She exhaled as quietly as she could while the Inspector clicked up the lid of the CD storage unit by the handbrake.

33

There was only one CD in there.

'Can I ask you something?' she said, turning to look at him. 'This has been assessed medium to high risk, hasn't it?'

'After hearing your statement, I'm escalating it to high,' he concluded heavily. 'The sea temperature was around eight degrees Celcius today. The fifty percent immersion survival time for a normally clothed person in reasonable health with no underlying medical conditions is two hours.'

'He wasn't in the sea, he was in a kayak – and he was wearing a wet suit.'

Laviolette tried to prop his elbow on the window, but there was too much condensation. 'How would you describe your relationship to Bryan Deane?'

'Friend of the family,' she said, automatically.

'Did suicide ever cross your mind?'

'No.'

'Said with conviction.' He was smiling again now, a light smile that broke up his face into a network of fine lines. 'Why not? You saw Bryan Deane for the first time today in over sixteen years, and you'd rule out suicide? What makes you so sure?'

'Martha. I saw them together this morning.'

Anna saw again – the tall girl in riding clothes with hair the colour she remembered Laura's being as a child, standing on the grass verge beside her father, not much shorter.

Bryan had his arm round her shoulders and Martha had gripped onto it while staring sullenly at Anna, hitting her crop against the sole of her boot.

'They seemed really connected. I don't know.' She shrugged irritably, aware that the Inspector was smiling at her still. 'I just can't imagine him leaving her behind.' She paused, turning to him. 'You're seriously considering the possibility that the disappearance is voluntary?'

'I don't know much about Bryan Deane, but I do know

that he's Area Manager at Tyneside Properties and that Tyneside Properties have had to shut down two of their branches in the past nine months. Then I hear that he owns an apartment overlooking the marina down at Royal Quays in North Shields that's been on the market for months. Then tonight – as I'm heading home, I hear Bryan Deane's disappeared, and I find that interesting.' He waited for her to say something, rubbing the condensation from the window and staring up at the Deanes' house. 'I wonder what's going on in there now,' he said. The downstairs had gone dark, but there were lights on upstairs. 'Not a lot of love lost between those two. Mother and daughter, I mean.'

Anna remained silent.

'A sad house,' he concluded tonelessly, turning to her. 'Why d'you think that is?'

'A man's disappeared.'

He shook his head. 'That wasn't what I meant. The sadness was underlying. Invasive.'

'Invasive?' She smiled.

'It's funny, isn't it – the things people end up wanting out of life.'

Ignoring this – it was too ambivalent, and she was too exhausted – she said, 'They were in shock.'

'Martha Deane was – yes.'

'And Laura Deane,' Anna insisted, unsure why she suddenly felt the need to insist on this when she hadn't believed it herself. 'There's no right way to show shock – you know that.'

'I think Laura Deane was enjoying the attention – to a point.'

Even though she agreed with him, Anna didn't comment on this. She'd sensed the same thing – as well as a mixture of anxiety and what could only be described as excitement coming off Laura, but she didn't mention this either. Partly because she felt the Inspector already knew these things, and partly because she hadn't yet made up her mind about Inspector Laviolette. She didn't know how she felt about Laura either, but there was definitely an old childish loyalty there, which surprised her. To put it another way, she didn't feel quite ready to sacrifice Laura to the Inspector – not until she was certain of a few more facts herself.

'And I'd like to see Bryan Deane's life insurance policy,' the Inspector added. When this provoked no response either, he said, 'Who are you protecting?'

'Myself.' Looking at the clock in the dashboard, she said, 'For the past twenty minutes I've been unable to shake the impression that I'm somehow under suspicion.'

'Of what?'

Then his phone started ringing. He checked the caller and switched it off, looking momentarily much older. 'I've got to go,' he said. Then, 'I might want to call you again.'

'DS Chambers has got my details.'

He hesitated then dropped the phone back into his coat pocket.

Anna got out of the car.

The rain was easing off, and she was about to shut the door when she said, 'Laviolette's an unusual name.'

'Not to me it isn't.'

She looked up instinctively at the house and he followed her gaze. There was a curtain moving at the window above the front porch, as if it had just been dropped back into place.

'D'you want to know something I noticed?'

She stood waiting by the car.

Even though the rain was easing off, her hair and face felt wet and there was a fine dusting of water over the front of her jumper still.

'Laura Deane's not half as upset by Bryan Deane's disappearance as you are.'

The yellow Ford Capri turned out of the Duneside development and headed north up the coastal road. There were soon high dunes running alongside the car beyond Anna's right shoulder as the beam from St Mary's lighthouse flashed precisely over treacherous waters and, inland, over a betrayed country that was only just getting to its knees again. It wasn't yet standing, but it was at least kneeling and this was what determined local councillors wanted people to know as they set about transforming the past into heritage with the smattering of civic art that had sprung up – like the quayside statue outside the apartment in Blyth that she'd taken a short-term let on.

She took the Links Road past the Royal Northumberland Yacht Club and warehouses on South Harbour before turning into Ridley Avenue, which ran past the recently regenerated Ridley Park. It was where the medical men used to live and practice and was once nicknamed Doctors' Row, even though the houses weren't built as one, low strung, continuous line of brick like the miners'. The houses on Ridley Avenue were detached with gardens to the front and back; gardens with lawns, and borders of flowers, not vegetables.

But the medical men were long gone and all she saw now were poky façades covered in pebbledash, while the original stained glass rising suns – still there in some of the thickset front doors – looked more like they were setting.

She drove slowly down Bridge Street and Quay Road before parking outside the newly converted-to-flats Ridley Arms overlooking the Quayside at Blyth Harbour. Her apartment – open plan in accordance with contemporary notions of constant surveillance – was the only one occupied, even though the re-development of the old harbourside pub into four luxury apartments (the hoardings advertising them were up on the main road still) had been completed nine months ago. But then the kind of people the apartments had been built for didn't exist in Blyth – in Tynemouth maybe or Newcastle, but not Blyth. Blyth wasn't a place people re-located or retired to; it was a place people were born in and stayed. Being born here was the only guarantee for growing to love a landscape so scarred by man it couldn't ask to be loved.

Someone close by was burning a coal fire. It was the smell of her childhood and it hung heavy in the last of the fret. What was left was clinging to the masts of the blue and white Scottish trawlers, but most of the harbour's north wall was visible now and there was a sharp brightness coming from the Alcan dock where aluminium was unloaded for smelting at the Alcan plant. Anna could just make out the red light at the pier end, as well as the thick white trunks of the wind turbines on the north wall – stationary, silent, and sentient.

She was back where she'd started.

# 4

Laura was above her, barefoot, wearing pink and white velour shorts and a grey T-shirt, which had grass stains on the back and a Bugs Bunny transfer on the front – cracked because it was her favourite T-shirt and it had been over-washed. A light tan took the edge off the cuts and bruises running the length of her legs – legs that were swinging away from the branch Anna's hands, hesitant, were reaching out for.

Anna wasn't trying to catch up; she was concentrating all her efforts on keeping going – up; up – and she wasn't barefoot like Laura. She was wearing red plastic basket weave slip-ons because she'd seen too many crawling things in the bark of the tree to want to go barefoot. The shoes had good grip – it wasn't the shoes that were slowing her down, it was her constant need to peer up into the tree in an attempt not only to ascertain how she was going to get up it, but how she was going to get back down.

Laura didn't need to do this – and only occasionally flicked her head upwards. She wasn't interested in the views either as they got higher.

But Anna was.

Anna kept stopping to take in the Cheviot hills in the distance and, down below, their two tents pitched on the fringes of the tree's shadow at the bend in the river. She could see Erwin, standing in the river with his trousers rolled up to his knees, fishing. Mary was lying on their green and blue check picnic rug on the bank, reading a book from the library – a wartime romance set in the backstreets of Liverpool. Anna could see the sun reflecting off her reading glasses.

The tree was oak.

They'd camped under it for the past two summers, but Erwin always forgot to mark the spot on the map so it took them a while to re-discover it each year. It was off the main road that cut across country to Jedburgh, down a single track road with four fords, and up a farm track. Anna had a feeling that Erwin forgot to mark it on the map on purpose because if they put a pencil cross on the Ordnance Survey map and gave the spot a grid reference it would somehow be bad luck and then it might really disappear. They'd found the spot by accident – if they left it alone, it would be there for them next summer.

The summer the Fausts took Laura with them and the girls climbed the tree turned out to be the last summer they'd ever go there, but they didn't know that then.

Oaks make good climbers, but not even Erwin could reach the lower branches of this one so he'd driven into nearby Rothbury and bought rope from a hardware store, hanging it from the lowest branch and tying in knots for hand and foot holds. Once they were up, Laura started rhythmically swinging away from Anna, leaving her to follow.

Now Laura was at the top, sitting with one arm round the trunk that was almost narrow enough for her to hug. She was peering down through the tree, her hair hanging round her, too thick even for the sunlight to get through.

Pleased with herself, she laughed suddenly and Anna saw Erwin, standing in the river, turn round and look up at the tree, his hand cupped against his forehead, shielding his eyes from the sun.

'Come and look,' Laura called out.

The sun was bouncing frantically off whatever it was she was holding in her hand – a penknife – then the next minute she leant into the tree and carved something into the trunk.

Anna started to climb again with renewed determination until a shadow – a large, loud, moving shadow – cut through the sunshine, and the branches at the top of the tree began to shake aggressively as if they'd suddenly woken up to the fact that two trespassers were among them. She heard shouting from below and, looking down, saw that Erwin was no longer in the river but on the grass, running towards the tree, his trousers rolled up at the knee still. Mary's book lay open on the rug and she was standing staring helplessly up at the sky.

There was a helicopter hovering above them – it had come to take Laura away only Laura was too busy carving her initials into the trunk of the tree to notice.

Anna tried to call out, but the helicopter was too loud, getting louder . . .

She woke up suddenly, and thought at first that the sound was the wind turbines on the north harbour wall – then she remembered. The sound she could hear – the sound that had cut through her dream – was the sound of helicopters. It was Easter Sunday and they were searching for Bryan Deane because Bryan Deane had gone missing.

The light in the bedroom was dull, which made her think it was still early when in fact – grabbing at the pile of clothes by the side of the bed and shaking them until her watch and phone fell out – it was almost half ten.

Putting on the watch, she lay back on the pillow for a

while, staring at the ceiling, then got out of bed, her legs heavy.

She walked to the window through the pile of clothes she'd dropped back on the floor and pulled up the blind. Pressing her forehead and the palm of one hand against the cold glass, she took in the rolling grey sky and sea, a fair part of which was taken up by one of the endless succession of super tankers either bringing coal from Poland or Norwegian wood pulp across the North Sea for the British press to turn into newspapers. Her mother, Bettina, used to work in the offices at South Harbour and Erwin, drunk, once told Anna that her father was a Norwegian from one of the ships.

It was dirty weather – squalid; nothing like yesterday – and the sea had an inhospitable rolling swell of about six feet.

A hard sea to survive in, Anna thought.

Through the glass she could hear the cabling on the trawlers moored to the quayside down below, ringing. The third trawler, *Flora's Fancy*, was making its way between the pierheads and out into open sea past the wind turbines, which were turning today – all except the one second from the end on the left by the old coal staithes. There was always one that stood still and silent no matter how hard the others turned.

Just then a red Coastguard helicopter flew over the trawler and turbines, heading straight out to sea before turning and looping southwards back inland.

Anna went into the kitchen and poured herself a bowl of muesli – making a mental note to shop at some point – as another helicopter went overhead.

It wasn't the Coastguard this time, but an RAF Rescue helicopter that would have come from the base at Kinross.

Then her phone started ringing.

She went into the bedroom where she'd left it – it was Laviolette, sooner than she'd expected. Forgetting what he'd said to her before slamming the door of the Vauxhall shut in the early hours of the morning, she asked quickly, 'Has anything come in yet?'

'Nothing. We've launched a full scale open search with MCA collaboration this morning. Conditions aren't great, but they're meant to be getting better. Boats have gone out from Tynemouth, Cullercoats and Blyth, and a couple of private fishing vessels have volunteered to assist.' He hesitated as if about to ask her something then changed his mind. 'But nothing's come in yet.'

In the silence that followed there was the sound of furniture moving, a child whining and Laviolette's voice, talking to the child, making an effort to soften itself.

'I can hear helicopters – down the line. Where are you?' he asked abruptly.

Caught off guard, she said, 'My flat. I just saw the Coastguard and RAF helicopters go out to sea.'

'You've got a sea view? South Harbour or Quayside?'

'Quayside,' she said, wondering how he knew she was in Blyth.

He paused, but didn't comment on this. 'I've got a feeling Martha Deane might try to contact you. If she does that I want you to let me know.' Without giving her time to respond to this, he carried on, 'Did you call Laura Deane yet?'

'No.' Anna wasn't sure she *was* going to call Laura Deane. 'Did she call you?'

'No.'

'Okay, well – we'll speak, and don't forget to call me if you get any visitors.'

Laviolette ended the call, and Anna, forgetting the half eaten bowl of muesli in the other room, decided to go for a run. She was about to leave the apartment when the phone started ringing again. This time it was Mary – Erwin had had a bad night, and wasn't any better this morning.

'Have you phoned the hospital?'

'They say to come in, but he says he doesn't want to. It's his breathing, Anna.'

'I'm phoning the hospital. I'll see if they can send someone to you and if they can't he's going to have to go in. Does he have a patient number – reference number – anything I need to quote when I phone?'

'I don't know,' Mary said, close to tears. 'I don't know any more. Don and Doreen have gone over to be with Laura – she still hasn't had any news. It's hard to believe –' Mary broke off. The improbability of Bryan Deane's disappearance had fractured her resolve with regards to Erwin's cancer, and right now she wasn't coping.

'Smoker's cancer' was how her grandmother, Mary, had referred to the small cell lung cancer Erwin had been diagnosed with. After nearly forty years underground on twenty to thirty cigarettes a day, Mary wasn't surprised, and implied that Anna shouldn't be either. It was how women of Mary's generation were used to losing their men. They hadn't wanted to tell her, but –

'But it might only be weeks, pet.' Mary's voice cracking ever so slightly.

It was the 'pet' that did it – not the news of Erwin's imminent death, but the 'pet'. Anna was crying; something she rarely did. Or at least, the tears were running, but she wasn't making any sound.

'I'm sorry, pet, but I thought you should know.'

Then came the hours of phone calls to the specialist and primary care team.

Erwin's cancer was 'metastatic', the medical term for 'hopeless'. There was no hope for Erwin. There was no point his having surgery or even radiotherapy because the cancer was no longer confined, but spreading. He'd been given the course of chemotherapy not as a potential cure, but to ease the pain of his ending.

According to the specialist, Erwin didn't want any more chemotherapy so they were putting him on morphine tablets instead.

That was when Anna had left London and headed north for the first time in just over a year. She'd had extensive conversations with various cancer specialists and had driven up the M1 feeling vaguely determined and prepared. Mary's phone call had enabled her to unplug herself from her London life in a way she'd been attempting but failing to for some months now, she realised.

As she pushed on at eighty miles an hour past Northampton, Nottingham, Leeds, York, Durham she wondered if this was what she'd been waiting for . . . an excuse to come back. But, come back to what?

When she pulled up in the late afternoon outside the council house that was her childhood home – number nineteen Parkview – Mary seemed confused, distant, and almost embarrassed.

She'd gone into the kitchenette to make tea and left Anna to face Erwin alone after calling out, 'Anna's here,' making it sound like she'd travelled hardly any distance at all.

Erwin was sitting on the sofa in the lounge beneath the framed copper engraving of the Chillingham Cattle. He was watching Tom & Jerry cartoons, his mouth open – smiling. His clothes looked too big and his skin was grey. There were some specks of dried blood on his upper lip from an earlier nose bleed, and he was wearing a cap because of hair loss from the chemotherapy.

'Granddad!' By the time she said it, she'd been standing in the lounge doorway for what seemed like ages.

He'd looked up – reluctantly – from the cartoon, still smiling, still rubbing his hands together where the skin had gone dry between thumb and forefinger.

'Alright, pet,' he said automatically, as if she'd just come from upstairs or the kitchenette. He tried to engage in her, but he wasn't really that interested. In fact, he was almost impatient, waiting for her to leave the room; the house . . . go back to London. The man who'd loved her all her life.

It struck Anna that neither of them wanted her here; that they were embarrassed about Erwin dying with her there. Alone, together, they knew how to behave with each other, and with death in the house, but they didn't know how to behave with her there.

She didn't know what to say and, leaving him in front of Tom and Jerry, went into the kitchenette, closing the door gently behind her.

Mary tensed, but carried on putting the teapot on the table next to the tea set that usually lived in the china cabinet in the lounge.

She sat down at the small drop-leaf table and poured their tea.

Anna noted, relieved, that the table was set for two.

Erwin, who'd never watched daytime TV in his life before, was left in front of Tom and Jerry.

'Why didn't you tell me sooner?' Anna said at last when Mary showed no signs of breaking the silence other than to ask if she'd had a good journey up, and how work was.

She finished her mouthful slowly, prudishly. 'We didn't know ourselves until recently.'

'Well, why didn't you tell me when you knew?'

'What could you of done?' Mary let out, angry. 'What can you do now? What are you going to do? What are you doing here?' she finished, exasperated and suddenly tearful. 'He's dying.'

'I know,' Anna said, angry herself now; raising her voice. Only she hadn't known; not really; not until she'd seen him on the sofa just now in front of Tom and Jerry. The man who'd been a father to her, and who'd been so strong still even at the age of fifty when she was born; who she'd always thought of as invincible.

The air cleared after that and Mary had been happy to take Anna through the small pharmacy lined up under the key rack – a gift from a school trip to Scarborough – on the kitchen bench beside the microwave: the slow-release morphine tablets, anti-inflammatory tablets, anti-sickness tablets and laxatives.

All the labels on the pots had been turned to face outwards. Mary was almost proud of them, and was waiting for some comment from Anna, who tried to think of something to say but couldn't.

Instead she got up to pour herself a glass of water at the sink, and saw through the nets at the window that it was the garden where the cancer had taken its toll. The house was as still and immaculate as always, but the garden . . . Erwin's shed was the only thing to rise out of the debris with any semblance of its former self. The plot that had fed the Fausts, their freezer, and many neighbours was laid to waste. The shed looked embarrassed – as though it was just about holding onto its dignity with the help of the crocheted curtain, white still at the tiny window.

Looking out at the garden, Anna finally felt afraid; afraid of what was happening here at number nineteen Parkview, and afraid of what was going to happen. Erwin and Mary had been there all her life; they brought her up when her mother disappeared off the face of the earth – grandparents who became parents again. She wasn't losing a grandfather; she was losing a father.

Erwin had an appointment at the hospital the next day,

47

and although they let Anna drive them because she was there, she knew they'd have preferred to go on the bus like they usually did.

They weren't doing any tests – it was just a consultation *to see how things were going to be at the end*, as Mary put it, re-arranging the brooch in her scarf.

Anna was left outside in a waiting area, on a blue chair next to a water dispenser and wire rack full of cancer care leaflets.

Erwin and Mary had gone into Dr Nadafi's room – Mary had long since got over her agitation at being assigned a 'coloured' man – and sat down in front of his desk. Before the door shut, Anna saw them taking hold of each other's hands beneath the desk, and her heart broke suddenly for them.

The waiting room, which had been empty, soon filled with young couples, children, a teenage girl and her parents.

Unnerved, Anna stood up to get herself some water from the dispenser, her hands shaking, aware that people were staring. She felt them wondering about her, briefly, then went to wait in the corridor – standing against an old radiator whose heat she could feel through her jeans.

'You didn't have to hang about,' Mary said when they came out, verging on angry.

'For C-christ's sake, Nan!' Anna was angry herself now.

'We could have got the bus home,' Mary persisted.

'I want to be here. Just let me be here.'

Erwin, looking stunned still from the consultation, said nothing.

'I need the toilet.' Mary set off down the corridor.

'Where's she going?' Erwin asked Anna, in a panic at the sight of Mary's retreating back.

'Just the toilet.'

Erwin nodded as Mary called back over her shoulder,

'Take him down to Out-Patients – we've got a prescription to pick up from the pharmacy.'

Anna started walking towards the stairs when Erwin grabbed hold of her suddenly and pulled her back, staring intently at her and chewing rapidly on the inside of his cheek.

It felt like the first time he'd even noticed her since she'd arrived the day before.

'Whatever she says – I want you to be here, you know, at the end.'

She cut him off. 'Granddad.'

'Please,' he insisted, keeping a tight grip on her arm, his breath rasping. 'I mean it.'

He hadn't really spoken to her until now, and, listening to him, she was aware of his accent – how German he sounded.

'Not for me,' he added. 'For Mary. You have to be there for her because I'll be leaving her alone.'

Anna put her hand over his, which was still gripping her upper arm. 'You know I will. You know that.'

'Hearing's the last thing to go,' he started to mumble, more to himself than her, 'isn't that strange? You've got to carry on talking to me even when I lose consciousness, even when you think that might be it. You've got to keep on talking because I'll still be able to hear you.'

'I will.'

He nodded and they carried on walking down the stairs, following the blue signs to Out-Patients.

Mary stood by the bedroom window at number nineteen Parkview, looking out for the nurse the hospital was sending them. Her poise of earlier weeks was shattered after having spent an entire night lying next to someone she was convinced was dying. When Anna, angry, asked her why

49

she hadn't phoned earlier, all she could think to say was, 'What was the point?' – unsure even what she'd meant by that.

'Where's the nurse?' Mary said irritably.

Anna, sitting in a G-Plan chair that was as old as the house and still upholstered in its original Everglade green, shut her eyes. She held on tight to Erwin's hand. His face was turned towards her, his mouth open – rasping. As soon as she so much as started to loosen her grip, his hand slid away from her down the side of the bed, and that scared her. The furniture in the room, like the carpet she remembered from childhood with its dense pattern of ferns, was still in good condition so had never been replaced. Neither Erwin nor Mary would have dreamed of growing tired of these things before they became threadbare.

Everything in the house had been earned and that's why the television set was covered with a blanket to protect it from dust when it wasn't being used; why the stereo was kept in the box it came in unless it was being played. Even now, the house was as clean and tidy as it had always been because for Mary and Erwin's generation cleanliness and tidiness were the only things separating them from the lost and the damned: the drinkers, the fornicators, the un-employed and the hungry.

'How was Laura last night?' Mary asked after a while.

Anna hadn't been expecting this. 'In shock.'

'It's funny – you can't have seen her in, what – fifteen years or something?'

'Sixteen.'

Mary turned away from the window to look at her, pausing. 'And yet, you and Laura, when you were growing up, you were like this,' she said, twisting her fingers together in spite of the arthritis. 'You were close to Bryan as well – at one time. He used to wait for you coming home from school – off the Newcastle bus, d'you remember?'

Anna did. She could see him now – waiting on the flower troughs outside the station, next to the Italian café, Moscadini's. They'd walk back from the station down to Hartford Estate together, sometimes talking, sometimes not – Bryan in something barely resembling a uniform and Anna in her navy blue and red Grammar School colours, the beribboned hat pushed in her bag. She'd been glad of the company – and the protection – because it was a risky and unpleasant business getting home to Parkview in a Grammar School uniform.

'He was forever in our back garden, drawing some miniscule insect with his magnifying glass.'

Anna stared at Mary. She'd forgotten that Bryan drew, and she'd forgotten all about his magnifying glass as well, which had a resonance for her she fought to remember, but couldn't right then.

'Have you got any of his pictures still?' she asked suddenly.

'Probably. Somewhere. I'm sure I put some up in the wash house. That poor child,' she added, lost in thought and barely aware now of Erwin's rhythmic rasping. 'He was as good as orphaned – the Strike on one side and suicide on the other. It was Bryan who found her, you know.'

'Found who?'

'His mother – Rachel. What a thing to come home from school to. You won't remember –'

But Anna did remember. She remembered because it had been a Monday – wash day – and Bryan had come running through all Mary's sheets, hanging from the line she had propped cloud high, and Mary had yelled at him until she'd seen his face, and the dark patch on his trousers where he'd wet himself.

Mary took him inside number nineteen and ran a bath

51

– and that was the first time Anna saw Bryan Deane naked; at the age of twelve, the day his mother died.

'It was hard on Bryan – he was Rachel's favourite. They said all sorts of things about Bobby Deane after that, but I don't think Bobby ever laid so much as a finger on Rachel, she was just lonely that's all – you know, that real loneliness; the sort you can't escape from. Bobby was a Union Official – he was working twelve hours a day and more. They said all sorts about Rachel as well,' Mary carried on, 'about how Bryan wasn't even Bobby's because there was a darkness to him that none of the other Deanes had.' She sighed.

'Bryan?'

Mary nodded. 'During the Strike, Rachel took to spending a lot of time with somebody Bobby sang with on the colliery choir. She liked to sing as well. I think it was just companionship, but it wasn't something you did back then. Men and women weren't friends. You stayed in your own home . . . your own backyard. You didn't take to wandering, however innocent that wandering might be. There were rules – and Rachel was never very good at rules; she used to say she felt suffocated.'

'So who was Rachel's friend?'

Mary hesitated. 'A widower, but a widower still counted as another woman's husband if you were married yourself, and Rachel was. He was a safety engineer at Bates.'

'What happened to him?'

'He died in an accident. You've got no colour,' she said suddenly to Anna.

'I'm not sleeping well.'

'I can tell. That's what make up's for, you know – the bad days.' Her eyes moved, disgruntled, over Anna's running clothes – noting them for the first time – before she turned to look out the window again.

An optimistically red Nissan was busy parking on the street below, and a woman was getting out and glancing up at the house.

'That hair.'

'What about my hair?' Anna patted her head.

'Not yours.'

'Whose hair, Nan?'

Short term memory loss and lack of concentration were meant to be side effects of the morphine they were giving Erwin, but if anything it was Mary who was suffering these symptoms on his behalf. The thought that Mary might be siphoning off some of Erwin's morphine crossed Anna's mind – and not for the first time either.

'Laura could have had anyone with that hair, and yet she chose Bryan Deane.'

'Or he chose her.'

'Maybe, but if you'd asked me all them years ago who was most likely to end up with Bryan Deane, I'd have said you were. Don't look at me like that. I used to see you together. You didn't grow up alone. I was there as well, remember?'

She glanced at Erwin, whose head had rolled back onto the pillow, exhausted, his mouth open and the breath rattling through it still.

'He stopped breathing last night, and I was so angry with him,' she said, becoming increasingly distressed. 'I was angry with him for making me that afraid. I'm angry with him for dying, Anna. I'm just – angry. I feel angry the whole time. Love hangs on strange threads,' Mary concluded, making an effort to control the tears.

Anna left Erwin – and Mary – with the nurse, Susan, who was in her late forties and who entered the Fausts' lives with fortitude, humour, the re-issued eau de toilette of Poison, and a portable oxygen canister.

Within minutes of her stepping inside number nineteen Parkview, normality had been restored and the terrors of the night vanquished. By the time Anna left, Erwin was breathing normally and Susan was sitting at the drop-leaf table in the kitchenette with Mary.

Anna got into her car and paused for a minute – pressing her forehead hard into the steering wheel before turning on the engine and driving out of the estate past the parade of shops where Mo's used to be. Curious about the shop that had featured so prominently throughout her childhood, she parked the car.

There were only two shops still open on the Parade – a fish and chip shop called The Seven Seas, and the convenience store that used to be Mo's – although this wasn't immediately apparent given the caging across the windows on the outside of both.

There was no longer a post office inside Mo's, but the security glass had been retained – behind which there was a till, an overweight girl in a tracksuit, a child, and most of the shop's alcoholic stock.

'Milk and eggs?' Anna asked, not particularly hopeful.

'Back of the shop – in the fridge.'

She felt the girl's eyes on her as she made her way towards the back of the shop, which smelt of underlying damp and rotten lino.

Anna recognised the lino – it had been there in Mo's time when there had been a baker's, butcher's, grocer's, hardware store, chemist and hairdresser's owned by Mo's twin sister on the Parade. It was where all the women on the estate used to go to get their hair done, including Anna when she was small. She hated getting her hair cut so much that Mary used to have to bring one of Erwin's belts with her to the salon so that they could tie her into the chair in order to keep her still.

She and Laura used to spend most of their summers walking between Mo's shop, the park and home. Anna could even remember the way Mo's used to smell – of sherbet, newsprint and hairspray from the salon next door. There had been a pink and green rocket outside whose presence it was difficult to justify given that nobody she knew ever had ten pence to spend on a rocket ride – the pennies they pooled together went on sweet things.

They would walk sluggishly, tipping back sherbet, towards the park the houses on Parkview overlooked to the rear. A park that had been in perpetual decline, and whose play equipment – erected on concrete in the hedonistic days before health and safety – was painted metal that got chipped and rusted, a fall off which resulted in broken teeth, fractured elbows, hairline cracks to the skull and tetanus jabs.

Anna would sit behind Laura on the metal horse as the sun moved across the sky, not speaking, surrounded by roses that never seemed to bloom, the horse's rusting saddle dying their thighs a feint red – until the big boys crawled up out of the sewage outlet where they kept their stash of pornography and sniffed glue. When the big boys appeared it was time to go home, but if they were out of glue, and walked in a straight line still with eyes that weren't red, they let Laura and Anna play chicken with them on the railway line that ran between the Alcan aluminium smelting plant to the north, and Cambois power station to the south – the power station whose four chimneys would have filled the horizon through her apartment windows at the Ridley Arms if they hadn't been demolished in 2003.

Until the summer Jamie Deane, Bryan's older brother, put his hand up Laura's skirt and Anna and Laura stopped going to the play park.

The memory took Anna by surprise, and for a moment she forgot what she was doing and stood staring into the fridge at the back of the shop. She'd forgotten all about Jamie Deane.

'You alright?' the girl shouted out.

Anna jerked in reaction to this, getting the milk and eggs out of the fridge and walking back towards the glass booth at the front. Distracted, she pushed the money across the counter, took her change and was about to leave when she said, 'You're not by any chance related to Mo are you?'

'Daughter.' It was said without hesitation, and without interest – as if nothing she ever heard or said would change her fate; this included.

'Say hi to her for me, will you? Hi from Anna – the German's granddaughter.'

'She's dead,' the girl said, without expression.

Anna quickly left the shop with an acute sense of depression – not only at the demise of Mo's empire, but at her lineage as well. Mo herself had been a large, bright, singing woman with a sense of humour that could cut you in two.

The same couldn't be said of her daughter.

She was about to get into her car when something caught her eye – a burgundy Vauxhall, parked outside one of the bungalows arranged in a semi-circle round the green that the Parade backed onto. Retirement bungalows – most of them in pretty good repair still, the gardens well tended.

While outdated burgundy Vauxhalls weren't exactly unique – especially not here on the Hartford Estate – Anna was certain that the one parked in front of the bungalows opposite was the one she'd been in the night before; the one belonging to Inspector Laviolette.

She got into her car and phoned Mary.

'You're not back at the flat already?'

'No – I stopped at Mo's.'

'Whatever for?'

'Milk. And eggs. Nan, you know the bungalows behind Mo's?'

'Armstrong Crescent?'

'I don't know. Nice gardens –'

'Armstrong Crescent,' Mary said again.

'Do you know anybody who lives there?'

Mary hesitated. 'It's where they re-housed Bobby Deane. After he started drinking.' She hesitated again, as if about to add something to this, but in the end changed her mind.

# 5

Bobby Deane, whose face had been all over the Strike of 1984 – 85, was sitting in one of the few pieces of furniture in the bungalow's lounge – an armchair that smelt of urine. The entire bungalow, in fact, smelt of urine, but it was strongest in the immediate vicinity of the armchair, which led Inspector Laviolette to the assumption that the armchair was the source, and if not the armchair then the man sat in it. Either way, the Inspector wasn't visibly bothered.

Bobby Deane watched Laviolette with moist, alert eyes, brightly sunk into a swollen, purple face. He had no idea who Laviolette was, and couldn't remember whether or not he'd spoken yet or how long he'd been in the house for – he only knew he was police. Bobby had no recollection of Laviolette's arrival either – he could have been there for years – and not knowing what else to do, simply stared at the man in the green coat making his way slowly round the room, sometimes smiling to himself sometimes not.

Laviolette was smiling as he sat down on the microwave against the wall opposite Bobby Deane's armchair – the only other available seating in the room – that no longer worked, but was still plugged in. 'Off out somewhere, Mr Deane?'

The tone was pleasant, but Bobby knew what police 'pleasant' meant.

He stared blankly at Laviolette then down at himself. He was wearing a padded blue Texaco jacket, shiny with neglect. His eyes ran over his legs then down to the floor where they picked out something purplish among the carpet's pile – his feet. Those were his feet down there, bare and without shoes.

He became aware of Laviolette's eyes on his feet as well.

'Sorry to interrupt – this won't take more than a couple of minutes.'

Where had he been going?

'Have you seen Bryan at all recently, Mr Deane?'

'Bryan,' Bobby echoed, thinking about this.

'Your son, Bryan?'

Bobby looked down again at the anorak he was wearing, and remembered – briefly. He'd put the anorak on because of Bryan, but when was that? It could have been years ago – he hadn't seen Bryan in years. All he remembered was sitting in the chair when he'd heard a car pull up outside. He'd gone to the window, lifted the yellow net and seen Bryan. He'd gone out into the hallway, slipping over something and bruising his left knee badly – he remembered the pain and the way he'd shouted out, 'Just coming!' as though Bryan was already in the house, speaking to him. Then he'd put the anorak on, and was about to open the front door when he'd looked down and realised that he didn't have any shoes or socks on.

So he'd gone into the bedroom to look for some socks – checking out the window to see that Bryan was still there.

The sun had been bright – he had a vague memory of brightness – and the bedroom windows even more filthy than the ones in the lounge, but he'd been able to see Bryan's big silver car parked on the road still and made out Bryan inside it. Only Bryan's posture was odd – his arms holding the steering wheel and his head resting on it – and Bobby had known instinctively then that Bryan was trying to decide whether to ring on the door or not.

Then Bobby had sat down on the mattress in the bedroom and fallen into one of the black holes he was more often in than out of these days, and forgotten what it was he was doing. He'd forgotten all about Bryan outside as well. At some point he'd got up again and gone to the window, without knowing why. His subconscious had taken him to the window to check and see whether Bryan was still parked there. Consciously, however, he had no idea what he was doing standing at the window or what it was he was looking out for because there was nothing out there as far as he could see – apart from a large girl in a pink tracksuit, smoking a cigarette on the green just behind the shops, staring at his house. When was that? Only yesterday? Had he been bare-foot in his anorak since yesterday?

But Bobby didn't mention any of this, partly out of habit – because the man sitting opposite was police and it was his policy not to answer any questions put to him by police – and partly because he was already in the process of forgetting.

'What's that? Did you just say something?'

'Have you seen Bryan recently?' Laviolette asked again, aware that Bobby Deane's vulnerability was making him uncomfortable.

'Bryan's my youngest son,' Bobby said slowly, uncertain.

'That's right,' Laviolette agreed. 'Have you seen him lately?'

'He's got a little girl of his own,' Bobby carried on, ignoring the question. 'What's her name?' he appealed, half-heartedly to the Inspector.

Laviolette smiled patiently. 'Martha.'

This time, the smile seemed to relax Bobby. 'Martha. He

brought her here once. It was a Saturday – he takes her to the stables at Keenley's, Saturdays.' There was spittle on his chin; the recollection was making him reckless – despite the fact that his audience was police – because he might lose it at any moment. There couldn't be anything wrong in this recollection – surely grandchildren were allowed to go horse riding if they chose, and sons were allowed to visit their fathers without breaking any laws.

'Did Bryan come yesterday?'

'I haven't seen Bryan in years. What was yesterday?'

'Saturday,' Laviolette responded, debating whether to be more specific or not. 'Easter Saturday,' he said after a while.

'It's Easter?' At first Bobby looked surprised – then resigned.

'Yesterday was Saturday. Did you see Bryan yesterday, Mr Deane?'

Bobby shook his head, running his left hand down the greasy chair arm and starting to pick at the foam. 'No. He never came in.'

'He never came in,' Laviolette repeated gently. 'So he was – where? – outside?'

'I don't remember,' Bobby said, suddenly deflated. 'I don't remember anything.'

'Mr Deane, your son's wife reported him missing yesterday – Easter Saturday – and we're trying to find him, that's all. We'd like to find Bryan so that he can go home.'

'You don't know where Bryan is?'

The Inspector got up, sighing. 'Well, if you do see Bryan – if you even think you see Bryan, will you give me a call?'

He gave Bobby Deane his card, waiting for him to read it.

Bobby sat turning it over between his thumb and forefinger.

'Is it alright if I use your bathroom?' Laviolette asked.

As he disappeared out of the lounge and Bobby Deane's

mind, Bobby sat clutching the air with his left hand. He was holding a piece of leather in his hands – reins, attached to a harness, attached to a pony he was pulling towards the sand dunes rising in front of him.

The pony, so sure of itself underground, was hesitant up here on top – it kept stumbling and stopping even though it was blinkered, bewildered. Bobby would have to pull hard then to get her to move, and yell irritably – until he remembered that the black and white pit pony was the reason for his own day up top as well, and then he'd give her neck a belligerent stroke. All the same, he couldn't understand why she hadn't gone running off – this was her one day a year up top. But then one day probably didn't make the other three hundred and sixty-four any better, he reasoned – in fact it probably made them worse. This reasoning didn't lessen his own disappointment, however. He'd so wanted to see the pony run. In the end, frustrated, he'd tethered it to a hawthorn and run up onto the dunes with the rest of the boys. He must have been – how old? – as old as Bryan's daughter the last time he saw her. So he ran with the others up onto the dunes, cutting his feet, which were bare, in the thick blades of dune grass.

He sat moving his bare feet now, in the carpet's filthy pile, while the Inspector checked the cabinet in the bathroom for signs of occupancy other than Bobby Deane's. There was nothing apart from a bottle of Old Spice, a cup of tea, a couple of buttons, and a penny whose copper had turned blue. There was a fraying yellow towel hanging from a nail in the wall, no sign of any toilet paper – and a bath full of water.

Laviolette let the bath out then crossed the hallway into the kitchen where there was a piece of board over the hob on the oven and a Calor Gaz camping stove on top of this. On the surface, lined up, were cartons of weed killer, a box of disposable gloves, and various tools. Somebody was using Bobby Deane's kitchen to cut Methadrone, and it smelt bad in here.

In the lounge, Bobby Deane age twelve had been running with the other boys down the dunes onto the beach. Now he'd taken the edge off his excitement, he thought he should go and check on his pony so he climbed back up and slid down the other side into the field and there, standing by the hawthorn bush and pit pony, was a girl. She must have been collecting some sort of berries because her mouth, her hands and her dress were stained almost black with them, and she was holding a flower in one of her hands. A carnation? Bobby stopped half way down the dunes, watching her stroke the pony.

When Laviolette went back into the lounge, Bobby was staring at the wall opposite where the bungalow's previous owner had left a barometer hanging – the needle was pointing to 'Fair'. He was smiling while clenching and unclenching his feet in the carpet.

'I'm going now, Mr Deane,' the Inspector called out.

Bobby stared at him in shock. Who was he? How long had he been standing there for, and what was he doing in his house?

'I'll ask Rachel later when she gets in from work,' he heard himself saying, automatically. 'Her shift finishes soon. I'll ask her – she'll know about Bryan.'

Laviolette left Bobby Deane's bungalow and stood in the front garden for a moment, thinking about Rachel Deane – who he remembered as a long, silent woman – and Rachel Deane's suicide. Then he crossed the immaculate garden belonging to the bungalow next door. There was a stone donkey on the porch, pulling a stone cart planted with purple pansies; the purple jarring with the yellow the front door was painted. He knocked and a tidy, sour-looking woman answered – promptly enough to suggest that she'd been watching his approach from behind the nets.

He showed his ID, introduced himself and explained that he'd been next door at Mr Deane's – aware that the woman already knew all this. Only the left hand side of her face and body were visible behind the door as her eyes, worried, searched the street behind Laviolette, torn between desperately wanting to know what the police were doing next door, and not wanting anybody to see the police on her own front step.

'I'd ask you in, but I've just done the floors,' the woman said, staring at the Inspector's feet, which weren't clean.

'That's fine, Mrs –'

The woman hesitated then said, thinly, 'Harris.'

'Mrs Harris.' Laviolette smiled. 'Mr Deane's son, Bryan, sometimes visits him Saturdays. I was wondering whether you happened to notice whether Bryan Deane visited Mr Deane yesterday?'

'What's all this about?'

'Just follow up to something – a family matter.'

'A family matter involving the police?' She waited, but the Inspector had nothing more to add to this, he just stood there smiling at her.

'Did you see Bryan Deane here yesterday, Mrs Harris?'

'He was here.'

'What time?'

'Around eleven.' She sighed. 'I noticed because it was the first time in ages I'd seen his car parked outside – and he was parked in my husband's spot. My husband's registered disabled – that's why we've got the bay outside. I was about to go out there and ask him to move – when he drove off.'

'So he didn't go into the house?'

She shook her head. 'He was parked there for, I don't

know – ten minutes or something – then he just drove off, like I said.'

'He didn't get out of the car at all?'

She shook her head again. 'No. And like I said, it's the first time he's been round here in months – maybe even longer. Not like the other one.'

'The other one?' Laviolette said sharply.

'There's another one – tattoos – he's been round a lot the past six months, and when he's round, the shouting that goes on . . . it comes through the walls. I mean, we have the television up loud anyway because of Derek's hearing aid, but when that lad's round we can hear everything, and the language . . . in our own home. We've been on and on to the council, but they're not doing anything about it.' She paused, waiting for an echo of sympathy from the Inspector, but it never came.

The Inspector wasn't following this. He was thinking hard about Jamie Deane. Mrs Harris had to be talking about Jamie Deane, who'd been in prison for twenty years – and who was released six months ago. The Methadrone production line in Bobby Deane's kitchen had Jamie Deane all over it.

'. . . and nobody deserves neighbours like that,' Mrs Harris concluded.

Laviolette stared at her for a moment, his mind still elsewhere. 'When you hear shouting through the wall – coming from next door – does it never occur to either you or your husband to knock and see if Mr Deane's okay?'

Mrs Harris looked bewildered.

'That would certainly be the neighbourly thing to do, don't you think? It might save on your phone bill as well – to the council.'

'Are you saying . . .' she began.

But Laviolette cut her off. 'What I'm saying, Mrs Harris, is this – has it ever occurred to you while you've been on the phone to the council to drop in the fact that you've got an elderly man living alone next door to you – with Alzheimer's?'

Mrs Harris was too shocked by the Inspector's anger to respond. All she could do was lay her hand against her collarbone and throat and watch him retreat across the immaculate garden, her eyes wide.

'I'm a good Christian,' she shouted hoarsely after him, afraid, when he stopped at the gate and turned.

'Does Mr Deane get any other visitors?'

'There's a woman up on Parkview who brings in shopping for him – Mary Faust – but that's only once a week,' she said quickly, her eyes wet. 'I'm a good Christian,' she repeated, not wanting the Inspector to walk away with the wrong opinion of her, before shutting her yellow door on the world.

Mo's daughter, Leanne, could have told the Inspector exactly when Jamie Deane visited his father in the bungalow on Armstrong Crescent because Jamie Deane's irregular appearances in the store over the past six months were the only thing that made life inside the glass security booth worth living for her. She knew everything there was to know about him – even things he didn't know about himself, like the way his eyes creased at the corner and got brighter when he laughed. Leanne knew everything.

Today though, Jamie caught her off guard.

She was busy reading a filthy text a friend had just sent her about Daniel Craig while talking to her daughter, Kayleigh, who was in the booth with her because it was Sunday, and who wanted to know what a zombie was – when she looked up and saw Jamie standing smiling through the security glass at her. The locket she'd been sucking on dropped out her mouth and fell wetly against her skin. That's exactly who Jamie Deane reminded her of, she thought – Daniel Craig.

'Haven't seen you in a while,' Leanne said, pulling her tracksuit top down nervously over her waist, breathing in and sliding off the chair.

'Missed me?'

She pulled her hair back over her shoulders and laughed.

'Put a pack of Bensons on the tab for me, will you.'

'Your tab's getting long.'

'I'll make it up to you.'

She was shaking as she got the cigarettes off the shelf and slid them through to his side, and thought she might cry when he stroked the back of her hand – briefly – with his forefinger.

Close to clinically obese, there was so much going on between chin and counter that all Jamie could do was stare vaguely but appreciatively at Leanne's mid-way bulk – emblazoned with the word SWALLOWS spelt out in sequins (a gift from the friend who sent the Daniel Craig text) – before heading out of the shop and back into his van.

Two minutes later, he was back.

'You can't of smoked the whole pack.'

Jamie, distracted, said, 'There's a car parked outside dad's – know anything about it?'

'What car?'

Abandoning Kayleigh and leaving the booth door propped open with a fire extinguisher, Leanne followed Jamie out of the shop, but didn't recognise the car parked outside Bobby Deane's bungalow.

'It might not be for your dad,' she said at last, pleased with herself for thinking this.

Jamie grunted in concession to this theory as her eyes slid over the chain caught in the crease at the back of his neck and she breathed in the smell of him – take away food, dog, dope, anger, and a sweetness that vanished as soon as she tried to define it, and that wasn't aftershave or the backlash of the dope.

'Any strangers been in the shop this morning?'

'No. Wait –'

'Who?' he demanded, irritable.

'A woman who knew mum.'

'Police,' he hissed, turning round suddenly and nearly knocking her backwards she'd crept so close.

She lifted her eyes with difficulty from his neck and watched Inspector Laviolette leave Bobby Deane's bungalow then ring on Mrs Harris's door.

'What the fuck's he doing now?' Jamie mumbled running, crouching into his van, which had Reeves Regeneration painted on the side.

He watched through the windscreen as Laviolette stood talking to Mrs Harris then Mrs Harris's front door shut and the Inspector got back in his car.

Soon after this the burgundy Vauxhall accelerated past Jamie Deane's parked van and Mo's daughter, Leanne, standing with her arms folded on the pavement outside the shop. Behind her, Kayleigh was pressing a tongue dyed red with lolly against the glass.

Jamie wound the van's window down. 'Has he gone?'

'Yeah – he's gone.'

'Get me a pasty.'

Leanne turned and walked automatically back into the shop, taking a pasty past its sell by date from the cold cabinet.

Jamie took it from her then put the van into gear without another word, without so much as even looking at her.

She stood on the pavement and watched him turn into Armstrong Crescent, her heart breaking.

\*

'What was he doing here?' Jamie yelled at Bobby, his mouth full of pasty, staring at the Inspector's card. He'd already been in the kitchen, and the stuff in there was untouched. 'I can't believe you let that bastard in here. Him!' he cried out, in frustration.

He knew that losing patience didn't work, but he hadn't yet discovered what did so in the meantime he carried on yelling at Bobby Deane who'd just had time – following the Inspector's departure – to walk into the hallway in search of a staircase that didn't exist in order to go upstairs to a bedroom that also no longer existed.

Perplexed at being unable to find any stairs at all, Bobby had gone back into the lounge and sat down in the armchair again when he heard the front door opening. The next minute a man walked into the room who he briefly recognised as one of his sons – he just couldn't remember which, and had no idea what his name was.

Then his son started yelling at him and then he stamped on his left foot, which was bare still, and the pain was such a shock to Bobby it blocked out the yelling for a while.

He became confused and as a result of this confusion, Jamie and the bungalow slipped entirely from his mind as he fell into a profound sense of unfamiliarity, which made him panic and want to leave the chair he was sitting in and go in search of the stairs again. If he could only find the stairs, he'd be able to find Rachel.

Rachel was upstairs waiting for him; she had something to give him – a flower – and the flower was beginning to wilt; it needed water.

He tried to get up, but was pushed back down.

After that, he kept his eyes on the man pacing in front of him.

There was a dense pain in his left foot that made him feel helpless – then he remembered, momentarily. 'I told him

Rachel would be back soon – that she'd know where Bryan was.'

Jamie stared at his father. 'Bryan? It was nothing to do with me then?'

'Who are you?' Bobby said, managing to get to his feet at last, in spite of the pain, and shuffling to the window.

'I'm your son, you stupid fuck – your son, Jamie.' He let out a few brief, frustrated sobs. 'And I did twenty years for you. Twenty years – and you've got no idea who the fuck I am.' He put his hand over his face.

Bobby, who was looking out the window, said, 'He's gone.'

'Who's gone you daft fucker?'

'Our Bryan was parked outside. I thought maybe he'd come to take me for a drive up the coast – I haven't seen the sea in a while – but he never came in. Why didn't he come in?' Bobby appealed briefly to Jamie, who was now smoking one of the Bensons he'd taken from the shop. 'Can I have one?'

'No,' Jamie yelled. Then, 'I don't fucking believe this. Twenty years and it's still Bryan. Bryan.'

Bobby looked down at the windowsill where there was a spider's web flecked with flies. 'Are you looking for Bryan too?'

'Why would I be looking for Bryan?'

'He's gone missing.'

'Bryan?'

'Bryan. The police are looking for him.'

Bobby turned back to the window, distracted by a woman next door who looked vaguely familiar, wheeling her bin out onto the pavement. The bin had the number eight painted on it, in white. Bobby wondered about the number and the woman, who was staring at him and who looked like she had a freshly pruned rose bush up her arse.

Laughing quietly to himself, he waved, but she didn't wave back.

In fact, she almost ran back up the garden to her front door.

Still laughing, Bobby mumbled, 'That's it – piss off back to where you came from.' Then, turning away from the window and seeing a man standing in the room behind him, smoking – who he was sure hadn't been standing there earlier – he said again, 'Can I have one?'

'Give over.' Jamie threw the cigarette into the fireplace's empty grate.

Bobby followed its course through the air and into the grate, waiting.

When the man left the room, he called out, 'Where are you going? I'm hungry.'

He followed him out into the hallway, desperately trying to think of a way to make him stay, suddenly terrified at the thought of being left alone. 'I'm hungry,' he said again.

Jamie paused at the front door, leaning back against the wall and accidentally turning the light switch on. He seemed preoccupied – bored, even.

Bobby was fiddling with the zip on his Texaco anorak, wondering where the door in front of him led to.

'You already ate,' Jamie said.

'When?'

'Just now. Can't you smell it still?'

Looking around him, Bobby gave the air a quick sniff. 'What did I eat?'

'Sunday roast – the full works . . . beef . . . york-shires . . . roast potatoes.' Jamie belched. 'Excuse me.'

'My stomach feels tight.'

'Cause you stuffed yourself silly, that's why.'

'But, I'm still hungry.' Bobby was starting to panic again now. 'Is it Sunday?'

Jamie pulled open the front door and Bobby saw the crescent of bungalows curving round the green. In the centre of the green there was a yellow bin, lying on its side. It looked like somebody had tried to set fire to it. Tilting his head slightly, which hurt, he could just make out the words *Wansbeck Council*.

'The man who was here,' he called out, suddenly, 'he was Laviolette's boy. That's who he was,' Bobby declared, his voice triumphant.

Jamie walked back towards him. 'I don't know what you're sounding so pleased about. I don't know how you can even bear to say that man's name.'

'I used to sing with Laviolette in the colliery choir – the Ashington Male Voice Choir. We went to Germany together with the choir.'

'And what else, dad? What else did you do? You don't even remember, do you?'

Jamie slammed him hard against the wall – the crown of his head catching the bottom of the electric meter.

Bobby, slumped against the wall, shook his head.

'Mum. D'you remember her?'

Bobby fought hard to catch at something flitting round inside his head; he shut his eyes and pushed his hand out to take hold of the flower proffered. 'Red carnations,' he gasped. 'The women were in the pit yard, waiting for us. They gave us flowers – carnations for heroes – to take the hurt out of having to go back after the Strike.' He shook his head sadly, the clarity and sharpness of the women's faces he'd summoned, already fading. 'But there were no heroes by then – everything was broken.'

Jamie shook his head in disbelief. 'Yeah, everything was broken.'

'I looked for her,' Bobby insisted suddenly, 'among the women with flowers, but she wasn't there. She'd already gone by then, hadn't she?' he appealed softly to Jamie, his eyes wet.

'Oh, she'd gone a long time before that only you were too busy with the bloody Strike to see.'

72

'She was tired – thirty-one pounds a week minus the fifteen the Government took off her saying we got paid by the Union, only we didn't. What does that make?' Before Jamie had time to work it out, Bobby said, 'Sixteen pounds a week. Sixteen pounds a week makes you tired – it would make anyone tired.'

'How the fuck d'you remember that – sixteen pounds a week – and not remember Roger Laviolette?'

'Roger Laviolette,' Bobby echoed happily. 'I used to sing with –'

'Yes, you used to sing with him,' Jamie yelled into his face, holding onto him by his anorak, which smelt terrible up close, 'and how is it that you remember the singing, but you don't remember the killing?'

'I never killed anyone,' Bobby said, frightened.

'Yes you did. You killed Roger Laviolette because of mum and him.'

'Wait – where are you going?'

But Jamie was no longer there.

There was washing hanging across the balconies of the flats above the shops and Bobby stared for a moment at a large bedspread with a picture of a leopard on it, before walking, barefoot, out the front door and down the overgrown garden path to the gate as a white van turned the corner out of Armstrong Crescent.

He was waiting for somebody, he was sure, but he was only sure for a few moments. Then he forgot who it was he thought he was waiting for.

Then he forgot he'd even been waiting, and no longer knew what he was doing standing barefoot at the end of the path, leaning against the gate – so he let himself out and crossed the street onto the green opposite, still curious about the yellow bin.

After contemplating it for a while, he looked about him

trying to work out not so much where he was going, but where he'd come from. Neither the bungalows in front of him nor the block of flats behind signified anything much. He only knew that his feet were cold and that the left foot hurt. Looking down, he saw that his feet were bare and that the one on the left was badly bruised.

The front door to one of the bungalows opposite was open and there was a woman staring at him from the windows of the bungalow next door to that.

If he just sat down in the grass and waited, it would probably be okay. What would come to pass would come to pass in a world that was as tired of him as he was of it.

A flock of seagulls flew overhead then circling the upturned bin and its contents, interested. They only came inland when the weather was bad out to sea.

Bobby tilted his head back and looked up at the sky, the fast moving clouds disorientating him further.

Was it today he'd been down to the beach and onto the dunes with the pit ponies?

Was it today he'd seen the small girl in the dress? It couldn't have been – this was no weather for dresses like that, and the dress had been stained with some kind of fruit, but it couldn't be blackberries because it was too early in the year for blackberries.

He looked around to check the trees and see whether they had leaves or not, but there were no trees on any of the horizons. There was no colour in the gardens opposite either – the only thing that stuck out was the yellow door in the bungalow where the woman's face was staring at him still.

Then it started to rain.

He pulled his collar up and carried on sitting there, unsure what else to do or where to go until a woman came walking through the rain. She was wearing a long waterproof coat, and a headscarf – and she had a blue carrier bag in her hand.

It took him a while to realise that she was walking towards him; walking fast, her shoes slipping on the wet grass.

'Bobby!' she gasped. 'What in God's name are you doing?' She turned round on the spot, taking in the flats and the back of the shops and the bungalows as he'd done earlier, only she was more stunned. 'How long have you been out here for? Where are your shoes? You've got a cut on your head – there's blood.'

She was on the verge of tears as she pulled him to his feet and led him towards the bungalow with its front door open still.

'I don't want to go in there,' he said, pulling his arms away from her.

'Get inside out of this rain, Bobby.' She pushed him forcibly indoors and he stood in the hallway listening to the sounds of water running, and soon there was steam coming out of the room at the end of the hallway.

# 6

The sky was clearing by the time Anna turned back down Quay Road towards the Quayside, and the sun now making its way through the disappearing clouds, was harsh. She was driving straight into it and so didn't see Martha Deane sitting on the bench opposite the Ridley Arms until she pulled up right beside her.

Martha had her bike with her.

Laviolette had been right – here was Martha paying her a visit and sooner even than he'd probably anticipated.

'How long have you been here for?' Anna asked as she got out of the car, squinting because of the light coming off the water.

'I don't know,' Martha mumbled, unsure of her tone. 'I can't stand it at home any longer, and . . . you don't mind?'

Anna sat down on the bench beside her, sighing and tilting her face instinctively towards the April sun.

'I don't believe her,' Martha said suddenly.

'Don't believe who?'

'Mum. I don't believe her about anything. Do you?'

Ignoring this, Anna said, 'How did you know where to find me?'

'I heard dad and Nan talking yesterday morning. Dad said you should have phoned him about a short term let – that he'd have done you a deal.' She paused. 'Nan said she told you to phone him.'

'She probably did. I don't know – I've had so much on my mind.'

This was a lie. She had phoned Tyneside Properties before coming north and asked to speak to Bryan, but found herself unable to – so hung up.

'Nan says your granddad's dying.'

'He is.'

'That's sad.' Martha threw something into the sea. 'I wanted to go out with them this morning on the search – one of the boats, helicopters, anything . . . I just want to be out there doing something. It doesn't feel like anybody's doing anything.' Her voice was loud – tearful – and the next minute she had her head on Anna's shoulder and her arms round her neck, pulling herself to her.

Anna put her hand stiffly on Martha's hair, and tried not to tense up. She could feel Martha's tears running over her collarbone and beneath her running vest.

When Martha stopped crying, she let her arms drop but kept her head resting on Anna's shoulder, staring out to sea, and after a while said, 'I came home late once from a hockey match, and dad's car was parked on the drive. It wasn't until I triggered the security light that I saw he was in the car still, just sitting in the car on the drive, in the dark.' She paused, thinking about whether she wanted to say what she was going to say next. 'He waved at me and acted like he'd just got home, but I knew he'd been there a long time.' She twisted her head on Anna's shoulder, looking up at her. 'He just looked so unhappy, and you know what I keep thinking? I keep thinking – what if he just couldn't cope any more with all the rows they've been having?'

Anna kept looking at the sea, aware that Martha was watching her. 'Everybody rows.'

'There's not a night in the past year when I haven't had to go to sleep with my headphones on to try and cut out the sound of them going on and on at each other about money – always money. That's what everything comes down to.'

Anna had a clear picture of Martha curled up in bed with her headphones on, and it was one of a deep loneliness she recognised from her own childhood; a loneliness she had carried into adulthood with her, as an inability to seek comfort – especially physical comfort.

Martha was picking at a frayed seam in her jeans. 'Did something happen between dad and you, like – a long time ago?'

'What makes you say that?'

'You knew – about his appendicitis – and he was so pleased to see you yesterday.'

'We barely spoke.'

'He doesn't get pleased about much these days, but he was pleased about seeing you.'

Anna paused. 'We grew up together and haven't seen each other in a while – that's all.'

'You, mum and dad used to all live next door to each other. I know from Nan how close you and mum used to be – like sisters, she said, right?'

Anna nodded.

'So how come mum and dad never – and I mean never – talk about you?'

'I can't answer that.'

'Well, that's how I know something happened.'

Martha carried on watching her without comment then suddenly said, 'I brought something for you.' She searched in her pockets for a while then handed Anna a photograph – of Bryan Deane sitting alone at a table in a restaurant overlooking a blue, white-capped sea. Despite the view, he was staring down at the check tablecloth. He wasn't smiling; he wasn't even looking at the camera, and she could barely make out his face.

'That's Greece last year,' Martha was saying. 'I took it. I've got a copy on my windowsill and I know it'll make me feel better – more hopeful – knowing you've got a picture of him as well. We can keep a vigil – I've got a candle in front of mine; a scented one – cinnamon and vanilla.'

Anna stood up.

'Wait – where are you going? We don't have to talk about this any more.'

'It's fine. I just need to eat, that's all.'

'Can I come with you?'

Anna hesitated, unsure whether she wanted Martha in her apartment. 'Does your mum know where you are?'

'I told her I was going to my friend, Ellie's.'

'For how long?'

'I didn't say how long I'd be – and I don't even have a friend called Ellie.' Martha shrugged. 'She doesn't give a fuck where I am.'

'Okay – but you'd better bring the bike in with you.'

Anna watched Martha drift round the apartment. 'Have you finished nosing around?'

'Almost.'

'Not the bedroom,' she called out.

'I've already done the bedroom. I'm in the bathroom.'

The next minute Anna heard the medicine cabinet being opened. She went down the hallway. 'Martha!'

Martha turned round, smiling. 'Impressive.'

'What's so impressive?'

'No medication – not even anti-depressants – nothing.'

'Why would there be?'

Martha ambled back into the living room and went over to the windows, which were streaked with rain again. 'Mum's been on and off Lithium for years – now she takes pills to help her sleep – Nytol. D'you have a boyfriend?'

'No – no, I don't. Why are you asking?'

Martha was about to say something when Anna's phone started to ring.

'Is my daughter with you?' Laura Deane's voice said.

Anna hesitated. 'She is – d'you want to speak to her?'

Martha had turned away from the window and was now staring at her.

'No – I need her to come home. Can you tell her to do that?'

Anna thought Laura was going to call off then, but she didn't. 'What's she been saying?'

'Nothing much – she's just pretty upset.'

'We had a row.'

Anna was silent.

Laura laughed. 'I bet she's been pedalling all sorts of shit about Bryan and me.'

'No – she's been fine,' Anna responded ambivalently, too shocked by Laura's tone to say anything else, and aware that Martha was watching her intently now.

'She thinks I'm stupid,' Laura carried on, 'telling me she was going to Ellie's house. I knew exactly where she was going, and she doesn't have a friend called Ellie. In fact,' she laughed again, 'Martha doesn't have any friends. She just sort of latches onto people until they get sick of her. There was a teacher at school last term she did the same thing to. She had to see the school counsellor after that. There's something else you should know about Martha – she lies a lot. I mean, she lies compulsively.'

Martha was staring out the window again and had her back turned to Anna.

'Laura –'

'I want Martha home – okay? I don't want you seeing her again and I don't want you round here either. I want you to stay away from us.'

'I needed to give a statement.'

'But you didn't need to do it here – in my home. You think I'm stupid as well, and you know what? That's always been your problem, Anna – you underestimate people.'

Laura rang off and Anna placed the phone carefully on the arm of the sofa, staring at it without seeing it.

A few minutes later, still in shock, she said to Martha, 'That was your mum – she wants you to go home.'

The intimacy of the past hour, which had taken her by surprise, had gone. All she saw was a child she wasn't responsible for, standing in her apartment looking out of her window – and she didn't want her there any more.

Martha kept her back turned to Anna. 'It's probably a maximum of ten degrees out there today – the sea temperature will be the same. When your deep body temperature drops to thirty-five degrees, you start to feel disorientated and confused. At thirty-four degrees, amnesia sets in. As your temperature drops from thirty-three down to thirty consciousness becomes cloudy until you lose consciousness altogether. If your deep body temperature gets down to twenty-five degrees then you're probably dead. She hates me.'

'Your mum? I'm sure she just –'

'No!' Martha shouted, adamant. 'She hates me. This isn't about her wanting me to go home it's about control, that's all. She needs to know she's got control over me – and you as well. You don't know her.'

She began hurriedly collecting her stuff, putting on her coat so roughly she ripped it.

'Let me drive you – it's pouring out there.'

'I'm fine.' Martha pulled the bike aggressively towards

her, opening the door to the apartment before Anna had a chance to get there.

'You'll get soaked.'

'It's only rain.' She paused at the top of the stairs for a moment, and they stared at each other then looked away.

'Do you want to know what she was doing before I came over here today?' Martha said. 'She was sitting on one of the barstools in the kitchen reading a *holiday* brochure. I mean, she's no great reader. That brochure – any brochure – is pretty much about her limit, and she's working hard at it. When I see her this morning, reading her brochure, I say, "You're not thinking of going on holiday are you?" and she says, "We'll see." And I say, "But, dad –" thinking, I really have got a point, and she just says, "Piss off."'

Martha was as sullen again now as she'd been standing beside Bryan yesterday morning, in her riding clothes.

Anna was aware that she was waiting for her to say something, and at last said quietly, 'I don't think she's all that keen on you coming over here.'

'Fuck that. Fuck her.'

They carried the bike awkwardly down the stairs together.

'You know what I think?' Martha said, wheeling the bike out into the rain. 'I think she pushed him over the edge, and that's why he's gone.'

'Gone?'

'He's gone,' Martha said again.

'Which is different to disappearing?'

'Completely.'

Anna stared out through the open front door at the Harbourmaster's office – a nondescript brick building with woodwork painted a depressing shade of blue – thinking.

After Martha had gone, she went into the bedroom and lay down on the bed, shutting her eyes, but a few minutes later was up again, looking for the running shoes she'd kicked off earlier. Then her phone started ringing.

'Busy?' It was the Inspector and Inspector Laviolette was the last person she felt like speaking to right then.

'About to go out for a run – why are you phoning me?'

'It's raining.'

'I like running in the rain. Has something turned up?'

'Not a sodding thing.' He sounded tired. 'Nothing . . . not a trace. Divers are going out tomorrow, then we're launching an appeal.' Before she could respond to this, he said, 'Has Martha contacted you yet?'

'No,' she said, without hesitation, waiting. The silence was on the verge of becoming uncomfortable when he said, 'Do you remember much about Bobby Deane?'

'Like what?'

'I don't know.'

'You think Bryan's still alive, don't you?'

'I'm not the only one.'

'I remember Bobby when the Strike was on. I remember going up to the caravan they had outside the gates at Cambois power station when the pickets were trying to get lorry drivers not to deliver coal.'

'Who did you go with?'

'Bryan – probably.'

They were silent for a moment.

'I was up at the power station during the Strike,' he said after a while. 'I'd just joined the Force.'

'You picked a good time.'

Laviolette laughed. 'It wasn't so bad at the start – we were all local boys, with some extra cork lining in our hats, shin pads and cricket boxes over our valuables, but there wasn't any trouble. Most of the drivers turned back. A few went through – there was abuse, but just verbal. Then there was this one driver who said he supported the cause, etc., turned his lorry round and drove off. Two minutes later, he was heading back up the road at well over seventy miles an hour, drove straight through the line and went crashing through the gates. One of the pickets went down and one of our boys went down as well.

'When the next lorry came along, everybody was worked up and there's no way we would have been able to hold our lines – there weren't enough of us – if it hadn't been for Bobby Deane, talking sense to his men, keeping them calm and telling them not to break through the line.' There was the sound of scratching on the other end of the line. 'I went to see Bobby Deane today – to ask whether he'd seen Bryan recently – only Bobby Deane's got Alzheimer's and should be in care.'

Anna thought about telling him she'd seen him parked on Armstrong Crescent, but kept quiet. Laviolette wasn't the kind of man you offered more information to than was necessary, and anyway, her head was suddenly full of deer – something to do with Bobby Deane and deer. 'Didn't Bobby used to poach deer over the border during the Strike?' she said out loud. She had a clear image of a slaughtered deer, hanging upside down, its dead eyes staring intently at her in the Deanes' wash house.

'We heard rumours that Christmas – venison pie at the free cafés. So that was Bobby, was it?' Laviolette seemed to like the idea of Bobby as a poacher.

Anna was too shocked at the recollection to say anything. Now she realised it wasn't Bobby Deane she associated with the slaughtered deer, it was Jamie.

'I found out today that Jamie Deane's about the only one who still visits his dad – although I'd call into question his motives. He's using Bobby's kitchen to cut his Methadrone in, and he's probably picking up his dad's pension and dis-ability as well.' The Inspector paused. 'What d'you know about Jamie Deane?'

Anna thought about Jamie Deane, whose name she hadn't heard in years. 'Why are you asking me?'

'No reason.'

'He was put away, wasn't he? I don't know how long for.'

'Twenty years. He killed a man, but never confessed to it. At the time people thought it was Bobby who probably did it and that Jamie was covering up for his dad.'

'Bobby?'

Ignoring this, Laviolette said, 'Jamie's been on probation for the past six months, and now his brother's missing.'

'You think Jamie Deane's got something to do with Bryan's disappearance?'

'Maybe. I don't know.'

'And?'

'Nothing. I just like talking to you – that's all. You don't trust me,' he added.

'I don't need to. You've got your own Sergeant.'

'Do you believe there's such a thing as a law-abiding citizen?'

'I believe there are six degrees of separation between a person who commits a crime and a person who thinks about committing a crime. I've got nothing to do with Bryan Deane's disappearance, Inspector.'

'I think we've all got something to do with it – just not in the way we think.'

# 7

There were no lights on at number nineteen Parkview when Anna pulled up outside, and nobody answered the door when she rang so she let herself in, automatically turning on the hall light and calling out softly for Mary. But there was no reply, and the house was full of an overwhelming stillness.

She ran up to the bedroom.

Thinking Erwin was asleep, Anna crept round the foot of the bed and sat down in the green G-Plan chair she'd sat in earlier.

After a while, she felt his hand, cold, trying to take hold of her. 'It's me – Anna.'

Erwin nodded, and gave her hand a weak squeeze.

'Are you in pain?'

'Always,' he smiled.

'Do you want more morphine?'

'In a bit. But not right now – just you stay sitting there,' he trailed off, his mouth too dry to say anything else.

She sensed his fear, in the way he was watching her, and the way he held her hand, and at the same time how interminable his ending had become to him.

The house felt emptier each day as his presence in it receded in proportion to the collapse of his will, which had been so strong and which had seen him survive capture at the age of seventeen – after only six months in the Luftwaffe's signal corps – and internment, first in Belgium then in England.

Now Erwin was barely there.

'Where's Nan?'

'Out in the garden.' Erwin shut his eyes. 'They say Bryan Deane's gone missing,' he whispered, slowly. 'I remember you two up at the club – how old were you, eleven? Twelve? – Saturday afternoons . . .'

'I don't remember that.'

'We'd go to the market in the morning then Nan would come home for some peace and quiet and I'd take you to the club with me, and Bobby Deane was usually there, and you and Bryan would play. You'd play for hours.'

'We would?'

'You got your first kiss at the club.'

She ran two fingers inadvertently over her lips as she remembered, suddenly, the smoky carpet smell of the club. All those Saturday afternoons spent among men talking, mumbling and drinking slowly until one of them said something funny, which everybody was obliged to at some point, and they'd all laugh – before falling silent again over their Federation Ale.

And Bryan . . . kissing Bryan under the table among all those legs and shoes, and how he'd tasted of sherbet and cigarette and childhood still.

Her first kiss.

She could taste sherbet now just thinking about it, and she must have been smiling too because Erwin's mouth was attempting a smile in return.

'You remember now, don't you?'

'How did you see?' she said, laughing.

'I wasn't at the table. I was at the bar getting in a round.'

Pouring herself a glass of water from the jug on the bedside table, she made an effort to transfer the memory of sweetness from sherbet to the lime and lemonades Erwin would buy her – as many as she asked for until she was nearly sick on the bus home.

'Joyce,' she said, remembering the conductress who was always on the bus home – the thinnest woman she'd ever seen, with tight curls covering her head. 'She liked you.'

'Everybody liked me.'

'That's why she used to let us on the bus for free, and we always had to sit downstairs because you were too drunk to make the stairs.'

'I was never drunk.'

'You were. Every Saturday without fail.'

They sat in silence after this until Erwin said with difficulty, 'I need to tell you about Bettina. I need to tell you about her before –'

'Granddad, it doesn't matter. Bettina doesn't matter to me.' She paused, slipping her hand out of Erwin's still cold grasp. 'And I want it to stay that way. I don't want you to say something that's going to make her matter to me.'

'You don't know what I'm going to say.'

'I don't want to know.'

'But that might change.'

They were silent, Anna wanting to leave now.

'There's a photograph,' Erwin persisted, his voice a croaking whisper, 'in the cupboard behind the dresser where the wallpaper's come away from the wall in the corner just under the coat rack.'

When Anna hesitated, he said suddenly, irritably, 'Just get the bloody photo – it's the only one I've got left.'

She went into the built-in cupboard behind the dresser and found the piece of loose wallpaper he was talking about.

'It's for you,' he said weakly when he saw that she had the photograph in her hand. 'Anna,' he tried to call out after her as she left the room, crossing the small landing to the bedroom at the back of the house that used to be hers – and her mother, Bettina's, before that. She'd avoided going in there since coming back because childhood bedrooms were dangerous places for adults to return to.

The curtains weren't drawn and through the window she could just make out the dark mass of park and the signal lights on the Alcan railway tracks running along the top of the embankment.

She sat down carefully on the edge of the bed without turning on the lights, aware of the black cat with a pink ribbon round its neck – Erwin had found it on one of the buses he cleaned – on the pillow behind her next to a night-dress case she'd embroidered at school. Hanging from a hook in the wall, just to the left of the mirror above the chest of drawers, were the necklaces she'd worn to adorn her burgeoning teenage body in the hopeful, intact years between puberty and the loss of her virginity – to a boy on a campsite in the South of France, she remembered briefly.

Then she turned over the photograph, able to see enough in the orange light coming in through the open bedroom door.

She didn't recognise the girl – Bettina at the age of twenty; fourteen years younger than she was now – but she recognised where the photograph had been taken. Bettina was standing down on the beach at the mouth of the estuary a mile north of the Hartford Estate, her head turned towards the photographer – Erwin, Anna guessed – who must have been standing on the bridge above; the bridge that carried the road over the estuary and ran up to Cambois power station. It was only possible to walk on this stretch of beach by the estuary at low tide and people looking for sea coal went picking further up the coast making this stretch a lonely place – ideal for someone wanting to take a walk without being seen. Erwin must have followed her that day – maybe followed her every day at a distance, keeping his eye on her. Anna could imagine him doing that; it was the sort of thing Erwin would do.

Bettina's dress was ballooning around her – not because of the wind, but because of her pregnancy.

Bettina was pregnant with her, Anna, in the photograph and Anna was shocked at how protective she felt towards the heavily pregnant girl who had essentially abandoned her at birth and who she'd never known – less than a stranger to her because she should have been so much more.

Erwin and Mary had loved Bettina with all the abandon of parents whose union the world around them had been slow to accept. They'd been carefree in their love because – up until the moment they found out she was pregnant – they'd thought love was enough for a child. It wasn't.

Mary never got over her confusion – a confusion which manifested itself in the way she loved Anna.

While Erwin threw his heart to Anna with the same eager abandon as he had to Bettina, Mary – colder, wiser, afraid – loved sparingly; carefully. After Bettina's pregnancy and sudden departure it was Mary who was left to soak up public opinion, and Anna who – ironically – offered her her only chance of social redemption.

Mary became watchful and ambitious (despite her grand-daughter's speech impediment), hiring a tutor – a thin, precise man who objected to people like the Fausts, but who needed the money – to ensure that Anna passed the Eleven Plus. Anna would have passed the exam anyway, but it wasn't in the tutor's interest to point this out. He gave Mary muted progress reports throughout the ten months they paid him for – creating the impression that there was something lacking in Anna that only he, the indispensable Mr Dudley, could give her – and was happy to accept her tearful gratitude when the offer of a scholarship arrived in the post.

First time round, the only thing Mary had been interested in as a parent was her daughter's happiness. Second time round happiness had lost its credence and appeal. The essential thing, she realised, was to arm her granddaughter against adversity. The downside to this was that she spent so much of Anna's formative years aware of who she didn't want her to become that by the time the danger was over and Anna was about to leave home for university – she had no idea who she had become.

While Mary had never stopped loving Anna, the prouder she became of her granddaughter the less she understood her.

There was nothing written on the back of the photograph and Anna was about to fold it up and push it in her jeans pocket when she stood up instead, opening the wardrobe door. Inside she saw a box for an electric kettle Erwin and Mary had had for at least twenty years.

She put the photograph under the packaging in the bottom of the box because she didn't want to take Bettina with her. She didn't want the responsibility Erwin had bequeathed her and was angry with him for attempting to make her complicit in this secret legacy.

Pausing on the landing, she thought about going into Erwin's room again to tell him what she'd done with the photograph then changed her mind, and went downstairs instead – out into the garden.

It had stayed fine for the rest of the day, and the twilight – just settling now over the garden – was long and generous, but she still had trouble at first picking out Mary, standing in the semi-darkness of the wash house, staring out through the window.

She could tell – from Mary's posture and the lack of light – that Mary had been crying, and that this was where Mary came to cry. The secret emotional life of a whole generation of women had been lived out within the sturdy brick walls of these perfunctory outhouses built for laundry, tears and – as in the case of Rachel Deane – far worse things, and for the first time ever Anna had an overwhelming sense of this. To the extent that she felt like a trespasser as she knocked on the door and went inside.

There was Mary's old Hoover twin tub machine, preserved beneath a blanket but rubbing shoulders with the small automatic machine that had usurped it. There was a stack of used paint cans against the far wall and above them a calendar from the Blyth Allotment Association for the year 2000. Hanging from a nail in the wall was her old bucket and spade, and a three-foot doll that had once belonged to her mother, Bettina, and that Anna had been given when she was about the same height as the doll. Its eyes moved and it walked and talked. It had terrified her as a child. It still terrified her, she thought, turning away from where it stood in the corner, leaning back on its heels with its arms outstretched towards her.

'Nan,' she said softly.

Mary, who hadn't turned round when she heard the door to the wash house open, turned round now, reluctantly. She stared at Anna, sighed, then turned back to the window while buttoning and unbuttoning the bottom button on the cardigan she was wearing.

'Sorry – you weren't in the house, and –'

'Just give me a few seconds.'

Anna was about to leave when Mary said suddenly, helplessly, 'Look at me,' – as if her appearance was about to jeopardise everything. 'I'm sorry –' She faltered. 'I needed a bit of respite.'

'It's fine,' Anna soothed her, kissing and holding her.

'Don't you get lonely?' Mary said after a while.

'I don't really think about it.'

'You need someone, Anna. What happened to that Frenchman – Alec?'

'We kept each other company, Nan, that was all. We enhanced each other economically and socially.'

'Where's the harm in that? There's plenty of people who live their lives like that.'

'What's so wrong in wanting to be with someone I know I'll be sitting holding hands with at the age of eighty while we listen to a doctor telling us that one of us is going to die?'

Mary shook her head, smiling.

'I was twenty-two when I met Erwin, and marrying him was the single biggest act of rebellion in my life. I lost my family over him. This love you're talking about – it doesn't just give, it takes away. It forces you to make choices, and sometimes it can leave you stranded . . . lonelier than you've ever felt in your life before. So lonely, you wish . . .' She trailed off.

'What?'

'You wish you'd never had it in the first place. Erwin wasn't my first love,' Mary said after a while. 'My first love was Bobby Deane. I never told you that before, did I?'

'Bobby Deane,' Anna said, shocked.

'You should of seen him back then,' Mary carried on, smiling openly at her – enjoying her shock.

'Bobby Deane,' Anna said again.

'It was before Rachel. I was tiny – sixteen or seventeen. It never meant anything much to him. Not like Rachel,' she finished, turning away to look out the window again.

Anna watched her cough into the sink then straighten up.

'That reminds me. I found one of Bryan's drawings – them ones he used to do. It was up on the wall behind those

93

blankets. The paper's got damp, but the drawing's not spoiled.'

It wasn't.

The brown and black ink drawing of a spider was intact, and underneath in unsure biro, was written: Agelena labyrinthica of Agelenidae family – 12 September 1986 by Bryan Deane.

'The date on it – that's a year after Rachel died.'

'You should keep it,' Mary said.

Anna sat down on the old stool Mary and Erwin used for decorating – staring at the picture.

'He must of used a magnifying glass for that. The detail –'

Anna didn't respond. The magnifying glass again; magnifying glass . . . 'The magnifying glass,' she said out loud to Mary. 'I found it that day.'

'What day?'

'In the garden – on the brick path near where the potatoes were growing. It was summer. I must have been thirteen?'

'What day?' Mary said again.

The magnifying glass had been irritating her since their conversation that morning, but Anna remembered now. 'The day Jamie Deane locked me in their wash house. I went round to the Deanes' house to return Bryan's magnifying glass, but he wasn't in. It was Jamie Deane who answered the door. You remember . . . I came home in such a state.'

Mary shook her head.

'You had that job up at the Welwyn electrics factory where Rachel used to work. It was so hot that day.'

So hot, she remembered her palms sweating as she turned the magnifying glass over and over in her hands, waiting in the overgrown and neglected front garden at number fifteen Parkview. She was on the point of turning away – she'd never rung on the door to number fifteen before because

94

Bryan always came for her through the back garden and knocked on the kitchen window – when the decomposing nets at the window were lifted then dropped. A second later the front door opened and Jamie Deane was standing there in bleached jeans and a black T-shirt – she could hear Iron Maiden playing inside the house.

By then she'd changed her mind, but it was too late.

'Is B-B-Bryan there, please?' She could hear herself saying it.

Jamie stared – then laughed and jerked his head at her to come in.

'What d'you want with Bryan?'

He didn't mimic her in the way most people did.

'Just wanted to return s-s-something of his.'

That's when he pulled the magnifying glass out of her hand and stared at her through it. 'And what's Bryan want with this then?'

The scene continued to play itself out – vividly – as she sat motionless on the stool, watched by Mary.

'Is he here?' she said, without much hope. Nobody seemed to be here at number fifteen – apart from Jamie.

She'd never been inside number fifteen Parkview before and was trying hard to hide her shock at the fact that there was no carpet on the stairs; that the wallpaper was scratched and shredded, and that the door to the lounge was peppered with darts.

Then Jamie called out, 'Laura – look who's here,' and Anna's shock intensified as an upstairs door opened – the Iron Maiden that was playing becoming even louder – and Laura appeared at the top of the stairs smoking and staring at her, without warmth.

Anna and Laura had barely spoken for the past few years. Doreen and Mary had, between them both, sporadically attempted to reinforce the friendship, but it hadn't worked.

Doreen was especially keen because Laura was doing badly at school, hanging out with boys much older than her and smoking. She shared all this with Mary knowing that Mary would understand because of what had happened to Bettina, and that she wouldn't hold it against her. The thing she didn't share – with Mary or anyone else – was that the happiness had gone out of Laura and it was this that was really haunting her. Where had the happiness gone? Who had taken it? The fact was, the Hamilton family was disintegrating and Doreen thought Anna would be a good influence on Laura, which was an honourable enough sentiment but the fact was Anna and Laura now existed in different worlds. Anna broke into a cold sweat if she got a verb ending wrong in a German vocabulary test while Laura was happy to hurl chairs across classrooms and set fire to other girls' hair in home economics.

In fact, Laura now terrified Anna as much as Jamie Deane did.

Jamie was still smiling at Anna in a slow, lopsided sort of way as he started to run his hand over her back.

She froze, staring helplessly at Laura, who remained at the top of the stairs staring blankly at her and exhaling.

'How old are you?' Jamie asked.

'T-t-thirteen,' Anna croaked.

'And still not wearing a bra?'

'She's got nothing to put in a bra that's why,' Laura said belligerently from her post.

'Let's have a look.' Jamie started to pull at Anna's T-shirt, dropping the magnifying glass on the floor and breaking it.

'No,' Anna yelled, instinctively knowing that whatever happened, she mustn't let Jamie Deane lift up her T-shirt.

'Alright – alright,' he said, laughing, and stumbling back towards the staircase.

Then he was staring at her again – they were both staring

at her, Laura and him, and it occurred to Anna that behind the blankness, Laura was scared as well.

'Bryan's in the wash house,' Jamie said suddenly.

Laura stood up on the stairs, throwing the cigarette down. It looked like she was about to say something but in the end changed her mind.

Anna ran through to the kitchen, out into the back passage and through to the garden aware of Jamie directly behind her. The wash house leant against the back wall of the house just as it did at number nineteen Parkview, and every other house on the Hartford Estate. It was where a lot of women still spent their Mondays only not here at number fifteen because there were no women at number fifteen Parkview, and she should have thought about that – she should have known then that the wash house was the last place Bryan would be . . . the wash house was where Rachel hanged herself, but all Anna could think about was Jamie Deane behind her.

The door to the Deanes' wash house had been painted green by number fifteen's previous tenants, and there was a piece of orange string with rabbit's feet tied into it nailed to the doorframe. She should have thought about that as well, but she didn't.

The door opened easily and she slammed it shut behind her, leaning against it and breathing hard. Then she heard Jamie turning a key in the lock and realised – too late – what was happening. That's when she remembered that it was the wash house where Bryan discovered Rachel Deane, hanging from the roof beam – and there were a pair of large, still round eyes staring at her through the dark.

She screamed, turned round and started to pull on the door, pulling on it so hard she broke the handle, dropping it at her feet.

'Laura!' she screamed out automatically, her eyes shut

now, pressing her face into something soft hanging from the back of the door – Rachel Deane's old apron? 'Laura!' she screamed again, her eyes shut still and breathing hard – not wanting to touch anything.

Then there was a tapping on the wash house window and turning to look she saw the eyes staring at her again, and what it was the eyes belonged to, which was also the source of the terrible sweet smell filling the wash house – a dead fallow deer hung up by its legs, which were bunched together with blue rope. The deer's head was hanging back and there was a yellow plastic washing up bowl on the floor, positioned to catch the blood coming from its throat. The deer must have been hanging for a while because there was no blood coming out of it any more. There were only the eyes, staring, and beyond them Jamie Deane's face grinning at her through the window.

After the first hour passed and she'd given up shouting and kicking at the door, she was almost glad of the deer. She had no idea how long she was in the wash house, only that the quality of light gradually changed and that at some point the door was clumsily unlocked and slammed suddenly open – so forcefully that in its juddering rebound it nearly shut itself again. Who was it who opened the door? Who let her out?

'Anna, pet?' Mary said, concerned.

Anna stared at her, aware that she was breathing hard. 'There was a deer hanging up in the wash house.'

Mary was nodding slowly at her now. 'Bobby used to hunt them over the border, in Scotland. He started when the strikes were on.'

'You must remember that day, Nan. You have to,' she insisted, looking at Mary, who she could barely see now in the doorway. Neither of them had made a move to switch on the lights. 'I was in such a state when I got home.'

'I think we should go back inside the house and have a sherry.'

'Don't you remember it at all?'

'I don't, no – come on.'

It was night outside as Anna followed Mary back indoors, turning on the light and watching her take the bottle of sherry out the cupboard, placing it with due reverence on the table.

Apart from the consecrated bottle of sherry, Mary didn't keep alcohol in the house. Life was too hard and the temptation of the bottle too strong, and so many men – women as well – had lost their reputation in the bottom of a bottle. You were only as good as your reputation – if you lost that, you lost everything.

So the unspoken rule was that you drank up at the club, in public and among friends. It was the only guarantee of being able to escape daily life – even if only momentarily – while at the same time preserving its sanctity.

Mary looked terrible beneath the unforgiving strip lighting in the kitchenette and suddenly, without knowing why, Anna realised that Mary had been lying in the wash house – about not remembering that day.

Mary looked up then – instinctively aware of Anna's eyes on her – before looking away again.

'Jamie Deane's out of prison.'

'Jamie Deane?' Mary sat down and tried to pour the sherry, but her arm wasn't steady enough. 'Can you?' she said to Anna, handing her the bottle.

'I'd forgotten he was even in prison. Did Don and Doreen not say anything?'

She passed Mary her glass of sherry.

'No,' Mary said, her tone implying that Anna should know how the situation was. 'Nobody's got anything to say about Jamie Deane any more.'

Anna nodded, drank her sherry, then put the glass back down on the table.

Mary's glass was empty as well.

Anna poured them another one, staring at the replenished glass and the thick amber liquid that slid sluggishly to one side when she tilted it. 'You knew about Jamie being out of prison,' she suggested quietly.

'I'm tired –'

'You knew.'

Mary drank the second glass of sherry, but held up her hand when Anna tried to pour her more.

'Is this the only alcohol you've got in the house?'

'You know it's the only alcohol we keep. I've seen him – Jamie.' Mary sighed.

Anna was shocked. 'You've seen him?'

'At Bobby Deane's.'

'What the hell were you doing at Bobby Deane's?'

'He's not well – he needs stuff doing for him.'

'And you've been . . . doing that stuff?'

Mary nodded sadly.

'Why?' Anna demanded.

'I told you why,' Mary responded angrily.

'He's got Alzheimer's.'

'How do you know?'

'Inspector Laviolette told me – he's been to see him because of Bryan. You need to contact social services, Nan. Where's Laura in all of this?'

'Bobby and Laura never got on. Laviolette?'

'You know him?' Anna asked, interested.

'Is he involved in this business with Bryan? That can't be right –'

'Why not?'

Mary fought briefly with herself then pushed her glass

forward for some more sherry. 'It's his father, Roger Laviolette, who Rachel Deane –'

'Had the affair with?'

'Spent time with,' Mary corrected her.

'The widower? What happened to him?'

'You don't remember?' Mary said, surprised. 'He died.'

'How?'

'Jamie Deane killed him.'

'You said Roger Laviolette had an accident.'

'Dying's an accident,' Mary said, uncharacteristically obtuse.

'But murder isn't.' Anna paused. 'Laviolette told me people thought it was Bobby who did it and Jamie who took the blame despite never actually confessing to it.' She didn't say that he'd failed to mention it was his father who was murdered.

'He said that – to you?' Mary shook her head. 'No. It was never Bobby. Bobby Deane never hurt anybody,' she said shortly.

Anna left Mary standing at the front door, one arm pulling her cardigan around her against the night, the other waving.

She got back to the Ridley Arms just after nine and put Bryan's picture of the spider next to the photograph Martha had given her, which she'd balanced against the wall on the kitchen bench. Bryan Deane . . . sitting sad and preoccupied in an island paradise Laura and he had paid a substantial amount of money to spend time in.

She picked up the photograph and read 'Cephalonia – Aug 2007' written across the back before putting it down, looking round the empty apartment and deciding to go for the run she'd been trying to have all day.

*

It was too dark to run on the beach so she stuck to the coastal road, her ankles bearing the brunt of tarmac. She passed the bandstand – still semi-flooded from all the recent rain – and defences from the last war, buried in dunes that rose in a high line now alongside her. When they dipped she could just make out the blockish silhouettes of the tank traps – that she remembered playing on as a child.

She carried on running – past the Shipwright's Arms Bryan failed to show up at the night before, and the Duneside development he failed to return home to – until she got to the harbour at Seaton Sluice where she stopped, breathing hard. The tide was on the turn and the sea was loud in her ears. There was something large and white lying on its side at the water's edge – an abandoned fridge that the tide must have brought in.

Still breathing hard, she bent over – pressing her forehead into her knees.

What happened to Jamie Deane after that day Mary claimed to have no recollection of?

There had been police at number fifteen Parkview, she remembered now. The police took Jamie Deane away, and that was all she knew – at the time she didn't really care why or where; she never really asked. So it must have been then – the day she was locked in the wash house – that Roger Laviolette was murdered.

What she did care about was Bryan, who for some reason she never understood stopped speaking to her after that. When the summer finally ended and they went back to school, he no longer waited for her in the litter-ridden flower beds by the bus stop.

She wondered, now, why she never challenged him about this, but it was impossible to revisit the perspective of her thirteen-year-old self. At the time, she simply didn't. At the time, she let him go.

That September Laura Hamilton and Bryan Deane started seeing each other in a way that made Anna and Bryan's old friendship seem childish and irrelevant.

Bryan never came into the garden again.

Anna stood up straight, looking around her.

This was where she usually followed the headland for a further two miles to the lighthouse, but she wouldn't manage that tonight. Reluctantly, with an air of defeat, she turned her back on the harbour at Seaton Sluice and started to run slowly back towards Blyth – the copper coloured towers of the Alcan aluminium smelting plant floodlit in the distance.

When she got back to the Ridley Arms, she shut herself in the bathroom. It was the first time she'd shut any doors in the apartment and she didn't just shut it, she locked it as well.

After a while, she turned on the shower then sat down on the toilet, staring at the locked bathroom door as, without warning, she started to cry.

# 8

While Anna sat on the toilet, crying, Laura Deane – drunk – walked into her daughter's room and stood staring aimlessly around her.

Martha, who was sitting at her desk working on one of the Victorian porcelain dolls she collected – that Doreen bought her in kit form – turned to look at Laura.

Laura was wearing a grey batwing jumper – the sort she used to wear when she was the same age as Martha, that had once again become fashionable – and a pair of tights.

Martha felt sick looking at her and turned away, back to the doll. She'd made up the calico body, pushing the stuffing carefully into the corners with the stub of an old pencil she kept specifically for this purpose, and was now in the process of attaching the doll's head, arms and feet to the torso. The arms and feet weren't too tricky because there were minute holes drilled through the porcelain, which meant these could be sewn on. The head was more difficult. It required gluing and she had to be careful not to get bits of glue stuck in the doll's hair.

The spotlight angled over the desk – the only light in the room – was hot on her hands as she concentrated hard on applying the glue to the doll's neck, willing Laura to leave.

But Laura didn't leave.

Martha heard her approaching the desk, her shadow falling over it – making it impossible for Martha to see properly. She tried to carry on, but couldn't and in the end laid the doll down, her face set.

'What's that you're doing?' Laura asked, slowly. Her mouth felt cluttered with the words as she made an effort to get them out in the right order. Talking to Martha was a complex task sober, drunk it felt like she'd just had a stroke.

She hung blearily over the desk, taking in Martha's hair – which had been tied in a plait – and resisting the urge to slip the band off the end and spread her daughter's hair across her shoulders.

'You've got beautiful hair,' she mumbled. 'You should wear it down more.'

Martha pulled instinctively away then continued to sit in silence, waiting for her to leave, as Laura's attention was taken suddenly by the tea light flickering on the windowsill, and the photograph of Bryan propped behind it.

'That's a horrible photograph,' she said, picking it up and frowning as she read the back. 'I don't remember taking that.'

'You didn't. I did.'

Laura put the photograph back on the windowsill – unsteadily – and continued to contemplate it.

'That was a good holiday. We had a great time in Cephalonia.'

'No we didn't.'

'I've got some lovely pictures from that holiday.'

'You did nothing but argue the whole time. I heard you – above the air conditioning.'

'There was stuff we needed to talk about.'

'You weren't talking.'

'We've tried to protect you, Martha.'

'Protect me?'

'It's complicated.'

'It's not his fault.'

'You've got no idea what I'm going through at the moment,' Laura said quietly.

'I'm going through it too,' Martha yelled as Laura left the room and went back downstairs.

She remained motionless at her desk listening to her mother in the kitchen opening another bottle of wine – then went downstairs herself.

'Piss off,' Laura said, without looking at her as she refilled her glass.

Martha remained by the breakfast bar, holding onto the edge of it. 'I don't believe you. I don't believe any of this.'

'What the fuck are you talking about?'

'Dad –'

Laura stared at her for a moment before breaking into uncontrollable laughter.

Martha watched her laugh until eventually she ran out of laughter.

'You need your head seeing to,' Laura observed, her teeth hitting the side of the glass.

'So you keep telling me. Anna's on my side.'

'Anna? What's Anna got to do with any of this?'

'She was the last person to see dad alive. She cares about him, and when dad saw her yesterday morning outside Nan's – he squeezed my hand so hard, I –'

'Shut up.'

'Something happened between them.'

'Shut up.'

'I know it did. Why won't you tell me?'

'Look at you.' Her eyes ran over her daughter, her mouth sagging open. 'What did I do to deserve you?' She drained her glass and poured herself another. 'One of these days they'll put you in a straitjacket, you know that, don't you? And I won't have any trouble signing that bit of paper.'

'Shit. No wonder dad went.'

'Get out! Get out now!' Laura yelled, throwing the glass at Martha. It smashed on impact with the breakfast bar, spraying Argentine Malbec over the floor and walls.

Martha ran upstairs as Laura knelt down on the floor among the broken glass, cloth in hand, mopping automatically, oblivious to her hair trailing through the puddles of wine that had arranged themselves tidily across the non-porous kitchen floor.

Upstairs, Martha – breathless – sat back down at her desk.

After a while, she picked up the doll's head, stroking the delicate features with the tip of her forefinger.

At some point Laura came upstairs, slamming shut her bedroom door and falling face down on the bed, narrowly missing Roxy whose head shot up, momentarily alert.


A white transit van with Reeves Regeneration painted on the side drove over the mini roundabout at the end of Bridge Street, Blyth. It followed the coastal route Anna had taken in her car the night before – Easter Saturday – because its destination was the same: number two Marine Drive on the new Duneside development at Seaton Sluice.

The roads were empty but the van was unable to increase its speed because there was an infestation of speed cameras along this stretch of road, which had been popular with joy riders in the late nineties – something the driver, Jamie Deane, had missed.

He turned up the radio as Metallica's Master of Puppets came on – under the impression it was playing solely for him – and started to thrash about in his seat, pulling viciously on the steering wheel in time to the music.

The world he'd left behind as a child had changed and

he didn't recognise the look of it any more, or understand the pace of it. Freedom, he'd come to realise, had its own horrors, and in the beginning it was these horrors that kept him sitting on the floor of his room with his back against the wall, in the Blyth hostel probation had put him in – not far from the Quayside. Unsure when he was meant to go to sleep or when he was meant to get up, he found it easier to just stick to the body clock he'd been running on for the past twenty years.

His counsellor – a woman called Janet, who blushed when she spoke to him – assured him that the symptoms he was suffering (and she could see he was suffering) were normal, but Jamie wasn't interested in normal and it was unrealistic of Janet to set him this fixed idea of normality as a goal when he was still struggling to achieve a sense of reality.

He just wanted to find a place he belonged, and if it wasn't this world, the one he'd been carrying inside him since he was fifteen, then which world was it?

There was too much colour, too many people, and too many cars, which was why he preferred going out at night. There was too much of everything, and his childhood haunts – the rows and their backstreets, the derelict corners – had vanished beneath tailored plots with honey-coloured houses like those on Marine Drive. The houses had fenced in front and back gardens, and drives – because everybody seemed to have at least one car. The world looked better, but it didn't feel better.

Janet encouraged him to sit his driving test, and then helped him to get a job with a contractor the council used for house clearance and waste collection – Reeves Regeneration. The department he worked for was Environmental Services, but the work was essentially rag and bone work, and he got to drive a van – the one he was driving in now. He wound down the window laughing wildly at the dunes running alongside, suddenly excited in a way he hadn't been for a very long time.

He pulled up outside number two Marine Drive, parking across the driveway and peering through the van's window at his brother's house with a happy curiosity.

He'd driven here many times over the past six months, but the reality of their lives – the detached house with all the windows and the big silver cars on the drive – had terrified him. Bryan and Laura had been children the last time he saw them. Since yesterday, however, the reality had changed and although the house looked the same from the outside, he knew Bryan wasn't there. Laura was in the house on her own, and this terrified him a little less.

The Thompsons – next door at number four – were just seeing off the last of their Easter Sunday guests, and Mr Thompson lingered in his front porch as Jamie Deane's white van pulled up outside number two. Mr Thompson didn't like the look of the white transit van, and would have liked the look of the driver even less – but was unable to see Jamie Deane, clocking him as he stood in his front porch.

In the early days of his career, Mr Thompson had driven a white transit van just like Jamie Deane's and didn't want to be reminded of it now, standing outside number four Marine Drive on Easter Sunday. The van had no business being there.

Just as Bryan Deane had no business disappearing like that, which had resulted in his missing a seminal episode of Gardeners' World on Alpines while he answered a series of absurd questions put to him by the police.

The Deanes, in fact, had irritated Mr Thompson ever since they moved in. They were loud in the garden, and when father and daughter played badminton they hit the shuttlecock over the fence. The girl was forever knocking on their door asking for it back, treading in his borders . . . crouching down and straightening up among his Delphiniums – many of them taller than she was – in her white shorts.

There was that time her throat had risen at him from the collar of her short-sleeve green blouse and he had been unable to take his eyes off it; had not been able to help himself, and all the time she'd carried on – in that knowing way girls did – as if she was playing a game that was new and strange to her with an imaginary friend she had no idea had the potential to become dangerous when provoked.

Mr Thompson wished it was the girl who had gone missing, and not the father.

Then his wife called him indoors.

Inside number two Marine Drive, Laura Deane's phone started to ring.

Outside number two Marine Drive, Jamie turned off the radio, but carried on singing – his phone pressed against his ear.

Inside number two Marine Drive, Martha laid down the doll she was putting the finishing touches to, and listened.

The unanswered phone made the house feel empty.

Then the ringing stopped.

Outside number two Marine Drive, Jamie rang off, aware that his irritation was rising. He started to tap his phone against the dashboard, keeping his eyes on the house and scratching nervously at his face. There were lights on upstairs and down. He'd try again, and if she didn't pick up . . . if she didn't pick up, then what? He could ring on the door, but he didn't feel like doing that just yet. He'd had the idea of doing this gradually, and had been proud of himself for deciding on restraint.

So instead, he got out his Oxford Dictionary of Quotations from the van's glove compartment, opened it at random and found one he liked. He read it out loud a couple of times in a slow monotone and without feeling, trying to memorise the words.

There were no other sounds in the house so Martha crept towards her parents' room and, opening the door, saw Laura lying diagonally across the bed with the duvet only partially covering her, and still semi-dressed in tights and a jumper. A box of Nytol lay open and untidy on the right hand bedside table.

Roxy jumped lazily to the floor and trotted out of the room past Martha, who was crouched down by the side of the bed checking Laura's pulse to make sure that she was only comatose and not dead. Close up, Laura was breathing – deep, steady and unpleasant smelling breaths. Martha pulled on her hair and pinched her upper arm hard, but she didn't stir.

Reassured, Martha picked up the mobile. The unanswered call registered on the screen as 'Caller Unknown'. She scrolled through the messages in Laura's inbox, but there was nothing untoward. There was a call from Bryan at 15:37 on Saturday. He'd tried phoning her again at 15:45, but she mustn't have picked up because it was logged as a missed call.

She was just putting Laura's phone in her pocket when it started ringing again.

Creeping quickly out of her parents' room, she ran down the corridor back into her own room.

'Laura? It's me – Jamie.' A pause. 'Go on – say something.'

Martha kept the phone pressed against her ear, and didn't say anything.

'Why don't you take a look out the window?'

Martha got up and walked slowly downstairs, tripping on the last tread and falling into a turquoise vase whose dried flower display was shaken, dusty, to the floor.

Through the centimetre gap in the lounge curtains, she could see a white transit van parked on the pavement outside beneath the street lamp, and made out a man, indistinct, turned towards the house, watching.

'There you are. Hello, Laura,' the voice said softly. 'It's been a long time and I just wanted to say – I don't know what I wanted to say actually, only that I heard about Bryan and that I'm here. As you can see.'

Martha called off and pulled the curtains together, hanging onto the edges of them.

The phone didn't ring again, and soon she heard the van pulling away.

She exhaled, aware that her heart was beating fast and – suddenly, forcibly – that Laura and she were alone in the house.

# 9

Laura woke up – clawing clumsily at the hair covering her face – to the smell of bacon cooking, and had an awful feeling that her parents were downstairs. What time was it?

She got out of bed – saw Martha standing at the end, staring at her – then got back into it again, pulling the covers over her this time and dislodging Roxy, who let out a muffled whine before running past Martha downstairs to the kitchen where Doreen was frying bacon, and Don, unsure what to do with himself, was sitting awkwardly at the breakfast bar fiddling with a basket, which had strange-looking fruit in it he couldn't have put a name to.

Laura shut her eyes. 'Roxy needs a walk. Why don't you take her down to the beach?'

Ignoring this, Martha said, 'Who's Jamie?'

Laura sat up, her hands grasping at the duvet, wide-eyed.

'Who is he?' Martha demanded. 'He phoned you on your mobile last night – I picked up.'

Laura's eyes flicked rapidly round the room until she located her mobile, which had been put back on the bedside table the night before – after Martha had put Jamie's number into her own phone.

Checking incoming calls, she saw that she'd received a call from the same unknown number twice – once at 00:03, and then again at 00:06.

'Why did you pick up?' Laura said, angry.

'I didn't know who it was, I just I heard your phone ringing and it was late, and I thought it might be important – about dad.'

'What did he say?'

'Who is he?'

'What did he say?' Laura demanded.

'I don't know – nothing.'

'He must have said something.'

'I don't know,' Martha yelled, tearful. 'He said he'd heard about dad. When I looked out the window I saw a white van parked outside.'

'Parked outside where?'

'In front of the house.'

Laura got out of bed and went over to the window.

There was no sign of a white transit van, only Don and Doreen's sparkling clean lentil-coloured Toyota that Don rarely pushed above forty miles an hour.

'If my phone rings again, you leave it alone. I don't want you touching my phone.' She stayed by the window, uncertain.

'Who is he?'

'It doesn't matter.'

'If you don't tell me, I'll go down and I'll ask Nan. I'll tell them he phoned.'

'No you won't,' Laura said, crossing the room and grabbing hold suddenly of Martha's wrist, twisting it hard. 'Don't you dare do that. His name's Jamie Deane, and he's dad's brother.'

Martha, shocked, pulled her arm away. 'Dad's brother? You're lying.'

'I'm not lying,'

'I never even knew dad had a brother. How come I never knew that?'

'He was in prison – for a long time – that's why dad never said anything. He didn't want you knowing.'

'What was he in prison for?'

'Beating somebody up – badly.'

'How long for?'

Laura hesitated. 'Twenty years.'

'For beating someone up?'

Pulling absently on her necklace, Laura turned away from Martha and walked back towards the window. 'The person died.'

She stared down at the street and saw Don on the drive, washing her car. She could hear him whistling as well, breaking off to say something to the McClarens who were emerging from the garage at number six – an endless stream of children and bikes. The McClarens spent most of their weekends in Lycra – involved in pursuits that were good for the cardiovascular.

The McClarens didn't shy from Don, on the drive washing Laura's car, because a disappearing husband wasn't the kind of thing to dent the social confidence of people like the McClarens – people who spent their summers, en famille, re-thatching remote village schools in places like Tanzania.

There was a camping table at the end of their drive with a sign sellotaped to it:

Daisy's perfume shop. Rose petal perfume only £2.

The jars of rose petal perfume – made by the youngest McClaren, Daisy, were lined up on top.

'You're scared of him,' Martha said suddenly.

Martha was right – Laura was scared. She wished Bryan was there only Bryan wasn't.

Breakfast was eaten in silence. Each one of them in turn tried to think of something to say, but in the end only Don succeeded – with a flaccid observation that the garden furniture needed a new coat of oil, which did little to initiate further conversation.

So they continued to eat in silence, aware that if Bryan had been there still, Doreen would never have cooked breakfast in Laura's kitchen.

With Bryan's disappearance, Laura had become their daughter again.

She needed them.

After years of there being nothing to do except stand on the sidelines and marvel at the life Laura and Bryan had built for themselves – now, at last, they had something to do.

After breakfast, while Don and Martha looked for Roxy's lead and got ready to take her down to the beach, Doreen – who was virtually blind – knelt on all fours in front of the oven with some wire wool, arguing with Laura about the amount of Nytol she was taking, and what she was mixing it with.

They were still arguing when Martha, hooking her arm through Don's, let Roxy lead them down Marine Drive past neighbours who'd barely been aware of her before (apart from Mr Thompson), but who had since heard about Bryan, and who now stared at her – Martha Deane, the girl whose father had gone missing.

She held tightly onto Don, pressing her face into his jacket, which smelt heavily of soap and aftershave.

'I don't like people staring,' she mumbled.

'They're not staring,' Don said lightly.

'They are,' Martha insisted, keeping close to him until

they'd crossed the main road onto the dunes where she let Roxy off her lead.

Don threw a couple of sticks for her, but she just watched them arch through the air and fall onto the beach ahead while continuing to pant expectantly.

'Daft dog – they're for you, they are,' he yelled, above the wind, hurling a stick into the sea this time. Roxy watched as the stick meant for her was pursued by an excited Border Collie who went crashing into the waves after it.

Don and Martha stood at the water's edge along with Roxy, watching the Collie in the sea attempt to retrieve Don's stick.

After a while Martha said, 'Why did nobody ever tell me I had an uncle?'

'An uncle?' Don said, not denying it so much as surprised to hear it put like that.

'Jamie – Jamie Deane.'

Don looked at her then shook his head. 'Who's been talking to you about Jamie Deane?'

'Does it matter?'

'Oh, well, it was going to come out at some point.' Don sighed and put his hand roughly on top of her head, wobbling it from side to side.

'Is it true he beat somebody up so badly they died?'

Don thought carefully about this.

'He's a bad lot, that's all.' Then, because this sounded too much like a judgement, and he wasn't one to judge, he said, 'That lad never seemed to have any luck.' He shook his head, laying Jamie Deane to rest because he didn't really want to think about Jamie Deane.

Martha, still able to hear Jamie's voice in her head, decided to let it rest as well. She could have asked Don more, but what Don had said and how he'd said it had taken the fear out of last night's call for her.

117

Now, standing on the beach in broad daylight with Don beside her, she just felt vaguely sorry for this uncle she'd never seen. Part of her even wondered – hoped – if he'd try to contact them again.

She pulled Don's hand out of his pocket and took hold of it, swinging it gently – aware of all the calluses on it, and how hard his hand felt in her own small hand. It was a hand that had seen decades of hard labour, and it was the gentlest hand she would ever hold. They stared out to sea, half expectantly – towards the horizon.

Neither of them was thinking about Jamie Deane any more.

Don slipped his hand out of Martha's, putting his arm round her instead and pulling her close as she started to cry.

'I want him to come back.'

Don didn't say anything, he just held her even tighter, rubbing at her arms.

After a while she pulled away, looking up at him. 'Your hair.'

'What about my hair?'

'It isn't moving. I mean, it's like gale force down here and your hair isn't moving at all.'

Don ran his hands over the Brylcream sculpted Teddy boy cut he'd had since before he started dating Doreen even, and smiled.

When they got back to Marine Drive, Bryan's car was being towed onto the drive at number two, watched by Inspector Laviolette who was leaning, relaxed, against the open door of his own car, smoking.

He stood up when he saw Martha and Don approach and started to walk towards them, sombre but smiling, his focus mostly on Martha – concerned that it might in some way be upsetting for her to see her father's car returned in this way.

'Alright, Martha?'

She nodded, waiting, pulling Roxy back hard to heel.

Behind them, Sergeant Chambers was talking to the man in the cab of the tow truck.

Laviolette had seen the CCTV footage yesterday and nothing had come up. He'd watched Bryan Deane park his car opposite St George's Church and get out, stretching and looking around him. He'd seen him get into his wet suit, lock up the car and take the kayak off the roof. Then Bryan Deane had watched the sea for four minutes, which was a long time, before making a phone call.

This was the phone call to his wife – Laura.

Laura had told them about it.

He made the call at 15:37.

Then he made another call – the missed call to Martha, who hadn't picked up – before putting the mobile in the boot of the car, and after this the camera lost sight of him as he disappeared down the cliff path, past the redbrick building housing the Toy Museum and Balti Experience – down onto the beach, Laviolette presumed.

He would like to have seen Bryan Deane on the beach; he would like to have seen Bryan Deane talking to Anna Faust on the beach, and kept watching half expecting – irrationally – to see the beach and Bryan and Anna because that's what he really wanted to see.

He watched hours of footage after that . . . the Bank Holiday traffic on the roads and pavements gradually decreasing . . . the parking wardens checking the ticket in the windscreen of Bryan Deane's car and booking it . . . twilight . . . the close of day . . .

Bryan Deane never went back to his car.

'You're done with it, then?' Don said, looking at Bryan's car, uncertain.

'We didn't find anything,' Laviolette said carefully, aware of Martha watching him intently.

119

He smiled blandly at her, thinking about the footage he'd seen and how his mind had picked up on something subconsciously – something important; something to do with the second phone call Bryan Deane made, the call to his daughter.

'Can I ask you something?' he said to her, smiling still. 'Your dad tried to phone you Saturday afternoon, didn't he?'

Martha nodded. 'I already told you that.'

'That's right,' Laviolette agreed. 'I was just wondering – I know you spend most Saturdays with your grandparents . . .' he nodded here at Don, who was staring warily at him '. . . and then you go home Sunday morning?'

'That's right.' It was Don who answered this, not Martha.

'Is it usual for your dad to phone you at some point?'

Don turned to Martha.

Martha was thinking about Laviolette's question – seriously considering it because it was a very good question, and one she had the impression Laviolette felt he should have thought of asking earlier.

'No,' she said after a while, looking directly at Laviolette. 'He never usually phones me while I'm at Nan's. In fact,' she added, 'Saturday was the first time I think he's ever tried to call me.'

For some reason this realisation made her smile – and warm to Laviolette in a way she hadn't until then.

Laviolette smiled back at her – he didn't doubt her and ask if she was sure, or ask her the question again. He didn't do anything other than nod silently.

'Dad phoning me – is that a good thing or,' Martha hesitated, 'a bad thing?'

Laviolette deliberated over this for what seemed like a long time because now he knew something about Bryan Deane that made him increasingly certain of one thing: Bryan Deane's disappearance was deliberate. He briefly revisited the idea of suicide while continuing to smile lightly at Don and Martha, but in the end pushed it aside.

'We'll see,' he said finally, in answer to Martha's question.

Martha stood gripping her bike's handlebars, listening to the sound of the TV through the walls as the garage door started to rise; the smooth electronic mechanism failing to conceal the sound of her mother's laughter. Don and Doreen had left at around three o'clock and now Martha, who'd finished her doll and decided to make a present of it to Anna, was cycling over to the Ridley Arms in Blyth.

Fifteen minutes later – barely aware of the long, slow sunset taking place around her – she turned into Quay Road, got off the bike at the entrance to the Ridley Arms and pressed on the buzzer for Flat 3. She buzzed another two times, but nobody answered so she crossed over to the other side of the road where the Harbourmaster's office was and, looking up, saw that the entire building was dark. There were no lights on inside the Ridley Arms.

She tried calling, but Anna didn't pick up, and was about to leave when the lights along the quayside came on. Turning instinctively towards them, she saw the Inspector's car parked where Anna's yellow Capri usually was, facing out to sea.

He must have seen her at the same time because he got out of his car and gave a broken wave. All Laviolette's physical gestures looked sad, Martha thought, watching him at a distance – like a succession of small, incomplete finales.

He waited by the car as she wheeled her bike over, unsure whether she was pleased to see him or not, but smiling anyway – a small, defeated smile.

'She's not in,' he said.

'I know – I just tried. She's not picking up her phone either.'

They looked up at the windows to Anna's apartment then Laviolette said suddenly, 'Was she expecting you?'

Martha shook her head. 'How long have you been waiting here for?'

He seemed surprised at the question then smiled at her again. 'Only about ten minutes or so.'

Martha didn't believe him. She didn't know why, but for some reason he was lying to her. 'Why did you want to see Anna? Nothing's happened, has it?'

'Why did *you* want to see Anna?' he asked.

A trawler with its lights on was making its way between the pier heads and into the harbour, and every now and then a single voice could be heard clearly above the sound of the engine.

'I've got something for her.'

The Inspector was watching the approaching trawler as Martha undid her rucksack and brought out the porcelain doll, holding it carefully in her hands while smoothing the hair down.

He stared down at the doll. 'You made that?'

She nodded, continuing to stroke the doll's hair.

'For Anna?'

She nodded again then turned to face him.

The Inspector smiled, and was completely unprepared for what Martha said next.

'You think dad's committed suicide, don't you?'

'No – I don't think that.'

'Yes you do.' After a while, Martha said, 'They argue all the time – mum and dad. She lied on Saturday when you asked her if everything was okay between them and she said everything was fine. It isn't. They've got no money and everything's pretty much going to shit. The other night she was going on and on at him because she was drunk – she's always drunk at the moment. She went on and on at him until he shouted back at her . . . I heard him . . .' light tears were rolling down her face, but she carried on speaking as

122

if unaware of them, '. . . that he'd be better off dead.' Martha paused, staring intently at the doll. 'What if she forced him to do something?'

'Like what?'

'I don't know,' Martha said, exasperated. 'But you should consider it – as a possibility.'

Laviolette pulled up the zip on his coat 'These things have their own rhythm, and right now the focus is on the search and possible appeal.' He started to look in his pockets for his car keys and when he found them said suddenly to her, 'Have you got lights for that?'

Martha shook her head.

It was dark now.

'I'll drive you home – we can put the bike in the boot.'

'What's this?' she said as he started up the engine and the car filled with the sound of choral music.

'Miners – singing.' He didn't tell her that it was an old recording and that one of the singing miners was his father. 'The thing you need to keep in mind,' he said, a few minutes later, 'is that there's only one person who really knows what happened to your dad – and that's your dad.'

'Your car's tidy.'

'You sound surprised.'

'I'm not talking about that sort of tidy.'

'How many different sorts of tidy are there?' He smiled through the windscreen at the road.

'I don't mean tidy like clean and tidy. I mean empty tidy, like even if you wanted to make it untidy, you wouldn't be able to because you haven't got enough stuff to litter it with. See what I mean?'

Laviolette, amused, thought about this – still smiling – then said, 'Yeah – I do.' He paused. 'You're right.'

They drove in silence for a while after this, Martha watching the wind move through the grasses on the dunes as the car crawled along. Then she turned to him and said, 'You're not married, are you?'

This time he took his eyes off the road to meet her gaze. 'What makes you say that?'

'I don't know – it just feels like there's only you.'

'You're a very astute young woman. I used to be married.'

'When?' she asked, interested.

'A long time ago – I wasn't much older than you are now.'

'Like mum and dad then – they married young.' She stared out the window again, glad she was inside the car and not out in the night on her bike. 'What went wrong?'

'Well, we should never have married in the first place – so it was more a case of nothing was going to go right anyway.'

'So why did you – marry?'

'I don't know. I really don't know.'

Martha leant back in the seat, turning her head to watch him. 'Are you still in touch?'

'No – no.'

'Vehemently said.'

Laviolette laughed.

'What? Did I say something stupid?'

'I can't imagine you ever saying anything stupid. Vehemently,' he repeated, trying not to let the fact that he was unsettled by her interest in him, show. He wasn't used to people being interested in him. 'I haven't heard that word in a long while.'

'It just came to mind.' She paused. 'I'm not sure if I like it – as a word.'

'Me neither.' Then Laviolette said quietly, 'I'm not even sure if she's dead or alive.'

'Your wife?'

He nodded.

'Why would she be dead?'

'She was a heavy drug user. Heroin.'

'Is that why things didn't work out?'

'It wasn't the drugs I had a problem with – it was the part of her that needed them.'

'It's the same thing.'

Laviolette gave her a quick look.

'I'm never getting married.'

'You're only fifteen.'

'I don't care. I'm never getting married. Whatever's there in the beginning – it always turns out the same. Look at you – mum and dad.'

She put her leg up on the dashboard, distant from him now. 'There's a moment – and it's hard to say when exactly it happens because it happens so gradually – when life becomes about owning rather than just being, and that's when things get complicated.' Laviolette paused. 'At your age, people don't expect you to own anything – they don't even expect you to own yourself.'

Martha turned away from him to look out the window, uninterested. 'Do you think anybody marries the person they're meant to?'

'Some people do.'

Laviolette turned into the Duneside development.

'On Saturday – when dad was dropping me off at Nan's – Anna was there, and it was the first time they'd seen each other in, like, sixteen years, and he was holding my hand so tight it went – numb,' she finished, gripping suddenly onto Laviolette's arm. 'Stop the car.'

'What's wrong?'

'The van – the one parked outside the house,' she whispered, 'it's dad's brother – Jamie Deane.'

Laviolette's hand remained on the gearstick as he peered through the windscreen at the van. 'Does he often come round to the house?'

Martha was staring so intently out the window that Laviolette, unsure whether or not she'd heard the question was about to ask it again when Martha said, 'Never. I didn't even know dad had a brother – until last night when he phoned mum, but she was too doped up to hear – so I picked up.'

'What did he want?'

Martha thought about this. 'Nothing. He just said that he knew about dad. I didn't say anything – I just let him talk. He thought he was speaking to mum. He sounded just like dad – on the phone. That was weird. Where are you going? Wait –'

But the Inspector was already out the car, running in a way that should have made him look ridiculous, but didn't – towards the white van, which juddered into life, pulling away sharply from the kerb and reversing over the 'Private Property' sign on the edge of number four's lawn before accelerating unevenly away – the van's exhaust scraping the blue gentians in Mr Thompson's rock garden.

Half way up Marine Drive the van jumped as the gears were changed. Thinking it was going to stall, Laviolette ran after it, but was left stooped panting over a drain as the van accelerated once more – watched by Martha who was smiling to herself, pleased. Jamie Deane had got away – from what, she didn't know, but he had got away and for some reason this made her suddenly happy.

Still bent over double, Laviolette twisted his head in the direction of number two Marine Drive, whose door was open.

The front door to number four was also open. It opened, in fact, at the same time as the door to number two, and

Mr Thompson – who'd been watching the white van long before the wanton act of vandalism – was now running in a lopsided fashion towards the rockery where he fell on his knees in the damp grass in front of his shredded gentians.

Laura Deane stood in the doorway to number two, her phone in her hand, and it was Laura Deane the Inspector made his way towards, still breathless.

For a moment her face was the most open he'd seen it – verging on vulnerable – and this, he realised, was due to fear.

But before Laviolette had a chance to speak Laura – who was watching Martha get her bike out of the Inspector's car and wheel it slowly past Mr Thompson next door, prostrate still before his gentians – said, 'What's Martha doing with you?'

Laviolette was about to respond to this when all three of them became suddenly aware of Mr Thompson getting numbly to his feet on the lawn outside number four, two dark patches of dew on his trousers at the knee.

'This is private property,' he hissed unevenly at them before stalking indoors with his left fist clenched, fully intending to write a letter requesting compensation for damages.

'Shall we go inside?' Laviolette suggested at last. 'I want to talk about Jamie Deane,' he carried on smoothly, noting the expression on Laura's face.

'My uncle,' Martha prompted her. 'The one I never knew I had?'

Ignoring this, Laura said, 'I'll open the garage so you can put your bike in.'

Laviolette waited in the hallway while Laura opened the garage door. He heard her talking to Martha. The tone was angry, but he couldn't make out the words and when they emerged from the garage Martha walked straight past him up the stairs, holding her arm as if it hurt, her face set.

'D'you mind if we go into the kitchen,' Laura said, looking suddenly tired.

He hauled himself awkwardly onto one of the bar stools – as awkwardly as Don had earlier – and watched her fill the kettle with water and switch on the gas.

'I'm putting the kettle on – I don't know why. D'you want tea? Coffee?'

'I'm fine thanks.'

'Me neither.' She switched off the gas and hovered restlessly for a moment in the corner of the kitchen. 'Actually, I'm going to have a glass of wine – it's been a long day. I don't suppose you're allowed one, are you?'

'I'm fine,' he said again, watching her uncork an already open bottle and close her eyes as she took the first sip.

'We decided not to tell Martha about Jamie.'

Laviolette didn't say anything.

'It was a joint decision,' she added. 'Are you comfortable talking about this?'

'Why wouldn't I be?'

'Well it was your –'

'How did Jamie feel about this joint decision?'

Laura shrugged irritably. 'Put it this way – he never tried to contact us either.'

Laviolette stared down at the reflection of himself in the polished granite surface of the breakfast bar. 'Until now.'

'I don't know how he found out about Bryan,' she said, watching him.

'Or why finding out about him should provoke an impromptu visit.' He looked up at her.

'D'you think he's got something to do with Bryan's disappearance?'

Ignoring this, Laviolette said, 'How did he know where you lived?'

Laura shook her head and looked afraid again. 'No idea. I've got no idea how he got the number either.'

'What did he say – on the phone? What did he want?'

'Nothing – apart from that he knew Bryan had gone missing, and that he was parked outside.'

'Did he threaten you in anyway?'

Laura gave a short laugh. 'Most women would find a man calling them to say they're parked directly outside their house threatening.' She paused. 'I feel taunted. Jamie was always good at that.' She stopped suddenly as she realised what it was she'd said.

'So you knew him well at some point?'

'As a child.' She poured herself another glass of wine.

'And as a child was it Bryan you knew first – or his brother, Jamie?'

Laura hesitated. 'Jamie, I suppose.'

'How was that?'

'I don't know. He just always seemed to be around.'

'Were you and Jamie ever together as in a relationship together?'

'Not really, no.'

'Not really,' the Inspector repeated.

'But you already knew that, didn't you, Inspector?'

'Yes, I did.'

'You know all about Jamie Deane.'

'I do.'

'So why are we doing this? Why are you even handling this case?'

'Because although you're answering my questions, you're not giving me anything here.' He brought his palm down suddenly against the granite surface, leaving a print.

Laura jerked in reaction to this, spilling some wine, as

Laviolette slipped off the stool far more gracefully than he'd got onto it, walked purposefully towards the patio doors and stared out at the garden – wondering briefly which of the Deanes was responsible for it, and trying to discern any real horticultural passion.

'How old were you and Bryan when you first started seeing each other?'

'I was thirteen. Bryan was fourteen.'

'What did Jamie think about that?'

'I don't know – he was in prison.'

Laviolette sunk his hands in his pockets and swung round to face her, 'Have Bryan and Jamie been in contact at all over the years?'

'Not that I'm aware of. Bryan's never said anything anyway.'

'Do you have much contact with your father-in-law, Mr Deane?'

'My father-in-law?' Laura repeated, surprised. 'We never really got on.'

'Your father-in-law's got Alzheimer's,' Laviolette said, aware that Laura winced every time he said 'father-in-law'. 'He shouldn't be living alone.'

Laura stared at him, impassive, but her expression changed to shock when he said, 'I went to visit him yesterday.'

'Why?'

'To ask him if he'd seen Bryan.'

'How would he know? He doesn't know who Bryan is any more.'

'Does Bryan visit him?'

'Occasionally – I think. He doesn't really talk about it.'

'Doesn't it weigh heavily on him – a father with Alzheimer's, living alone?'

'They fell out years ago. It's complicated – but then, that's families, isn't it? They're complicated.'

She looked out the kitchen window at the McClarens' cat – a mink-coloured Burmese attempting to catch a fly by the Hebe.

'Are you a family?' she asked him.

The question was strangely but accurately put. 'Your daughter asked me that on the way over here in the car.'

'She did?'

'What do you think?'

'I don't know – maybe once, but not any more.'

He nodded.

'That's sad,' Laura responded.

He turned away from her, back to the garden, and watched a cat – the McClarens' cat – sprint from the fence onto the lawn where it stood, one paw raised, alert and absorbed in its own agenda. It flicked its head quickly in his direction, just to the left of his shoulder as if there was somebody standing directly beside him; somebody he could neither see nor feel. Then it looked away. Behind him, he heard her say, 'People on the outside don't understand, do they – the work that goes into a marriage?'

'I ran out of energy – the energy required to undertake the monumental acts of heroism needed to keep us together.'

He crossed the kitchen aimlessly then stopped, feeling suddenly stranded. He wanted a glass of wine now, and had to put a lot of effort into stopping himself asking for one.

'In the beginning you can't imagine anything ever going wrong, can you? You see other people – couples; families – and you think, I'm never going to let that happen to me . . . us. But somehow stuff does go wrong, and one day you look around you and realise that you're just like every-body else – clinging on.' She stopped speaking and started to twist the wine glass nervously in her hand.

Laviolette was watching her trying to decide whether she'd taken herself by surprise speaking like that or whether the whole scene – this speech included – was pre-meditated. Then he decided that he didn't care – her words had a resonance to them he found hard to resist.

He looked quickly at her. For the first time since meeting her, he realised that he was thinking of Laura Deane as a victim rather than . . . rather than what, he wondered? The word that came to mind was 'conspirator'.

'What are you going to do?'

'About what?'

She hesitated. 'Jamie – coming round here.'

'Feeling threatened isn't the same thing as being threatened. I can't stop him coming.'

'Why are you protecting him?' she said harshly, frustration changing her tone. 'I can't believe you're protecting him – after what he did.'

'What did he do?'

She stared at him in disbelief. 'He killed your father.'

'I don't know,' Laviolette said, thoughtful. 'I've spent such a lot of time thinking about that over the years, and I'm not sure he did.'

'But that's why he went to prison – for twenty years.'

'What if he didn't go to prison because he murdered my father, but because all those years ago, a girl lied? That would be a very different matter, wouldn't it?'

Laviolette drove down the coast to Tynemouth, turning left at the Priory onto Pier Road and the bulk of headland known as the Spanish Battery. Although there were houses here – his own included – and the white clapboard headquarters of the Tynemouth Volunteer Life Brigade (anchored to the headland by steel guy ropes to prevent it from being carried away in the frequent storms), the headland felt severed from the land rising behind it; a severance reflected in the poise of the Admiral Collingswood statue (Nelson's second in command at Trafalgar), whose face was turned resolutely seawards. The Spanish Battery was named after the seventeenth century Spanish mercenaries who manned the guns on the headland in response to the Dutch threat at the time. Laviolette had, for some reason, always had a soft spot for those Spanish mercenaries.

He parked outside number four Old Coastguard Cottages – an old stone house that was also home – the headlamps illuminating the long grass that was rolling in one of the headland's perpetual winds. Even after he'd switched off the engine, he could still feel the wind rushing under and over the car, rocking it from side to side.

He continued to sit in the dark car, aware that the last thing he felt like doing right then was walking into number four Old Coastguard Cottages and asking Mrs Kelly how her day had gone – how his son, Harvey, who she looked after, had been. He didn't want to listen, smiling, to the account of their day, rent with the small seismic details Mrs Kelly insisted on giving him because Mrs Kelly was a gem . . . a real find, and Laviolette knew that these small seismic details were borne of the love she had for his son; a love that let him off the hook. He felt responsible for Harvey, but he didn't love him.

He thought about the conversation he'd just had with Laura Deane, and how today – for the first time in years – he'd spoken about his wife, and not just once but twice: first with Martha then Laura Deane. In fact, Laura Deane reminded him a lot of Lily – what Lily could have been in the right hands. He'd told Martha that he had no idea whether she was living or dead and he hadn't said it to be barbaric. Years ago when he first lost her, he might have done, but not now.

He shut his eyes and saw her briefly – thin, blonde, scruffy, and bruised. He hadn't loved her, which made him the last

133

person she should have entrusted herself to . . . agreed to marry.

He swung his gaze away from the house back out to sea. There was a couple walking tightly together along the pier below the cliff on which stood the priory's ruins. A couple taking a walk . . . he knew that normality could conceal the most incredible acts of sedition, but tonight he chose to believe that the couple taking a walk were nothing more than what they seemed: a couple taking a walk, and wondered what it would be like to walk with someone along the pier at the end of the day. How did people get to the stage where they could just take a walk together like that?

Sighing, he got out of the car, bracing himself against the wind and the cold as he made his way across the small garden separating his house from the road. Instead of going to the front door, he stood outside the window whose curtains Mrs Kelly rarely drew before he came home – an old superstitious habit she'd acquired over the years being married to a fisherman.

Through the window he saw Mrs Kelly and Harvey sitting on the sofa together – Harvey was a lot taller than Mrs Kelly – watching what looked like a costume drama on TV. There was a tray on the coffee table in front of them with cheese and biscuits on it, and some paper covered in the 3-D shapes Harvey was forever drawing. Harvey, perched on the edge of the sofa, was rocking gently backwards and forwards. Mrs Kelly sat still with her hands clasped in her lap.

He couldn't remember when or why he'd painted the walls of his house yellow; when or why he'd chosen the carpet he had, but somehow it all hung together. He'd constructed a life for himself out of a series of inescapable facts, and number four Old Coastguard Cottages looked like someone's home.

Mrs Kelly twisted her head instinctively towards the

window and, smiling, waved at him as if the fact that he was standing out in the garden peering in through the window at them was the most normal thing in the world.

He didn't know how long he'd been standing there, but thought suddenly of Bryan Deane's four-minute vigil above Longsands on Easter Saturday – the one he'd watched on the CCTV footage. Bryan Deane's four-minute vigil had been motionless and yet during those four minutes Bryan had departed one life and entered another.

Once Mrs Kelly had put Harvey to bed for the night and left, Laviolette went up to the small room at the top of the house he used as a study. It was tiny, and full of stuff too meaningless and personal to go anywhere else in the house. It felt like a student's room – one he was renting inside his own house – and he often spent the night up here on the sofa.

There was a skylight in the roof, but no windows – the lack of a view calmed him.

He had a cardboard box by the desk full of objects he'd collected over the years that had got broken – tea pots, desk lamps, Harvey's toys – that he often found himself repairing before realising that they no longer had any purpose in his life, and so were returned, repaired, to the box where they got jolted to the bottom, broken once more.

A therapeutic cycle of needless activity. It made him think of the factory Lily used to tell him Harvey could work in when he got older – a place where they made people like Harvey spend half the day making wooden crates and the other half smashing them up with rubber mallets.

People like Harvey.

He also had things up here he shouldn't have – like copies of interview tapes from the investigation following his father's murder, and it was one of these he put on now, dated 7th August 1987.

He sat down on the sofa that was covered in a crocheted blanket he had a feeling his mother must have made – maybe while she was dying.

The room was a deathly blue and beige that always made him feel depressed, but he was able to think clearly there – he'd never sought to understand the connection between depression and lucidity.

Putting the tape player on his lap, he pressed play then leant back against the sofa – arms behind his head; his eyes closed.

Inspector Jim Cornish – now Superintendant – started speaking.

Jim Cornish was old school – a lumbering heavyweight who was far more mentally agile than he appeared, and renowned for the dogged pursuits he used to lead. The tape didn't make for easy listening. Jamie Dean's incoherent screaming – he must have been fifteen at the time – followed by silences so taut and sullen they made Laviolette's ears pop.

But Jamie stuck to his story – despite being locked in a tiny room with Cornish and his protégé, Tom Kyle: a notoriously violent man who was relocated in the early nineties when they had to shut down the Berwick Street station where the interviews had been conducted. Berwick Street had a reputation – over half the people who went into it never came out, and in the end it was easier just to close it down than clean it up.

Jamie Deane sensed he was fighting a losing battle – that came across despite the screaming and the silences – but he stuck to his story: he claimed that he'd spent the afternoon of 7th August 1987 having sex in his bedroom with Laura Hamilton. He went over it again and again. He didn't go stupid on them, and he didn't cave in.

Neither Cornish nor Kyle got to him.

The thing that got to him was the loss of his only alibi – Laura Hamilton.

Laviolette took out the Jamie Deane tape and put in the Laura Hamilton one.

He listened to Cornish tell her that Jamie Deane claimed he'd spent the afternoon of 7th August 1987 having sex with her.

Laura Hamilton, terrified, denied this then burst into tears.

Cornish and Kyle took their time with her because the social worker sitting in on the interview was pissing them off, and they enjoyed putting uncomfortable questions to the attractive thirteen-year-old. The interview was halted here – when it resumed, Laura was calmer.

She sensed that what she was saying wasn't falling on deaf ears; that they wanted to believe her, and that escape from the interview room, police station, and darker side of life was imminent. She relaxed, becoming almost flirtatious – especially with Kyle.

When Jamie heard that Laura denied having spent the afternoon with him, he broke in half, and that's when Cornish and Kyle nailed him.

A job well done.

Laviolette turned off the tape, but kept his eyes shut, thinking of his own recent interviews with Laura.

He was convinced of one thing: Laura knew how to lie.

But knowing this brought him no closer to answering the two questions he would have been happy to exchange what was left of his life for answers to:

If Bryan Deane wasn't dead, where was he?

If Jamie Deane didn't kill his father, then who did?

# 10

Anna heard the post through the letterbox, and went slowly downstairs – stopping suddenly halfway. There, on the doormat at the bottom of the stairs near the front door, was Bryan in a red T-shirt, smiling up at her from the front page of *The Journal*, which Mary had delivered. Running down the last few steps, she grabbed hold of the paper.

It was the same photograph as the one she had in her kitchen at the Ridley Arms – the same restaurant; same checked tablecloth; same white-capped sea. The only thing that was different was Bryan, who was smiling. She pictured Laura going through the albums of Deane family life, trying to decide which pictures – pictures taken in innocence – to give the police, who would have asked for photographs of Bryan smiling because Bryan was the victim rather than perpetrator of a crime. Photographs published of perpetrators never showed them smiling.

Over the past few days Anna's world had become so small that now there were only four people in it: herself, Mary, Erwin and – sporadically – Susan the nurse. Erwin had barely been conscious at any point during the past forty-eight hours and between them, Mary and Anna had been keeping a constant bedside vigil, sleeping in alternate two hour shifts in Anna's childhood bedroom.

They moved in a silent circle through the house – from Erwin's room, down to the kitchenette where they ate, back up to the bathroom where they washed then into Anna's room where they slept. Only Anna found it hard to sleep – especially during the daytime – and so stood looking out the window with a mixture of outrage and envy at the children in the garden of the Deanes' old house, number fifteen, on the trampoline sucking ice pops mid-air as they bounced in their school uniforms.

She watched the man next door at number twenty-one haul grow bags across his patio and plant them up with tomatoes and was as amazed at this as she was by the children on their trampoline. She was amazed that these things could be accomplished when death was so close to them. Hadn't they realised that a man was dying in pain in an upstairs bedroom close by?

It seemed extraordinary to her that buses still passed the windows of number nineteen Parkview with passengers; that there were people who could simply get on a bus and go wherever it was they needed to go because they weren't living with death.

It felt as if she and Mary would just continue to exist like this forever more, moving in the same silent circle through the rooms inside number nineteen Parkview, no longer able to tell the difference between grief and exhaustion.

She went into the kitchenette to pour herself a cup of tea, and that's what she was doing when the front doorbell rang. She jerked the teapot with shock at the sudden sound – scalding herself – and went to answer it, her left hand throbbing.

It was Martha Deane.

'Who's that?' Mary called out from the top landing.

The sound of the doorbell must have woken her up and she made her way wearily downstairs, stopping when she saw Martha.

'It's alright, Nan – you go back to bed.'

Mary hesitated before disappearing back upstairs.

Anna passed her hand over her brow, exhausted, before turning back to Martha.

'I'm staying at Nan's – she said you were here. What happened to your hand?'

'I burnt it – just now, on the kettle. Look, I meant to phone you – after the appeal – but my grandfather's much worse, and I'm not really sleeping.' She rested her head against the front door. 'I don't know what's going on at the moment – I'm not really myself.'

Martha bit on her lip, anxious, then turned away without saying anything – walking off down the garden path.

'Martha!' Anna called out after her. 'Martha – wait.' She caught up with her at the gate.

'It's okay,' Martha mumbled, pulling her arm slowly out of Anna's grasp.

Anna wasn't even aware she'd grabbed hold of her. 'Has something happened?'

'It's seeing his picture everywhere. I can't stand all those people – strangers – seeing him.'

'You know what?' Anna said, 'I could do with some air – d'you feel like a walk? We could go down onto the estuary if the tide's out.'

'Okay.' Martha sounded pleased.

So this was where she was, Laviolette thought as he parked his car outside number seventeen Parkview behind Anna's yellow Capri. He got out and looked up at the house as he made his way towards the Hamiltons' front garden where there was a sign sellotaped to the gate, which said

*No takeaway leaflets or junk mail please*. He rang on the doorbell and waited.

It was Don who answered, in trainers and a tracksuit – and not because he'd been running – a roll up cigarette in the corner of a mouth that still held the lines of its youthful sensuality.

'Alright Inspector?' Don said, worried.

'I tried phoning –'

'I never hear it when Doreen's got the TV on.'

'Nothing to worry about.' Laviolette paused, but Don's face didn't relax. 'I was just in the area and . . . mind if I pop in for a few minutes?'

Don hesitated then nodded. 'Sure, sure – come in,' he said, taking the cigarette out of his mouth, suddenly eager to show the Inspector some belated hospitality.

Laviolette followed him through to the kitchenette at the back of the house, which smelt heavily of cigarette smoke. He imagined that this bothered Laura Deane – especially when Martha came home smelling of it after having spent the weekend at her grandparents.

'Afternoon Doreen,' he called into the lounge as they passed.

Doreen was sitting only inches away from Jeremy Kyle's face on the TV screen, which had some sort of magnifying attachment over it.

'She won't hear you,' Don said, putting the kettle on. 'Tea?'

Laviolette sat down at a small drop-leaf table identical to the Fausts' next door at number nineteen – both tables had been purchased in the Co-Op's furniture department during the sixties. There was an ashtray in the middle full of stubs.

Don made tea and the two men sat drinking it, comfortable in their mutual silence – in a way that reminded

Laviolette of how comfortable his own father used to be with silence; a trait he'd inherited and that he used to great effect during interrogations.

'I just wanted to check in with you – following the appeal,' he said after a while.

'We didn't watch it.'

'I can understand that.'

Don looked at him. 'Doreen didn't feel like going out today, but we're going for a drive tomorrow – maybe up Rothbury way,' he added, distant. 'Laura wanted to go into work – I wasn't sure it was a good idea, having to meet all them people . . . customers and what not.'

'Routine . . . habit . . . they're stronger allies than we give them credit for.'

'Allies,' Don repeated, unconvinced. 'To tell you the truth, I think the whole appeal thing was worse for her than Bryan's actual disappearance. D'you mind?' He gestured towards his tobacco tin. 'Want one?'

'I'm fine.' Laviolette watched Don roll himself another cigarette – with great delicacy – using a small red roller, and holding it between his thumb and forefinger in the way men used to smoke.

'Nobody's contacted you?' Laviolette asked. 'Since the appeal?'

'Like who?'

Laviolette picked up his cup and started drinking his tea again. 'Like Bryan.'

Don laughed then, unsure why he was laughing, stopped. 'You're serious,' he said, watching the Inspector.

'Has Bryan tried to contact either yourself or Doreen, in confidence, since his disappearance? It can happen in families.'

Don continued to watch him in disbelief. 'Bryan's dead.'

'We don't know that.'

142

'He disappeared ten days ago. He went out to sea in his kayak, and he never came back. He's drowned – dead.'

'We've got no evidence of that.'

'And you've got no evidence otherwise either. Now you listen to me. It's a tragedy – a great big fucking tragedy – and we need to be left in peace to grieve. This is my son-in-law we're talking about – my daughter's husband – granddaughter's father – family. My family. We need to get over this. Appeal –' Don spat.

'You're angry.'

'Yeah,' Don agreed, 'yeah, I am. Bryan's dead.'

'Maybe,' Laviolette conceded.

'Definitely,' Don said, finishing his cigarette.

The sound of wailing came from the TV in the other room.

'There are some things we need to investigate further – unfortunately.'

'What's there to investigate for Christ's sake?'

'Financial strain.'

'Meaning what?'

'We need to establish –'

'What?'

'Whether Bryan's disappearance –'

'Death –'

'Was connected to this.'

'In what way?'

'In an intentional way.' Laviolette stopped and looked across the table at Don. Don was a physical man, and right now he was just about holding onto the threads of the conversation. Laviolette knew that if he pushed him much further he'd explode.

Don stared at him. 'You mean – suicide?'

Laviolette nodded as Don drew his right hand down into his lap, leaving his other hand curled lifelessly on the kitchen table.

The next minute he started to sob loudly.

'God,' he mumbled, helpless, his shoulders shaking.

'I'm sorry,' Laviolette said.

'How can you think that?'

'I have to think everything.'

'They're good people, Laura and Bryan. They lead good lives . . . they've worked hard for what they've got, and you come round here, and –'

'I know that.'

Don looked up suddenly, passing his arm harshly across his face. 'Alright, love?' he said to Doreen, who was standing in the doorway to the kitchenette staring at them both.

'What's happened?'

'Nothing's happened – it's fine. Go back to your programme.'

'My programme's finished,' she said, watching Don get to his feet and go over to the window, turning his back to them as he carried on sniffing and wiping at his face. 'Don?'

Laviolette started to make his way to the front door, but Don caught up with him, pulling hard on his arm. 'Don't you dare talk to Laura about this. You let her be. You let her be, d'you hear me?'

'I'll be in contact, Don.'

'Know who you remind me of – your bloody father, that's who.'

It was after this that Laviolette – gloomy, preoccupied – saw Anna and Martha.

Anna and Martha walked down Parkview towards Longstone Drive, glancing at number fifteen where Bryan used to live as they passed.

There was a new front door with frosted glass panels, and – apart from an exhaust pipe under the privet hedge – the front garden had been filled with gravel and looked tidy.

'Dad never talks about his family – I ask him about stuff sometimes but he won't talk about the past.'

A woman in slippers and a long T-shirt with Daffy Duck on it came out of the side passage door and put some cartons in the recycling bin, squinting down the path at them.

'Did you ever know my uncle, Jamie Deane?' Martha asked suddenly. 'I didn't even know I had an uncle until he phoned Easter Sunday and I took the call. Nobody told me.' She paused. 'He sounded just like dad.'

They carried on walking – past the large, detached redbrick house on the corner of Parkview and Longstone Drive, built by the council as a children's home.

'What did he want?'

'I don't know – he thought he was speaking to mum. He's only been out of prison six months.'

Anna saw Laura, at the age of thirteen, sitting sullen and scared at the top of the stairs in the Deanes' house.

'Did you tell her he'd phoned?'

Martha nodded. 'She didn't really say anything. She just looked scared. Why didn't anybody tell me dad had a brother?'

'He killed a man, Martha – that's a difficult thing for a family to talk about.'

They'd reached the stile at the end of Longstone Drive, which they crossed, jumping down onto the footpath that led to the estuary.

The footpath ran down the side of a field of oil seed rape, on the brink of yellow. The slip road to the new bypass rose up across the end of the field and the traffic on it was loud.

'You should be careful, Martha,' Anna called out, above the sound of distant traffic.

Martha laughed and Anna followed her down the path.

'Did you tell Inspector Laviolette about Jamie phoning?'

Martha nodded, running her hands through the tall grasses

lining the path, beyond which there were wild roses, hawthorn and brambles. Every now and then different coloured butterflies rose to shoulder level from under Martha's hands, before dropping back into the grass again.

'What did he say?'

'Nothing much.'

They got to the road bridge – where the photograph of Bettina that Erwin gave her was taken. There was sand underfoot now as the path followed the River Wansbeck's mouth so Anna slipped off her shoes.

'This was my walk – when I lived at Parkview. You get to the sea quickly – away from all the houses and stuff.'

'Did you come here with mum?'

'No – this was my walk when I was at the Grammar School. Your mum and I weren't really speaking by then.'

They rounded the lip of beach at the river's mouth and were suddenly able to see the coastline stretching south – down to the windmills on the north harbour wall at Blyth where the Ridley Arms was. They walked to the water's edge leaving footprints in the wet sand, the wind picking up their hair, pulling it back off their faces.

'That whole summer, we made plans – your mum and me. We weren't going to let things change between us just because we were going to different schools. It was a summer of oaths and promises that didn't make any difference in the end. My world changed in a way I'd never anticipated, and for the first time in my life, I was unhappy.' Anna paused. 'Unhappiness does things to you; it has a deeper more lasting effect on a person than happiness. I went into myself. I wasn't really there for your mum, and I think she could have done with me being there.'

'Why?'

'Because,' Anna said, realising this for the first time, 'I always had been.'

She rolled up her jeans and walked into the freezing North Sea as the waves broke over her ankles.

Martha stood watching her for a while before eventually taking off her shoes and socks as well, and joining her in the water, resting her head on Anna's shoulder.

'People used to come here in the Strike to collect sea coal and driftwood – anything that would burn. We'd go up to the slag heaps at the power station as well and stand watch while the others filled prams, carts . . . buckets. Those were different times.'

They walked back slowly along the estuary, in silence, until beach gave way to grassy scrub again, and they stopped to put their shoes on. They crossed the field of oil seed rape and the stile where the footpath ended, jumping down into Longstone Drive.

'That was a children's home when I was growing up,' Anna said pointing to the detached red brick house on the corner of Parkview that they'd passed earlier. 'The kids from there used to run wild.'

Martha looked up at the house.

'I think it was an end of the line place for the kids who got passed around until there was nowhere left, but there – St Jude's hostel.'

'Is that what it was called?'

'No, it's a joke – St Jude's the patron saint of hopeless cases. There were never more than around ten children living there. I always remember this boy who was there for a year – he must have been twelve or something – and he only had half a head of hair. I always wondered about him – because of the hair.'

They were on Parkview again – almost at number seventeen – when Martha said unexpectedly, 'Mum hates the fact she comes from this place. Did you know she once –' She stopped talking, looking up the street.

Following the direction she was looking in, Anna saw –
simultaneously – Inspector Laviolette outside number
seventeen, and Laviolette's car parked on the street behind
her Capri.

'Anna,' he called out, seeing her.

They walked up to him, Martha holding onto Anna, clearly
upset.

'Don't worry – nothing to report. I've been touching base
with your grandparents following the appeal.'

He gave Martha a thin, bright smile. Then he turned to
Anna. 'Been out for a walk?'

Before she had a chance to respond, he jerked his head
in the direction of number nineteen, and said, 'How are
things?'

'Much worse.'

All three of them hesitated, waiting for someone to say
something, when Don – who was standing on the doorstep
drying his hands on a tea towel – said, 'Are you coming in,
Martha?'

There was nothing to say after that and Anna watched
as Laviolette got into his car and Martha disappeared inside
number seventeen.

Once Martha had gone, Anna walked over to the
Inspector's car.

He wound down the window. 'Are you okay?' He'd already
asked her this, but there was an intimacy to it second time
round that unnerved her.

'I need to ask you something. It doesn't seem right –'

'What doesn't seem right?'

'You being assigned this case – with the history between
you and the Deane family and Jamie Deane on probation
now.'

'Who've you been talking to?'

'It isn't right.'

'It isn't right,' he agreed. 'That's why I've been assigned this case.'

'Enemies?'

'Enemies,' he repeated.

'I'm sorry to hear that.' She paused. 'And you know that Jamie's attempted to contact Laura – are you worried?'

Laviolette sighed. 'I don't know. I'm inclined to think that Laura's done more harm to Jamie than he could ever do to her – or any of the other Deanes for that matter.'

He left her standing on the pavement next to the spot where his car had been parked.

Laura Deane was standing with her arms folded inside a long cashmere cardigan, staring absentmindedly through the salon window at Tynemouth Front Street. Sorrow suited her. She felt relatively calm, and there was a fruitful buzz coming from the salon behind her. People she worked with and people she knew had been coming in all morning. People had been kind, and she'd allowed herself to be visibly moved by their kindness, which people liked. It made them feel as if they were getting something for their sympathy.

She glanced down at her hands – manicured by Liz that morning – which so many people had taken hold of and held. The scent of so many differently perfumed embraces rose from the threads of her cashmere cardigan where they'd been temporarily trapped, released by the movement of her arms as they fell suddenly to her side.

A white transit van with Reeves Regeneration on the side had pulled up on the kerb opposite – right next to the bus stop. The door opened and Jamie Deane stepped down into the road, oblivious to the lunch time traffic. Grinning, he held up a copy of *The Journal* with Bryan's picture on the front. Laura could see the red of Bryan's T-shirt from where she was standing.

Aware that Kirsty on reception had also noticed him, Laura said, 'Who's that?'

'Some nutter. D'you want me to call the police?'

Laura didn't answer, and they both carried on watching as Jamie got back into the van, yelling something at a man in a blue car who'd sounded his horn at him.

Mo's daughter, Leanne, stared sullenly at Laviolette as he pushed the bacon, eggs, loaf of bread and butter across the counter, smiling patiently at her as she counted the handful of change he gave her. He continued to smile as she dropped most of it on the counter and started counting again, the shop lighting bouncing harshly off her carefully oiled hair, pulled back in a bunch.

'All there?' he said.

She nodded, slammed the till drawer shut and watched him leave the shop, get back in his car and drive away.

Then she called Jamie, who didn't pick up. She remained sunk heavily over the counter, lost in admiration at the stars that had been airbrushed onto her nails.

When her phone started ringing, she grabbed at it.

'What is it?' Jamie demanded.

'That copper's just been in here,' she said, enjoying herself. 'The one who came to see your dad that time.'

'What did he want?'

'I don't know.' Leanne ran her tongue quickly over the nails on her forefinger. 'He just bought some stuff – bread, bacon –'

Jamie cut her off. 'I don't give a fuck about his shopping list – where'd he go?'

'I don't know.'

'Well go and see if his car's parked outside dad's you dumb fuck – then phone me back.'

\*

Laviolette pulled up outside number eight Armstrong Crescent, watched through nets by Mrs Harris at number six, and Leanne – under instructions from Jamie Deane – from the fire exit at the back of the shop.

He knocked on Bobby Deane's door and waited, turning instinctively round to see Leanne – across the green at the back of the shop – staring at him. He waved, and she disappeared. Then the front door to Bobby's bungalow opened.

For a moment Bobby's eyes rested with intent on the Inspector, as his mind sought out Laviolette. Then he gave up. He was holding a copy of *The Journal* in his hand with Bryan's picture on the front.

Laviolette held up the bag of food.

'What's that?' Bobby asked, not really interested.

'Lunch.'

Bobby thought about this. 'Are you Meals on Wheels? Did you come yesterday?'

Laviolette hesitated then nodded.

'I'm hungry,' Bobby said, still unconvinced, his eyes on the bag as the Inspector walked past him, into his house.

'Can I go through to the kitchen?' Laviolette asked.

Bobby nodded and followed him.

The kitchen felt cleaner than it had last time, and there were no signs of Jamie's Methadrone production line.

'D'you remember me?' the Inspector asked.

Bobby shook his head. 'What's in the bag?'

'Bacon – eggs. Have you got a frying pan?'

'I don't know.'

'D'you mind if I look for one?'

'Okay.'

Laviolette started opening cupboards at random until he found a pan in the one under the sink along with a couple of Pyrex dishes, some plates, a plastic jug, stainless steel toast

151

rack, six egg cups, a pair of scales, and an old Happy Meal toy. There was also a basket of cleaning fluids.

The pan had once been non-stick and smelt strongly of the countless cans of soup that had been heated in it.

Bobby remained in the kitchen doorway and watched as Laviolette fried the bacon, with difficulty, in the small pan. 'The food used to come in tin foil trays.' He paused. 'You wore a red sweater with words on it.'

'Well this smells better than any ready meal, doesn't it?' he said to Bobby, who didn't respond.

He was wearing slippers today, Laviolette noted, and no coat, and hadn't referred to the fact that his son's photograph was on the front of the newspaper he was holding.

Laviolette finished cooking the bacon, putting it on a Pyrex dish in the oven to keep it warm, and decided to scramble the eggs he'd bought. There only seemed to be one set of crockery so Laviolette put his food on the dish he'd been keeping the bacon warm on then took everything through to the lounge followed by Bobby, who stood at a loss in the centre of the room, his eyes on the steaming food.

'Why don't you sit down in your armchair?'

Bobby shuffled over to the armchair and Laviolette put the plate of food in his lap, pulling *The Journal* gently out of his hands.

'You've got it?'

Bobby nodded and sat holding the plate, staring enraptured at the food.

'It feels hot.'

'It's not too hot, is it?'

'No – no.'

Laviolette disappeared back into the kitchen to get some cutlery for them both then, sitting down on the microwave he'd sat on during his last visit, they started to eat in silence, Bobby staring at a fixed point on the floor as he chewed.

'You're eating as well?' he asked after a while.

'Is that okay?'

Bobby nodded, and carried on eating – almost shyly now.

Laviolette waited until they'd finished before picking up the newspaper Bobby had been holding.

'This looks like Bryan,' he said, sounding surprised. He wanted to get Bobby's attention without agitating him. 'Doesn't this look like your Bryan?'

Bobby stared over his empty plate at the photograph of his son, smiling under foreign skies.

'Bryan,' he said, giving Laviolette his plate and taking the newspaper off him. 'Bryan,' he said again, looking hard at the picture – in the same way he had looked at Laviolette earlier. 'That's not Bryan,' he concluded.

'It is Bryan,' Laviolette insisted, gently. 'He's gone missing – that's why he's in the papers. We're trying to look for him.' Laviolette started to read the piece out loud and after a while Bobby pulled it out of his hands, excited, staring at the photograph – suddenly absorbed by it.

He was about to say something when Laviolette heard the front door opening, and stood up thinking it must be Jamie Deane.

'That's not Bryan. He's far too old,' Bobby was saying. 'Bryan's only fourteen,' he concluded, triumphant as Mary Faust walked into the bungalow's lounge, staring from Laviolette to Bobby, shocked. 'And he's not missing, he's been round at Mary's all afternoon. You ask Mary – she'll tell you,' Bobby carried on, excited. 'Tell him, Mary,' Bobby commanded, not at all surprised to see her standing there.

'Mrs Faust,' Laviolette said, taking in the keys she was holding in her hand still.

'I've come round to check on him,' she said, awkwardly, her eyes on the plates. 'You made lunch?'

Laviolette nodded. 'I wanted to talk to Bobby about Bryan

153

– Bryan being in the papers. We've been talking about Bryan, haven't we Bobby?'

Ignoring this, his eyes on Mary, Bobby said, 'Tell him about Bryan.'

Mary turned obediently to the Inspector. 'Bryan's been with me all afternoon,' she said, uncomfortable.

Laviolette stared at her, puzzled, and before he had time to say anything, she picked up the plates and took them through to the kitchen, staring at the sink as it filled with water.

He watched her wash and dry the dishes in silence, stacking them on the kitchen surface – until Bobby appeared, suddenly anxious, holding the newspaper still.

'Rachel loved Bryan. She loved him best out of all of us, and that's why he took it so hard when she . . . when she . . .'

'You loved her didn't you Bobby?' Laviolette said, suddenly overwhelmed by this fact. 'You loved your wife very much.'

Bobby was panting in short sharp rapid breaths that made Laviolette worry he was about to have a heart attack.

'Stop it,' Mary said forcefully, drying her hands on the tea towel. 'He's not well.'

'No, he isn't well. He needs round the clock care.'

'I try to come at least once a week, but it's difficult with Erwin ill,' Mary said helplessly.

'He needs professional care.'

'I've tried talking to Don and Doreen about it, but he's not really their responsibility. I can't do any more. Family matters are private, but – look at him.' Mary's face was crumpling.

'Who are you?' Bobby asked her suddenly, interested.

'A friend, Bobby,' Mary said, close to tears. 'A friend.'

'I'll be back soon,' Laviolette said, taking hold of Mary's hand. 'And if he says anything at all – about Bryan – I need you to phone me. Anna's got my number. And I'm sorry for your troubles,' he finished ambiguously.

When he left the bungalow, Mrs Harris from next door was waiting for him. 'So that's what it was about – the other day. Bryan Deane's gone missing,' she concluded, triumphantly, before the thin smile slid sideways off her face. 'Or he's on a beach in Spain somewhere.'

Laviolette watched her thoughtfully for a moment before nodding, and taking his leave of Mrs Harris – who remained in her front garden, arms folded, virtually motionless, until Jamie Deane's van pulled up fifteen minutes later.

When he got home Mrs Kelly and Harvey were out at a yoga class Harvey was responding well to – becoming something of a class pet – run by a friend of Mrs Kelly's who had recently qualified as an Yyvengar yoga instructor.

Laviolette went straight up to his study, thinking about Mary Faust and Bobby Deane, and what Bobby had said about Bryan being round at Mary's. He thought about phoning Anna, but what was she going to confirm that he hadn't seen with his own eyes – Mary Faust's husband was dying of cancer and she still found the time to visit Bobby Deane. There must have been something between them once.

It was difficult to follow Bobby because time was no longer linear for him: his magnetic fields were constantly shifting and the North Pole could turn up any time, any place. It was only now, Laviolette realised, that when Bobby – insistent, almost irate – had said that Bryan was with Mary, that he was talking about the afternoon of 7th August 1987. He'd completely forgotten that Mary Faust was Bryan's alibi: Bryan had been with Mary the afternoon his brother, Jamie, beat a man half to death and then set fire to him. Mary was Bryan's alibi: Bryan spent that afternoon in the garden at number nineteen Parkview, drawing insects.

He found the interview tape he was looking for and was soon listening to Mary Faust's voice, dry, uncertain, wanting to be helpful.

He'd listened to the tape before, but only a couple of times – not like the Jamie Deane tapes that he virtually knew by heart.

Mary, nervous under the circumstances, but sensing that the environment wasn't hostile to her, went into some vague, unnecessary appraisal of Bryan's skills as a draughtsman.

'Was there anybody else with you yesterday afternoon, Mary?'

Gently asked by Jim Cornish.

Hesitation on Mary's part then, 'No. Just me – and Bryan.'

The interview was short because Inspector Jim Cornish wasn't interested in Mary Faust – the questions he asked were barely rudimentary – and he wasn't interested in Bryan Deane either. Inspector Jim Cornish had made up his mind and Jamie Dean, he decided, was guilty, for all sorts of reasons his brain was linking rapidly and at random ranging from Bobby Deane's role in the Strike to the fact that Jamie Deane had two records for GBH.

Laviolette rewound the ten minutes' worth of interview he'd just listened to, playing it again.

It was so simple he'd overlooked it, but listening to the tape now, he realised that Mary Faust was lying – why and about what, he wasn't sure, but she was definitely lying.

Cornish would have sensed it, deep down, which was why he hadn't probed. She was vague about the time she finished her shift at the Welwyn, but by then Jim was too worked up to uncover anything other than the statements he'd decided in advance he wanted to uncover. The overriding force at work in all the interviews and interrogations was Jim's need to indict Jamie Deane. Failing that, he probably would have pushed for Bobby Deane, but Bobby Deane had been hundreds of metres underground that day with about twenty alibis and even Jim Cornish might have had trouble buying twenty alibis – not that he could have bought any of those men. So he went all out for Jamie Deane.

Laviolette heard noises lower down in the house – cupboard doors banging, voices, the TV . . . Mrs Kelly and Harvey were back from yoga.

Mrs Kelly called out, 'Hello?'

He got up and opened the door to the study.

'Alright, Mrs Kelly?' he called down the stairs.

From where he was standing in the doorway, he could see the top of her hair – there was a one inch crown of grey where the dye was growing out. For the first time, he wondered whether Mrs Kelly – who had intimated to him in the past that she spent a lot of money on the upkeep of her hair – got her hair done at Laura Deane's place, Starz Salon, on Front Street.

'You're home,' she said, turning her face up towards him. 'D'you want me to bring you a cup of tea up?'

'It's okay – I'll come down. I'm only going to be a few minutes more.'

She nodded and disappeared.

He remained in the doorway, listening to her tread on the stairs as she descended back down to ground level and Harvey.

Then he went back into the study, but he was no longer thinking about Mary or Laura or Bobby or Bryan, he was thinking about Jim Cornish.

Laviolette would never forget Jim Cornish in 1984, his face smashed with drink and laughter, saying to him, 'You're never thinking of joining up and putting yourself in uniform now in the middle of a strike with a scab for a dad, you daft bloody fuck.'

Jim Cornish had his eye on him right from the start, and

157

while Jim Cornish bothered a lot of people, Laviolette was the only one who made the mistake of letting it show.

During the Strike he'd put in to go to Ashington Pit where there were mostly local police, but instead he was sent to Bates where his dad worked as a safety engineer – was still working, driven in every day in a bus with mesh at the windows and a driver they nicknamed Yasser Arafat because of the scarf wrapped round his head to conceal his identity. Laviolette was recognised by men on the picket line as the son of Roger Laviolette, the safety engineer still going into work – as Jim Cornish knew he would be.

When that stopped entertaining him, Jim sent Laviolette up to Cambois power station where strikers were no longer allowed to speak to lorry drivers delivering coal, and after that he was taken on night patrol booking men on the picket lines who could no longer afford to tax their cars – inciting them so that they could then charge them with breach of the peace and obstruction, which meant they'd be banned from the picket lines. At one point, Laviolette remembered, there were more men banned than there were picketing and although Jim was one of those behind all of this – and more, working alongside police imports they brought in from the south to do the really nasty work locals on the force refused to do, and goading officers to press their payslips up against the windows of cars and buses as they passed – it was impossible to pinpoint his face or to say afterwards with any real conviction that you'd seen Jim Cornish do these things.

Jim was a chaos monger – Laviolette had seen him in his element, sweating on the soft tarmac of a July street as he beat a half naked protestor into the gutter, the half naked protestor then turning and beating Jim Cornish into the same gutter with the same frenzied exhilaration. Neither of them was aware of the Strike any more – whatever was going on between Thatcher and Scargill and their own two egos was going on between Thatcher and Scargill. On the ground there were pickets and there were police. The protestor beat Jim Cornish into the gutter because Jim was in uniform and because he no longer had the energy left to screw his wife or the means to feed his children; he had energy only for this and that's why he was doing it. Jim Cornish had no reasons – he enjoyed being beaten by the protestor almost as much as he enjoyed beating the protestor because these were his times.

Decency and order had gone. Civilisation as they knew it was over because civilisation needed work to go to and a home to return to, but there was no work and most homes had been destroyed.

Laviolette had seen the post-war generation explode onto the streets because peace hadn't felt like it was meant to and in their new Secondary Modern Schools teachers hadn't shared with their pupils the things they'd learnt from war. In fact, they pretended war had never happened and just taught them the things they themselves had been taught about loyalty to the empire and society and the nation. When the Strike came, people saw suddenly that none of what they'd been taught was true and that there was no sense in order.

Order had its own particular smell; a smell Laviolette remembered from his childhood when his mother was still alive – fried cabbage, oil heaters, coal fires, hairspray and cheap perfume, which combined was the smell of order.

That order never returned after 1985.

# 11

Bryan Deane's kayak – the one that bore him out to sea, never to return – was washed up at high tide on the beach at Whitley Bay the day of Erwin Faust's funeral. It was found at around five thirty in the morning by a woman who worked as an anaesthetist at Ashington hospital, out walking her dog. The woman, who was in her fifties, stood beside her panting Jack Russell and contemplated the red P&H Quest kayak on the early morning beach, which was full of birds. It was already a beautiful day, and as she stood contemplating it, she fought to remember the significance of the kayak. Then, when she did remember – a man had gone missing in it around Easter time and Northumbria Police had launched an appeal – she fought with her conscience over whether she could be bothered to contact the police, which would involve giving a statement and being late for work. In another couple of hours, the beach would be full of people. Somebody was bound to notify the police, and anyway *this* kayak might not even be *the* kayak.

She turned and carried on walking up the beach towards St Mary's lighthouse, listening to the quiet wash of the waves. Then, sighing, stopped and looked back at the red kayak resting on its side in the sand, no longer the magnificent intact red it had been the Easter Saturday Bryan stood holding it, next to Anna Faust on Tynemouth Longsands.

It was the kayak. She knew as soon as she saw Flo running towards it; she knew as she turned and walked back towards it now, holding her mobile.

Laviolette arrived at Whitley Bay within the hour. He sent Sergeant Chambers to the Italian café on the Promenade, and stood contemplating the kayak, which lay a lot further from the water's edge now the tide had retreated, abandoning it to the Inspector's gaze. Constable Wade – now DC Wade – who had been at the Deane's house Easter Saturday, took a statement from the female dog walker and was about to join the Inspector again when she saw him look away from the kayak and out to sea in a way that made her hesitate before crossing the sand towards him.

'All done, sir,' she said.

'You make it sound conclusive.'

'Well at least we've found the kayak.'

'But what about Bryan Deane?' He turned to face her. 'You think he's dead don't you?'

'I do, sir, yes.'

'Why?'

'Common sense,' she said, staring out to sea.

'Common sense,' he repeated, looking quickly at her, amused.

As Laviolette stood on the beach at Whitley Bay, Anna helped Mary fold away the sofa bed she'd been sleeping on in the lounge downstairs at number nineteen Parkview. Mary watched Anna fold the duvet into the box and put the pillows and linen back in their bag before taking them upstairs.

'We just need to get through today,' she said, taking in

Mary, motionless in the middle of the lounge in her dressing gown and slippers, her hair flattened by the net she slept in, and her jaw hanging loose without the false teeth to give it shape. 'We just need to get through it,' she said again.

Mary nodded, distracted, and she was still standing in the same spot when Anna came back downstairs.

After breakfast, which was eaten in silence, Mary watched Anna clear up, without comment while Anna stared through the kitchenette window at the weeds flourishing in the otherwise barren garden, which in previous years had been filled with a burgeoning crop of broccoli, runner beans, summer cabbage, potatoes, spinach and sweet peas.

'We should get dressed,' Anna said, turning round to face Mary and when Mary didn't respond, she took hold of her elbow and pulled her gently to her feet before leading her upstairs, into the bathroom. 'Maybe you should wash your face.'

'I don't wash my face,' Mary said, watching the sink fill with water. 'I get those facial wipes – they're lovely and soft on my skin.'

Anna left her in the bathroom with the door open and went to get the suit they'd chosen in Newcastle at the weekend from the wardrobe in Mary and Erwin's room.

The bed was made, empty.

She hadn't been sure, after Erwin died, what she was meant to do with the bed linen. It seemed to her that something ceremonial should be done with it; something to mark the fact that the linen had borne the passage between life and death, but she didn't know who to ask because she'd never buried anybody before.

In the end she folded the bedding into a bag and left it in the wash house.

She unzipped the M&S suit bag Mary had been more pleased with than the suit itself and laid it out on the bed, suddenly aware of Mary standing in the doorway, watching her.

'You changed the bedding.' She paused. 'Where's the other set?'

'The wash house.'

'That's my spare set,' Mary commented, staring at the bed.

'Well, your good set's in the wash house.'

Mary nodded.

'D'you want to get dressed in the back bedroom or –'

'I want to get dressed in here,' Mary said, shuffling decisively into her bedroom. 'Erwin was always such a tidy man.' She looked around her. 'Hung everything up – all his clothes – never left things lying around. I never had to clear up after him.'

Anna laid the suit out on the bed. 'If you need anything, I'm just next door,' she said, going into her own room and shutting the door behind her.

She sat down on the end of the bed looking out the window at the cloudless sky and feeling the warmth of the midsummer sun where it fell on her knees and thighs, and could have crawled back into bed and slept the entire day away because she couldn't imagine it ever ending, this public death.

Erwin's private death had been unendurable enough. There were the moments they thought he'd gone then some part of him would flutter . . . quiver . . . his left eyelid or his throat, while she and Mary knelt on either side looking as if they were pinning him down; trying to prevent him from flying away.

Then the moment did come and it was as though everything in the room rushed suddenly to the foreground. From the pale green lampshade and crocheted runner on the bedside table to the Wilbur Smith book from the library, and the Casio watch laid out carefully across the cover (obscuring the man in a Safari outfit with cocked rifle).

163

Erwin had decided to die.

Even though there hadn't been much of it left at the end, there had been enough for them to feel his life, stopping. They knew he'd gone even though he was lying on the bed between them still. The nurse, Susan, had said that was how it would be, but Anna hadn't wanted to believe her, because she was jealous of Erwin's death, and needed it to be unique. But Susan had seen it all before.

All they were left with after Erwin's irrevocable departure were the things he no longer needed, and it was terrible: clothes, shoes, coats (with shopping lists in the pockets still) . . . the Penguin biscuits in the larder . . . the shed full of tools . . . a cassette of Westminster Cathedral Choir in the tape player . . . a newspaper that had slipped under the sideboard with his biro jottings on the sports pages from when he'd last played the pools . . . the bottle of eau de cologne with its blue and gold label, which had been the one smell from his childhood he was able to buy in England.

Through the bedroom wall she heard the coat hanger clanging against the wardrobe doors, and started to slowly get dressed herself.

Fifteen minutes before the hearse and car were due to arrive, Don and Doreen rang on the door. They were travelling with them in the car. Don gave Mary and Anna large, hard hugs then told Mary to get the sherry out and as all four of them stood drinking to Erwin, it was as if something lifted momentarily.

'We really appreciate this, Don,' Anna said, 'especially given what you're going through at the moment.'

Don shook his head. 'We're going to get you through this, Mary,' he announced, 'even if we have to do it drunk.'

It was then that the hearse and car pulled up to take them to St Cuthbert's where Mary and Erwin had been married.

'They're here,' Mary said quietly, suddenly mortified at

the sight of the empty sherry glass in her hand, and aware that she wouldn't have noticed the cars pulling up at all if it hadn't been for the sun bouncing off the long black roofs. Looking outside, she realised suddenly that the street was full of people. There were people lining it on either side; people standing on the garden wall. People had come to say goodbye not just to a man, but to an entire generation – a generation that was leaving them and taking the world they'd lived in with them.

People had come to pay tribute to the German, and when Mary stepped out the front door into the sun the silence was thick with respect.

Laviolette walked back across the beach to the Promenade and got another coffee from the café before climbing the bank onto the headland next to the mini golf course where his car was parked.

He sat drinking his coffee, the sun brilliant on the sea to his right then, sighing, phoned Laura Deane to tell her that he thought they'd found Bryan's kayak.

Laura, sounding pleased to hear from him – for the first time as far as he could recollect – stood at the salon's reception desk absently stroking her neck and said lightly, 'Inspector – I was about to call you. My doctor said I should think about taking a short break and I wasn't sure whether or not I needed your . . . permission.'

He exhaled loudly. She was flirting with him and he was aware that, like most women, Laura Deane was probably more proficient at flirting with men she disliked than those she liked.

'I'm not sleeping,' Laura carried on, 'and since the appeal I keep getting these anxiety attacks. There's a name for them . . . I can't remember . . . I feel like I'm about to black out then I start to fall. I fall –' She paused.

Laviolette had the impression she was holding her breath.

'Where were you thinking of going?'

'The other side of the world.'

'For a short break?'

'No more than ten days.' She paused again. 'I thought coming into work and carrying on would make it better, but – I'm tired of carrying on, and I'm not coping. I'm not coping with anything.'

He drew his hand absently through the dust on the dashboard then, sighing, said, 'I phoned to tell you that a kayak matching the description of Bryan's kayak was washed ashore this morning at Whitley Bay.'

'This is bad news, isn't it?' she said quietly. 'Do you need me to come down to the beach?'

'No – it's fine.' Laviolette hesitated. 'Unless of course you want to?'

'I don't know. I don't know what to do.' She started to cry. 'What am I meant to do?'

'Whatever you want to do – whatever's best.'

'I don't want to see the kayak. I don't want to come down to the beach and see the kayak.'

'That's fine. D'you want to have a think about it and phone me back in half an hour?'

'No, I don't. I want to get on a plane and pretend none of this is happening.' She broke off. 'Is that selfish of me?'

'Would Martha go with you?'

'If I can persuade her to, which I doubt.'

Laviolette was silent. He *almost* believed her – there wasn't enough of a reason to disbelieve her.

'You don't think I should go?' Laura prompted him when he didn't say anything.

'I'm thinking about Martha – there's going to be media exposure here with the discovery of the kayak. When would you go – if you go?'

166

'Tomorrow morning – it's a cancellation. I need to confirm within the next thirty minutes.'

'Tomorrow morning,' Laviolette repeated, thinking. 'Okay – go,' he concluded heavily.

'Really?'

'Yes, really,' he laughed suddenly, in spite of himself.

They both stayed on the line, unsure how to end the call.

'Inspector? You said that the kayak matches the description of Bryan's kayak – how sure are you?'

'It's Bryan's kayak, Laura.'

As Mary walked down the aisle at St Cuthbert's Church, holding tightly onto Anna's arm, she glanced down at her feet, trying to comprehend the time that had passed since she'd last walked down that aisle just over fifty years ago. Her ankles, then, had been the ankles of a twenty-two-year old, and covered in a pair of nylons she had to put nail varnish on in two places to stop the ladder running any further. She'd worn a pale blue suit and brown war issue shoes, and unlike today the church had been empty because she was marrying a German POW.

She'd been waiting on tables in the café that was now Moscadini's – where Bryan used to wait for Anna after school. Erwin had been working for a firm of painters and decorators who'd been hired to paint the café. They'd noticed each other immediately, and Mary had somehow known what was going to happen as soon as she saw him that first time, tall in overalls that didn't belong to him. In fact, Erwin didn't look like he belonged to himself at all after the years spent in camps.

What happened afterwards had been effortless . . . until Bettina, but then Bettina was the great tragedy of their lives.

They sat down at the front of the church, which was full. There were people standing.

Looking down the length of the pew – the scent of the

lilies unbearable this close – she was sure there was somebody missing; somebody they were still waiting for, and now
there wasn't any room. She felt Anna squeezed up against
her, and started to panic.

'Move up,' she hissed.

Don turned to her, confused, unsure what to do.

'There's no room for Erwin.'

Don looked at Anna, who nodded at him before taking
hold tightly of Mary's hand.

'It's alright, Nan.'

'He'll want to be here at the front with us.'

'It's alright.'

Then Mary saw the coffin in front of them, and remembered. 'I forgot,' she whispered wetly into Anna's collarbone.
'I forgot.'

There in front of her was the coffin containing the remains
of a man who'd last been in the church as a groom, and it
was at the realisation of this that Mary started to cry. She
wasn't crying at the thought of Erwin in particular, but at the
terrible inevitability of growing old and how awful it was that
the girl she'd once been should be trapped inside the old body
she'd seen in the mirror that morning, and that there was
nothing she could do about it.

They started to sing the first hymn, which wasn't a hymn
at all, but a carol – 'Silent Night' – and they sang it because
it was Erwin's favourite. Anna never forgot him telling her
that the third Christmas he spent as a prisoner of war, they'd
been given permission to walk to the small village church near
the camp, and stand at the back for midnight mass. The priest
giving the service allowed them to sing 'Silent Night' in their
own language, and there wasn't a single protest from the
congregation, who turned round when the prisoners started
to sing, and saw nothing but row after row of homesick boys.

*

The sunset that evening was long and vast. Winter's solitary dog walkers and runners, who remained loyal to the beach throughout the year's coldest days, suddenly found themselves making way for people wanting to hold onto a day that had at last felt like the first day of summer. The anaesthetist who found the kayak that morning at Whitley Bay, had to call Flo to heel three times as children – and some adults – ran wildly towards the incoming tide.

The wind was strong enough for kites, surfers and windsurfers and at the café where Laviolette bought his coffee – run by the descendents of Italian immigrants – there were queues for ice cream. The anaesthetist stopped and looked around her, trying to remember where it was exactly that she'd found the kayak because there was no sign of it now.

As she stood on the beach, trying to remember, Laura Deane drove along the coastal road through Whitley Bay towards Seaton Sluice, a Neil Diamond CD that Bryan had bought her for her last birthday playing loudly. She had the window open and as she sang along, the wind blew strands of hair into her open mouth.

The last time she'd listened to the CD had been on the way to work the Saturday Bryan disappeared – Easter Saturday – but Laura wasn't conscious of this fact. It was a beautiful evening, and tomorrow morning she was flying to Montevideo. She felt suddenly younger than she had in years.

An hour after Laura drove north along the coastal road, Anna, still in black – she'd exchanged her funeral suit for running clothes – ran south through the rapidly greying twilight along the last line of beach not yet covered by the tide. The wash of the waves was loud and the air felt cold now on her skin.

Mary had fallen silent around half seven, lowering herself

stiffly onto one of the dining chairs that had been pushed back against the lounge wall, and staring across the room at a spot of carpet near 'the shrine' as Erwin used to call it – a coffee table with a collection of photographs on it chronicling the triumphs and highlights of Anna's life and career. In most of them she was either holding an award or shaking somebody's hand, and the photograph in pride of place – the one that came closest in Mary's mind to compensation for the absence of snapshots of babies and husbands – was the one of Anna shaking Prince Edward's hand.

Mary wanted to be alone.

'Do you want me to bring the bedding down before I go?'

She shook her head. 'I'm sleeping upstairs tonight.'

Anna hesitated then, for the first time in weeks, drove back to the Ridley Arms – glad to be alone herself. She lay along the sofa in the clothes she'd worn all day and, exhausted, fell asleep.

By the time she got to the harbour at Seaton Sluice, it was almost dark so she cut up onto the headland and ran back along the road. As she passed the Duneside development, she thought about the Deanes, and about Martha, who she hadn't been in contact with for weeks.

She carried on running, past the bandstand and harbour sheds on the outskirts of Blyth, aware that she hadn't eaten properly all day, that she felt lightheaded, and that her heart was pulling in a way that made her stop suddenly, worried that she was about to black out. She walked until her breathing became more regular then, when she got to Ridley Avenue, broke into a slow, even run again.

She could hear her phone ringing as she opened the street door to the apartment and, thinking it might be Mary, took the stairs two at a time, but it wasn't Mary.

'Is now a good time?' Laviolette said.

'Not really,' she answered heavily, walking to the fridge

170

and getting a carton of milk out. 'My grandfather died. The funeral was today.'

'I'll phone another time.'

'No – it's fine.' She fell onto the sofa and lay, staring out the window at the Quayside lights. 'It's fine,' she said again.

'You're sure?'

'What's happened?'

'Bryan Deane's kayak was washed up this morning. We got a call at six from a woman out walking her dog on the beach at Whitley Bay.'

Anna felt something wet spreading across her chest. 'Shit.'

'You okay?'

'I just spilt milk everywhere. Shit. Can I phone you back?'

'It doesn't matter. I just wanted you to know – about the kayak. And I'm sorry, really sorry, about your grandfather.'

After coming off the phone to Laviolette, Anna stood under the shower for twenty minutes before collapsing into the bed that had remained unmade for weeks.

She slept so heavily that she woke up the next morning in the same position she'd fallen asleep in.

She spent the morning cleaning the flat – something she hadn't done properly since moving in – and putting various loads of washing through the machine, and it wasn't until she stopped for lunch that she became aware of the fact that she'd lost her reason for staying up north.

On her way out to see Mary, she pulled a flyer out the letterbox.

'Sorry to hear about your grandfather.' Roy the Harbourmaster was standing smoking in the office doorway, one hand pushed in his trouser pocket. 'My wife's cousin was at the funeral.'

He looked away, distracted, down Quay Road towards the roundabout where a lorry was trying to reverse.

Anna screwed up the flyer and was about to throw it in

the bin next to where she'd parked the Capri when her mind – which had been running ahead and drawing conclusions without her being aware of it – concluded that the paper was too good a grade for it to be a flyer. She smoothed it out on the roof of the Capri, which was hot from the sun, her heart pulling in the same way it had towards the end of her run the night before.

This was no flyer.

Somebody had drawn a butterfly, intricately executed in pen and ink, and written 'Erwin Faust R.I.P.' underneath.

'You alright?' she heard Roy's voice, calling out.

She turned round, her hands over her eyes to shield them from the sun, and waved at him before walking over to the office.

'Did you see anybody other than the postman put anything through my door?'

Roy thought about this. 'There's been nobody round here.'

She felt him watching her as she walked back to the car, putting the drawing in the glove compartment.

She should destroy the drawing, but not right now.

Right now, it gave her something to hold onto in a world that had been empty for too long.

Bryan wanted her to know he was still alive.

An hour after checking into the Hotel l'Auberge at Punte del Este, Laura Deane left her room and – despite several wrong turnings along uniform corridors that epitomised everything everybody who came here had paid for: the luxury of forgetting – eventually found what she was looking for: Suite 87. She knocked three times, her left hand and forehead pressed against the door, her eyes shut. There was no answer so she knocked again, her breath caught in her throat as she waited for the door to open – unable to hear any movement on the other side.

Then, without warning, a voice called out from inside, 'Come in.'

She pushed the door open slowly, looking around her with scared eyes.

A man with blond hair – thinner than she remembered – was sitting by the window staring at her. He didn't look like he was waiting for anything or anybody.

'You're here,' she said, hesitant, shy and tearful.

'You thought I wouldn't be?' he sounded half amused; half sad, and she knew – from the way he said it – that he'd thought about not being there.

Despite his utterly changed appearance, the man in front of her bore remarkable similarities to Bryan Deane – gestures, the voice – and her eyes would have found him immediately in a crowd, but nobody here in this hotel in Uruguay had any idea who Bryan Deane was. The name on the passport he'd handed to the Ukranian on reception gave his name as Tom Bowen, and over the next ten days – despite starting off afraid of each other – Laura found out a lot about Tom Bowen.

Unlike Bryan Deane, Tom Bowen didn't get tired or depressed; he didn't talk about suicide or come home on a Friday night and announce that he was spending the weekend walking in the Lake District, alone. He didn't spend hours sitting on the edge of the bed holding a sock in his hand, staring at the wall; he didn't scream down the phone at people in call centres thousands of miles away trying to manage his credit card debt; he didn't sit in silence over a plate of trout and broccoli then start to quietly and in-explicably cry; he didn't get out of his car and kick in a van's door because it had taken his parking space; he didn't sit in the ensuite in darkness, pretending not to be home. Tom Bowen didn't look at her with hollow eyes or wake up sobbing or go on walks that lasted days.

Tom Bowen looked at her and held her and was there.

Tom Bowen made her feel weightless.

Tom Bowen made her laugh.

Tom Bowen made her not care about anything other than Tom Bowen.

Laura had been waiting for Tom Bowen ever since she first laid eyes on Bryan Deane at the age of thirteen.

The next morning, a Ukranian cleaner – sister to the Ukranian on reception – went into Suite 87. She'd been cleaning in hotels since she was fifteen and knew that licit and illicit love made rooms smell different. Suite 87, which she cleaned thoroughly and without expression – the lack of expression itself an expression of her experience – smelt illicit. The people who had spent the night here were not married – to each other anyway. These were her observations, made without judgement, but with a momentary wistfulness that gave her face – for less than a second – a thin brightness.

# 12

It was a hot day in mid September. Martha left the music block where she'd had her last lesson of the day and joined the flock of girls in blue shirts heading down past the tennis courts towards the school's main gates as the bell for the end of school rang. She was sweating – had been sweating all day in the airless classrooms whose open windows brought in nothing apart from the occasional bee – and the strap of her bag, heavy with books, was digging into her shoulders.

The school coaches were lined up on the road outside the gates ready to take girls back to Hexham and Alnwick where they were picked up by parents and driven to outlying villages. The grammar school had a county-wide catchment area. The coach drivers in wing-tip sunglasses and short-sleeve shirts – all short; all balding – stood talking and laughing, hands in pockets, as girls ate ice creams in small groups by the coaches' open doors, catching the cold air from the air conditioning.

Martha used to get the coach home in year seven – there was one that ran to Tynemouth where she'd wait in the salon for Laura to finish. There were coach prefects, but they did little to make the journey any more endurable for girls like Martha so she'd been going home on public transport since year eight – the metro to Whitley Bay then the bus.

By the time she got to the gates, the coaches were starting to leave, and that was when she saw him – while waiting to cross the road.

The dog standing beside him – in the shade under a dusty horse chestnut – was white. His hair was blond and he was thinner. He had on a Pogues T-shirt she'd never seen before, but it was definitely him.

He wasn't looking at her – he was looking at a group of girls in her year standing about a hundred yards away, laughing and making frantic arrangements for the weekend with friends. Why was he looking at them? He knew her; knew she wasn't one of those laughing girls.

'Dad!' Martha cried out.

She saw the laughing girls turn and stare, but she didn't care.

Her arm was up in the air – she felt the underarm seam of her shirt split – waving wildly.

He saw her then.

Suddenly he was looking straight at her, and the dog by his side, restless, let out a bark.

He didn't react – he just looked scared then worried before starting to walk away.

'Dad!' she screamed this time, running into the road as one of the coaches pulled away. She was forced to stop, and as the coach drew heavily past her, she saw her reflection slipping along the length of its white body.

By the time the coach accelerated – taking her reflection with it – he'd disappeared.

She ran across the road and got to the chestnut tree where he'd been standing, staring about her, helpless. She stayed there for another hour before eventually starting to walk in the direction of the metro station, her eyes everywhere.

But she didn't see a blond man in a Pogues T-shirt with a white dog walking beside him.

Laura left Starz Salon at around four, statuesque in white linen. Between the salon and the car, she saw three people she knew and passed through them in a bright hurry, waving energetically and pulling Roxy after her.

These people – who had sent flowers, personally delivered their condolences, expressed sympathy, offered support, and held onto Laura when words gave way to tears – stopped and stared. She'd moved through them so fast she left a wind blowing behind her that ruffled the feathers of decency. Her brightness took the warmth out of them and their feelings towards her.

They started to talk, making whispered observations that were as brief as they were insidious: Laura Deane looked like she'd found something rather than lost something.

Sitting on a stool on the other side of the salon window, Kirsty on reception drew a series of concentric circles absently round that day's date in the appointment diary then glanced up at the clock on the wall in front of her and wrote down the time. After this she flicked back through the last couple of months. There were times written against all the days, including Saturdays but excluding Sundays when the salon was closed: since getting back from Uruguay Laura left the salon every day at around four o'clock with the same air of nervous anticipation.

After getting in her car, Laura drove through heavy after-school traffic towards North Shields, singing along absently to songs that came onto the radio until she reached her destination: Royal Quays Marina. She parked the car in the

usual bay – number 87 – because she'd always been superstitious and like most superstitious people, enjoyed the
resonance of pattern and order that superstition gave to
the seemingly random act of life.

Leaving Roxy in the car with the shower radio tuned in
to Planet Rock, Roxy's favourite station – she bought the
shower radio specifically for Roxy to listen to in the car
because Roxy liked to lick the speaker when songs she
recognised were playing – Laura crossed the car park, instinctively looking up to see if there was anybody on the balcony
of their flat – flat fourteen – but there wasn't.

On the balcony next door, she made out the head of the
Polish woman who lived at number twenty-three, bent over
a book, but she lost sight of her as she disappeared into the
lobby of the Ropermakers Building.

The lobby had a communal smell to it that reminded her
of school, but she didn't have to wait there long because
the lift was always on the ground floor. She'd been coming
here nearly every day for the past two months and never
yet seen anybody either getting out of or into the lift, but
then that was hardly surprising given that only forty percent
of units had been sold, and most of these – their own included
– were running into negative equity.

It was their friend, Greg – Bryan's colleague at Tyneside
Properties – who'd talked up the Royal Quays development
and put the idea of an investment property into Bryan's
head – initially proposing joint ownership then backing out
at the last moment. Wise Greg.

They only managed to let it for six months before the
property market crashed. Last year they put it on the
market, but withdrew it in January when they realised that
they weren't going to sell the flat in the foreseeable future,
and anyway by then Laura had conceived of a different
use for it.

178

Flat twenty-one in the Ropemakers Building at Royal Quays Marina was where Tom Bowen was going to live.

She stared at herself for a moment in the lift's mirror before the doors jolted unevenly open onto an empty corridor, lit by a south facing window at the end with a view over the marina. A door slammed shut somewhere in the building then there was silence, cut through by her footsteps as she walked down the corridor to flat twenty-one, letting herself in.

The windows in the flat were shut.

It was hot, smelt of food and sex from the day before, and felt empty.

It was also a mess, but Laura never felt the compunction to clean here that she did at home. Part of her liked the mess.

The flat had estuary views – views they'd paid a premium for, but that failed to retain their leverage during the economic downturn.

Leaving the windows shut, she moved through the rooms of the flat to confirm what she'd somehow instinctively known as soon as she walked in – Tom wasn't there. The reason she left Roxy in the car when she came here was that Tom often looked after the Husky belonging to the Polish woman next door and Roxy and the Husky didn't get on, but there was no sign of the Husky today. There were drawings across the sofa and coffee table – the ones on the coffee table pinned down by cups. Tom was taking a life drawing class on Tuesday and Thursday nights and his drawings covered most of the available surfaces.

She let herself out onto the balcony, saw the Polish woman reading still – and a cargo ship in the distance, moving through the mouth of the Tyne – and went back inside. She put the kettle on, watched it boil, then opened the fridge and took out one of the bottles of white wine she'd brought with her the day before, pouring herself a glass. She stood drinking it, anger passing to worry, passing to anger again. Where was Tom? The romance of the past few months, which had started at the Hotel L'Auberge in Punte del Este – a glorious, rolling, all consuming romance – broke suddenly as she stood silently drinking her glass of wine in the flat's tiny kitchen.

For the first time since Bryan's disappearance, she found herself thinking – what would happen if Bryan really did decide to disappear?

Anna was asleep on the sofa when Laviolette rang, the sun falling across her back. She'd fallen into a habit of going to bed around ten and sleeping until two or three in the morning when she'd get up and maybe eat something then go onto the computer for a while before going for a run at six. After the run, she had breakfast and drove over to see Mary. She came home in the afternoon and slept.

Laviolette had left three messages for her since Erwin's death – nothing to do with Bryan Deane, just well intended enquiries after her general health and state of mind, neither of which were good.

She hadn't returned any of them, but he didn't bring this up – he didn't ask her how she was feeling either, he just said, 'Can you help me with something?'

'What?'

'I'm heading to fifty-one Perry Vale, Whitley Bay – following up a Missing Persons.'

She laughed. 'They've assigned you another one?'

'OAP – sixty-two – reckons his wife's gone missing. He says she went out for a walk yesterday morning and never came home. Uniforms went round yesterday and took a statement, but there's something . . . I don't know.'

'I don't work for Northumbria Police, Inspector.'

'I just want you to observe, Sergeant.' He paused. 'Where

are we now? September? You're into month six of your one month's compassionate leave – that's very understanding of the Met.'

'They want me to have an evaluation before I go back to work. At the moment I'm not even up to the evaluation.'

'So what are you going to do?'

'I don't know.'

'Come on – it's a beautiful day. You need to get out more – it'll help you sleep at night.'

Anna knew she was going to go.

Laviolette knew she was going to go.

She walked heavily over to the windows, her back and upper arms aching from the position she'd fallen asleep in on the sofa. She'd become dependent on the North Sea being outside her windows, and even though the Thames flowed past the new development in Greenwich where she rented a flat, it had none of the angry restlessness or empirical unpredictability of the North Sea.

'How do you know I'm not sleeping at night?'

'I can hear it in your voice.'

'What did you say the address was?'

'Fifty-one Perry Vale, Whitley Bay.'


It was Constable Wade who answered the door.

She looked surprised to see Anna.

Laviolette obviously hadn't said anything, and Anna wondered if this was the way he worked – keeping people in the dark. In evaluations it was the kind of behaviour they linked to paranoia and an inability to communicate – she'd worked in an investment bank's Personnel department running employee risk assessment profiles for six months when she first left university.

'The Inspector wants me to observe,' Anna explained, trying to put Constable Wade at her ease.

Constable Wade would never have openly criticised the Inspector – and made an effort now to neutralise any facial expressions – but she couldn't help repeating, 'Observe?'

Anna smiled and nodded, and the next minute DC Wade – who could only have been in her mid twenties – was grinning back at her.

Fifty-one Perry Vale smelt as if old people lived there. Anna followed DC Wade into a lounge where the Inspector and an elderly man – Mr Larcom – were sitting on a red three-piece covered in raised velveteen flora. There was a red and gold coffee table with a plate of Rich Tea biscuits on it and some cups of tea.

Sergeant Chambers was standing by an electric organ in the corner of the room, holding a cup of tea awkwardly in his large hands, and looking unhappy.

'You made it,' Laviolette said, smiling at Anna and introducing her to Mr Larcom simply as, 'another colleague – Anna.'

Anna didn't look at Chambers and Wade, instead her eyes swept quickly round the room and the thing that struck her was the lack of photographs. There was a sideboard, but there were no photographs on top of it.

'D'you want to take a look round the house?' he said to her over his shoulder before turning back to Mr Larcom and helping himself to another biscuit.

This time Anna saw Chambers and Wade exchange glances, which the Inspector also saw but chose to ignore.

'They searched the house yesterday,' Mr Larcom said, aware that Anna was watching him. 'And these two,' he jerked his thumb at Chambers and Wade, 'they did it just now.'

All the Inspector said in response to this was, 'Don't worry – we'll just carry on talking down here.'

Anna went into the kitchen and started opening cupboards as quietly as she could: instant coffee, Bistro gravy granules, mustard powder, Oxo cubes, Saxo salt – the war generation's staple store cupboard ingredients. She wasn't enjoying herself – why had she agreed to come?

She went upstairs.

The lilac bathroom was as clean and tidy as the rest of the house, the bathmat damp still – with talcum powder impressions of what must have been Mr Larcom's feet.

The Larcoms' bedroom was silent and gloomy despite the sun outside, and the spare room smelt damp, and felt as though it hadn't been slept in for years. The whole house, in fact, felt strangely vacated.

She thought about Mr Larcom downstairs. There was no urgency to his worry over his wife's disappearance. He only seemed mildly disorientated and confused – probably at the number of strangers he'd had in his house over the past two days.

The Inspector was right, there was something . . .

Her mind had picked up on something here upstairs.

She went back onto the tiny landing and looked around her then, distracted, went downstairs again – smiling encouragingly at Mr Larcom, who'd been too busy listening to her move around upstairs to respond to the Inspector's questions.

Still smiling, she squeezed between Sergeant Chambers – who didn't move – and the sideboard, and looked out the single patio door at the garden, which couldn't have been more than three metres square – laid to lawn. There was a shed at the end and a wheelbarrow balanced against it.

'Mind if I take a look at the shed, Mr Larcom?' she said, opening the patio door before he had time to respond.

'We did the shed just now,' Chambers put in.

'I'll only be a few minutes. Is it locked?'

183

'No – it's not locked,' Mr Larcom said, sounding sad for the first time as he said this.

The Larcoms clearly weren't gardeners.

The shed was used as more of an overflow attic than anything else.

She paused, noticing a heap of blue harnesses on the floor in the corner behind an old push mower – the only piece of gardening equipment there was in the shed. They were the type of harnesses used by removal companies for large items of furniture.

She shut the shed door, crossed the lawn – and saw Mr Larcom watching her through the patio door.

Laviolette smiled placidly at her as she went back inside, his mouth full of biscuit, looking like he'd just informed Mr Larcom that an insurance premium was due to be paid out.

Constable Wade looked sombre, professional and solidly alert.

Sergeant Chambers looked like he was itching to rip someone's head off and play football with it.

Mr Larcom just looked surprised all over again to find these strangers in his house.

'D'you mind if I take one last look upstairs?'

It was Laviolette she was looking at as she made the request. He seemed pleased – with her request? Himself? The situation?

She went back upstairs, stopping on the top tread, her hand on the banister.

There was something wrong here on the landing; a humming sound – dull, electrical – coming from the ceiling, which her eyes ran over now. A white cable running out of the loft hatch had been messily pinned across the ceiling and down the wall where it ran into a plug socket in the skirting board.

There were marked impressions in the carpet from where – Anna guessed – a ladder must have stood.

She stayed motionless at the top of the stairs for a few minutes more, her eyes fixed on the loft hatch, before calling down. 'Inspector? Inspector – d'you mind coming up here for a moment?'

The Inspector and Mr Larcom appeared at the foot of the stairs.

'It's alright Mr Larcom, you can stay down here. Constable Wade!' Laviolette called out, waiting until she had lead Mr Larcom back into the lounge before joining Anna upstairs.

'I've got a feeling that's an extension lead,' she said, running her fingers over the cabling, 'going up into the loft. He's got some sort of electrical appliance plugged in up there. Can you hear that?'

They stood listening until their ears picked out the faint humming sound.

'I think we need some ladders.'

'I think we do.'

They smiled at each other and went back downstairs.

'Mr Larcom,' Laviolette said brightly as they walked into the lounge where everyone was in the same position as before, 'd'you mind if we get your ladders out the garden shed?'

Mr Larcom stared at them. 'My ladders?'

Laviolette nodded. 'We just want to take a quick look round the attic.'

'Why?'

'Because we didn't do that this morning.'

'I'll get them,' Mr Larcom offered wearily, hesitating before stepping through the garden door onto the patio.

Laviolette jerked his head at Chambers to follow him.

They returned a couple of minutes later with the ladders.

'You want to watch when you put them up – the spring's starting to rust. Sometimes you think they're fully open and they're not.' Mr Larcom paused. 'And the hatch to the attic

185

is hinged.' He paused again. 'The hinges are on the right, and there's a light cord hanging from one of the rafters – you can't miss it.'

Leaving Mr Larcom downstairs with Constable Wade, they went upstairs – Chambers carrying the ladders.

'D'you want me to go up?' he offered when they got to the top landing.

'You and Anna. Anna first – this is her lead.'

Anna hesitated before starting to climb. The hatch opened easily and she realised that it was easier than most lofts to get into because the hatch had been widened in a way that hadn't been immediately obvious, standing beneath it.

She stood up, found the light cord and pulled it, looking round the illuminated attic space while she waited for Chambers.

There was a large chest freezer two metres away, filling most of the space. This was what the extension cable was for.

With a grunt, Chambers swung himself up and was soon standing beside her, looking at the chest freezer while trying to suck a large splinter out of his left index finger.

He turned round and spat among the rafters, shaking his hand. 'Got it. Shit,' he added.

Anna wasn't sure if he was referring to the splinter or the chest freezer.

'How the fuck did he get that up here?'

'Those straps – in the shed.'

'I didn't see any straps,' Chambers said, aggressively.

Anna ignored this, crossing the boards that had been laid across the three rafters separating them from the chest freezer.

'We used to have one of these,' he said.

'So did we.' Anna thought about the chest freezer Erwin

186

used to have in the side passage at number nineteen Parkview for overflow from the vegetable patch.

'Can't think what the hell my mum used to put in it.' He sighed, looking behind him at the open hatch where the Inspector's head had appeared. 'Seriously though, how the fuck did he get this up here?'

He was about to say something else when Anna opened the lid of the freezer.

They looked down then up at each other as Anna let the lid drop with a bang. She started to laugh.

Chambers looked at her, concerned, then started laughing himself – the back of his hand over his mouth. 'Shit,' he said, laughing even harder as Laviolette finally managed to haul himself up into the attic, picking his way awkwardly across the boards towards the chest freezer. 'Sir, you'd better come and take a look at this,' he said.

'What am I looking at?'

Anna, no longer in hysterics, managed to say, 'Mrs Larcom.'

And there lay Mrs Larcom, on top of a surprising amount of frozen food, twisted on her side, and fully dressed – the hem of a flesh coloured slip showing beneath a green skirt. There were wrinkles in her tights, at the ankle, and she only had one slipper on. The other slipper was resting on top of a box of arctic roll. She was wearing a pair of clip-on earrings, and a necklace and her hair was full of frozen peas and sweetcorn. There were peas in the hollows of her face. It looked like she'd been dropped into the freezer in a hurry, and the force of her landing had burst the bags of frozen vegetables.

Even looking at her from this angle they couldn't see any wounding and, shutting her eyes, Anna gave in to an impression that she'd probably been drugged by Mr Larcom – there may even have been accomplices. He could have got her to climb up here on some pretext, given her a paralytic then pushed her into the freezer, shutting the lid and leaving her to freeze to death. Possibly.

Mr Larcom was waiting for them, expectant, when they got back downstairs. He looked sad – as though he'd given things his best shot, but wasn't all that surprised that he hadn't quite pulled it off.

'We found your wife, Mr Larcom,' Laviolette announced.

'You did?' He nodded slowly to himself then said, 'We've been married forty years. What's forty years? Silver? Diamonds?' For some reason he appealed to Anna at this point. 'We were never close though. I've been planning this ever since I retired twelve years ago. Oh well, I suppose it's kept me busy. I needed the money, you know?'

Mr Larcom seemed much calmer now – relieved almost.

'What did you need the money for?' Sergeant Chambers asked, genuinely curious.

'A woman I've been seeing – Romanian woman; she cleans down at Jesmond Dene . . . those big places down there. I wanted to make a go of it with her.' He was speaking slowly, looking at them all in turn, and hoping it all made sense. 'Seventy-seven's not so old these days, is it?' He grinned suddenly then, looking upset for the first time, 'She won't get into trouble over this, will she? She had nothing to do with any of it. I've got my pension, you see,' he explained patiently, 'but I needed the money settled on Brenda.'

'Life insurance?' Laviolette prompted.

'That's it,' Mr Larcom nodded, pleased that they were following him.

Laviolette leant against his car, which was parked half way up Perry Vale.

'What was that?' Anna demanded.

'Life.'

188

'I'm not talking about Mrs Larcom. Mrs Larcom . . . shit.'
Anna started laughing again.

'It's good to see you laugh. It's good to see you.'

Ignoring this, Anna said, 'I'm talking about you getting me over here.'

'You weren't picking up your phone.'

'I'm grieving.'

'I was worried about you.' Laviolette smiled at her.

'Stop smiling.'

'Okay.' But he didn't stop smiling.

'You've got no right – to be worried about me.'

'I wanted to take your mind off things.'

'With Mrs Larcom?'

'I'm looking for a new Detective Sergeant.'

'You've already got one.'

'Skipper here is relocating to Teeside.'

She glanced behind her at Sergeant Chambers, who gave her a brief consenting nod.

'Can I ask you something Inspector?' he said. 'When you call me Skipper – is it because you're fond of me or because you can't stand the sight of me?'

'It's because I can never remember your name.'

Chambers nodded thoughtfully.

'You knew, didn't you?' Anna said suddenly to Laviolette. 'When you phoned me – asked me to come over – you'd already seen the extension lead running up to the loft hatch.'

'What makes you think that?'

'You knew about the extension lead – you wanted to see how long it would take me to notice.' She paused then said again, 'You knew.'

Laviolette shrugged. 'Neither Chambers, Wade or any of the uniformed officers noticed the lead.'

'So it wasn't their day.'

'Do you want a drink or something?'

189

'You knew about that extension lead,' she insisted.

He smiled suddenly at her, and it felt like the first real smile she'd seen on his face. 'Come on – a drink.'

She hesitated, about to accept – she *did* want a drink – when her phone started ringing.

It was Martha Deane.

'Some other time,' she said, pulling herself away from the moment – with relief, she realised afterwards as she got back into the familiar Capri, her phone ringing again.

Laura had been looking forward to her meeting with Bryan's old colleague, Greg Bolton at five that afternoon, but now she was distracted by the fact that for the first time since they'd started meeting there in the afternoons, Tom hadn't been at the marina flat. She'd arranged the meeting with Greg the day before after a brief, flirtatious call to him. Their encounters had always been mildly flirtatious, and although initially Greg had been sombre because it was only the second time they'd spoken since Bryan's disappearance, he soon found himself responding to her habitual flirting.

Greg Bolton had been made acting Branch Manager – not that Tyneside Properties were exactly going to advertise this fact, but they did need somebody to run the branch in Bryan's absence.

Greg was coming to value the house because Laura was thinking about putting it on the market – selling the house was something she and Bryan had talked about before his disappearance on Easter Saturday. It was something she'd been afraid of for the past two years, but now it was actually going on the market the only thing she felt was an incredible sense of relief.

Greg knew the house – him and his wife, Patsy, were frequent guests at number two Marine Drive – but he enjoyed the guided tour Laura gave him.

Laura had spent time wondering how to play things with Greg, and as she drifted through the house, listing the obvious features with a genuine pathos, she could see that she'd been right to adopt sadness; a sadness that gave her an allure . . . a weight she hadn't had before.

He didn't tell her that the market had flat-lined, and he didn't tell her that if she did go ahead with putting number two Marine Drive on the market, she wouldn't get anything close to what they'd paid for it – because Laura knew all these things. He just told her to think about it; to be really sure.

'It's a beautiful home,' he said, following her back downstairs and helping her to regain her balance as she slipped on the last tread.

They'd just walked into the kitchen and Laura, poised near the fridge, had just responded to his comment with one of her own – 'It's not a home any more' – when Martha burst through the front door. Dropping her rucksack onto the floor near the breakfast bar and – seeing Greg with his hands on the bench behind him, leaning back and smiling, and her mother hanging onto the fridge door in the process of hauling out a bottle of wine – said, breathless, 'I just saw dad.'

Greg and Laura didn't move for what seemed like minutes afterwards.

'I saw dad,' she said again.

Laura arranged her hair carefully over her right shoulder, and turned to smile wearily at Greg, who didn't smile back.

Confronted by the cataclysmic, a vague sense of horror had settled over Greg, immobilising him at a moment when he most felt like running – number two Marine Drive had lost its appeal.

'You remember Greg, don't you Martha?' Laura persisted brightly.

'I saw dad – I saw him,' Martha yelled, her face suddenly red, the muscles on her neck defined, her eyes wide, and scared. 'He was standing under a tree outside school. He was just standing there. He had blond hair and there was a dog with him, but I knew immediately – it was him.' The next minute Martha burst into tears. 'Say something!'

Laura's smile had gone.

'Martha!' she called out as Martha, running and still crying, left the house.

She turned back to Greg, clutching the fridge door in one hand and the bottle of wine in the other, but couldn't think of anything to say.

On the other side of the fences lining the back gardens of Marine Drive, cars on the coastal road swerved to avoid the girl in school uniform running, oblivious, through the traffic. A van driver supplying custom-made blinds yelled something incoherent at her retreating back as, blue shirt billowing around her now in the wind from the incoming tide, she fled down past the play park and onto the dunes.

But nobody stopped.

As the speedometers flickered back up to forty and beyond, the girl became nothing more than a speck of blue and red on the line of dunes in the wing mirrors and rear-view mirrors of traffic heading north.

Martha sat down in a hollow above the beach.

She wasn't crying any more, but her eyes were wet and stinging from the wind that had blown the last of the tears away, and she was sweating heavily. She drew her knees up and sat hugging them as she listened to the sea's incoming roar.

After a while she phoned Anna.

Anna parked the Capri on the headland by the Kings Arms – a three-storey stone building painted white, overlooking the natural harbour at Seaton Sluice, which local history claimed was the birthplace of the industrial revolution.

She could see Martha, in her school uniform – sitting in the bus stop by the old customs house where she'd told her to wait.

Martha had seen Anna – was standing up, waving, and making her way towards her, running the last few hundred yards and slamming into her as she'd done on the drive outside her house the night Bryan disappeared.

'Let's go onto the beach,' Anna said after a while.

Holding hands, they slid down the steep grass bank onto the harbour-side, following it round – past a red fishing boat swinging sharply from side to side – onto the beach. They walked slowly, in silence, following the line of debris from the last high tide – the sea had almost reached it now. The wind was strong down on the beach, but warm – and they had to shout to make themselves heard.

'What did he look like?'

Martha stopped. 'He looked like dad.'

'I mean – had he changed his appearance in any way?'

'He had this weird blond hair, and there was a white dog with him – a big white dog. I don't know what the breed was,' Martha said, worried, 'but all I saw was dad. To me he looked just like dad.' When Anna didn't comment on this, she added, 'And he looked sad – I never saw him look so sad.'

Ahead of them there was a group of school children hurling bits of driftwood at each other. Without saying anything, they turned and started heading back towards the harbour.

'He's alive, Anna,' Martha said, suddenly excited as the wind blew the last of the shock away, and young enough not to see any difficulties or obstacles in this potential fact. 'He wants me to know he's still alive.' She broke into a run, running hard along the beach until – out of breath – she was forced to stop and wait for Anna, who was walking towards her thinking of the drawing that was posted through her door the day of Erwin's funeral. That was over two months ago – she hadn't seen, heard or received anything else since.

Part of her wasn't convinced Martha had seen Bryan.

Part of her was still open to the possibility that it was Martha who'd sent her the drawing – using the spectre of Bryan to remain connected to her.

But all the other parts of her wanted more than anything to believe that the man Martha saw standing under the chestnut tree outside school, and the person who sent her the drawing the day of Erwin's funeral – was Bryan Deane.

'What did your mum say?'

'Fuck her.' Martha drew her foot through the sand in a long arc then looked out to sea for a moment, distracted by the memory of Greg in the kitchen. She'd almost forgotten about Greg.

'D'you think we should tell the Inspector?'

Anna thought about this. 'I don't know.'

'Why?' Martha demanded, immediately distrustful – as if Anna's comment was indicative of doubt on her part.

Anna knew what Martha was thinking. 'Because,' she explained, 'so far, you're the only one who knows, and I've got a feeling that your dad wants as few people as possible to know he's alive.'

Martha, who'd been listening carefully, smiled suddenly. 'Okay,' she said, 'we'll keep him for ourselves.'

There was a simplicity to what she said that was dangerous in itself. But Anna nodded, smiling at the complicity of it, and the next minute, feeling a lightness she hadn't felt in years, caught hold of Martha's elbow and said, 'Race you to the harbour!'

They started to run, the wind behind them now, the boats in the harbour restless, rocking, tired of their anchors.

In the heavy silence following first Martha then Greg's departure, Laura stood motionless in the hallway until the quality of light started to change, casting longer slow-moving shadows over the beige walls.

Eventually she came to, startled by the sound of the doorbell ringing in the empty house and looking about her with something close to anguish. She hadn't yet switched on any lights inside the house.

Falling into the doorframe as she made her way to the front door – badly bruising her left shoulder – she stared at her wind-torn daughter.

'Where the hell have you been?' she shouted, louder than she meant to and catching Mrs McClaren – who'd just returned from swimming lessons and who was in the process of emptying her car of children – staring at them.

Mrs McClaren hesitated then waved.

Laura didn't wave back; instead she grabbed hold of Martha's thin arm and hauled her indoors.

'Where the hell have you been?' she said again, whispering now even though there was no point because they were indoors.

Martha stared at her the same way Mrs McClaren had done just seconds earlier – as if they had components inside them that were superior to those inside Laura herself.

'Are we going to talk about this?' Laura demanded.

Martha walked past her, in silence, up the stairs.

Laura followed; the door to Martha's room slammed in her face – she pushed it open so forcefully that CDs started to fall out the rack on the wall.

'You don't believe me,' Martha said at last, 'so what's the point?'

Laura picked up the CDs from where they'd fallen onto the floor, putting them back in the rack – some of the cases had come apart.

After a while, watching her, Martha said, 'I saw him outside school – he was standing under a tree on the opposite side of the road. He had a dog with him,' she concluded, flatly.

'What sort of dog?' Laura asked.

'Big . . . white.'

'Have you told anybody else?'

'I don't want to talk about this any more,' Martha said sullenly. She swung away from Laura, but she could feel her mother's eyes on her still. 'What was Greg doing here?'

'Greg?' Laura, distracted, sounded surprised at the mention of his name. 'Oh. I'm thinking of putting the house on the market. It's something we discussed – dad and I – before –'

Martha was shaking her head, and Laura knew what was coming next. She stood up.

'No,' Martha said, her voice loud with disbelief. 'No!'

Laura started to leave the room. 'You're right,' she called back through the open door, from the top of the stairs. 'I don't believe you.' She paused. 'A big white dog?' She started to laugh.

# 13

Later that night – after telling Martha she was going to a Pilates class – Laura drove back along the coastal road towards the Royal Quays Marina at North Shields on a bottle of Pouilly-Fumé.

She parked the car in the usual bay and, looking up at the waterside flats, saw that the Polish woman was no longer reading on her balcony and that the balcony door to their flat was open, which meant that Tom must be there.

The purchase of the marina flat – an investment neither of them had the stomach or imagination for; not really – had, within a very few months, come to signal their downfall financially as the property plunged into negative equity and they were left unable to either sell it or rent it.

The edge of life together as they knew it emerged suddenly on the horizon, beyond which lay an abysmal darkness.

The darkness had always been there, but now they could see the edge the threshold between them and it had gone. For months Laura found herself holding her breath while Bryan moved slowly, silently about the house – without expression, hovering somewhere between occupied and preoccupied. He'd respond to her with polite intonations that left her wondering, most of the time, whether he was about to make them tea or saw his own head off with the bread knife.

Their marriage was no longer the blood sport it had always been.

They'd had their last fight.

Bryan's disappearance had been Laura's idea – it was the only thing she could come up with to prevent him from actually disappearing. She knew it was a risk, him living in the marina flat after they got back from Uruguay, but she wanted to keep him close while he experienced the freedom of death.

She hurried now across the car park and into the Ropemakers Building, taking the lift up to level three where their flat was, and letting herself in.

Tom was outside, smoking on the balcony, his arms hanging over the steel railings as he stared down at the marina and River Tyne. There was a stillness to him that was different to the stasis she'd known before, in the months leading up to his disappearance – it was a stillness full of the promise of movement.

The dining table was covered with sketches that were weighed down, but the edges kept curling up and crackling in the breeze that passed through the flat, lifting the curtains hanging at the balcony door into the air. The Husky – the big, white dog Martha had seen outside school that afternoon – lay along the sofa in a block of evening sunshine.

They'd decorated the marina flat themselves like it was their first place together. All memory of the four-bedroom detached house on Marine Drive and the life they'd lived there was painted over – in cornflower blue, it was eventually decided.

'Blue's my favourite colour,' Bryan had said, awkwardly. Laura, quietly stunned, 'It is?'

She felt like crying when he said the word 'blue' – it was something he should have said twenty years ago; that she should have encouraged him to say, but never did.

With this revelation, she conceded – the flat became Bryan's flat – and they painted it blue, to music they used to dance to, played on LPs that – along with Bryan's old record player – had been retrieved from the attic on Marine Drive and driven over to North Shields like childhood contraband.

They painted drunk and stoned and everything they touched – including each other – was charged with the eroticism of potential. The rows and disputes they had in the flat led to reconciliation rather than retribution, and although the reconciliation sometimes took place in the bed that Laura had bought new bed linen for from Bainbridges in Newcastle, it also took place on rugs in the living room, the kitchen floor, up against the fridge door – where she discovered the newfound pleasure of climaxing with her back up against stainless steel – the bath, the dining table, the sofa and somewhere close enough to the front door for her nipples to freeze in the draught coming under it.

They'd got to this point – love again – Laura thought, as she turned the key in the door, aware that if she opened it to find Laviolette standing there, she wouldn't care as much as she should, because she'd had this: they'd become magnificent again, in each other's eyes.

The terrifying banality of things that used to plunge them into life-threatening rows at number two Marine Drive – running out of milk, a blocked sink, a mysterious scratch on the fridge door – Laura embraced in the flat as proof of a romantic negligence.

Two weeks before Easter Saturday she'd brought over some bin liners full of clothes she told Mrs McClaren she was taking to charity shops. These clothes that Bryan had worn at number two Marine Drive, looked different on Tom Bowen when worn against the cornflower blue walls of the marina flat. Likewise, Tom not only noticed what she was wearing – he noticed what she wasn't wearing. It had got to the point at number two Marine Drive when Bryan was able to conduct a conversation with her walking naked round the bedroom – about getting the gutters cleaned after autumn's fall.

Tom turned round instinctively then, his eyes thin as he exhaled the last of his cigarette before throwing the stub over the edge of the balcony.

'The door,' Laura said.

He shut the door, catching one of the curtains in it so that it carried on flapping on the other side of the glass.

Laura stared at him, waiting for him to speak.

But he didn't say anything.

Distracted, he walked over to the table and thumbed through a couple of his sketches.

'What were you thinking?' she hissed at last, dropping her handbag onto the sofa by the Husky and crossing over to him, pulling hard on his left arm – anger giving way to relief now that he was here in front of her again. 'This afternoon – what were you thinking?' she demanded.

He sat down, staring absently at the dog stretched out on the sofa still.

'I needed to see her. I miss her,' he said, letting out a soft sob that turned into a cough – he was coughing a lot since starting smoking again.

The sob shocked Laura.

He was upset, disintegrating in front of her, and she couldn't think of anything to say apart from, 'It's going to be fine.'

'God – Martha. What were we thinking? What *were* we thinking?'

'It's going to be fine,' she said again, barely aware of what she was saying.

'How's it going to be fine?' He stood up, and went over to the balcony doors and his posture as he stood there staring out to sea made the flat feel suddenly tiny.

'We've got this far,' she said bravely.

'And it feels too far.'

'We're nearly there, Bryan.'

He smiled briefly and turned to look at her, unconvinced, 'But it's still not far enough, is it? Not yet.'

'They've got to pronounce you dead sooner or later – this can't go on indefinitely. The hardest part's behind us. You disappeared.'

'I know I did, and I miss me, Laura. I miss me.'

'No you don't,' she said sharply, keeping her eyes fixed on his. 'And neither do I.'

The only thing that had kept their marriage up and running at Marine Drive was their ability to lie to themselves and each other. Now the only chance they had of seeing this through was in telling the truth.

She stood up and joined him by the balcony doors. 'I can't stop thinking about you. I haven't felt like this since I was eighteen, Bryan, and eighteen's a long time ago. We're going to make this work. We're going to do all the things we talked about. This is our second chance and we have to look after it.'

He stood limply beside her, his arms hanging down, and for one awful moment she thought he was going to burst into tears like he'd done when she picked him up that Easter Saturday and driven him to Newcastle's Haymarket Bus Station, as planned. Only things hadn't gone quite as planned – almost didn't happen at all – because of the fog that day.

'It's not too late.' She finished the sentence with more of an inflexion than she'd meant to so that it was left hanging

201

between them, an unanswered question. 'Everything we need is here in this flat.'

He smiled sadly at her and passed his hand down the side of her face. 'Apart from Martha.'

She put her hands over his, pressing it against her cheek.

He was holding her now, absently kissing the top of her hair as she watched the sun lower itself fatly onto the horizon.

The tension had gone, and Laura felt as if the moment contained her entire life and that her entire life had somehow managed to fit itself into this sun filled room.

'I was so scared this afternoon,' she said, after a while. 'The flat was empty and I didn't know where you were, and I thought, what if you just decided to go? What if this time you really had disappeared?'

She needed him to say something; reassure her, but he just pulled gently away, distracted again now.

He opened the balcony doors, breathing in the night air, and for some reason, watching him, she felt affronted – it was as if he was trying to curtail any further intimacy.

'You won't do it again, will you?' she persisted.

He stepped onto the balcony, resuming his earlier pose by the railings. 'Won't do what?'

'Disappear like that.'

He didn't answer at first, staring intently up at the sky as if trying to find something new up there. When he eventually turned to her, it was to say, 'Did you go to Erwin Faust's funeral?'

And at the mention of the name, Faust, there was Anna – where she always was – standing there between them.

Martha was sitting on the sofa watching TV with the sound off while listening to one of Bryan's Led Zeppelin CDs. She'd drunk almost half a bottle of vodka and was feeling vaguely sick when the doorbell rang so she got up slowly, aware that her head was starting to hurt.

She saw – simultaneously – the man in the front porch and the white van parked on the street, and realised who it was.

They stood staring at each other, neither of them moving.

Jamie's face wore a large uncomfortable smile that gradually slid off in a way that made it look as though he was rapidly being emptied of himself. He continued to stare at her, his eyes wide and shot through with red, the two veins on either side of his forehead, pronounced.

'Laura,' he said hoarsely, leaving his mouth hanging open in his unshaven face.

Martha, unsure, remained holding onto the door, watching the spider's web that was tattooed across the left hand side of his neck ripple as he stretched out his hand and ran it over her hair.

She somehow stood still until he lifted his hand from her head, running it instead over the silver number two in the brickwork to the side of the door – illuminated by a small uplighter – as if all this pleased him.

'I'm Martha,' she whispered.

'Martha,' he repeated as the street lights blinked on to orange. 'The daughter.'

He caught his lower lip beneath his teeth then his face broke into a smile, and everything was suddenly brought back up to speed. 'Fucking terrified me, you did,' he carried on in the same hoarse voice, 'when you first opened that door and I saw you standing there.'

'Sorry,' Martha apologised.

'The hair . . . everything. I wasn't expecting that. It made me feel – I don't know – somehow wounded.' He shook his head at her then swung away, his eyes running over the other houses on the street. The spider's web was broken up now by the creases in his neck as he tilted his head back to exhale, and his hair was so short she could see the white skin of his scalp. This provoked a rising pity in her, and she was too young to realise that pity was a dangerous emotion, so stayed standing in the doorway – able to hear Led Zeppelin playing on the sitting room stereo still. 'But not the eyes,' he said, swinging back towards her. 'You've got kind eyes.'

He got a pack of Benson and Hedges from his pocket and sat down on the edge of the porch.

Martha watched him light up – flicking the ash into one of Laura's ornamental bays.

'Is she here?'

Martha hesitated then shook her head.

'Know when she'll be back?'

Martha shook her head again then carried on watching him, her head hurting now. She saw Mrs McClaren run past – resplendent in neon Lycra – raising her arm in a wave, but didn't wave back.

'They never told you about me, did they?' he said, squinting up at her. 'You had no idea I even existed.' He stood up and ran his hand over her hair again, which made her spine tingle and her stomach feel strange.

Without knowing why, she felt an overwhelming urge to step onto the porch, take hold of him and dance down the drive. She could picture them, clearly, dancing up Marine Drive, across the main road and over the dunes onto the beach.

'You phoned – Easter Sunday. You phoned mum's mobile, but I picked up.'

'Easter Sunday,' Jamie repeated, thinking about this. 'That was you?'

Martha nodded, pleased. 'You sounded so like dad, I thought –'

'That was you?' Jamie said again, interrupting her. His

eyes were as wide open as they'd been when she first opened the door, only more preoccupied. 'Did you tell her I'd phoned?'

'I told her.' Martha hesitated. 'She said you'd been in prison – but that doesn't explain why she was so scared.'

'Did she say why I was in prison?'

'You killed a man.'

'She told you that?'

'No – a friend did.'

Jamie contemplated her blankly.

'Well your friend was wrong. I never killed nobody.'

'Then, why –'

'I lost my alibi.' Before Martha had time to comment on this, Jamie said, 'They knew I hadn't done it.'

'Who?'

'The police. They wanted me because I already had a string of convictions for GBH. They told me again and again what I'd done and how I'd done it until I started thinking maybe I did do it. I had to keep on telling myself, I couldn't of done it because the afternoon that man was killed . . . I spent that afternoon with Laura. We were together.' He looked suddenly agitated. 'We were together that whole afternoon.'

Martha didn't feel well. 'Mum was your alibi?'

Jamie pushed his hands in his pockets and started nodding rapidly in the same way he had earlier, when she first opened the front door.

'She lied. She told them that afternoon never happened, but we were there – the two of us – in that room. I know it happened. That afternoon changed everything.'

# 14

Martha was sitting in Sally Pearson's office. She knew why she was there and was in the process of shutting herself down – something which had the unnerving effect of making people think she'd literally vacated herself.

First her eyes went dead then all expression left her face, and finally she let her body sink in on itself.

Even Miss Pearson's professional brightness lost its glow at the sight of her.

'Martha,' she exhaled, her long earrings shaking.

Sally Pearson was the school's educational psychologist.

They were sitting opposite each other at a table with a vase of stargazer lilies and an arrangement of sea shells between them. The room smelt of flowers, perfume, dust, nail varnish and futility.

Martha stared at the sea shells while Miss Pearson worked hard at maintaining her bright smile.

Out the corner of her eye, Martha saw her splay out her hands, check her nails then quickly curl her fingers back together. She was wearing an engagement ring she hadn't been wearing the last time Martha saw her.

'Is it too hot in here? Shall we open the window?'

Miss Pearson got up and opened the window with difficulty.

Martha watched her struggle and felt a fleeting pity she managed to suppress by reminding herself that no matter how professional Miss Pearson tried to appear, she couldn't conceal the fact that she didn't like Martha very much.

'That's better,' she said as she sat back down, glancing at her watch. 'Which shell is it that you're interested in? This one?'

Miss Pearson picked up a shell at random and turned it round in her hands.

Martha could feel sweat collecting behind her knees and felt a sudden desperate urge to wash her hands. She often got this urge when she was nervous.

Miss Pearson fixed Martha with eyes that were becoming increasingly unsettled.

'Your mother phoned the school this morning. She told me that you claim to have seen your father yesterday after school – outside the main entrance.'

Her mouth twitched fatally, and Martha watched, fascinated, thinking she was about to start laughing.

'I don't claim to have seen him. I saw him.' Martha swallowed loudly. 'Why is it that people are held to account for telling the truth far more than they are for lying?'

Not expecting an answer, she looked away, concentrating on the shells again, silent.


Laura met Laviolette at the entrance to the priory ruins, and they walked from there down onto the beach at King Edward's bay. The beach was full – a patchwork of small, temporary encampments that Laura and Laviolette surveyed from the curving promenade.

People enjoying the last of the Indian summer glanced at them as they made their way laden, shouting, down onto the sand – the children running ahead, their faces open wide with excitement.

Laura felt a pang she couldn't put a name to that she tidied quickly, efficiently away.

'Has Martha contacted you at all?'

'Martha? No.' Laviolette stood with his hands clasped, his arms balanced on the promenade railings, the metal hot from the sun.

He spoke with his usual slow, easy manner, but Laura sensed his alertness as he continued to stare down at the beach, watching a group of children approach the rock pools with nets.

'I was worried she might have done.'

'Worried?' He turned to face her, but her sunglasses concealed the better part of her face.

'She says she's seen Bryan.'

'When?'

'Yesterday – outside school. I wasn't sure if she'd already phoned you or –' Laura fell silent. 'I contacted the school this morning to let them know.

The Inspector straightened up, his hands on the railing still.

'Why did you phone the school?'

'I want her to see the psychologist – she's very good. Martha's seen her before. Martha lies, Inspector. We were told she does it to control things she doesn't have any control over.'

'You think Martha's lying about having seen Bryan?'

Laura laughed in disbelief. 'Of course she's lying. She didn't see Bryan – she couldn't have.'

'Why not?'

'Because he's dead, that's why,' she finished angrily, turning away from him and starting to walk back up the steps when he caught hole of her arm.

She studied his fingers briefly where they were gripping her, before slowly pulling her arm away.

'Bryan's dead,' she insisted. 'I'm trying to come to terms with it. I'm trying hard, and some days are just about bearable. Martha's got to start living with the fact sooner or later.' Laura paused, and when the Inspector didn't say anything, added, 'I just wanted to warn you. I thought it was the right thing to do.'

Laviolette nodded, preoccupied. 'Warn me?'

'I thought she might have phoned you,' Laura said again, 'and that you might start deploying people . . . resources . . . when you don't know Martha.'

People arriving at the beach and people leaving, stopped and stared, but Laura couldn't see their eyes. Like her, most of them were in sunglasses. They looked like beetles all of them, their heads flicking suddenly in her direction. Some of them recognised her from the appeal, but nobody said anything, they just stood there, staring, poised somewhere between curiosity and judgement.

As she watched Laviolette's retreating back, the shirt wet, clinging to his spine, she felt the onset of one of the anxiety attacks that she'd been having at least three times a week since Bryan's disappearance. Hot, breathless, tearful she pushed her way up the steps onto the cliff top path, but when she got there it was as if all the buildings – even the thirteenth century priory ruins – had turned to face her and were conspiring to topple and bury her alive.

Laviolette parked the car on double yellows under the shade of a burgeoning hornbeam. He was excited. Excitement wasn't something he often felt, but he was excited now.

The heat was forcing women – they were all women – out of the cars lining the road outside the Grammar School entrance, and they stood in well-groomed groups talking, laughing, waiting. These women took care of themselves; had time on their hands that Laviolette, watching, guessed it was sometimes an effort to fill. They wanted to belong – to what they weren't quite sure, but the overall plan was that they and their children should belong. He thought of Laura Deane. Some of the women he could see through his windscreen had been born belonging; others had to work at it. He imagined that quite a few of the ones working at it had seen parents die of exhaustion before they got to claim their pensions, which was probably enough for them to have made vows never to grow so old so young themselves. Their mothers would have been too busy working to take them to school, and their mother's mothers probably went to school barefoot with a potato in their pocket.

Quite a lot of them would remember being hit as children by parents trying to teach them the difference between good and bad, which was a love of sorts even if those same parents were too exhausted to show any other sort. The heat finally forced him out of his car as well and, sensing movement, a group of women close by – all dressed in white – turned towards him, but all they saw was a man in his late forties emerging from an outdated burgundy Vauxhall. They turned away.

Laviolette smiled affably at their backs, and sat down on the crumbling brick wall surrounding the hornbeam – a wall that was in the process of being destroyed by the tree's roots.

He looked along the length of road filled with cars, coaches and two competing ice cream vans, and wondered where exactly Martha had seen Bryan the day before. There was an elderly man in a cap and braces watching his Jack Russell pee against a car tyre, and two shirtless builders, laughing, but none of these were Bryan Deane.

From somewhere inside the large stone building opposite, behind the glossy black railings, bells started ringing.

There was a pause. The women shifted expectantly, and the leaves on the hornbeam started to move, making the shadow on the pavement by his feet move with them as a breeze picked up.

He stood up instinctively as the women's laughter and conversation became louder in an attempt to meet the sounds now filling the air – of twelve hundred girls leaving a building they'd been compelled to remain inside for seven hours. The red and blue uniforms spilt onto the street, flowing in all directions. Laviolette felt momentarily overwhelmed. How was he going to find Martha in all this?

The women dispersed – plans made, news exchanged – their focus now on the girls as they stood by their cars shouting and waving. The flood was thinning, but there was still no sign of Martha.

He was looking instinctively at the girls leaving school alone, the girls without a pack, with curled postures and eyes – when they lifted their heads to check for traffic while crossing the road – that were unnervingly alert. That was Martha, he thought, realising for the first time how fond of her he'd become.

Then someone sounded their horn and that's when he saw her, looking up like the rest of them, but more expectant. She looked through the slow moving traffic at a white transit van parked about one hundred metres away.

Jamie Deane.

Laviolette started walking towards it as Martha appeared on the pavement in front of him. She was smiling, and as the passenger door swung open the radio could be heard, playing loud.

'Martha!' he called out.

She couldn't hear him above Jamie Deane's radio.

'Martha!'

This time she paused, her bag swung back over her

shoulder as she looked down the street. Then she saw him, and hesitated – momentarily confused before pulling herself quickly up into the van.

Laviolette broke into a run as Jamie Deane started to manoeuvre the van out of the parking space. He got there just before it pulled away, and banged once on the window.

Martha's face – pale, agitated – stared at him through the glass, and beyond her he saw Jamie Deane for the first time in twenty years.

Martha turned away and said something to Jamie that made them both start laughing hysterically as the van jumped forward and joined the rest of the traffic on the road.

Laviolette jogged alongside it for a while until he had to stop, sweating and breathless. He watched it disappear from sight, blinking to keep the sweat from running into his eyes.

Jamie hadn't planned to pick Martha up from school – he'd been making a delivery in the area and passed a primary school just as all the children came running out of their classrooms into the playground. He parked the van for a moment and watched them navigate their afterschool freedom before turning the engine back on and pulling away – with something close to contentment.

It was then that he thought of Martha.

He had no idea what time she finished, but it was likely to be somewhere between half three and four. He was there at three thirty, parked up a side street. When the bell went, he drove round the corner and got a spot opposite one of the ice cream vans just as someone was leaving. He sat with the engine running and the radio playing, nonplussed by the volume of girls in uniform. After twenty years living in and among uniforms, he wasn't daunted at having to pick out a face in a crowd.

The unstructured hours of his new life made him anxious

and depressed – his counsellor had warned him they would – so he was pleased once he'd set himself the task of picking up Martha from school. He had somewhere he needed to be and something he needed to do.

He was only just discovering the real horror of imprisonment – that it made you terrified of freedom.

Martha. His niece, Martha. Martha had been a shock to him; he'd been wholly unprepared for the effect she had on him. While he'd been inside Laura, Bryan and others – but mostly Laura – had remained imaginatively real to him, but he had no real concept of Laura and Bryan's daughter because she'd never really existed for him.

When the door to number two Marine Drive opened the night before, he really did think it was Laura standing in front of him, framed in the doorway. After twenty years, it was entirely possible and reasonable to him that he should find her exactly as he'd left her and it took him a while to come to terms with the fact that the girl he thought was Laura was in fact Laura's daughter. It was then that he saw her walking through the school gates and started to energetically sound his horn.

Her face did exactly what he wanted it to when she saw him: it opened up – surprise followed by pleasure. He was so happy he was virtually bouncing in his seat by the time she'd crossed the road and got to the van. He leant over the passenger seat and threw open the door for her and that's when she hesitated.

He let out a sound midway between a laugh and a choke, suddenly terrified she was about to change her mind, but then she jumped up into the seat, slamming the door shut and locking it. A second later there was a man outside, banging on the window. Jamie tilted his head to stare at the man's palms, which looked swollen and white against the glass – like those of a drowned man.

'It's the Inspector,' Martha said, in shock. 'Laviolette.'

At the sound of the name, Jamie burst out laughing, the tattooed web on the side of his neck taking the strain of the sudden hysteria.

Without knowing why, Martha started laughing as well.

The sight of the Inspector, sweating on the pavement as they pulled away, struck her suddenly as the most absurd thing in the world. She pressed her left hand into her stomach – she was laughing so hard it was bruising her muscles – watching in the wing mirror as the Inspector continued to reduce in size by the second until he disappeared altogether when they turned right at the end of the road.

After this, they felt silent.

Martha sat clutching her rucksack on her lap, looking around the van, out the window and eventually at Jamie.

'Where are we going?'

'I don't know – where do you want to go?'

'Norway,' Martha said decisively.

Jamie, who'd been smiling happily, stopped smiling and gave his nose a few vicious rubs as he tried to work this one out.

'I've always wanted to go to Norway,' Martha carried on, 'it's just across the sea – I'd like to see the fjords.'

He kept flicking her nervous glances while trying to keep his eyes on the road.

She watched his face tense as he thought about this then laid her hand suddenly on his arm, 'But not today,' she reassured him.

Then his face broke suddenly into a smile again.

Martha stared out the window thinking about a lot of things at once – including Norway.

'How was school today?' he asked after a while.

For some reason the question made her laugh.

'Good? Not good?'

'It's never good.' She carried on staring out the window as they passed a gas works on their left.

'That bag of yours looks heavy.'

'It is,' she said, looking down at her rucksack. 'Books – games kit.'

'So what is it, O'Levels this year or whatever they call them?'

'GCSEs – some this year, some next.'

'How many are you taking?'

'Twelve – including Mandarin.'

'What the fuck's Mandarin?'

'Chinese.'

Jamie laughed. 'Seriously?'

'Seriously. China's emerging as a market leader.'

'Listen to you,' he said, pleased. 'So the Chinks are taking over the world?'

'Maybe – in a couple of years' time.'

He smiled happily to himself, thinking about this.

Five minutes later they turned onto Tynemouth Front Street, the priory ruins rising ahead of them.

'I know where I am now.' He twisted his head as they passed Starz Salon. 'Your mum's place. We could call in.'

Martha didn't say anything as they turned the corner past the priory and started to head down the hill. 'Wait. Stop here.'

Jamie pulled up outside St George's church.

'I want to get out. I want to walk on the beach.'

They got ice creams from the van parked opposite – run by a woman called Kath – which doubled up as a mobile library; the shelves at the back of the van were full of books Kath was happy to lend or exchange.

Kath was sitting outside the van on an old stool, smoking and reading 'Mrs Dalloway'. She waved – recognising Martha.

'Alright, pet?'

'Hi Kath – this is my uncle Jamie.'

'Alright, Jamie?' Kath said automatically.

Most people were bothered by Jamie when they met him for the first time. They felt a subconscious mental, spiritual and physical aversion; the sort of aversion healthy, intact people instinctively feel towards the damaged and abused – who have been forced to acknowledge things about the world and the people in it that the majority would rather spend their lives never knowing.

Martha hadn't been bothered by Jamie.

Kath wasn't either.

She was a terse woman who valued her private thoughts.

Her eyes didn't linger on his tattoos; they were happy to confront his eyes.

Jamie waited for her to recoil in the way he'd got used to people doing on the outside and that made him feel – for the few seconds it lasted – as if all the breath had been drawn suddenly out of the world.

But Kath didn't recoil, and he rewarded her with a smile very few people saw; one that – for as long as it lasted – gave his eyes an extraordinary depth.

They headed down the steps cut into the cliff, Martha taking off her shoes and socks as soon as they got onto the beach where there was a wind blowing that at long last lifted the heat.

'You should take your shoes off.'

Jamie hesitated before sitting down on a rock and pulling his trainers off awkwardly. His feet were white and he wasn't wearing any socks. Martha could see the impressions of holes across the top of his feet where the eyeholes from his laces had been digging in.

'Is that better?' she said as he joined her and they started to walk away from the crowds congregating round the

216

beach café, Crusoes, towards the sea, which was a long way out.

They stood paddling, the water lapping sluggishly round their ankles – Jamie flinching sporadically and checking behind him – as if life was taking place just over his shoulder at a forty-five degree angle.

There were hardly any waves and the water only came to the waists of three children far out to sea, trying to clamber onto an inflatable green dinosaur.

Jamie was watching them intently as if their game would help him to understand something he'd been trying to understand for a long time.

Martha was watching them as well – remembering what it was like to play in the sea at that age, and not have to think about her body.

After a while, she said, 'Last night – when I said you sounded like dad on the phone? I meant it.'

'You were close?'

'We *are* close.' She paused, lifting her foot out the water. 'He's still alive. I saw him yesterday. I was coming out of school and he was standing under a tree not far from where you were parked.' She paused again. 'I didn't see him today.'

Martha caught hold suddenly of his arm with both her hands and rested her head against him. 'He had blond hair, and he looked so thin. He had a dog with him – a Husky.'

'Did you speak to him?'

Martha shook her head, staring out to sea still, which was empty now – the current had taken the children and their dinosaur elsewhere.

'He wanted me to see him. He wants me to know he's still alive.'

Jamie remained silent, thinking about this.

He ran his hand over her hair a couple of times then they started to walk back up the beach, people wondering in the absent way people did – about the schoolgirl and ill-looking man with tattoos. Martha felt their eyes on them, but Jamie remained oblivious, lost in thought. She didn't need to ask him whether he believed her – she could tell he did.

'Have you told anybody else?' he asked her. 'The police?'

Martha was about to respond to this when she saw a woman in a white jumper running across the sand towards them.

'Martha!' Anna called out.

She'd been standing at the water's edge – only a couple of metres away – when she'd turned and seen them.

'It's okay,' Martha said automatically, trying to reassure Anna, who was staring at Jamie because he looked a lot more like his brother, Bryan, than she remembered. 'It's okay,' Martha said again.

Anna felt a wave of something close to pity pass over her as she laid eyes on Jamie Deane – who she'd last seen when she was a terrified thirteen-year-old; only a couple of years younger than Martha was now. She wondered if Laura knew her daughter was down on Tynemouth Longsands with Jamie Deane, who she could feel watching her now – without any particular resonance. He didn't recognise her.

'Anna Faust,' she said, pausing awkwardly in the interlude following the introduction. She saw his face flicker with effort as he sought to remember her, and was about to say something when Martha said, 'He didn't do it, Anna. Tell her,' she commanded Jamie.

But Jamie remained silent, his eyes on Anna.

Martha, frustrated, carried on, 'He spent twenty years in prison for something he never did – because mum lied. The afternoon that man was killed, she was with him. She was with him the whole time.'

Looking from Martha to Jamie, Anna saw again Laura Deane sitting on the top of the stairs that day – sullen, scared – inside number fifteen Parkview.

'You,' Jamie said, becoming suddenly conscious of who Anna was. 'I remember you. Bryan's little friend.'

'I knew it,' Martha put in.

'Why little?'

He shook his head. 'I don't know. For some reason I always thought of you as little. I remember you,' he said again, pleased. 'Funny,' he carried on slowly, more to himself.

Anna watched them climb up the steps past where the Grand Hotel used to stand before it was burnt down, back onto the cliff top road, unable to move from the spot. She was still standing there thirty minutes later when Inspector Laviolette arrived.


Laviolette drove along the coastal road towards Blyth. He wanted to talk to Anna, who he'd given up trying to call, and was just passing the Toy Museum when he saw her canary-coloured Capri parked not far from where Bryan Deane parked Easter Saturday, although she couldn't have known this.

He parked as close to the Capri as he could and left a note under the windscreen asking her to wait for him in the car if their paths didn't cross.

Then he stood for a while near the bench he'd seen Bryan Deane standing next to on the CCTV footage, and decided to conduct his own four minute vigil while scanning the beach and sea for Anna. It was low tide and there were no waves so she wouldn't be surfing, but there were people in the water, swimming – mostly children.

His eyes picked out solitary figures as he checked his watch.

Two minutes had passed – two minutes that felt like ten, but then time was relative. It struck him again how long four minutes could be.

Then he saw her – he was sure it was her; at the water's

219

edge in a white jumper, her hair blowing. Unlike most of the solitary walkers on the beach, she had no dog with her.

She'd made an impression on him – enough of an impression for him to recognise her at a distance of over two hundred metres, and the sense of recognition was something he felt in his stomach. This made him afraid in a way he hadn't been for years – decades even.

He checked his watch again.

Ten minutes had passed – ten minutes that felt like two.

He went down onto the beach using the same steps Jamie and Martha had, crossing the sand marked with their footprints still, towards Anna standing in the shallows, her shoes in her hand.

He tried calling out her name, but the wind, which was much stronger this close to the sea, tore it out of his mouth and carried it away.

She must have seen his shadow on the sand, drawing alongside hers – the two shadows stretching out from their owners at a forty-five degree angle – because she turned to look in his direction then, surprised to find herself no longer alone.

She smiled suddenly at him as if it had taken her a while to remember who he was.

He smiled back, trying to work out whether she was genuinely pleased to see him or not. 'You were thinking about Bryan Deane,' he said suddenly.

'Yes,' she agreed, 'I was.'

'Is that why you came here?'

'Yes,' she said again, staring down at her left foot as she drew it through the water.

The tide had turned; it was coming in now, and the waves were picking up and beginning to rush in the way they had a reputation for doing along this stretch of coast. It was a dangerous reputation to ignore, but summer after summer

220

the coastguard were sent out to rescue tourists who'd taken a chance against the incoming tide at Holy Island and got stranded on the causeway.

'How did you find me?' Anna said after a while.

'What makes you think I was looking for you?'

She laughed lightly and, without saying anything, they turned and started walking back down the beach at an angle, the tide was coming in so fast.

'I saw your car parked on the cliff top. I was coming to see you anyway,' he conceded, 'but this saved me the journey. Do you want to get a beer or something?'

She hesitated then, nodding, followed him to Crusoes, the Longsands beach café where they managed to get a table outside on the decking. When he went in to get the beers, she slung her feet over the rope railing, tilted her head back and let her eyes shut.

Laviolette re-appeared a couple of minutes later. 'I've never been here before,' he said.

'Any reason why you should have?'

'I live in Tynemouth.'

'I didn't realise,' she said, watching him.

'In fact, apart from the investigation, I can't remember the last time I took a walk on the beach.'

'Well, you took a walk just now.'

'I did,' he agreed, smiling at her – pleased.

They sat in silence, watching people arrive and leave the beach.

'You're going to miss this,' Laviolette observed, 'when you go back to London.' Then, when Anna didn't respond, 'The offer still stands. DS Chambers is moving back to Teeside to be near his wife's family.'

Anna nodded, smiling. 'You make it sound so simple.'

'It is simple. You're only renting in London – you haven't got a place to sell.'

Anna pushed her chin down onto her chest, thinking about this.

'Have you never thought about coming back?'

'I've thought about it.'

They fell silent again.

'Is that what you wanted to see me about?'

Laviolette shook his head as a woman came out to clear the table next to them.

'We're closing – ten minutes time,' she said.

Neither Laviolette nor Anna responded.

'Martha's seen Bryan.'

Without commenting on this, Anna turned to watch a father attempt to organise his family into a game of beach cricket, the long legged teenage daughter refusing to listen, no longer interested in being a part of this tribe she'd grown up in because that wasn't where life was at any more. The breakaway years . . . too old to run away from home, too young to officially leave.

Anna found herself staring at the pouting, sullen girl before turning her attention back to Laviolette.

'She already told you,' he said, watching her.

Anna nodded. 'Yesterday. When did she tell you?'

'She didn't.'

'So who did?'

'Laura Deane – this morning. When were you going to tell me?' Laviolette asked softly, without pausing.

'I don't know. I don't know whether I believe her.'

'Do you want to believe her?'

Anna didn't say anything. 'What did Laura say?'

'That Martha lies a lot; that she didn't want me wasting time and resources chasing a ghost.'

'Only you don't think it's a ghost Martha saw.'

'I think Martha wasn't meant to see Bryan, but she did.'

'That's one way of looking at it, I suppose.'

'Here's another way – Laura phoned the school this morning and had Martha referred to the psychologist. Assuming Laura knows that Bryan's still alive – she also knows that Martha's telling the truth. Do you see what I'm saying?'

The boy on the table next to them, reading a book and waiting for a girl, glanced up at them – then at his watch, then back down at the book.

'There's a child somewhere in the middle of all this, and she's losing ground as we speak,' Laviolette explained in a strained undertone, 'so whatever it is you know; whatever it is you're thinking; whatever it is you're feeling even – now's the time to share.' He was leaning forward, watching her intently. 'D'you want to have dinner with me?'

Anna stood up. 'Not tonight.'

'Where are you going?'

'Let's carry on walking.'

He followed her up the road beyond Crusoes that led onto the cliff top, and they carried on walking uphill towards the headland where the priory was.

They passed a group of school children sitting propped in the shade against the wall of the new public conveniences, eating chips and ice pops – using them as props to flirt with.

'When we were children,' Anna said, 'Bryan used to draw. He was a brilliant draughtsman. It's a damning testimony to the school he went to that they never picked up on it. After his mother died he used to draw in our garden – insects and stuff; mostly insects.'

They walked past the entrance to the priory and turned down Pier Road onto the Spanish Battery.

'They really were brilliant – the drawings. I mean, he had a real talent,' Anna insisted, as if Laviolette was disputing this. 'The day of Erwin's funeral, somebody posted a drawing through my door – of a butterfly.'

'Bryan?' Laviolette said, looking straight at her.

'It had to be.'

'And since then?'

'Nothing.' She met his gaze. 'Nothing.'

'He wanted you to know he was alive,' Laviolette stated, feeling the tension and aggression that had been building up, release, as he paused for a moment to watch a group of rowers from the Tynemouth Rowing Club launch an eight-man boat into the sea from the small bay on the south side of the priory. The rowers' silent collaboration gave a grace and coherence to the launch that made Laviolette feel calm to the extent of peaceful.

He could feel Anna beside him on the pavement, but she'd lost her relevance as he watched the departure of the rowers, wishing he was among them; one of the eight men. The desire was so strong that he felt like the one who'd been left behind once they'd gone.

Disorientated, he turned back to Anna.

'Why didn't you tell me about the picture?'

'It came the day of Erwin's funeral, and –'

'And?'

'I'm not convinced it's Bryan. It could be Martha.'

'If you thought it was Martha, you would have told me sooner. Have you got the drawing still?'

Anna nodded.

'Why don't you want anybody else knowing Bryan Deane's still alive?'

'I don't know.'

'How did he know you were at the Ridley Arms?'

'I don't know.'

'Where d'you think he is?'

'I've got no idea.' This time she held his gaze. 'I know how this works. The kayak's been washed up – there's been nothing new since –'

'Apart from the drawing.'

'The drawing might not have been him. Everybody presumes Bryan drowned – nobody's interested and they're not going to give you any more resources.'

'So we're on our own.'

'With what?'

'The fact that Bryan Deane faked his own death – with the co-operation of his wife – because the life they've been living didn't work out and they need the life insurance payout to start over again.'

'You're probably right.'

'You know I'm right.'

'Nobody cares.'

'I care. You care – and Bryan Deane cares enough to jeopardise everything in order to let you and Martha know he's still alive, that's how much Bryan Deane cares.'

'And why do you care so much?'

'Because I'm tired of people lying,' Laviolette said before starting to walk again, taking the path that led down from the Battery onto the pier.

'Ice cream?' he asked as they passed the van parked in the small car park on the lower slopes of the Battery.

Anna stared at him as if he'd said something profane then shook her head.

The pier at Tynemouth wasn't a resort pier; it was a long curving cement barricade with a small automated lighthouse on the end. It took a lot of battering from the sea, but renowned feet had walked its length – Harriet Martineau, Charles Dickens, Lewis Carroll, Thomas Carlyle – as well as those less renowned who came, regardless of age, because the sea didn't care who they flirted with, who they groped or what they shot up on.

Laviolette and Anna walked the pier in silence, the incoming tide wetting them with spray as it hit the man-made defence.

They passed a couple heading back towards land, who they smiled at and exchanged greetings with. The only other people on the pier were two Russians from a ship docked at North Shields, who asked them to take their photograph – standing against the rusting railings surrounding the lighthouse at the pier end, their arms around each other.

When the Russians left, Anna and Laviolette sat down on the warm cement – their legs hanging over the side only metres above the churning water.

'Why did you come back up north?'

'My grandfather was dying.'

Laviolette nodded. 'And?'

'You really want to know?'

'I really want to know.'

Anna breathed in deeply, watching the swell on the thick dark water beneath her feet. 'Someone I was working with – I'd been working with him for two years on the same case – committed suicide. Afterwards, I started suffering from these attacks. I knew what they were – I've seen it happen to people I've been close to. I could be sitting in front of the computer and without warning I'd be overcome by . . .' she tried to find the right words, 'this sense of imminent collapse. When this happened I knew I had to get somewhere where I could be alone – usually the toilets.' She saw herself in one of the sickly pink cubicles where she would either chew on her knuckles as she sobbed, hoping to stifle the sound or – when the attack was acute – find herself vomiting down the toilet. 'It's like being in a permanent state of grief – with nothing to grieve over. The attacks didn't go unnoticed.'

'You're too good at your job, aren't you?'

'They didn't put it quite like that, but that's pretty much what it amounted to.'

'And did you feel better, coming north – in spite of the cancer that brought you?'

Anna's lips had gone thin, in the way they did when she was concentrating. 'I felt better until the morning I saw Bryan Deane for the first time in sixteen years. That's when I knew –' she broke off, seeing herself again sobbing behind the wheel of the Capri while watching a toddler play with a Doberman in the house opposite number nineteen Parkview, 'that what was happening to me had been sixteen years in the making. Everything I'd purposefully walked out on; everything I thought I'd left behind had been secretly keeping pace with me all along, and I'd run out of storage space.'

Laviolette didn't say anything.

They watched the sun go down in silence, spreading a lazy line of orange along the surface of the sea.

'I saw you once – you and Bryan. A long time ago.'

Anna, whose head had fallen unconsciously against his shoulder, pulled herself up straight. 'Easter Saturday was the first time I ever saw you in my life.'

'I said *I* saw *you*, I didn't say you saw me – you couldn't have been more than eighteen both of you. It was a Friday afternoon, and it must have been raining outside because you walked into the Clayton Arms soaked through.'

'The Clayton Arms?'

'Up at Bedlington station. Friday afternoon used to be strippers and that's how I know it was a Friday I saw you – because there were two girls on stage that day wearing nothing but their tits.'

'What was I doing at the Clayton Arms?'

'You came in with Bryan, and you were the only other girl there. You looked at the stage for a bit then you went running out.'

Laviolette didn't tell her the rest of it: how he'd run outside after her that afternoon, straight past Bryan Deane and into the rain; how he'd seen her in the distance, running away from them all.

227

'How the hell d'you remember that? And h-h-how d'you know it was me?'

'I recognised you as soon as I saw you Easter Saturday at the Deanes. The first time I see you, you're with Bryan Deane. The next time I see you, sixteen years later, you're looking for Bryan Deane. Only this time I'm the one coming in from the rain.'

'Who said I was looking for him?'

'Isn't that why you came north?' he said, getting awkwardly to his feet with the support of the railings round the lighthouse where the Russians had stood to have their photograph taken.

Anna didn't say anything – she was too preoccupied still by the memory of Bryan and her at the Clayton Arms.

'Where d'you think he is?' Laviolette asked after a while.

'I've got no idea.'

'Close enough to wait for Martha after school.'

Laviolette looked down at his feet as a high wave colliding with the pier left a trail of spume over them. 'You said – Easter Saturday – that all of us are involved one way or another,' Anna said.

'The living and the dead.' He gave her a quick, shy smile. 'Bobby Deane. Rachel Deane.'

The waves were getting higher and the pier was wet from sea spray with small rainbows bouncing off it where the sun still reached.

'Rachel Deane was having an affair with my father – you knew that?'

'Not until recently. Nan told me.'

'People said that's why she killed herself – because she couldn't leave Bobby Deane and she couldn't leave my dad, and she had to leave one of them. The mathematics of staying with both of them was –'

'Inappropriate,' Anna suggested softly.

'Hellish,' Laviolette corrected her. 'Bobby came to see us after Rachel died, I'll never forget that. He came round the back, straight through the door into the kitchen, drunk but not dead drunk. Dad had the radio in pieces on the bench – he was in the middle of trying to mend it – and when he turned round, the screwdriver in his hand still, his face just dropped. Bobby was huge – felt huge then anyway and dad was a lightweight. The thought of what Bobby had come to do to him terrified him, you could feel the fear coming off him and the violence coming off Bobby, and dad was sort of crumpling up before Bobby even got close.

'I remember thinking, this is it, and feeling relieved. I also remember realising that dad was far more afraid of Bobby Deane than he'd ever been in love with Rachel Deane.'

'How old were you?'

'How old?' He stared at her for a moment, too lost in the memory to respond. 'Nineteen? Twenty?' he said, seeing himself standing by the bench next to the dismembered radio, as if it was that Bobby Deane had really come for and he was meant to be guarding it. 'Twenty,' he decided, staring at her but not really seeing her. 'Just married, and new on the force, but it never occurred to me to do anything about Bobby Deane standing in our kitchen because right then all I was thinking was – what did Rachel see in him? And I'm not talking about Bobby.

'So there I was thinking, this is it, then the next minute Bobby just flopped, pulled out one of the kitchen chairs, sat down in it – lifeless – and started sobbing. He wasn't crying, he was sobbing. It was as if, somehow, we'd been his last hope and he'd been expecting to open our kitchen door and find Rachel in there with us, but she wasn't and when he saw she wasn't he finally gave up.

'I'll never forget the sight of his hand curled on the table as he sat there motionless, sobbing. After a while – it seemed like hours, but it couldn't have been – he started wiping at his face, and he said to my dad, "Why did you give her a choice? Why didn't you just take her away from here? You should of just taken her away – she'd of been alright then."

'I can remember him saying it – I can remember him saying every single one of those words, at a loss.'

They stared at each other for a moment before Laviolette turned and started to walk away.

Anna followed, drawing alongside him again.

'I knew then that Bobby Deane had said everything he'd ever have to say to my dad, which was why – when dad was murdered – I knew it wasn't Bobby Deane. He was taken in for questioning and when he realised they were holding Jamie as well, he tried to plead guilty.'

'To protect his son,' Anna put in, aware that she'd become cold in the past ten minutes. The heat had gone out of the day and the air was cooling rapidly.

'They thought about letting him frame himself for it, but he had too many alibis – even for them. So they went for Jamie instead.'

She thought about Jamie and Martha on Tynemouth Longsands earlier. 'Jamie was inside for twenty years!' Anna shouted.

'And guess who put him there?'

'His alibi – Laura.'

'Some alibi.'

A wave crashed over the pier then, soaking Laviolette's back and Anna's right hand side. The water was cold; running off her face.

'How did you know Laura was his alibi?'

'I didn't – until today. I met Jamie and Martha on Longsands earlier – just before I met you.'

'So that's where they went.'

'You were following them?'

Laviolette shook his head. 'I tried to meet with Martha – after school. I saw her get into Jamie Deane's van.'

He carried on walking.

'Where are you going?' she demanded.

'Home.'

'Where's home?'

He pointed to the headland rising above them where the pier joined the land. 'On the Battery.'

He could see Coastguard Cottages, and Mrs Kelly's car parked outside. Harvey would be in the house, drawing one of the thousand cuboids he drew every day – that none of the line up of professionals who'd seen him could explain. It was enough for Mrs Kelly – who didn't need an explanation as to why Harvey drew cuboids all day long – to ensure that he had a constant supply of pens and paper and therein, Laviolette thought, lay the answer.

He was aware that he wanted to take Anna up to the house.

Anna was eroding his need for privacy.

She was doing it unconsciously and inadvertently, but she was doing it and he wasn't sure where this left him.

'Are you going to invite me up?'

'I already did. I invited you to dinner. You said no.'

He walked away and she watched as, in between waves, he got smaller.

A few more seconds passed before she broke into a run – along the pier through the breaking waves after him.

231

# 15

As they walked into number four Coastguard Cottages, Anna realised that she had no idea what to expect. She knew, from the conversation they'd just had, that Laviolette had married at twenty and that there was at least one child because she'd heard a child when they'd spoken on the phone. Which was why, when they entered the kitchen, she interpreted the scene in the way she did.

It wasn't until she was introduced to Mrs Kelly – rolling pastry on the bench next to the oven, flustered by the interruption and more shocked by Anna than Anna ever could have been by her – that she began to realise what Laviolette's life was.

Harvey was about six feet tall, in his early twenties, and sitting at the kitchen table with a box full of striped drinking straws and a sellotape dispenser. There were three identical 3-D cubes lined up in front of him and he gurgled, distracted, when he heard Laviolette mention his name. He didn't look up.

Anna thought back to the Easter Sunday when Laviolette had phoned. The child he'd been trying to feed while on the phone to her – the child she'd mistaken for a toddler – must have been Harvey.

Once Laviolette had established with Mrs Kelly – shy to the point of silence now in Anna's presence – that there would be enough steak and kidney pie to go round, he led Anna upstairs to the study at the top of the house.

'How d'you manage?' she said, taking in the small box-like room crammed full of books and files that she guessed Laviolette spent most of his time in when at home. It smelt of carpet, sunlight, coffee and elastic bands.

'Mrs Kelly.' He smiled flatly, preoccupied – trying to work out whether he'd made the right decision bringing Anna here; whether or not he wanted her here. 'She had to have a knee arthroscopy this time last year and I paid for her to have it done privately so that she could be out in three days,' he heard himself saying automatically, still preoccupied.

Anna, about to sit down on the sofa, hesitated. 'It's okay,' she said.

He looked at her startled.

'I don't have to stay.'

'It's fine,' he said, shaking his head. 'I wanted to show you something.'

She sat down on the edge of the sofa as Laviolette got the tapes out from their usual place – aware that this was the first time he'd ever listened to them with anybody else; aware of Anna's eyes on him, and deciding against any sort of introduction.

'Where's Harvey's mother?' she said, watching him.

Laviolette stopped and turned towards her, the tapes in his hands, staring at her as if she'd said something in a foreign language he used to speak and that he hadn't heard spoken since he was a child.

'I don't know,' he said, still staring at her. 'We separated

233

– a long time ago. Actually, it wasn't even that formal – it just got to a point when she was no longer with us.'

Anna knew, from the way he said it, that he hadn't tried looking for her, and that this was something – as he grew older – he'd come to regret. Not necessarily for his sake, but for her's.

'I can't even remember when she left.'

'What was her name?' Anna didn't know why she was asking – it was irrelevant, but for some reason she wanted to know.

He paused before answering. 'Lily. It wasn't Harvey. I mean, Harvey was a shock and we were young, but it wasn't just Harvey. There was other stuff.' He paused again. 'My father was brilliant with Harvey. I was closer to him the two years before he died than I ever was – because of how he was with Harvey. He was only two when dad died – he was there when he was killed.'

'So Harvey knows,' Anna said, quietly.

Laviolette looked at her, realising this for the first time. 'He does, doesn't he?'

Then he pressed 'play' on the machine and the small room at the top of number four Coastguard Cottages was full of the sound of a child's voice – Laura Hamilton, age thirteen.

It was also the voice of Anna's own childhood; the voice that had chattered with her as they'd turned cardboard boxes and old curtains into ships with sails, the voice that had suggested they swapped leotards for the weekly tap and ballet classes they went to at Mrs Miller's Academy; the voice that had discussed in detail whether they should spend the ten pence they had between them on two sherbet dips or ten one penny sweets in Mo's shop. She remembered the way their hands smelt after a ride on the park's iron horse and how that last summer they went camping

234

together, they'd practised kissing in the green tent at night so that they'd know how to do it when it came to the real thing.

Anna sat on the edge of Laviolette's sofa, neither of them looking at each other, thinking all these things and feeling a thick, ebbing sorrow because the child on the tape – her best friend, Laura Hamilton – had already forgotten these things. The two adult male voices aggressive, cajoling, tittering, were asking her how many times she'd had sex before with Jamie Deane. Where did they do it? Did her parents know? She was underage. It was illegal. Anna couldn't picture the interview room or the officers conducting the interview, all she could see was Laura – perched at the top of the flight of stairs inside number fifteen Parkview, her hair hanging over her face.

'It happened that day – the day he locked me in the wash house – where Rachel Deane committed suicide,' she said to Laviolette, unaware until she spoke that the tape had stopped. Laura's voice was no longer filling the room.

Jamie and Laura had probably spent other days that summer doing the same thing, but somehow Anna knew it was that day – the day she'd gone round with the magnifying glass to number fifteen Parkview – that Roger Laviolette was murdered.

'I went round to return something of Bryan's, but he wasn't there. Laura was though, and that shocked me. We weren't friends any more by then.'

Without saying anything, Laviolette slid one of the desk drawers open and pulled out a bottle of Nicaraguan rum, pouring them both a glass.

Anna sat absently tilting the amber liquid. 'There was a dead deer in there, hanging upside down – its eyes staring.'

She drank the rum and held out her glass – it had a white banner painted on it with the words 'Good Luck' in red.

'Who let you out?'

'Of where?'

'The wash house.'

'That's the only thing I can't remember.'

'Jamie?'

'It could have been. I don't remember.' She drank the second glass of rum. 'Who gave you this case?'

'The man who conducted that interview we just listened to. Superintendant Jim Cornish.'

She kept her eyes on him as he filled their glasses again. 'You've got other tapes?'

'I've got all the tapes.' He wondered if she knew Mary had been interviewed.

The Jamie Deane interview was as unbearable as always to listen to.

Halfway through Anna got up and turned off the machine. 'He didn't do it, did he? Where was he interviewed?'

'That wasn't an interview – it was an interrogation.' Laviolette paused. 'Berwick Street.'

Anna thought he was going to add something to that, but he didn't. He carried on swinging lightly in his chair from side to side, staring at the spot on the sofa where she'd been sitting.

She knew about Berwick Street – whether you'd been there or not, everybody growing up on the Hartford Estate knew about Berwick Street.

'You said they brought Bobby in?'

After listening to the Bobby tapes, they sat in silence.

Anna felt one of the waves of depression she often got after conducting interviews herself when the answers she got didn't collectively amount to a resolution. If Bobby Deane didn't kill Roger Laviolette – and Jamie Deane didn't – then who did?

Stretching, she got up slowly from the sofa and crossed

the room to the desk where Laviolette was sitting. She stared at the tape machine for a moment before rewinding the Bobby Deane tape. She kept stopping it and pressing 'play' until she got to the right spot.

Unsure what she was doing, Laviolette listened for about ten minutes before Anna pressed 'stop' again.

'There,' she said.

'What?'

'Listen.' She rewound it and pressed 'play'. This time she let the tape run for five minutes before stopping it.

He could feel her watching him.

'Did you hear it?'

He shook his head and she played the same five minutes again.

'He stops claiming he's guilty.'

'Yes, but before he changes his mind they stopped the tape.'

'I can't hear it.'

She rewound it another three times. 'You hear the cough?'

Laviolette nodded.

'The dynamic of the interview changes after that cough. Somebody coughed to cover up the sound of the tape going off. What did they say to him when the tape stopped running?'

'They must have been making a deal.'

Anna nodded, thinking. 'Listen to the way he's speaking after the break. His tone —'

'He's still lying,' Laviolette commented after they'd listened to the five minutes for the tenth time.

'I agree. But he's lying in a different way.'

'Different way – how?' Laviolette yawned, unaware until then of just how exhausted he was.

'When people lie to protect themselves, it's different to when they lie to protect others. After the break in the tape,

Bobby's lying to protect someone else – he knows who did it. He knows who killed your father.'

Laviolette thought about the last time he'd visited Bobby Deane in his bungalow on Armstrong Crescent. 'Bobby Deane doesn't know his own name any more,' he said.

Mrs Kelly brought their supper upstairs on a tray. She didn't come into the study – she left it outside the door.

They ate in silence, and afterwards – with a bottle of wine drunk and onto rum again – found it easier to talk about things they would have found it hard to talk about sober; things they carried around with them every day; things that made them who they were, and that it was a relief to acknowledge.

When Laviolette asked her what she was doing that day in the Clayton Arms with Bryan Deane, it wasn't painful to remember or an effort to talk.

She settled back in the sofa – the square of sky visible through the skylight, dark now.

'That day . . .' She shook her head. 'I hadn't spoken to Bryan since I was thirteen. It was summer – the last summer. I was leaving in September for London, and Bryan had become nothing more than the boyfriend of the girl next door.' Anna laid her head on the sofa's armrest.

'I was in the final stages of re-inventing myself that summer – nobody from nowhere. The accent had gone even then, before I left – eroded. I'd gone from running *back* home from school as fast as I could – to running *from* home to school as fast as I could. None of my friends were ever invited back to number nineteen Parkview.

'Laura was working at Mo's sister's salon by then, and Bryan . . . I heard he was working as well, but nobody knew what it was exactly that he did. We hadn't spoken in years. I think it was only just this side of legal – was he collecting rents for somebody? I don't know. Put it this way, he acted like he'd lost his boundaries, like he was operating beyond the opinion of others. I never saw him with anyone apart from Laura at that time. He felt . . . contaminated in some way. I'm surprised he managed to keep himself clean – has he never had a record?'

'Nothing,' Laviolette said.

'He drove a car nobody in a hundred-mile radius could have afforded, and it's the car I remember because it was outside Laura's house that day and Bryan was sitting in it. He must have been waiting for her. I was walking back from Mo's and he asked if I wanted to go for a drive . . . after five years never saying a word to each other.'

'You said yes.'

'Without thinking. I didn't ask where we were going. I didn't say anything.'

Anna fell silent, remembering how the breeze – and Bryan's eyes – had felt on her face.

'He felt much older than eighteen,' she said. 'We drove into Tynemouth as the storm clouds rolled in, got some beer from an off licence on Front Street, an went down on the beach.'

'Which beach?' Laviolette asked.

'Longsands.' She hesitated. 'There's no connection. We haven't tried to contact each other – not once – in sixteen years.'

'What happened on Longsands?'

'We talked – that's all. We talked about everything in the way people do maybe only once or twice in their lives because . . .' her eyes slid away from him, round the room and up to the skylight then back again, 'those are the kinds of conversations that make or break lives.'

They were silent for a moment, aware of a faint ticking sound coming from somewhere in the room.

Laviolette guessed that it was one of the clocks in the repairs box. It must have started working again of its own accord. Distracted by the clock, he heard her say, 'I've never really felt whole again since that afternoon. Can one afternoon do that to a person – break them in that way?'

Laviolette was contemplating her – aware that he was probably the only person she'd spoken to about that afternoon on Longsands.

'Why did you never try to contact him afterwards?'

'I don't know. He never tried to contact me either.' She fell silent again, already regretting haven spoken to Laviolette. It was uncharacteristic of her, and she wasn't that drunk. Lying along the sofa, she continued – silently – to track her way back into the memory of that afternoon.

The storm never broke, but the threat of it was forcing people off the beach, and the beach was emptying – something they only noticed when they finally stopped talking and looked around them.

A few minutes later, they got to their feet and, taking hold of each other's hands, walked down to the water.

They started kissing, in increasingly deep water under a grey sky.

'Bryan wanted to go up to the priory, and . . . Do kids still go up to the priory?'

'Kids will always go up to the priory to do their business.'

'I said no. I tried to persuade myself that I was thinking of Laura and that I'd done enough damage already, but I wasn't thinking of Laura – neither of us was. I was just scared. Bryan was furious. We drove home after that – via the Clayton Arms. I remember walking into that bar full of men – the storm clouds had broken by then and we were soaked through from the rain. I had no idea what we were doing there.' She broke off. 'That's when you must have seen us.'

'Why did Bryan take you there?'

'He was angry with me.'

'That's not an answer.'

'There were two women on stage. Bryan told me that the brunette was my mother.'

'Was she?'

Anna shrugged. 'It could have been. She left just after I was born, and I'd only seen her once since.' She remembered running out of the Clayton Arms and trying to make it to a drain, but the drains were flooded in the downpour so she was sick on the pavement instead. 'He phoned me – the next day – to say he'd made it up. He didn't know why. I didn't know whether to believe him and anyway, the damage was done – it's the only image of Bettina I've ever had, whether I want it or not: a half naked brunette, drugged on a smoky stage. It was as if he was using the idea of her to counterbalance something between us.'

'Counterbalance?' Laviolette was staring at the carpet near her feet, swinging the well oiled chair rhythmically from side to side still, in a way that made it whisper.

'A darkness that was in both our lives – I don't know. It was as if he was trying to say that we weren't so different after all, but then – I never said we were.'

'Then you left,' Laviolette said quietly.

'I left. Bryan stayed. By the time I came back from my first term at King's – Christmas – Laura Hamilton was three months pregnant and about to become Laura Deane.'

'Did she get pregnant on purpose?'

'Probably, but it doesn't really matter, does it? Bryan stayed.'

'Did you go to the wedding?' he asked, curious.

'No. I went to Damascus with a Syrian called Khalid. It didn't work out in the long term, but then neither of us expected it to.'

'Were you invited – to the wedding?'

'I can't remember. By the time I left university, the Met – along with most of Britain's police forces – were launching a major drive to recruit women (on paper, anyway) in an attempt to revamp an organisation shot through with endemic corruption.'

'And oestrogen was the answer,' Laviolette put in.

'I was interviewed on Woman's Hour – along with another female recruit. Mary still has the –'

Before she finished speaking, he said, 'Why did you come north?'

'I came looking for Bryan.'

'And that was before he disappeared,' Laviolette observed.

Anna kept what happened the day after that to herself – for herself.

The day after she'd refused to go up to the priory with Bryan, she let him take her to a house in North Blyth, which felt as though it was being used as a squat. She didn't ask about the house; she didn't ask any questions. This time, in contrast to the day before, they barely spoke; they just went upstairs and made love on a mattress Bryan spread their clothes over in an attempt to cover some of the more sinister stains. There was a curtain still at the window that Bryan managed to draw despite the pole hanging at an angle.

Anna had never felt so naked in her life before, and never so naked since.

They knew, as they were making love – which they did three times, sleeping in between as day turned to night – that this was the moment all other moments in their life would be judged against.

'Come to London with me.'

'To do what? Clean the streets? This is my place.'

'I can't stay.'

'I know you can't.'

'I have to go.'

'I know.' She remembered Bryan pushing the hair from her face, the night air around them thick with the smell of industry – the power station, the aluminium smelting plant.

She was back where she'd started.

# 16

It was just after ten in the morning and Laviolette was sitting opposite Jim Cornish, Superintendent, in Jim Cornish's office. There was twenty years of service and a desk full of golf trophies between them, as well as ranks of photographs positioned so that the person sitting in the chair Laviolette was currently sitting in was forced to contemplate them, as Laviolette was doing now. There were a lot of Jim shaking hands with people, and a collection of more personal, family shots. Jim had four children – two girls and two boys – but there was only one photograph showing all four. The rest were of the eldest son, Richard – mostly of him playing rugby – and the two girls, whose names Laviolette couldn't remember. They were displayed to provoke reassurance in those Jim liked, and envy in those he didn't.

The younger son, Dom, had left home at eighteen with a black man, and moved south. He committed suicide five years ago at the age of thirty, but Jim never talked about Dom – nobody did, in fact, apart from Jim's wife. Jim's wife had been on anti-depressants ever since while Jim just carried on with his year-on-year affairs, which he'd been doing ever since the birth of his first child, rugby-playing Richard.

Jim Cornish had started his career at the notorious Berwick Street station where the Deane interviews were conducted. He would hold mattresses over people in the cells while beating them half to death – and he was one of those who remained miraculously untarnished after Berwick Street was exposed, probably because he proved so adaptable to whatever new legislation, and faces accompanying it, was wheeled in. One of the main reasons Jim was so successful at adapting was that he had no self-belief – he was happy to assume, without question, the convictions of others – and he'd always managed to keep his sights on the bigger picture, which had to be upheld at all times, and at all costs.

Jim Cornish didn't view justice as an arm of the law; he viewed it as the enemy. He knew what people wanted – he had a talent for that – and tried to ensure they got it. If people wanted their rapists to be six foot Jamaicans, he made damn sure they were. Who wanted to know that a rapist could also be a married white collar worker in his mid fifties with three children? Nobody. So why spoil somebody's day with an inconvenient and complicated truth. It was self-indulgent and childish.

Jim advised his officers against many courses of action, but there was very little he actually condoned. As far as Jim was concerned, the law's only purpose was to uphold order, and self-denial never changed the world. Laviolette had watched Jim rape a woman once during their early years on the force, but if either of them were embarrassed by that now – if either of them even thought about it as anything other than the caprices of youth – it wasn't Jim.

It was a woman who brought about this morning's summons, and that woman was Laura Deane. It was a formal complaint – Laviolette was harassing her daughter.

Jim's eyes kept flicking between his computer screen and

the papers on his desk before resting momentarily on his Detective Inspector.

'So what's going on?' he said at last.

Jim used to speak almost entirely in profanities but since becoming a latter-life church goer following Dom's suicide – at the invitation of the Chief Superintendent – he made an effort.

'Martha Deane reckons she saw her dad outside school the other day.'

'Reckons,' Jim said, staring down mournfully at his desk. 'What do you reckon, Inspector?'

'That we need to investigate the claim.'

Jim shifted in his chair, leaning neatly over to one side so that he could look at Laviolette on the diagonal rather than front on – while trying to decide whether he needed to be wary of him or whether he could just feel sorry for him.

'Problem is, this particular claim comes from a distraught fifteen-year-old who's just lost her dad.'

'We don't know that.'

'Come on!' Jim exploded – a mini explosion that was quickly contained but that sent a pen he wasn't even aware he'd been holding, across the desk. 'This is a classic empathy sighting. Plus the kid's been seeing the school shrink – compulsive lying or something.'

'Probably inherited,' Laviolette put in.

Jim paused, momentarily confused. 'Compulsive lying,' he said again, 'and that's her own mother talking.'

'And what if it's in her mother's interest to say those things because she doesn't want anyone knowing her husband's still alive? Do you want to know what I'm thinking?'

'No,' Jim said loudly, leaning forward now and jerking his finger at Laviolette. 'No, I don't want to know what you're thinking because your thinking is costing us too much.'

'Bryan Deane faked his own death so that the Deanes can claim on the life insurance.'

Jim started laughing – all tension between them momentarily gone. 'Yeah, I can see that, but who cares? Is that the kind of stuff you lose sleep over? They're consenting adults.' Then he stopped laughing. 'Conspiracy theories, Laviolette. Who are conspiracy theories for? The unloved and the unemployed, that's who, and you're only one of those things at the moment.'

'Are you threatening me?'

'No, I'm just tired of you. You never change. Your working methods aren't . . . I don't know . . . I'd call them into question. A lot of people would.'

'Like who?'

Jim waved his hand expansively to one side. 'There's no order to your work, and that's what we're about here; that's what police work is: order. You've got no anchor. You're not a religious man –'

Jim's eyes dropped automatically to the photographs on the desk in front of him as if those were the just rewards of his religion, which didn't explain Dom's suicide at the age of thirty, but then Jim Cornish wasn't the sort of man who sought explanations.

'Mrs Deane said the way you've conducted the investigation so far has made her feel persecuted. She's not happy. If she gets any unhappier, I may be forced to take it further.'

'Since when have I ever been wrong about anything?'

Jim's eyes were on him now, seriously considering this until he found his angle. 'Since when has that been a skill?' he said, impatient. 'It's when not to be right – you've never learnt that. If you won't play the game, you've already lost your chances of winning by one hundred percent.'

Laviolette sat half listening to him, thinking that this was how he probably spoke to his children in the study at home – Jim was bound to have a study in his house where he acted out the whole paterfamilias thing before downloading that evening's porn – when they made a bad decision.

Something else Laviolette realised – too late – was that Jim Cornish was most people, and most people trusted Jim Cornish not because he was trustworthy (he was inherently untrustworthy and had a penchant for getting blood on his fists in dark rooms), but because he was like them.

Laviolette wasn't like them.

Jim was watching him, an amused expression on his face. 'What did I say to you, when you first joined the force?'

'You only said one thing?'

'Think of truth as the deformed child we keep locked in the cellar.'

'Well, at least there's a cellar – that's good to know,' Laviolette said.

Jim Cornish stopped smiling. His eyes ran briskly over the golf trophies, photographs and office walls – the things he held dear; the things he had achieved. Then he stood up, his hands in his trouser pockets. 'You asked me just now – when have you ever been wrong about anything? Well, you just got wrong,' he announced.

Laviolette stood up as well so that the two men were facing each other. 'About what?'

'Bryan Deane's body is in the mortuary. It was washed up this morning. You should go and take a look. DC Wade's down there with Laura Deane as we speak.' Jim grinned at him, knowing that the part that would get to Laviolette most was the fact that DC Wade had been told before him.

'It's over,' Jim said, still grinning.

*

Laura Deane and DC Wade were just leaving when Laviolette got there, which had probably been the intention. He stopped by the double doors they walked through – still swinging with the momentum of their departure – suddenly, profoundly irritated. He'd wanted to be in the room when Laura Deane and her dead husband were reunited and she made the identification; he'd wanted to be there very badly, and now he'd missed it.

Laura stopped when she saw him, turning so that he got full frontal exposure to her grief. She didn't say anything, she just brought her hands away from her face and let them hang by her side as she stood there so that he could see the unevenly red skin, swollen in all the right places, the make-up – expensive as it was and marketed with a no-run guarantee – beginning to run round the eyes. She let her face do the talking, and the face said, 'Look at me – this is what a woman looks like when she's just had to indentify her drowned husband's body. I'm in shock, and now I'm officially grieving. You can't touch me.'

Once she saw that he understood, she turned away from him back to DC Wade's firm embrace.

DC Wade, embarrassed, twisted her head round and nodded briefly at Laviolette before leading Laura Deane – a slow-moving combination of white, beige and gold – up the corridor.

Laviolette remained standing there long after they'd gone.

Someone emerged from a door close by – and for a second he could hear rock music playing on a radio – stared at him then disappeared through another set of doors, leaving him alone with the inescapable smell of chemicals and a total lack of natural daylight.

A few minutes later, he was looking down at the bloated corpse of a drowned man. The small, tiled room was full of the infinite sadness of departure Laviolette had often felt

249

when confronted with death. There was also nausea – faint, but it was there – because there was nothing human about the remains; they were just remains.

He pressed his back against the tiled wall, his fingertips splayed to either side, contemplating the real possibility that this might be Bryan Deane.

What if it was?

What if it wasn't?

Wouldn't it be kind of wonderful just to go with it – ignore the light he'd seen in Laura Deane's eyes and choose only, in retrospect, to see the grief?

Wouldn't it be kind of wonderful to agree with everyone that death by drowning had really been the forgone conclusion all along, but that protocol had been followed and deployed?

Wouldn't it be kind of wonderful to close the case and move on . . . allow Jim Cornish to shake his hand and squeeze his shoulder?

Wouldn't it be kind of wonderful to just let go?

Wouldn't it be kind of wonderful to stop fighting?

He let his head drop back against the cream-coloured tiles that always provoked in him a shuddering foretaste of violence, as if he expected at any moment to see them sprayed with blood. Then he shut his eyes, but as soon as he shut them Laura's perfume, undercut by a wall of chemicals, became even stronger.

He didn't want the corpse lying in front of him to be Bryan Deane.

He didn't want the search – no, it was more than that; it was a quest that had been going on for over twenty years – to finish here today, like this.

He didn't want the Deanes to win, and he didn't want Anna – he thought about her perched on the edge of the sofa in his study last night – to lose her reason for staying.

250

He didn't want the story to end here.

Sighing, he took a step closer, thinking again about the light at the back of Laura Deane's eyes. It had only been there for a split second, but it had the effect of changing her expression completely – from one of grief to one of triumph.

Laura Deane thought she'd won; was suddenly sure of it – standing outside in the corridor, staring at him.

Then he remembered something Anna had said about Bryan having had appendicitis surgery. Looking down, he saw no sign of a scar.

He phoned Yvonne – an old friend he'd known since first joining the force, and the only person he could trust right then. Yvonne had never been promoted above the rank of sergeant because she'd never asked to be – if she had, she would have been; people didn't say 'no' to Yvonne, who was in a league of her own not even Jim Cornish could touch.

Yvonne knew everybody and operated way beyond the perimeters of her job description. She had an entry in the Guinness Book of Records for having the largest thimble collection in the world, and both she and her husband – a retired officer who spent his time on planes escorting illegal immigrants home – collected porcelain figurines.

'I hear you've got a body,' she said – brusque; wry.

'Yeah, I'm with it now – only it's not *my* body.'

'It isn't?'

'I'm sure of it.'

'Based on?'

'Nothing much other than the absence of an appendicitis scar. Yvonne – I need you to run a check – all missing persons reported in the last six months.'

'Because?'

'This isn't Bryan Deane.'

Laviolette banged open the double doors and started to

run – along the corridor and through the building, its daylight levels increasing as he ran – until he was standing in the car park in full sunlight, breathless.

He wanted to know where Laura Deane had gone after identifying her missing husband in a mortuary.

But there was no sign of a silver Lexus 4x4 parked anywhere.

Laviolette walked, distracted, to where his own car was usually parked, and stood staring at the black Volkswagen Polo in front of him, waiting for it to transmogrify into a burgundy Vauxhall Cavalier.

But it didn't.

Then he remembered that he hadn't been able to get his usual spot that morning, but couldn't remember where he had actually parked his car – he was going to have to check all one thousand bays.

He started to walk through the car park.

By the time he'd located the Vauxhall – somewhere he had no recollection of leaving it – he'd tried Laura's mobile, the landlines at number two Marine Drive, Starz Salon, and Don Hamilton. Laura clearly hadn't told her parents about the body in the mortuary.

Laura Deane was nowhere to be found.

He tried Anna's mobile, but she wasn't picking up either – so phoned the house. It had been too late and they'd drunk too much the night before for Anna to drive back to Blyth, so she'd spent the night on the sofa in the study. He hadn't seen her before leaving that morning – she'd still been asleep.

Mrs Kelly picked up. He could hear Harvey, in the background, irate. 'Is Anna there?'

'Anna?' Mrs Kelly – distracted by Harvey who was outraged that his pipe cleaner cuboid was refusing to stand level on the table – was at a loss.

'Last night?'

'Oh. Anna.' Mrs Kelly said the name shyly. 'She left.'

'When?'

'Not long ago.'

'Did she say where she was going?'

'No, she didn't really say anything. Just a minute –' He heard her trying to calm Harvey. 'I was going to do a stew for tonight – is that okay?' she said, hesitant.

'Fine – that's fine.'

'Oh, and Harvey's got his appointment in North Shields later – so we won't be back until six.'

Mrs Kelly's mention of North Shields was entirely incidental, but it triggered something in Laviolette. He'd forgotten about North Shields, and that was something he shouldn't have done.

The Deanes had a flat in North Shields that they rented out – at the Royal Quays Marina.

Anna had woken that morning on the sofa in Laviolette's study, in Laviolette's house with a feeling of empty panic at having given something away, drunk, that in daylight she regretted, and daylight was staring down at her through the skylight as she swung her legs over the edge of the sofa into a sitting position, staring down at her bare feet in the carpet as if they had nothing to do with her.

Laviolette had left without waking her.

Uncertain, she went downstairs and attempted to talk first to Harvey then Mrs Kelly. Harvey was easier, but Mrs Kelly did offer to make her coffee. She had the impression they were waiting to go out – had been waiting for some time – but that Mrs Kelly didn't want to leave her in the house alone. Anna also guessed – from both Harvey and Mrs Kelly's reaction to her presence – that visitors at number four Coastguard Cottages were a rarity. She tried to think of some way to reassure them both, but in the end gave up.

She took her coffee upstairs with her after telling Mrs Kelly she'd be leaving in ten minutes, and sat on the sofa in the study again looking round the room more intently now she was alone in it. She thought about Harvey – downstairs – and what Laviolette had said about him being there the day Roger Laviolette had been killed. A minute later, she was pulling down the old projector box with the interview tapes in it, from the shelves.

The cine projector was in the box still, the clearly labelled tapes slotted down either side of the incommodious machine. Anna found herself wondering – like she had with the car when she first met Laviolette the night Bryan disappeared – if the old projector was even his, and if it was, what had it been used for? She couldn't imagine – from the things he'd said the night before – that the early years of his married life were times anyone would want to capture and replay.

They'd listened to all the tapes, Anna realised, apart from the one she'd just come across – the one she'd seen Laviolette hesitate over the night before, and withhold. Anna stared down at the tape, which had her grandmother's name on it: Mary Faust.

She wanted to play it on Laviolette's machine then and there, but could hear Mrs Kelly on the stairs. So she'd taken it with her – without hesitation – feeling entitled to it while wondering briefly how long it would take for him to miss it.

Why had police interviewed Mary after Roger Laviolette's death?

It was starting to rain, but Laviolette barely noticed as he dialled DC Wade's number.

'What have we got on the Deane's flat – the one at the marina in North Shields?'

There was a pause on the other end of the line. 'I'm sorry, sir, I'm not following,' Veronica said at last.

'The Deanes have a flat,' Laviolette said, tersely, articulating each word, 'in North Shields at the Royal Quays Marina.'

'I understand that.'

'What did Laura Deane tell us about the flat?'

'You want me to look in the case file?'

'Yes, I want you to look in the case file.'

'But, Inspector, this morning –'

'This morning, what?'

'The mortuary,' DC Wade said, helplessly, anxious to resolve the situation without dispute. 'I was there in the room with Mrs Deane, sir. I was there.'

Laviolette was trying not to lose patience. He didn't want to push her too hard, even though that was his inclination, because if he pushed DC Wade too hard, she might go running to Jim Cornish, and this situation that Laviolette was playing out right now was just the sort of situation Jim was looking for.

'We all want this case closed, Wade, but there's the coroner's report still to come and while we're waiting on that, I just want to review the case file – make sure we asked everything we were meant to when we were meant to. I don't want anything coming back to haunt us when this is closed, that's all,' he concluded.

'So it's not an investigative request as such?'

'Not as such, no. It's –'

'Administrative?' she suggested helpfully, happy to have made sense of the Inspector's request at last. He was being thorough, that was all.

'So you want me to check what went down on file regarding the North Shields property?'

'Please.'

'I'll take a look.'

Veronica phoned back twenty minutes later.

'What did you find?'

'Nothing much. Mrs Deane confirmed they had a second property let through Tyneside Properties – we cross-checked with them. That's it.'

'Great, we can sign that off then.'

'So – that's it?' Veronica said, relieved.

'That's it.'

When Laura walked into the marina flat, Tom was standing by the dining table, absently shuffling some drawings into a pile.

'I wasn't expecting you,' he said, his mind elsewhere.

He walked past her into the kitchen and started to methodically load the dishwasher. She remained where she was in the middle of the living room and watched him load it in the same perverse way he'd always done, which meant that everything had to be rinsed in the sink afterwards because it never got washed properly.

She'd stopped letting him stack the dishwasher at number two Marine Drive for precisely this reason, but here she'd felt no compulsion to do that.

The silence was awkward.

It was a silence that needed words, that tried seeking for them, but that couldn't find any.

'D'you want a tea or coffee?'

'I brought champagne,' she said, moving at last over to the kitchen doorway and leaning against the frame.

'Champagne?' He didn't understand.

'You died today – it's almost official.'

He carried on drying his hands on the tea towel. 'I did?'

'I saw you over an hour ago, laid out in the mortuary. I identified you. I cried.'

She was poised, watching him, waiting for him to get it.

'You did?' he said, in the same distant tone.

'You drowned. You got washed up in the harbour at

Cullercoats. A fisherman found you.' She paused, still waiting. 'Bryan – there's no catch. We've just got to wait for the coroner's report. Then –'

He walked slowly past her, still holding the tea towel, and sat down on the sofa in the living room.

'So – we're nearly done here?'

She nodded, sitting down on the coffee table, on top of a pile of his drawings and taking hold of his hands. Instead of bringing them together, the body in the mortuary had somehow come between them.

'What did he look like – this drowned man?'

'Like – nothing.'

He pulled his hands out of her grasp and fell back against the sofa, preoccupied.

'Please, Bryan,' she said, suddenly scared. 'We're this close.' She held up her thumb and forefinger so that they were almost touching, trying to bring him back to her. 'This close.'

He turned to her. 'To what?'

Laura shifted position carefully – it was as if everything had suddenly become breakable. 'Everything we talked about.'

'What did we talk about?'

'Don't be cruel – not now. It's too late for cruelty.'

'Seriously,' he persisted. 'I can't even remember any more, what it was we set out to do – what any of this is about.'

He stood up, preoccupied, and went out onto the balcony where his attention was taken by a young woman pushing a buggy out of the building and across the car park. There was a toddler in the buggy, asleep, her arm flung over the side so that the teddy she was holding hung out. A second later he watched it fall to the ground. The mother hadn't noticed, and he found it upsetting.

'Bryan?' Laura said, joining him on the balcony.

257

'A kid just dropped it – look,' he said, pointing to the teddy lying face down in the car park below.

Laura glanced at it without interest, waiting for him to turn back to her, but he didn't.

He walked straight through the flat, leaving the door open.

'Bryan? Where are you going?' She could hear him running down the stairs, and a few moments later he appeared in the car park below.

Laura saw him pick up the teddy from where it was lying, and dust the muck off it then jog after the young mother, calling out and waving the bear.

'Excuse me,' Laura heard him say, breathless, eventually drawing level. 'You dropped this.'

'Oh.' The mother nodded, surprised – pleased – as Bryan peered, smiling, into the buggy.

Laura remained on the balcony, unaware that she was crying, watching as the mother shunted the buggy forwards again, leaving Bryan standing in the car park.

He felt unaccountably relieved that he'd managed to return the teddy – a bear in a dress – to the sleeping child, and that the sleeping child would never know she'd lost it.

He felt unaccountably relieved that the bear was no longer lost.


Maureen at Tyneside Properties was standing at the back of the office talking to a decayed looking man in expensive clothes with a light covering of auburn hair that straggled across his cranium – a property developer whose small complex of four luxury mews houses in Gosforth they were hoping to sell. But she recognised the Inspector as soon as he walked in because everybody at Tyneside Properties – apart from the young man smiling affably at the Inspector now – had been interviewed after Bryan Deane's disappearance.

'Inspector!' she called out, more irately than she'd meant to.

The property developer turned to him, momentarily curious, but the curiosity soon passed. He'd known Bryan Deane relatively well. Tyneside Properties sold all the units on another of his developments four years ago, down near the Quayside, and got above asking price on all of them. They'd spoken once about branching out into the commercial property market, but Bryan had lost the inclination to make that kind of money and the developer – who'd spent very little of the past twenty years sober – was no player.

Maureen approached – in a red suit with brass buttons running the length of it. The suits she'd worn in the late eighties and early nineties – when she first knew Bryan – that made her look like an estate agent, now made her look like an air hostess, and Maureen had always worn make-up like a transvestite; something that had never ceased to entertain Laura Deane.

'Inspector,' she said again, smiling this time.

'Can I just have a few moments?'

They went into the small kitchen where brown brick walls were covered in health and safety regulations, an aerial photograph of the coast from Tynemouth up to Blyth, staff targets, a sole postcard from the Isle of Wight, and a poster of an airbrushed woman in a wide brim hat eating a cherry. There was also the front page of *The Journal* from the day Bryan Deane's picture had been published. Someone had scribbled something in blue biro across it and up close, Laviolette saw that it read: Fess up, Greg, just how badly did you want that promotion?

He turned to look at Maureen, amused.

'That shouldn't be up there,' she said, mortified, pushing past him and ripping it down. She placed the offending article on top of the microwave. 'Greg's been made temporary

Branch Manager. It's a tasteless joke, it's –' Words failed her. 'Please –' She waved her arm at the bank of outdated office chairs, gesturing at Laviolette to take a seat.

'I need to ask you something about the Deane's flat – the one in North Shields.'

Maureen nodded, and stopped smiling.

'Mrs Deane told us the property was rented, and we just need a bit more information regarding that.'

Maureen looked thoughtful. She didn't know what she'd been expecting when she saw the Inspector, but it wasn't this.

'When I saw you, I thought you might have some information for us – not that you'd be needing some *from* us.'

Laviolette thought of the body in the mortuary and smiled sadly. 'Unfortunately not.'

'Can I get you a tea or coffee or anything?'

'I'm fine.' He watched her put the kettle on anyway. 'The Deanes' flat is down at the Royal Quays Marina in the Ropemakers Building.'

'I'll have to take your word for it,' she said, 'it's Justin who works on lettings. Did you meet Justin? No, you wouldn't have done,' she carried on before he had time to answer, 'he's only been with us a couple of weeks.'

'I need to know when the flat was let, for how long, and who the tenant is?'

Maureen listened to this while regarding the Inspector, as steam from the boiling kettle rose up behind her.

The kettle clicked off, but the steam carried on rising.

'That's quite specific information you want,' she pointed out, uncertain, waiting for him to back up the request with something that would explain the personal visit to retrieve such seemingly irrelevant information. When no such explanation was forthcoming, she said, 'They were bloody lucky.'

'Lucky?'

'The Deanes – with the rental of the marina flat in the current climate.'

She realised from the Inspector's expression – too late – that she'd ended up inadvertently saying more than she'd meant to.

'There've been a lot of repossessions at the marina.'

'How long's it been let for?'

'I'd have to check the contracts file – I'm not sure.' She paused. 'Have you not heard anything at all since the appeal?'

'Nothing.'

'It's hard to believe, isn't it?'

She disappeared into the office, reappearing a few minutes later, and remained standing near the door. 'It was let mid-February,' she said, her hand holding onto the door handle still.

Laviolette was aware that his posture had become tense and that his left shoulder hurt. He wanted a name.

'It's a twelve month let and the deposit plus rent were paid up front.'

'Is that unusual?'

'Depends.' She paused. 'There was only one name on the contract – a man called Tom Bowen.'

'Tom Bowen,' Laviolette said, smiling. He wanted to say it out loud, and as soon as he said it, the image of the morning's bloated corpse slid off the table it had been lying on, and floated away. Tom Bowen was a good name; a vivid name. It sounded like a name belonging to someone who was still alive. Bryan Deane might be nowhere, but Tom Bowen was somewhere. Tom Bowen was living at flat twenty-one, the Ropemakers Building, and he'd been there all along.

Maureen hadn't left her position by the door, and looked relieved when the Inspector stood up to go.

Laviolette, feeling suddenly light-headed, asked for a

photocopy of the contract, which – after only a moment's hesitation – Maureen did herself, on a double-sided setting.

He was about to leave with the contract when Greg walked in, gave Laviolette a professional smile – clearly not remembering him despite having been interviewed for over an hour by DS Chambers and himself – and said to Maureen, 'I'm parked on doubles, and I'm late for the Marine Drive viewing – can you chuck me the keys?'

He gave Laviolette another brief, open smile although this one tapered slightly towards the end.

Maureen didn't look at him at all. She went to the key cupboard on the back wall of the office near the fire extinguisher and took out the keys, throwing them lightly to Greg.

'Back in about an hour,' he said, giving Laviolette a quick look before jumping back into his car, which he'd parked directly outside Tyneside Properties.

'Laura – Mrs Deane – has put the house on the market,' she said, worried that she hadn't mentioned this before. 'You already knew?'

Laviolette nodded slowly and took his leave.

As Laviolette drove through the rain into Tynemouth along Grand Parade, he saw Anna's yellow Capri parked in the same place it had been parked since yesterday, and knew immediately that this was where she'd come when she left Coastguard Cottages.

Despite the weather, there were surfers in the water – not many – but enough at this distance for them to look like a small colony.

He parked and walked down onto the beach via the small slip road full of recycling bins that led down to Crusoes – the café they'd had a drink at the previous evening.

The beach was empty as he walked towards the sea,

stopping about five metres from the water's edge. The surfers looked strangely androgynous in their wet suits, even up close, but he saw her immediately. She had none of the aggressive intentness most of them had, she just wanted to be there in the water doing what she was doing, and it gave her a beguiling grace; a purity almost. He knew he didn't understand what he was seeing, but he felt it.

She'd seen him and was heading towards him, gaining height and straightening up. She came to a standstill a couple of metres away from him, stepping easily off her board and catching it up before the next wave came.

She didn't look surprised to see him, and she was smiling – a wet, exhilarated smile that had nothing to do with him.

He jumped back as a wave caught at his shoes and, laughing, her face relaxed and the unsettling exhilaration left it.

They started to walk back across the beach – towards Crusoes.

'We've been stupid,' he said when they were far enough from the sea to talk comfortably.

'About what?' she said, sniffing loudly and not particularly interested.

'There's a body.'

She stopped walking. 'Since when?'

'Yesterday. A fisherman at Cullercoats Bay found it sandwiched between his boat and the harbour wall.'

'Bryan?'

'Enough people want it to be – including Laura, who came in this morning to identify it.'

'Did you see it?'

Laviolette nodded. 'Did you ever see a drowned body?'

'Once,' Anna said, automatically. 'How was Laura?'

'I saw her just after the identification.'

'And?'

'She identified it as her husband's body.'

There was a pause.

'And?'

'I'm waiting on the coroner's report. How about you?'

'I don't know. There's a body now. What if this time he really did die?'

'It's not him.'

'I need proof. I need something . . . it's just supposition,' she shouted over her shoulder as she carried on walking. 'I hear nothing but supposition.'

'It's more than that.'

This time she stopped.

'There was no appendicitis scar on the body.'

'A scar like that wouldn't show if a body had been in the water that long. You'll have to do better.'

'The Deanes have an investment property Bryan Deane bought just before the crash. I told you about it, it's at the Royal Quays Marina.' He broke off. 'Right now it's like the Empty Quarter down there, but the Deanes managed to let their flat in February this year – through Tyneside Properties.'

Anna was staring at him. 'You think that's where Bryan's been hiding?'

Laviolette nodded. 'And I think that's where Laura Deane went after identifying her husband's body at the mortuary this morning.'

Anna looked away from him towards the sea, which was depositing a line of something on the beach – large, grey-white objects that lay stranded and quivering in the wet sand before being picked up by the next wave and deposited again, each time a little closer to them. Jellyfish – hundreds of them -stretching along the waterline as far as the eye could see.

'She identifies her husband's body then she gets in her car and drives directly to their flat at Royal Quays Marina – currently rented to a Tom Bowen.'

She looked up at him. 'Tom Bowen?'

'That's the name of the guy who's renting the marina flat.'

'You think Tom Bowen's Bryan Deane?'

'It's him, Anna, I know it's him.'

'No, you don't know it's him.'

'It's him,' Laviolette said, grabbing hold suddenly of her arm. 'Anna –'

Pulling her arm free, she started walking again.

'Where are you going?'

'Crusoes. I left my clothes with Sheila on the counter so I can get changed out of this,' she said, pulling on the collar of the wetsuit. 'This isn't an investigation – it's a manhunt.'

'Come with me.'

'Where?'

'The marina.' He started walking towards her.

'You'll never get a warrant for that.'

'You don't want that body in the mortuary to be Bryan Deane.'

'I don't work for you. You've got your own people.'

'Not any more I haven't. They've assigned me to an armed robbery case in a supporting role.'

'I'm sorry,' she said frankly, meaning it.

The sea was following them up the beach, and they'd instinctively started to raise their voices again in order to be heard above it.

'I want you to come with me because you're the only one who'd recognise him.'

'What makes you think that?' she said, starting to walk away.

'You told me – last night!' he yelled after her retreating back.

Anna and Laviolette sat in Laviolette's car in the marina car park, looking up at the Ropemakers Building. They'd spent ten minutes driving round the car park, but there was no sign of Laura's Lexus.

Some of the balconies had garden furniture and pot plants on them, but most didn't.

Their attention was taken by a balcony door opening half way up the building. A woman with short hair dyed purple stepped outside – it was one of the balconies with furniture and pot plants – and lit up, staring absently at a fixed point in the distance. She was joined by a man they couldn't see clearly, who remained near the doors. She turned to face him leaning her elbows on the railings – and continued to smoke.

They stood there contemplating each other until suddenly exchanging a brief, hard kiss before pulling away. The man put his hand on the woman's right breast, but she lifted it off, kissing it. She dropped the cigarette into one of the pot plants and they went inside.

The balcony doors remained open, the white curtains blowing out, and there was something relentless in the way the curtains kept blowing that prompted Laviolette and Anna to get out of the car.

As they crossed the car park full of puddles after the day's five minute rain storm – which had been almost tropical in intensity – and entered the Ropemakers Building, a white Husky trotted through the curtains and onto the balcony where the couple had been standing.

It ran round the balcony a couple of times, its nose to the ground, sniffing the decking before lying down suddenly on its side in a temperamental patch of sunlight, its eyes rolling up towards the sky, its tail knocking rhythmically against a pot full of bamboo.

They moved fast, through the lobby – which smelt damp – and up the metal and wood staircase, too impatient to use the lift; aware now of a renewed sense of urgency. The

266

building felt empty, and when Laviolette rang on the bell to the Deanes' flat – flat twenty-one on level D – they could hear it echoing inside.

They waited – Anna watching the enlarged shadows of raindrops running down the window at the end of the corridor, moving across the floor.

There was no answer.

After pressing his ear to the door and trying the handle, Laviolette rang again – knocking as well this time. Drumming his fingers on the door he instinctively knew wasn't going to open he went along the corridor to flat twenty-three and rang on this door instead.

There was no answer here either, but he did hear movement on the other side. Briefly distracted by the sound of voices in the stairwell, speaking what sounded like Chinese, he waited for them to fade before ringing again. This time a woman's voice – foreign – simply said, 'Yes?'

This was followed by a dog, barking.

'Police,' he called out.

He looked at Anna.

The door opened and the tall woman with purple hair – who they'd just seen out on the balcony – was standing there in a black and gold dressing gown, her face startled-looking despite the heaviness around her eyes. The dressing gown wasn't tied, but pulled protectively round her.

There was a dog standing behind her – a Husky, whose neck she was holding onto.

Anna was staring at the dog, and the dog was staring back at her – unblinking.

The back draft of the smell of sex hung momentarily in the hallway.

Sex in the afternoon – it had been somehow instilled in Laviolette since childhood before the breakdown of decency and order, without anybody ever referring to the subject directly – was for teenagers, newlyweds, the unemployed, and the wealthy, or you were paying for it.

'Yes?' she said again.

'We're trying to get hold of Mr Bowen – in the flat next door?'

'Next door?' She took a step closer and looked vaguely up the corridor.

'Flat twenty-one – nobody's answering.'

'Oh – Tom. I don't know him.'

'Apart from the fact that he's called Tom.'

She shrugged. 'Maybe he's at work.'

'He works?' Laviolette asked quickly.

The woman stared at him for a moment then shrugged again. 'I don't know.'

Laviolette detected movement behind her eyes. He didn't doubt that what she was saying was true, he just didn't believe her.

'You're Russian?'

'Polish,' she said with a faint smile – as if his diagnosis amused her.

While she was still smiling, he said, 'I couldn't trouble you for a glass of water, could I?'

She stared at him – then Anna.

There was the sound of a toilet being flushed in the flat behind her, but what Anna guessed to be the bathroom door remained shut. The door to the bedroom was also shut.

'It's no trouble.' She gave him another faint smile.

He followed her in and she stopped, turning round to face him, making an effort to conceal the tension in her face. 'I've got a spare bottle – I'll fill it.'

Laviolette waited in the flat's tiny hallway, light-headed and fractious for a moment before walking into the lounge-diner, leaving the front door open behind him.

Anna followed.

268

She thought she heard a door open behind her and, turning round, caught a glimpse of a man with blond hair – the man from the balcony – disappearing through the bedroom door.

'So you've got no idea when would be a good time to catch your neighbour?' he said, startling the woman from her crouching position on the kitchen floor where she'd been looking for an empty water bottle in the cupboard under the sink.

She stood up. 'Not really, no.'

'Is he around in the evenings?' Laviolette persisted.

'I'm sorry – I really have no idea,' she said, exasperated.

They watched each other for a moment then Laviolette swung away from her with a smile, taking in the room behind him while she poured him a glass of water from the tap.

'I thought I had a spare bottle, but I couldn't find one.'

She gave the benches a quick wipe with a yellow cloth while he drank the water, drifting over to the fridge where there were a couple of drawings held up by alphabet magnets.

They were life drawings – in pen and ink – of a woman lying on her back with one leg hooked up and an arm flung over her head. Laviolette looked from the drawings to the woman cleaning the benches.

'That's you?' he asked.

She nodded.

'They're good,' he said, adding, 'Anna – come and take a look. You don't mind?' he said to the woman.

She shook her head.

'Somebody gave you these?' Laviolette asked, watching Anna, who was staring thoughtfully at the drawings.

'Somebody in the class. I do four classes a week – it's good money,' she said quietly then, in the same quiet voice – before he had a chance to ask any more questions – she said, 'what did you say your name was?'

'I didn't. Detective Inspector Laviolette.' He didn't introduce Anna. 'If you see Mr Bowen, will you tell him I need to speak to him?'

She nodded, moving past them towards the front door.

After taking one last look around the lounge diner, he followed her.

There were no tell-tale signs of male occupancy in the flat – the blond man and purple haired Pole weren't a couple, of that he was sure; so either she was cheating on someone, or he was cheating on someone, or they were both cheating on someone.

When they got back to the car Anna said, 'She was telling the truth,' echoing Laviolette's earlier sentiment.

Laviolette nodded. 'I agree. So why don't I believe her?' He stared up at the balcony, whose doors were open – the curtains blowing still. 'What were you thinking – when you were looking at the drawings?'

'That they could be Bryan's.'

'And?'

'They could be Bryan's.'

'You think it's worth checking to see if Tom Bowen's enrolled in any life drawing classes?'

Anna nodded, but she wasn't thinking about the drawings any more – she was thinking about the man she'd caught a glimpse of, disappearing into the bedroom inside flat twenty-three. He'd looked at her – only for a split second – but he'd definitely looked, and she'd felt the look across the back of her shoulders.

'What are you thinking?' Laviolette asked, watching her.

She turned to face him. 'Nothing.'

# 17

The viewing at number two Marine Drive had finished and Greg was just leaving when Laura pulled up on the drive. The strain of the day was taking its toll, and she felt as if she'd been wearing herself for too long. For the first time since reporting Bryan missing on Easter Saturday she wanted the one thing that up until then she'd been most afraid of: to be alone.

She turned off the engine and stared at the dashboard of the Lexus she'd insisted on, aware of a sudden, overwhelming sadness. She felt sadder than she'd ever felt in her life before and with the sadness came a sense of lifelessness.

There was a knocking sound on the car window and, looking round, she found Bryan's former colleague, Greg, smiling in at her.

Reluctantly she wound down the window. 'What are you doing here?'

'There was a viewing,' he said, uncertain. 'I spoke to the receptionist at the salon – told her to tell you.'

Laura continued to stare at him without speaking.

Then without warning, she hooked her hands under the bottom of the steering wheel and, shoulders shaking, started to cry.

Greg stood looking awkwardly around him. He couldn't just leave her like this, alone in the car, crying. Her hair was hanging forward, concealing her face, and the ends of it were trembling. Her knees were pressed together and the fabric of her trousers had gone dark in the places where tears had fallen.

'Come on,' he said, made suddenly decisive by a pity he felt in his lower abdomen. 'Let's get you indoors.'

Numb, she let him pull her gently out of the car.

'My handbag –'

'I've got your handbag,' he said, steering her towards the front porch. He put the keys he'd used for the viewing into the lock and opened the door.

Without another word, she walked down the hallway and disappeared into the lounge.

After a moment's hesitation, he shut the front door behind him and followed her.

She was lying in the corner of one of the sofas, her head flung back, staring at the pelmets that framed the heavy curtains.

At a loss, but unable to leave, he hung in the centre of the room he'd stood in barely fifteen minutes ago pointing out the solid oak floor and fireplace to a Mr and Mrs Reddington.

'I went to the mortuary this morning – a body was washed up in Cullercoats Bay and the police wanted me to identify it.'

'Shit, Laura – I had no idea,' Greg mumbled – running a hand through his hair – helpless. He didn't have the words or emotional palette to deal with this, but Laura's collarbone along with most of the skin around it – revealed to him because of the way her shirt had fallen open at the neck – had gone red after the outburst of tears in the car, and he couldn't take his eyes off it.

'I'm so tired,' she said, more to herself than Greg, shutting her eyes and letting her head fall even further back, her throat long.

For some reason, as soon as her eyes shut, Greg felt a sense of entitlement he'd never felt before. It was as if eight years of longing combined with eight years of dissatisfaction with his own lot in life came suddenly to a head in a moment of stillness that contained all possibilities.

Why not?

Laura remained motionless on the sofa with her eyes shut, and he continued to watch her – intently now.

Neither of them made a sound.

Did she know he was watching her?

There was something abysmal about all of this that didn't suit Greg – or the neutral tones of the décor for that matter – but it was too late now.

Laura had become so still that he wondered if she'd actually fallen asleep, and felt a brief sense of relief that vanished immediately as she arched her neck even further back before dropping her head to one side and opening her eyes to observe him.

Without thinking, he crossed the room, knocking his left knee on the corner of the coffee table as, crouching he pulled her roughly off the sofa and onto the floor. When she didn't resist or even react, he felt a brief anger – absurdly – towards his wife, Patsy, as if she had failed to protect him from this.

Then grunting and later whining, he laid bare the bones of an ultimately banal fantasy he'd nurtured for eight years – while still wearing his suit. He didn't even take his shoes off. It took three meaningless minutes and yet its horrible intimacy would haunt him for the rest of his life.

Their failure to exchange a single word or look afterwards.

The sight of Laura laid out on the lounge carpet.

His clumsy attempt to wash himself at the sink in the downstairs bathroom.

The rush to leave.

The vague sense of having committed a crime, but against whom, he couldn't have said.

Hearing crying from the other end of the hallway and knowing he wasn't going to do anything about it.

Knocking over the vase of dried flowers by the front door then the front door opening without him having to touch it.

Thinking he was about to see Bryan walk through the front door only to be confronted by someone who looked remarkably like him, but whose neck was covered in a web of tattoos . . .

Greg ran.

He got into his car, locked the doors then started the engine, his hands shaking as he drove out of Marine Drive.

Ever since that first time, there had been a complicit understanding between them that Jamie would pick Martha up from school. The arrangement gave his days a shape he hadn't been able to give them himself after twenty years inside.

When he first started work, he took whatever shifts they gave him, but after meeting Martha he always requested the six to two so that he could pick her up from school. His request for specific shifts was something Janet, the counsellor, was told about, and when she brought it up in one of their meetings and he said that an old friend of his needed someone to pick her kid up from school, Janet looked pleased. When she asked how old the child was and Jamie said fifteen, she didn't look so pleased. He tried to think of something to say that would make her look pleased again, but became so agitated, he knew the only favour he could do himself was to remain silent.

Since Martha, he woke up in the morning without the paranoid feeling of invisibility.

He was real.

He was alive.

He knew the names of all her teachers, and who took her for which subjects; the teachers she liked, and those she hated.

He knew her timetable – and that on Tuesdays when he picked her up, her hair would be wet because Tuesday afternoons she had swimming squad.

Laura had no idea any of this was happening.

He'd never once anticipated Martha when he was inside, and now he couldn't imagine having any sort of life without her.

She was waiting for him in the usual place – on the low wall circling the chestnut tree where she was convinced she'd seen Bryan that time.

She smiled when she saw him – she always smiled – and did her funny running shuffle towards the van, pulling her various bags after her.

'What are these?' she said as she got in, picking up the brochures on her seat.

He flashed her a smile as she pulled her hair back over her shoulders and started to flick through them.

'You said you wanted to go to Norway.'

'When?' she demanded, excited.

'I don't know yet. I need to see about money and . . . stuff.'

They drove slowly towards Seaton Sluice, Martha commenting on the brochures, reading bits out loud. Then she asked him about his day, and John – who he worked with. He'd once told her that John had an artificial limb, and after that she always wanted to know about John. Sometimes he told her about things that had really happened; sometimes he just made stuff up. It didn't really matter as long as he made her laugh – he loved making her laugh.

Then there were the dark days when he lost sight of himself; the days he couldn't face that he spent in his room sitting on the floor with the curtains drawn. On those days he had to set the alarm to remind himself to pick her up from school. He'd be silent and unable to talk and she'd know not to try to speak to him.

Tonight as they turned into Marine Drive – he always drove her to the front door and waited until she was inside – she slipped the brochures into the pocket in the door and was about to say something when she noticed Laura's car parked on the drive alongside another unfamiliar one.

'Mum's home,' she said flatly, her eyes skirting over the Lexus. The presence of the Lexus was strange in itself – Laura was never home at this time.

Martha looked at him, scared. 'Are you coming in?'

Jamie nodded as she picked up her bags, opened the van door and slid uncertainly to the pavement.

What happened next, happened fast, and even though everything around her looked the same as it always did, nothing felt right. She put her keys in the lock, but it was already being pulled open from the inside and there was a man standing in front of her she recognised, and the man was looking at her but not really seeing her. Then Jamie pushed past her and the man just ran out of the house like he was running away from something.

Without moving from the spot, she turned and watched him bundle himself into his car while trying to remember his name. Greg – the name came to her as his car reversed off the drive.

Indoors there were muffled, indistinct sounds coming from the other end of the hallway, which suddenly seemed much

276

further away. She called out, 'Jamie!', and he appeared a few seconds later, framed in the lounge doorway.

'It's okay,' he said, and even though his face didn't look as if it was okay, she let herself be pushed up the stairs by him and into her room because instinct told her she didn't want to see what he'd seen.

'What's happening?'

'Nothing's happened – just stay there.'

She nodded and sat down slowly on the edge of the bed, holding her school bags still as images of Norwegian fjords from the brochures she'd been reading in the van on the way home slipped through her mind.

Jamie stood staring down at Laura, who was lying on her side with her trousers round her ankles, her arms and legs useless looking, her head turned to one side. For a moment he felt nothing then with a rush that was almost audible, everything caught up with him and he let go suddenly of something he'd been holding onto for twenty years. In that instant he felt such an overwhelming mixture of fury and pity towards the woman lying at his feet, who had once been Laura Hamilton, that he could have killed her.

Checking the hallway behind him to make sure Martha wasn't there – it was Martha now, he realised, that he needed to protect at all costs – he knelt down awkwardly beside her as she rolled onto her back and stared up at him, her face older, swollen and unreadable.

She wasn't shocked at finding him kneeling beside her, and made no attempt to help as he pulled up her pants and trousers.

'You're her mother,' he hissed angrily.

She stared at him, uncomprehending.

'Martha. Martha can't see you like this.'

'Martha?' Laura started to raise herself on her elbows,

her head swaying, but Jamie picked her up suddenly, balancing her momentarily on one knee before standing up, the muscles in his neck thick with the effort.

She hung onto him because there was nobody else to hang onto.

'I feel sick.'

'You're drunk.'

'I'm always drunk.'

'Who was he?'

'Greg. He's called Greg.'

'Who's Greg?'

She shook her head, clinging onto him as he carried her upstairs. 'It was horrible –'

He carried her into the en-suite and told her to get undressed.

She stumbled obediently out of her clothes and let herself be pushed into the shower.

Jamie sat on the edge of the bath as steam started to fill the bathroom and Laura disappeared into it.

Pulling a large white towel off the rail, he stood up and opened the shower cubicle doors.

She was propped in the corner, her head against the tiles and her eyes shut, water from the shower streaming over the left hand side of her body. He didn't know if she was crying or sleeping. She was beautiful, but the woman's body didn't make him feel powerless in the way the girl's had – not because the skin was different or the shape was different but because the innocence which had been her glory had forsaken her.

She came to, sliding her head round on the tiles and peering at him through the jets of water with panda eyes where her eye make-up had run. Leaving the shower running, she stepped out into the towel, let herself be wrapped up in it then led into the bedroom where she stood shivering as he pulled down the blind.

Laura continued to stand there as he rubbed her body and hair roughly with the towel then, holding up the duvet, motioned for her to get in. She lay in bed staring at the radio clock whose red digits told her it was 17:57, but this didn't really signify much apart from marking the twenty minutes that had passed since Jamie picked her up from the lounge carpet.

They looked at each other carefully then looked away.

'You should sleep,' he mumbled.

She turned onto her back for a moment before sitting up and pulling the duvet around her, her hair sticking to her shoulders in thick, wet strands.

He cast his eyes quickly round the room, looking for something he might recognise – other than his brother's wife – but there was nothing.

His eyes came to rest heavily on her again.

'Are you going to kill me?' she asked in a small, flat voice.

Jamie laughed. 'If I was going to kill you I'd of done it by now. No,' he said, slowly shaking his head as if it was too much of a burden for his body to carry. 'Twenty years, Laura,' he exploded suddenly, the veins on his neck standing up as if those twenty years had come rushing in to choke him. 'And you forgot all about me.'

'I didn't forget – I put you out of my mind. When you're thirteen, twenty years is forever and thirty-three is never meant to happen.'

'But it does happen, and here we are.'

Laura sat rigid not daring to move. 'I was thirteen, Jamie,' she whispered.

'And because you never came to visit me – because I never laid eyes on you once in those twenty years, you never grew up. You stayed thirteen, and you stayed with me. You've been wearing that pair of red shorts and that yellow blouse you wore that afternoon for twenty years.

I've been in that afternoon for twenty years because you never came to see me . . . you never came to tell me that you'd grown up.

'No matter where they put me, it was always the same – as soon as it was lights out, I could hear Iron Maiden playing, and the crackle of the posters on the wall because of the breeze coming in through the window catching at them. I spent every night beneath the Paddington Bear duvet cover my mum never got round to replacing, and that none of us thought to after she died.' He stared at her as he walked slowly across the room and sat down on the end of the bed. 'I've been smelling you on me for twenty years.'

'I was frightened. I was so frightened of you.'

'I'd never of hurt you, Laura. I never hurt you, did I? Did I?' he insisted.

'I don't know any more,' she said tearful and confused, 'I was just so frightened. All the sex stuff . . . I didn't want anybody knowing about that. I was terrified of mum and dad finding out and when the police interviewed me they told me what you'd said about us – what we were doing that afternoon. They said I'd have to stand up in front of all those people and tell them what we were doing, and I couldn't do that Jamie. I couldn't do it. I was a child.'

Jamie sat rubbing at the duvet cover, trying to understand the implications of this. 'We were both children.'

'I didn't know what was going on; I didn't know what I was saying.'

'But you said enough –' He sat up and stared straight at her.

'I just wanted the police gone. I wanted you gone – the whole afternoon gone,' she whispered.

'But you kept coming round to the house that summer.'

'Bryan,' she said helplessly, lifting the right hand up in the air then letting it fall back to the duvet again. 'I was

280

forever hoping to see Bryan, but he was never there. It was hopeless.'

He looked at her, amazed. 'So Bryan was there – even then?'

She nodded slowly at him, her eyes expecting him to understand.

'I thought he came after, but he was there before me? So we never had that afternoon? We never even had that?'

'It was easier to pretend it never happened.'

'I used to hold onto the memory of you so tightly I thought you must be getting short of breath out here. Twenty years,' he added in disbelief. 'Twenty years of pretending you weren't in my bedroom with me that afternoon? Twenty years of pretending I never took those red shorts and yellow blouse off you? You lied to yourself.'

Watching him, Laura felt a horrible sort of wonder take hold of her as she finally realised. 'You were in love with me that much?'

'And you lied to the police,' Jamie carried on, ignoring her now.

An impatience she couldn't risk flickered across her eyes. 'Stop it. Stop saying that,' she demanded, quietly.

'They knew you were lying. You knew you were lying. Who was it? You know, don't you?'

Neither of them had seen Martha, standing in the bedroom doorway.

'Stop it!' Laura shouted, putting her hands out and holding onto his arms, knowing the gesture wouldn't stop him.

Jamie stared at her. 'You know who it was, don't you?'

Then he realised that he knew as well – that he'd known all along.

Laura saw him realise. 'It doesn't matter any more,' she shouted, scared. 'They found Bryan.'

'Who found him?'

'He drowned – I identified him this morning.'

'She's lying,' Martha said in a clear voice from the doorway as Jamie, who hadn't realised she was in the room until then, saw the reflection of her in the doorway.

'She's lying,' Martha said again.

She'd changed out of her school uniform into a pair of shorts and a T-shirt and her hair was loose round her shoulders.

He looked from the woman in the bed to the girl in the doorway – then himself, in the mirror.

For a moment the woman and girl became one and the same person before separating again, and he made his choice. He never wanted to do anything that would compromise the trust of the girl standing in the doorway whose reflection he couldn't take his eyes off because her trust in him was *his* glory.

'I saw him,' Laura was saying loudly. 'It was him.'

But Jamie wasn't listening as he stood up to take hold of Martha, who was running across the room towards him. He saw himself, in the mirror, with his arms wrapped round her, buried under the hair that had filled his dreams for twenty years. Only Martha was real. He was holding onto somebody who was real.

Jamie had gone. It was 3:00 a.m. and Laura was dreaming. She was in the small, tiled airless room she'd been in that morning, and the drowned body was on the table in front of her. She was just about to speak to someone who was in the room – someone she couldn't see, but who she knew was standing just behind her; whose presence she felt – when a shiver passed through the bloated, discoloured remains in front of her. She didn't see the body shiver, she felt it – in the same way she felt the presence of the person standing behind her, but just as she was about to turn to them and

282

ask if they'd felt it too, she became aware that the other person had gone. She was alone in the room with the body and the body was slipping sideways off the table it had been lying on and attempting to half slither, half crawl across the tiled floor towards her – something amphibian that should never have been brought up out of the water, and that was now attempting to get back, taking her with it. She could hear it slapping against the tiles then the next minute it went dark and the creature disappeared – there was only the sound of it. Then the sound stopped and the lights came back on. She kept checking her feet and legs half expecting to see the creature grasping wetly at her, but there was nothing on the floor. Instead, she felt the presence of the other person behind her again – the same presence she'd felt before.

It was 3:00 a.m., and it was all still here Bryan thought, using keys he hadn't used in months to let himself into his home. He walked into the kitchen and peered through the patio doors at the garden. It had been here all along.

Up until that morning – when Laura told him about the body she'd identified – returning to life as Bryan Deane remained a possibility. If Bryan Deane was officially dead, that was no longer an option. He'd had the idea, this afternoon, of walking into the nearest police station and announcing that he believed himself to be a missing person. It was the third time he'd almost turned himself in – the first time was only weeks after his disappearance when he was living rough up near Rothbury, and the second time was after seeing Martha outside school, which had broken his heart.

He'd gone to Martha's room first and, resting his head against the doorframe, contemplated his daughter while trying to overcome an urge to wake her so that he could feel her eyes on him and watch her face when she saw him. He remembered her sleepwalking as a child between the ages of nine and twelve – something they'd never found an explanation for – and how he'd followed her eerily slow moving, unconscious figure through the early morning hours half expecting her to lead him straight out of this world.

Then he saw the photograph propped against the window – the one she'd taken of him in Cephalonia – and the candle burning beside it, and for the first time began to have some real sense of the magnitude of what it was they'd done.

He'd come to warn them – wake them.

If he woke them now, they could all leave together, and yet here he was creeping about the house, terrified of doing precisely what it was he'd come to do.

Here he was standing over his wife, in their bedroom, watching as she turned her head on her pillow. She was dreaming; had always been a heavy dreamer – he'd forgotten that and, standing motionless beside the bed he used to sleep in, in the bedroom he used to fall asleep in every night and wake up in every morning, he felt a prick of tenderness towards her he hadn't felt for years. Crouching down until his face was on a level with her, he traced over the lines and shades of her unconscious face, which had a softness to it he never saw when she was awake.

A softness that enabled him to glimpse the girl he'd turned to when there was no-one else left to turn to – the girl he'd abandoned himself to before marriage – before the rest of their lives. Things went wrong after that – things they never thought about let alone spoke about because there was never time, and over time it became easier to just carry on. So that's what they did because that's what people do . . . they carry on and on and on.

There were moments over the years whose insignificance had an eerie vastness to them, when – standing in a supermarket queue or drying his hands in some public toilet somewhere or filling the car at a petrol station while watching the digits on the screen flicker and lose meaning – he recognised what was going on. He had two lives inside him – the one he was living and the one he could have lived, but wasn't that the same for everyone? How did that help and what on earth was he meant to do about it?

Then there were the debts, which had worked like a corrosive on the building that was their marriage – a building which had somehow managed to stay up despite the absence of any blueprint; a building which, throughout the years, Laura had been constantly adding rooms to in order to ensure that he never found his way out.

A better man could have loved her for that alone.

He stood up, pausing as his knees cracked loudly and looking around him at the outlines of familiar furniture in the light coming under the bedroom door from the hallway. Everything was the same as it had always been – the only thing that had changed was that he was missing from it.

He caught sight of himself then in the mirrors on the wardrobe doors and wondered who that man was standing in his bedroom – the blond hair shining strangely in the light from the hallway.

He remained in the doorway a minute more before turning away and walking back downstairs.

He left number two Marine Drive, and the Duneside development, crossing the road and walking past the play park and into the dunes, lying on his stomach in the damp sand and grass. He could just make out the candle burning in Martha's bedroom window, and a few seconds later the candle reached the end of its burning time and flickered out. He rolled over onto his back, staring up at the threads of cloud moving fast across the night sky – and the stars, which Martha once told him had already died by the time they came to lay eyes on them.

He'd made up his mind.

# 18

Laviolette was in his pyjamas still when Mrs Kelly arrived that morning. She ran her eyes over him – surprised then concerned – but didn't say anything. He stood in the kitchen doorway for a moment, aimless, watching her get Harvey's breakfast together while chatting nervously to Harvey who was drawing cubes with a neon marker at the kitchen table. She was nervous because Laviolette was watching and making an effort to understand the scene so that he could find some part to play in it.

Once Mrs Kelly had handed him his mug of coffee, he gave up and went back upstairs to his study where he phoned DC Wade to say he'd be in late. He didn't give a reason and, despite the hesitation in her voice, she didn't ask for one. Afterwards, he sat blowing on his coffee and contemplating his downfall – something he found curiously satisfying; cathartic, even.

He wasn't surprised that such an inauspicious career made up of seemingly insignificant incidents – failure to take a bribe here, failure to tamper with evidence there, failure to intimidate a witness here, failure to get blood on his fists in a dark room there – should culminate in this moment because a fact he'd come to realise over the years was that the more trustworthy he became the less likely those he worked for were to actually trust him.

Given his case record, they had to give him Detective Inspector, but they made it clear at the time that he'd reached his ceiling.

The way he'd handled the Bryan Deane case – the fact he'd been given it at all – had been pivotal, and it had been clear after yesterday's meeting with Jim Cornish that someone somewhere had decided his moment had come.

He sat in his old office chair, gently swinging it from side to side while starting to idly scrawl a frame round the bits of sellotape stuck to the surface of the desk – with a biro advertising a local insurance company. He thought about the day his father died – how he'd got the call and how he'd gone home to find Jim Cornish standing in the burnt out kitchen, and how his standing there had shocked and infuriated Laviolette almost more than what had happened.

The fire brigade was still there cleaning up when he arrived.

The smells of his childhood had vanished under the smell of smoke, burnt MDF, burnt lino, burnt vinyl and burnt flesh – his father's remains were under sheeting on the floor.

There were people everywhere, but wherever he turned the only face he saw was Jim Cornish's.

Turning away from him, Laviolette saw – through the door leading to the garden – Harvey's blue buggy tipped on its side.

'Harvey?' he said, to nobody in particular, feeling sick.

'Ambulance took him to hospital – burns unit,' Jim Cornish added, shaking his head.

'It's not serious,' another officer put in. 'He's fine – it's just routine. I can drive you there.' He swung, uncertain, towards Jim.

'What happened here?' Laviolette said at last. 'Who did this?'

'It could have been anyone,' Jim said, fixed on Laviolette now, 'I mean – given the state of things round here. The tensions –'

'The tensions,' Laviolette repeated stupidly.

'Everyone knows you've got two wages coming in here – and what with you in uniform.'

'Dad's a safety engineer,' Laviolette said. 'He's not NUM, he's NACODS. The National Union of Colliery Overmen, Deputies and Shotfirers decided not to strike.'

He remembered his father telling him, explaining patiently that if maintenance below ground wasn't kept up geological conditions would deteriorate to a state that would make it impossible for the pits to re-open. Going on strike would work against the cause.

Jim Cornish closed his mouth and puffed out his cheeks and didn't say anything – as if Laviolette wasn't getting the point.

A corner of the sheet covering Roger Laviolette's charred remains was caught under the toe of his boot.

'A neighbour says she saw a boy come in the back door here this afternoon, and we think we've got a match – to the description.'

'Who?'

'Jamie Deane.'

'Jamie Deane?' Laviolette repeated in the same stupid way as before.

Everybody standing in the burnt-out kitchen knew who the Deanes were, and everybody knew about Rachel Deane and his father. He could tell from the other officer's face that Jim Cornish wasn't meant to tell him about the neighbour's allegation, but it was too late now.

Laviolette knew that if Bobby had got to Jamie first, he

would have told him to say he was with him that afternoon, but Bobby didn't get there first.

Jim Cornish took Jamie Deane to Berwick Street station and Jamie told him the truth – that he'd spent the afternoon with Laura Hamilton; he could smell her still on his skin, crouched in the corner of the room with his arms wrapped round his head.

Laviolette was driven to the hospital to see Harvey, who they were keeping in overnight for observation. Everything had been choreographed to perfection. After the hospital, he was driven in the same car straight to Berwick Street station – in silence, with nothing to distract him from the image of Harvey lying curled in his hospital cot clutching the Sooty puppet he always slept with, the side of his face covered in a dressing from where he'd fallen against something or been pushed – nobody was clear about this.

Jamie Deane was lying in the same position as Harvey when Laviolette got to the station – only Jamie Deane was sandwiched between a large mattress and a brick wall in a dark room, and the team looking after him was headed by Jim Cornish.

The boy was all smashed up and Laviolette knew that he'd been brought to Berwick Street to smash him up some more; that it was permissible – expected of him, even. And that Jim Cornish desired this particularly.

On his way to the cells past the badly painted blue walls and dusty pot plants living out suspended life sentences, he passed Laura Hamilton and her parents – he didn't know then who she was, all he saw was a girl of about thirteen with long blonde hair, supported on either side by her parents – all three of them looking terrified.

'It's him,' Jim Cornish said, when Laviolette walked into the room, scraping his hair back into position. 'He just lost his only alibi.'

The face that peered up at Laviolette from behind the mattress had long ago stopped trying to differentiate between friend and foe, and was now working on the premise that anybody who walked into that room was foe.

Fifteen looked smaller than it sounded – especially lying crumpled behind a stained mattress on the floor.

The face was pale and discoloured.

It didn't look like a face that could have done what it was meant to have done to his father, but at that moment Jamie flinched and Laviolette felt a sudden charge of exhilaration – the sort he'd often seen on other men's faces during the Strike, whatever side they were on.

He'd never seen anyone flinch from him before, and it gave him such a rush that he finally let go of the parts of an upside down world he was still valiantly trying to hold onto.

It got to the point where Jamie Deane's body was no longer moving of its own accord, but only in response to his blows, and nothing had ever felt so good.

At some point Bobby Deane arrived at the station with a group of men – there were twelve of them altogether. Laviolette heard them as a distant roar, but had a sudden, clear picture of Bobby Deane in a corridor out there somewhere while only metres away, his son . . .

He looked down then at Jamie Deane – a long way down by his feet as if he was seeing him now for the first time, and seeing him, he was violently sick over the mattress lying on the floor that he'd asked Wilkins to take away.

Laviolette looked down at his desk in the study at four Coastguard Cottages – surprised to see that he'd scribbled a sequence of numbers, and even more surprised when he recognised them as his mother's Co-Op account number. The number he used to give the cashier when he was sent out for the groceries.

He was still staring at the numbers when his phone rang five minutes later.

It was Yvonne.

'They've got a problem,' she said, toneless. 'I ran a check on all missing persons –'

'And?'

'A couple of months ago, a girl called Alison Marsh had an argument with her boyfriend. He walked out, and she didn't hear from him so left it. After a while, she started leaving messages, which he never returned. She cried herself to sleep every night for weeks –'

'You just made that up,' Laviolette interrupted her.

'Yeah,' Yvonne agreed, 'I just made that up. But she did start phoning his friends only they reckoned they hadn't seen him either. Alison thought they were lying – covering for him – and was on the verge of dying of a broken heart when the boyfriend's mother phoned asking if Alison had seen Brett, because she hadn't heard anything from him in weeks. Alarm bells started ringing then, and a couple of days later Alison and Brett's mother filed a Missing Persons with Newcastle police. Friends and family have heard nothing since then.

'Tell me about Brett,' Laviolette said, his eyes fixed still on the numbers he'd scrawled into the desk.

'He shouldn't have argued with his girlfriend.'

'Something else.'

'Male – Caucasian – thirty-three years old on his last birthday.' Yvonne paused. 'You're smiling.'

'Did Brett have any defining features?'

'Defining as in features that would clarify, beyond a doubt, that there was no way Brett could be mistaken for Bryan Deane – or vice versa?'

'Yeah, those kind of defining features.'

'He had a moth – not a butterfly, a moth, Alison was

particular about that – tattooed on his left ankle over the Achilles tendon. Laviolette? If you're going to do what I think you're going to do –'

'Yvonne,' he said, 'can you still remember your mother's Co-Op account number?'

She responded, without hesitation, 'Five-one-six-two-five.'

Then the line went dead.

Bull & Dunnings offices – where Alison Marsh worked – were in a moderately sized building of steel and blue glass that already looked outdated, on a side street behind the Laing Art Gallery. On the rare occasions that he found himself in Newcastle with time to spare, Laviolette always did one of three things – went to the Hancock Museum, took a walk down Grey Street to the Quayside or went to see the Winslow Homer paintings at the Laing. There used to be a Mexican restaurant nearby that he ate at regularly with a social worker he dated seriously in his early thirties, but the social worker and Mexican restaurant had since disappeared.

A young woman with a pair of scissors in her hands was on reception, behind an elaborate flower display. When he got close enough to ask for Alison Marsh and explain that he worked for Northumbria Police, he saw that the woman was around eight-months pregnant and that she was cutting out a frieze of teddy bears – presumably destined for a nursery wall.

She didn't ask to see his badge and, after watching him for a while from under her fringe, asked if he wanted something to drink.

He shook his head, smiling, and continued to shuffle restlessly round the shabby lobby waiting for Alison Marsh to appear.

Behind the security door to the left of reception, Alison left the safety of her carpet-lined booth decorated with reminders scribbled on neon post-it notes, and tokens from a life more personal – and went into the lobby where Laviolette was waiting for her.

They shook hands and Alison's eyes, which looked scared, remained fixed on him as he introduced himself and asked to speak to her in private.

'It's bad news,' the pleasant dependable-looking girl who was Alison Marsh stated, quietly, turning to the receptionist. 'Lindsay, can you book meeting room three for the next . . .' she turned back to Laviolette, 'thirty minutes?'

'We won't need thirty minutes.'

'I might.'

'It's booked,' Lindsay announced.

Laviolette could tell from the way she walked through the maze of hollow corridors lined with old black and white prints of Newcastle landmarks that she was fairly certain why he'd come.

'What d'you do?' he asked her.

'I'm a conveyancer. I work with a team of conveyancers,' she added, unnecessarily, speaking in the way Laviolette was used to hearing people speak when they were in shock.

'This is about Brett,' she said, standing just inside the door to meeting room three, holding the handle still.

'I'm afraid so.'

She sat down at the long beige table with a tray of glasses in the middle and a plastic folder someone somewhere was probably looking for. She sat turned slightly away from him, her left hand on the table, her right in her lap, and started to cry.

'D'you mind getting me something for my face?' she said after a while, unevenly.

He left the room, found a ladies toilet, knocked loudly on the door, and walked in past a woman doing her make-up who watched him in the mirror, outraged, as he disappeared into a cubicle and emerged with a roll of toilet paper.

Although she was in exactly the same position he'd left her in, Alison was no longer crying when he got back to meeting room three – she was sitting very still, and the room felt emptier than if there was nobody there at all. This moment had changed her forever, and Laviolette was tired of changing people, he realised.

She turned to him, looking to him for guidance because she had no experience of moments like these. He could tell, from her face, that she already felt marked – set apart. The usual rapid, random thoughts ran through his head, prompted by a curiosity that had remained intact, unlike a lot of officers who'd been on the force as long as he had. Was it Brett who'd bought her the necklace she was wearing? What time did she set her alarm for in the morning?

'This isn't over yet, is it?' she said, already sounding a little less lost.

Laviolette shook his head. 'Unfortunately not – I need you to come with me.'

'Now?'

She got unsteadily to her feet and allowed him to take hold of her left elbow, which he could feel through the fabric of her shirt. They went back into the corridor where she looked around her, bewildered, as if the layout of the building she'd worked in for eight years had been reconfigured while they were inside meeting room three. The familiarity had been taken out of her world and now she was looking at him as if he was the only thing she recognised.

'Where are we going?'

'I'm sorry, but we need you to identify Brett for us. You might want to pick up your things – tell someone you're going.'

She stared at him flatly, no longer horrified.

Laviolette knew what was coming next and he was tired of this as well, he realised – tired of being the one who always knew what was coming next.

DC Wade was waiting for them at the mortuary.

He'd asked her to be there.

At this point, she either went to Jim Cornish to clear the request because she knew that Laviolette shouldn't be doing an identification on a body that had already been identified – or she kept quiet and showed up when and where he told her to show up.

She'd chosen to keep quiet and show up, and he couldn't pretend not to be happy about this.

Alison Marsh, looking as if she'd been rushed out of one life and into another she never knew existed, let DC Wade hold her as they went into the small, tiled windowless room Laura Deane had walked into the day before.

He'd told her on the drive over that the body had been washed up at Cullercoats, and the only thing she'd said in response to this was to comment on the rain, which had started suddenly – breaking violently over them just outside Gosforth.

Alison remained pressed close to DC Wade as an assistant called Shona showed her the left ankle.

They all saw the moth attached still to skin that no longer looked like skin.

Alison nodded, her hand gripping DC Wade's forearm.

'D'you need some air? D'you want to take a breather?'

Alison nodded again, but remained where she was.

After a few moments silence, and without saying anything Laviolette nodded at Shona to uncover the face.

'That's not him. Brett,' she said, in the same breath.

There was a suspended sense of relief in the room that

Laviolette often felt at positive identifications when something no longer identifiable as human, was given a name.

'We argued,' Alison said, starting to cry, looking helplessly round the room at all of them for some sort of atonement.

# 19

The weather had turned.

Autumn, which had felt more like a late summer that year, was passing into winter and Anna felt the pinch of it with a quiet exhilaration as she ran down onto the beach. A grey sky was hung out over the sea, the wind picking up the waves and dropping them. She knew what seas like these felt like because they were her seas; the seas she'd grown up with. These were seas you fought with.

As the wind ripped through her now, grazing her face with sand it had lifted from the dunes and spray it had skimmed from the breaking waves, she started to feel – finally – that elusive sense of belonging she'd been searching for since Easter. This grey country with its occasional days of respite when it felt as though someone had unearthed stock-piled boxes of sunlight and, overjoyed, emptied them all at once, might just be her country after all.

She didn't know whether it was the oppressive bleakness she remembered from childhood, so often mistaken for being inarticulate by outsiders – or the growing intimacy with Laviolette – but she'd never told anybody the things she told him –

She carried on running, wiping at her face which was wet with sea spray and the drizzle now starting to fall.

The only other person on the beach was a bundled-up woman down at the water's edge, yelling at a black Labrador standing watching her, motionless.

Then she saw him – the blond man who'd been in the Polish woman's flat yesterday when she and Laviolette went to the Ropemakers Building.

Then she recognised him – and it was confirmation of what she'd somehow known since then even though it was only a glimpse she'd caught of him, passing through the hallway.

Not knowing what to do, she carried on running, feeling sicker each time she landed on the sand, the wind in her ears hurting and disorientating her.

The man walking along the edge of the dunes towards her had blond hair and was taller than she remembered. He looked nothing like Bryan Deane – who used to have brown hair with auburn tints when the sun shone down on him. She'd seen the auburn standing next to him outside number seventeen Parkview, Easter Saturday.

But she knew it was him.

She kept on running.


Jim Cornish and Laviolette were in Jim Cornish's office. Jim was sitting behind his desk in the same position as the day before while Jim's wife and children, encased in various combinations inside various frames, were staring at Laviolette in the same unnerving, unsmiling way: rugby playing Richard, suicidal Dom, and the nameless girls referred to simply – by Jim himself – as 'the girls', denoting their supporting role within the family.

Laviolette was regarding Jim, who didn't look as if he'd moved at all since the day before, which had the odd effect of making Jim himself as well as Jim's accessories – the photographs and golf trophies – seem somehow less real; caught out, almost.

Jim was furious.

He didn't show it, but Laviolette could feel it as he watched Jim rub his thumb slowly backwards and forwards along the edge of the desk.

Laviolette had come straight from the mortuary to torment him.

It was a long time since anybody had attempted to torment him, and Jim was having trouble working out why it was that Laviolette had chosen this particular course of action.

After a while, aware that one of them had to speak otherwise the moment was at risk of slipping silently out of his grasp, Laviolette said, 'Brett Taylor had a tattoo – a moth just above the Achilles tendon on his left foot.'

'Says who?' Jim demanded, quietly, from the middle of a migraine that had been brewing since yesterday, and started in earnest about thirty minutes ago.

'The Missing Persons report.'

'Which you . . . just happened to have to hand?' Jim moved his lips into a long, narrow smile, which made them change colour.

He jerked his hand instinctively to his forehead, pressing down hard on the bridge of his nose with his fingertips, and momentarily shutting his eyes.

'Brett Taylor and Bryan Deane were the same age, same height, and matched similar descriptions, living. Worrying similarities –'

'Worrying,' Jim echoed, laughing. He carried on laughing for what felt like quite a while after that, his eyes on Laviolette.

'For the purposes of identification,' Laviolette finished. 'How many drowned corpses have you seen?'

Jim started at the question before giving it some serious thought. 'Two,' he said almost a minute later. Jim had always been precise, and particular about precision not only in himself, but in others as well – regardless of whether or not they were telling the truth. There was nothing vague about Jim.

'They all look the bloody same,' he concluded loudly.

Laviolette nodded. 'That's why I was concerned about Laura Deane's positive ID. A defining feature – like Brett's tattoo – helps. Laura was probably too upset to notice. It happens,' he added, expansively.

Jim stood up suddenly, shunting his chair back harder than he'd meant to so that it travelled across the carpeted floor fast, just reaching the wall behind Jim's desk where one of the wheels gave a faint tap on the skirting board, which Laviolette noticed was badly chipped.

Jim observed him with his mouth open, sinking his hands in his pocket and making an effort to control his breathing, but his face didn't relax and his eyes remained protruding without expression fixed on Laviolette.

He said, 'What d'you want?'

'Why did you assign me this case?' Laviolette surprised himself; this wasn't what he'd been going to say.

Ignoring the question, Jim said, 'We've got two missing persons – descriptions match – and only one body. We can work it out mathematically.' He raised his head slightly and jerked it towards the corner of the room as if there was a third party with them. 'What d'you want?' he asked again.

'I want you to tell me who killed my father.'

Jim started laughing again – loudly, genuinely.


Bryan watched Anna run past, a feverish smile on his face that nobody was there to bear witness to.

He'd spent the night on the beach, in the dunes, and his

body told him he was unwell. There was sand in his hair, his clothes were damp and he was varying between hot and cold – intermittent shudders passing through him. He'd woken in a hollow in the dunes well after first light to a grey, inhospitable day and the sound of children playing nearby. After using the car park toilets, he watched a woman turn a roundabout with two children on, laughing – until the woman became aware of him. There were many things lonely men weren't meant to do, and staring at children in a play park was definitely one of them.

He started to walk, heading along the dunes north towards Blyth, the Alcan towers and wind turbines at Blyth Harbour becoming closer. Even this far from the waterline, the air was full of sea spray – he could feel it on his face and hair. There was nobody on the beach apart from a woman with a Labrador, the dog standing expectant in the rolling waves, which were churning and breaking continuously – an even heavier grey than the sky. He pushed his hands in his jacket pocket, cold, only to find himself sweating a minute later.

Then, looking up, he saw her running along the beach towards him. It had to be her – it was right that they should meet on the beach like this. He saw her head turn in his direction and stopped, waiting. She seemed to hesitate for a moment, but then carried on running. He stood watching her, and it was how she'd always made him feel – like nothing more than an observer. The smaller her retreating figure became, the more bereft he felt. He'd been lonely most of his life since losing his mother, but it was only ever Anna who'd had the ability to remind him of this loneliness that had, over the years – and without him being aware of it – come to define him.

It occurred to him, standing there in the wind and drizzle that was starting, that all he had to do was run after her; catch her up, but he knew he wasn't going to do that. She had to turn and come back to him – retrace her steps – at some point. Nobody could run in one direction forever. The world might no longer be flat, but there were still edges a person could fall off.

He turned and carried on walking north, in the opposite direction – convinced, at last, that this was the only way they'd ever meet.


'You knew Jamie Deane was innocent – he had an alibi you chose to break. Why?'

Laviolette watched Jim slide some papers with his fore-finger across the desk and scan them with a heavy sigh.

'D'you remember Laura Hamilton – before she became Laura Deane?'

'Of course,' Jim said, pleasantly – it was no effort to him; he didn't begrudge Laviolette demanding this memory of him. 'She was a sweet thing – a very sweet thing. I imagine she still is – from her voice. I've only spoken to her on the phone.'

Laviolette saw Laura, walking up the corridor towards him at Berwick Street station, propped between Don and Doreen. 'She was only thirteen.'

Jim didn't dispute this; he just carried on smiling pleasantly at Laviolette, waiting for him to make his point.

'You forced her to lie – about being with Jamie that after-noon. Why? Why did you want it to be Jamie Deane that badly?'

As he sat down again Jim shook his head, pulling his hands up and clasping them behind it – with an affected boredom Laviolette could almost have believed if the eyes hadn't remained so alert. 'We didn't. That wasn't our choice.'

'So whose was it?'

'Bobby's – Bobby Deane's,' Jim said, distracted, his eyes running over the photographs on his desk. He flicked a quick look at his watch. 'I've got somewhere to be in six minutes.'

Ignoring this, Laviolette said, 'How?'

Yawning, Jim let his arms fall. 'We thought about nailing it on Bobby for a while, but it wasn't going to stick – not even when he realised we had Jamie, and he wanted it to stick.'

'The neighbour said she saw a boy go into the house through the kitchen door.'

Jim waved this to one side. 'And her description matched at least one of the Deanes. It made sense – everyone knew your father and Rachel Deane were screwing around. Everyone –' He was staring straight at Laviolette now, his arms laid out on the desk in front of him. 'Motive was never an issue; it was more a question of which Deane? We rounded up Bobby and Jamie, but we couldn't find the other one – Bryan. Nobody knew where he was, but we had two of them and we only needed one. We put the situation to Bobby – told him what had happened with your father, and that we were thinking of charging him. He gave us the name of at least twenty alibis. I can still see his face as he listed them, name after name – angry; triumphant. He thought he'd won.'

'It should never have been a game.'

'Maybe not,' Jim conceded, pushing his lips together. 'But we were young, and –' He gave a short laugh. 'The opportunity presented itself.' He looked at his watch again. 'I've got to be somewhere in three minutes. We called his bluff. We had Jamie in the other cell, and we put it to Bobby then, after he'd drawn over twenty alibis out the hat – that if it wasn't him, which it couldn't have been, it must have been Jamie who killed your dad.'

'He didn't know you had Jamie until then?'

Jim shook his head, laughing. 'He went – Fuck, you can imagine – broke Kyle's nose and started to tear his ear off. . . .' Jim was laughing uncontrollably now, 'before we managed to restrain him. He'd walked right into it.' Jim rubbed at his eyes, wheezing as the laughter came to a halt. 'God, that feels good – can't remember the last time I laughed like that.'

Laviolette stood motionless, staring at him. He could almost feel Bobby's fury – the horrible realisation of his own impotence – across a distance of over twenty years; the realisation that he'd absolved himself only to implicate his own son.

'Of course he backtracked then,' Jim carried on, enjoying himself now and no longer requiring prompts from Laviolette, 'but it was too late. We told him we had a witness, and that the description she gave us of the boy entering your kitchen could have matched either of his boys.'

The break in the tape, Laviolette thought. The break in the Bobby Deane tape that Anna had picked up on the night before.

'But Jamie had an alibi.'

'Yeah,' Jim agreed.

'You believed him?'

'Course we believed him. I might not be a very nice copper – in your book – but I'm a bloody good one. I'd done enough interrogations to know the truth when I heard and saw it. Jamie Deane had been doing exactly what he said he'd been doing all afternoon – screwing his girlfriend. No doubt about it.' Jim stood up. 'We told Bobby it was definitely one of his boys – that we were having one of them.'

'You asked him to make a choice?'

Jim nodded, looking suddenly serious. 'He chose Jamie.'

'And that's why you broke Laura? That's why you broke his alibi?'

'At least we gave him a bloody choice,' Jim yelled suddenly. 'Christ,' he spat, in conclusion to his outburst. Then, after a while, he said quietly, 'People talk about women

305

crying, but in my time I've seen more men cry than I ever have any woman.'

Laviolette looked at him. 'So you knew it wasn't Jamie? And Bobby knew it wasn't Jamie?'

'It was Bryan who killed him.'

'And you all knew?'

'We all knew – Bobby knew.' Jim picked his jacket off the back of his chair, holding onto his shirt cuffs and pulling it slowly on.

'But why did he choose the innocent son?'

'It was his choice. You know the story in the Bible – about Joseph being the favourite son. Well we each have our Joseph; it's human nature.' Jim paused here without intending to. 'We told him he had twenty-four hours to find Bryan an alibi – and to find Bryan. He was back in hours.'

'Who was Bryan's alibi?'

Jim finished shrugging his jacket on, turning to glance briefly at his reflection in the glass doors of the bookcase. 'Mary Faust. You knew that already. Can I go now?'

He walked past Laviolette to the office door, holding it open. 'Are you staying or going?'

Laviolette stayed where he was, thinking.

'I'm meant to be somewhere – thirty seconds. They're fitting me with a pacemaker next month. I don't run any more.'

'Alison Marsh gave us a positive ID on the body at the mortuary. She was sure anyway, but the tattoo placed it beyond a doubt. I drove her there myself. DC Wade acted as witness. Should I contact Laura Deane or . . .?'

Jim held onto his office door. 'Nobody comes out of something like this completely clean. Not even in private. Why does Jamie Deane's innocence matter so much to you now? Twenty years ago the only thing you asked for was the mattress to be taken away.' He let go of the door and stepped up to Laviolette as it clicked quietly shut. 'You didn't care then. That boy was barely breathing when you finished with him. You could have been a very different man, Laviolette.'

'Maybe, but I like myself the way I am.'

'You do?' Jim said, genuinely surprised.

Since his death, Mary had been prescribing herself Erwin's morphine. She'd also taken to carrying the tablets around with her whenever she left the house because these days anything and everything had the potential to terrify her while catastrophe seemed so inevitable and imminent it often left her breathless. Carrying the morphine around with her made her less afraid, and gave her back the dignity robbed her by fear. As soon as she shut the gate to number nineteen Parkview, she tapped her pocket to check for the now familiar rattle before – reassured – embarking on whatever journey she needed to embark on in pursuit of life's necessities despite life itself having ceased to feel necessary.

People she met – young and not so young – seemed to be under the impression that because she was old, her loss could be counted as bearable. It wasn't. Life had become unbearable, and the one person she felt like telling was Erwin, who was no longer there – and that, she realised, was one of the defining cruelties of grief: the cause of it was also the only cure for it.

She stood in the kitchenette, unaware of the time, listening to the quiet house. Houses were never silent – she could hear an isolated drop falling from a tap in the bathroom, the muffled clank of the old fashioned toilet cistern and the click of the central heating installed in the early nineties – but number nineteen Parkview had definitely become quiet as she moved, uncertain, through it leaving barely any trace. She'd found that if she waited until midnight before going to bed, she could sleep through until at least four – maybe five. She ate breakfast in the kitchenette while it was still dark, the blinds down and the orange light humming overhead. After that she sat in one of the rocking chairs in the lounge, waiting for dawn. Sometime after dawn the family in the house next door – number twenty-one – stirred; the man first if he was on the early shift at the Nissan factory; heavy footed. Then came the sound of the child – running feet, slamming doors . . . TV. The walls were thin and she heard most things that went on in the house next door, reassured by the rhythms and noises of their family life.

Once their TV went on, Mary put on hers, watching it without really understanding any of it, unsure how much longer she could carry on like this.

The first few weeks after the funeral, Don and Doreen had been good to her – having her round to lunch most days. If Don was playing golf, she'd pop next door and watch the Jerry Springer show with Doreen. Don drove her to the supermarket Friday mornings, and took her up to the club for a white wine and soda Friday nights, but she didn't like to lean too heavily on people – it wasn't how she'd been brought up.

It was a grey day today and with the kitchenette light on she was able to see – clearly – her reflection in the window as she pushed a strip of tablets into the pocket of the powder blue Mac she'd bought with Anna in Newcastle.

Outside, Don was getting into his car with his golf caddy, wearing a pair of plaid trousers that would have looked ridiculous on a more competitive man, but Don was so ready to laugh at himself that others rarely had to.

Mary could tell from the way he greeted her that he knew where she was going, which was why – without any preliminaries – Don was able to say to her now, 'Mary – he's gone. I was about to come and tell you.'

Mary stared at him as he watched her, uncertain. 'Bobby – he's gone.'

'Bobby?' she said. It was a long time since she'd heard Don say his name. 'Where?'

'Somewhere he can get the right sort of care. Social services have been trying to contact Bryan – Laura told us.' Don hesitated, unsure what else there was to say. An apology – expression of sympathy – didn't seem appropriate. 'Are you alright?'

Mary nodded dumbly as, after another moment's hesitation, Don got into his car.

She watched the car disappear then went back indoors, her hand shaking as she tried fitting the key in the lock. Shutting the front door behind her, she went into the kitchenette, and stood there in her Mac still, in darkness, for she didn't know how long.

She was at a loss.

Eventually, without being conscious of having come to any sort of decision, she turned on the light and filled her pockets with the remainder of the dwindling morphine supplies – as well as everything else Erwin had been prescribed that was still on the bench. Crouching with difficulty, she got a freezer bag out of the box under the sink and filled it with pills, carefully sealing it.

She caught sight of herself again, briefly – in the reflection in the window. So this is what it looks like, she thought – after almost half a century of marriage, this is what the end looks like.

She left the house for a second time.

Don's car was still gone.

She walked to Armstrong Crescent at around the same time as usual, letting herself in. She felt, instinctively, the curtains twitching in the bungalow next door, but Mary had the measure of the Mrs Harrises of this world; the gossip

309

mongers and fire starters who, unsatisfied with their own lives and unsure how to go about getting the ones they felt entitled to, destroyed the lives of others instead.

She went inside, automatically calling out, 'Bobby?'

It wasn't that she doubted Don; she just couldn't believe that Bobby had really gone, but as she walked through rooms as empty as those at number nineteen Parkview, she knew it was true.

They'd taken most of his clothes from the wardrobe and chest of drawers, but not all of them. Looking about her it was difficult to see what else they might have taken – he didn't have much. She sat down, exhausted, on the side of the bed, which had been left unmade, thinking about the day Roger Laviolette died.

Her mind turned unconsciously to that day because it was the last time Bobby had needed her; really needed her. She'd been his first thought that day – after he was released from Berwick Street station.

He hadn't turned to anybody else.

She'd been downstairs in the kitchenette at Parkview. Anna was upstairs in the bath, upset still, and when she'd looked through the window there was Bobby standing in the garden near the rhubarb, his face the wrong colour and loose looking.

She went out to him.

Roger Laviolette was dead and Bobby had come to her.

At first she thought it was a confession, but then he told her – pulling her after him into their wash house – that he'd just come from Berwick Street station; that a neighbour had seen one of his boys enter Roger Laviolette's house.

'Which one?'

'They've got Jamie,' he said, helplessly, turning to pull on her arms in the twilight.

'Who have?'

310

'Police.'

'It was Jamie who did it?'

He shook his head. 'It wasn't Jamie – no.'

'It couldn't have been Bryan – the neighbour must of got it wrong.'

He looked at her then, and seeing her face started to cry.

She'd been too shocked to react as Bobby stood in the wash house sobbing and clinging to her.

'No,' she said spontaneously. 'He couldn't of –'

'He did.'

'No.' Again.

'I've got to hand one of them over. I've got to give one of them up.'

He'd pulled away from her then. It was getting darker by the minute, but she could make out his face – and eyes.

'But Bryan did it, Bobby. It was Bryan.'

'I can't give them Bryan, Mary. Not Bryan. She'd never forgive me.'

'Rachel's dead, Bobby.'

'I'm not giving them Bryan.' He took hold of her again then, pulling her close – and she let him, knowing she'd do anything he asked her to.

'Where is Bryan?'

'Home.'

'You've seen him?'

Bobby looked away. 'Tell them he spent the afternoon here – with you and Anna. Tell them that.'

He'd come to her because he knew she would; he'd come to her because he couldn't help knowing – even after Rachel; even after Erwin – what he'd once been to her and still was. He'd been powerless that night Rachel walked into the dance hall. He'd known what it had done to Mary and he'd have done anything to lessen the hurting, but there was nothing he could do. Where Rachel was concerned, he was powerless. When Rachel walked into the dance hall that night he remembered her in her pinafore at the foot of the dunes, feeding his pit pony. He knew he'd been waiting for her ever since.

And Mary knew exactly what that felt like.

An hour later when Jamie came banging into the bungalow on Armstrong Crescent looking for his father – shouting out his name and thumping so hard on the walls that the barometer in the lounge jumped off its hook and fell to the floor – he found Mary asleep on the bed in her powder blue Mac still, halfway through Erwin's prescription drugs. There was a thin line of saliva curling out of the left hand side of her open mouth, and her left shoe had fallen to the floor, revealing a foot that had been misshapen in youth by dancing in badly fitting shoes.

Jamie stared down at her, worried, but not upset – trying to work out what she meant. He didn't know what to think – or who she was.

By the time it occurred to him to check her breathing, Inspector Laviolette was pulling up outside the bungalow.

Laviolette saw Mrs Harris positioned in her usual spot, and waved.

The front door was already open and he pushed it back, walking quickly, silently through the bungalow until he came to Bobby's bedroom at the back.

'Jamie,' he exhaled, taking in Mary Faust on the bed, and Jamie Deane lying beside her.

Jamie spun round, terrified – recognising Laviolette properly for the first time – and got clumsily to his feet, momentarily losing his balance. His hand went out to Mary's left leg – which had been balanced precariously on the edge of the bed – for support.

The leg slipped over the edge and the rest of Mary followed until she was lying face down on the carpet, her arms twisted uncomfortably under her.

'It wasn't me!' Jamie shouted, backing towards the wall.

'I know – I know that now.' Laviolette crouched instinctively – as he would have done with a frightened child – trying to make himself less immense. It wasn't until he'd said it that he realised he wasn't talking about Mary – lying face down on the floor between them both.

Jamie, backed up against the wall, stared down at the Inspector, his eyes wide.

He was taller – bigger altogether – than Laviolette, but he'd retained childhood's perspective on his childhood tormentor.

'I didn't do it –'

'I know that, Jamie, and I'm sorry – I'm so very sorry.'

Jamie kept glancing from the Inspector to Mary Faust, concerned – not about Mary's state, but about the implications of that state on him. He didn't know what Laviolette was doing here in the bungalow on Armstrong Crescent after all these years, and he didn't know whether to believe him – or not.

Laviolette shuffled, crouching, over to Mary – worried that Jamie would run.

'She's still alive,' he said, checking her pulse. He glanced up at Jamie. 'How long have you been here for?'

'I didn't do it,' he protested.

'Of course you didn't,' Laviolette tried to calm him, 'I'm just trying to ascertain how long she's been lying here for. We need to phone for an ambulance. Either you can do that – or I can do it.'

Jamie tried to think about this, but he was too confused still, and becoming more irate by the second.

'Jamie we need to do this now.'

Laviolette remained crouched on the floor, his left hand on Mary's neck.

'Who is she?'

'A friend of your father's.'

Jamie glanced at Mary – Laviolette's response didn't explain much. 'You phone for the ambulance.'

He watched as Laviolette made the phone call, his movements slow and deliberate as he took the phone out of his pocket and dialled, his eyes never leaving Jamie's face.

'Where's your dad?'

Laviolette moved slowly, awkwardly, to a standing position holding onto the wardrobe doors, the hangers clanging emptily on the shuddering rail.

'He's gone,' Jamie said blankly, staring into the virtually empty wardrobe. Then again, in disbelief – looking to Laviolette for an explanation – 'He's gone.'

'Social services,' Laviolette said, thinking of the phone calls he'd made.

'Why?'

'He wasn't well, Jamie. He needs round the clock care.'

'You sorted it up – with social services?'

'It needed doing, and nobody else –'

'Why?'

'Because I could.'

'I don't believe you,' Jamie said, suddenly decisive.

'He'll have been taken to one of two places – it won't take long to find him.'

'I don't want to find him – I want to kill him.' Jamie's eyes rolled upwards and his face opened as he let out a brief laugh. 'What did you think? I was only fifteen – I didn't know what twenty years meant. I let them put me away so that they wouldn't put him away. I thought he'd love me for it. I let them put me away because of the promise of that love.' Jamie was shouting now, but he was shouting carefully – he wanted somebody other than himself to understand what he'd gone through. 'I thought it would be enough to last me twenty years – that promise – but it barely lasted me one. It barely lasted me one,' he said again, 'because he never came to visit me. My father never came to visit me – not once – after what I'd done for him, and when I get out – when I come here after twenty years – he doesn't even remember me; doesn't even remember my fucking name. It wasn't me.'

'And it wasn't him either, Jamie. It wasn't Bobby. Bobby never killed my father.'

Laviolette stopped speaking as he realised what it was he'd said.

Jamie looked suddenly bereft at the thought of not only his own, but his father's innocence – after all these years. Bobby's innocence affected him even more than his own. 'How d'you know?' he asked. His mind felt strangely empty, but there were things he should be asking – important things. He was missing the point – he was always missing the point. He got everything and everybody wrong and he was tired of trying to live with the consequences; profoundly tired. He was so exhausted, in fact, that he could have lain down on the bed he'd found Mary on and slept forever. But before he did – and he could feel the bones starting to relax already at the thought of the bed – there was something he needed to know. His eyes, heavy lidded, rested on Laviolette and with an effort he said, 'So if it wasn't me, and it wasn't him then who –' He broke off, realisation shaking off the soporific effects of shock. 'You know who it was, don't you?'

He crossed the room and took hold of Laviolette, who'd been anticipating contact, but there was nothing he could do to brace himself against Jamie as he was pushed back against the wardrobe with such force that the wardrobe fell against the wall.

Laviolette lay sprawled inside.

'Bryan,' Jamie said. 'It was Bryan, and you knew. He knew as well, didn't he – my father? He knew it was Bryan.'

Laviolette had caught his leg on something metal inside the wardrobe. He felt a sharp, stinging pain and a line of blood – wet – running down his calf. He heard the sound of ambulance sirens carried irregularly by the wind.

'Bryan,' Jamie said again. 'Why did he give me up when it was Bryan who did it? Why?'

'They made him choose one of you – it was an impossible choice.'

'And he chose me – even though he knew I was innocent. He chose me, and that's what I've got to start living with now after the twenty years I've already done. This is the real life sentence starting.'

Laviolette could see, through the bedroom curtains, the lights of the ambulance parking outside. Any minute now, paramedics would be there in the room with them, moving – green and efficient – through a twenty-year-old story.

Jamie was shaking his head. 'Laura said a body was washed up.'

Laviolette knew what he was going to do next, and that he shouldn't – for all sorts of reasons. What he didn't know was why he was doing it. Was it because of the scared, broken child who'd peered up at him from behind the mattress all those years ago, and who had been haunting him for too long? Was it because of what Anna had told him about Bryan Deane the night before, and how she'd looked the morning after, asleep still on the sofa in his study? Was it because of the way he'd come home that night twenty years ago to find Jim Cornish in filthy boots moving through his house? Was it the memory of the sheet covering his father's humped remains? Or was it because he was tired of other people deciding how this was going to end for him?

316

'A body was found, but it wasn't Bryan's. He's still alive.'

'Where?' Jamie demanded quietly.

Through the wardrobe doors, beyond Jamie, he saw paramedics enter the room, rapidly assess the situation and somehow manage to attend to Mary, push Jamie towards the bedroom door, and pull him carefully out of the wardrobe in an effort not to tear any more of his leg. The pain was worse, standing.

'Where?' Jamie said again from the door.

'Royal Quays Marina – North Shields. The Ropemakers Building – flat twenty-one.'

It felt as though the room was suddenly full of people, but Jamie had gone.

Jamie had at last gone.

It wasn't until he saw Mary being wheeled through the bungalow towards the ambulance parked outside that he realised he should tell Anna. Anna needed to know about Mary.

Half way down Quay Road, Anna stopped running.

He was sitting on a quayside bench straight ahead, watching the wind turbines while being watched in turn by Roy the Harbourmaster, propped slackly in the open doorway to the office, finishing a cigarette.

Hearing her footsteps, Roy turned – his eyes thin as he inhaled.

He gave her a silent wave then, seeing that her attention was directed towards the man on the bench, turned to contemplate him once more himself.

The day wasn't warm and although she'd been sweating only minutes before, was cooling off rapidly.

The rigging was ringing loudly against the masts of the trawlers and the trawlers themselves were rocking in wide arcs. Waves were breaking over the feet of the turbines, and beyond the north harbour wall the sea wasn't even making an attempt at hospitality.

She carried on walking, aware of Roy watching her as she passed, and just then the man on the bench – it *was* Bryan – turned instinctively towards her.

He didn't smile.

He watched her until she was close enough to press her thighs into the back of the bench he was sitting on.

The eyes were wide and bright, the cheeks more sunken and defined than she remembered from Easter, but she looked into his face in the same way she had all those months ago when she'd been looking for signs of Bryan Deane.

He smiled now – a thin, feverish smile.

'Hello Anna.'

'Hello Bryan.'

They contemplated each other, less inhibited than the last time when he'd still been alive.

'You're not surprised,' he said, getting stiffly to his feet, placing his hands over hers where she was holding onto the back of the bench. 'Does anything ever surprise you?' He continued to smile, happy.

The sound of the wind turbines beating loudly, close by, made her feel as if they weren't on land at all, but the deck of some strange machine preparing to take off.

'You knew I hadn't really disappeared.'

'I didn't want it to be true.'

Roy remained in the doorway to the Harbourmaster's office, unashamed at his curiosity, watching them until they disappeared into the Ridley Arms.

He flicked his head up briefly as the lights in the upstairs apartment went on – a warm, white defiant light that didn't do much to counteract the grey day. But still, ships at sea would be able to see it – if they were headed landwards.

He coughed for quite a while after throwing the stub of

318

his roll-up down the drain. Then, straightening up, decided that there wasn't much happening on the quayside – so went back into the office feeling as though some weight he hadn't been aware of until then had been lifted. He definitely felt lighter; renewed almost.

He set to work again with a satisfied sigh.

Laura knew the flat was empty as soon as she opened the front door and stepped inside. She also knew that this time Bryan really had disappeared.

Nothing reasonable led her to this conclusion.

There was nothing out of place; no signs of definitive departure, and nothing for her to read. It was as if the air in the flat had absorbed his intentions, and it was these intentions that she could feel as she stood in the middle of the lounge-diner, staring about her, her bag and keys in her hands still.

If she added up the hours spent here in the past few months they wouldn't amount to very much, but it felt as though over half her life had been lived in those hours. Here, between the cornflower blue walls they'd painted themselves, she was neither Laura Hamilton or Laura Deane. She was nobody's daughter, wife or mother, but simply Laura. She'd come to know herself intimately here in a way she never had before. What did she do with that knowledge now?

She crossed the room and opened the balcony doors, stepping outside. The day was one of those infectiously grey days. She breathed in, shutting her eyes. As she exhaled slowly, she opened them again taking in the car park down below, the boats in the marina, the River Tyne wide here near its mouth, and the North Sea beyond, but it was as if nothing she laid her eyes on held any relevance to her any more.

319

She needed to cry, but couldn't. She was too furious.

The realisation that she was furious took her by surprise, and explained the tightness she felt in her chest.

Smelling cigarette smoke then, she turned and saw the Polish woman in her dressing gown on the balcony next door, staring out at the same things she'd been staring at.

Then she turned to stare at Laura, exhaling heavily.

Laura couldn't think of anything to say, and was about to go back inside when the Polish woman said, 'He's gone, hasn't he?'

Laura nodded, dumbly, watching the descent of the woman's cigarette butt over the edge of the balcony.

'D'you want to come round?'

Less than a minute later, Laura was standing in the corridor about to knock on the door to flat twenty-three when it was opened from the inside.

Without thinking, she let the woman wrap her arms around her, pressing her head gently against her shoulder. She smelt of sleep, old perfume and cigarette smoke, and she had her back up against the hallway wall as Laura collapsed, sobbing, into her.

After a while the woman managed to pull her gently into the lounge.

Laura stood in the kitchen doorway watching as the woman poured water from the kettle into a glass and handed it to her. The glass was full of something red.

'Raspberry tea,' she explained, seeing Laura's face.

Laura nodded, her attention taken by the drawings on the fridge door. 'These are you?' she asked, studying them.

'I'm a life model – at the college.'

'Bryan did these, didn't he?' she said, realising – too late – what she'd said.

'It's okay – I know who you are . . . who he is.'

'He told you?'

The woman shook her head. 'I guessed. Then he told me.'

'What did he tell you?'

The woman hesitated. 'Everything.'

Laura turned away from her – back to the drawings.

'That's how we met – at the art college. Then we realised we were neighbours.'

Laura didn't respond to this, but she was listening, and understood what it was the woman was telling her – out of what desire, she couldn't have said, but it wasn't cruelty – and that she'd somehow known all along.

'It meant more to me than it ever did to him – he never lied to me about that. He said it would never have happened if he'd been Bryan Deane still. He kept his distance.'

'By fucking you?' Laura said, sharply, taking a sip of tea and handing the glass back.

'Even then.' The woman stood, absorbed by the drawing, finishing the tea. 'He wasn't used to spending so much time alone. The nights were difficult, and he missed your daughter. He missed her a lot.' She hesitated. 'I had a son – he was eight when I left him behind. We had that in common – our missing children. We spent most of the time talking about our children. I think it was that and the loneliness more than anything. Sometimes it was very bad; I got worried about him.'

Laura's eyes skimmed the Polish woman's flat, not resting on anything – not really taking anything in as she tried to imagine Bryan here; their intimacy.

'I was waiting for you – out on the balcony today. I was worried when he didn't come back last night; I wanted to tell you.' The woman broke off. 'You know where he is,' she said suddenly. 'What are you going to do?'

Without saying anything, Laura turned and walked through the flat towards the door.

'What are you going to do?' the woman called out again.

Laura opened the door and stopped, turning to her. The air in the corridor outside was much colder, and damp smelling. 'What name did you use? What name did you call him by?'

'Tom. To me he was Tom. What are you going to do?'

'I'm phoning the police.'

The woman watched Laura run up the corridor to the staircase at the end. She stayed there listening to her shoes on the stairs, the regular clatter getting fainter and fainter as she neared ground level. Even fainter still, she heard the thud of the lobby door banging itself shut after Laura ran outside. She didn't hear anything after that, but she carried on waiting in the open doorway to her flat – feeling the cold now – for what, she didn't know.

Laura felt the belated nausea as she got into her car. Breathing in slowly, she tipped her head back and shut her eyes, waiting for it to pass. But it didn't. A second later, she was leaning out the car, vomiting over tarmac. Her head pounding, she saw that she'd splashed the side of the car parked next to her.

Searching in the door pockets, she found an old piece of tissue covered in lipstick prints and drank the remains of a cold latte pushed in the drinks holder. Then she stared up at the balconies lined one above the other, expecting to see the Polish woman – Tom Bowen's cure for loneliness – standing on her balcony, but she wasn't. Laura saw that she'd left the balcony doors to their flat open, but what did that matter any more? There was nothing left to steal up there.

Balking at the taste left in her mouth, she got out her mobile and dialled Laviolette's number.

Laviolette was sitting in the back of the ambulance parked in Armstrong Cresecent when Laura phoned. He was having the cut on his leg stitched.

'I know where Bryan is.'

Her voice was clear and steady – as if what she was saying no longer held any significance for her.

'Where?' Laviolette demanded, quietly.

'He's with Anna. Anna Faust. He's gone to her.'

Laviolette shut his eyes, and heard the paramedic who was stitching him up say, 'Only a few more to go,' under the impression that he was the cause of Laviolette's pain.

'You realise the implications of your telling me this?'

'I realise.'

'All the implications? I'm going to have to make arrests, Laura.'

'I realise.'

Laviolette's eyes remained shut. She didn't know what she was saying. How could any of them know the implications?

The nausea had passed and with it the headache as Laura, feeling calmer than she had in years, pulled out of the parking bay and drove towards the marina exit. As the barrier lifted and she checked for traffic on the main road, she failed to notice the white transit van pull up at the barrier behind her.

She hadn't noticed it earlier either, following her from Tynemouth to North Shields on the A189.

Jamie had sat in his van and watched her disappear inside the Ropemakers Building. Shortly after that he'd seen her appear on the balcony and start talking to a woman with purple hair standing smoking.

As he pulled out of the marina it occurred to him that at one point – a lot of years ago when they were children still – he thought Laura was going to lead him to himself. The least she could do now was lead him to his brother.

*

323

'Look at us,' Bryan said.

'Look at us,' Anna echoed, in her running clothes still, watching him, in his coat still – moving about the room taking in everything.

He stood gazing silently at the panorama for a moment before turning his back on it. 'Do they bother you?'

'What?'

'The wind turbines.'

'I like them. They make me feel watched over.'

He nodded, watching her; taking her in again – something he kept doing. 'You should have phoned me. I told Doreen to tell you.'

'She did.'

'I could have found you somewhere.'

'I like it here.'

'Always so independent. But then you wouldn't want to be beholden to anybody, would you – especially not me.'

She stood motionless behind the kitchen bench. 'I did phone,' she said at last. 'I phoned Tyneside Properties and asked to speak to you – then put the phone down. It's been sixteen years, Bryan. Sixteen years is too long to make a phone call about –'

'Real estate?'

'Yes.'

'So how much is this costing you?'

'I don't know.'

He shook his head then pointed to the drawing on the bench, saying, 'You got it. What did you think?'

She paused. 'I was relieved – hopeful. More than that.' He was standing close to her. 'I dream about you – often.' He lifted up her hands and pressed their palms together. 'I didn't want to believe you were dead.'

He studied their hands carefully. 'I was worried you might tell.'

'Who?'

'The police. The inspector.'

'Laviolette,' she said looking at him, but he didn't look at her; he kept his eyes on their hands, which were clasped now, mid-air.

He looked at her then, pulling away, drifted over to the bench where the photograph of him in Cephalonia was propped. 'Where did you get this from?'

'Martha. She gave it to me. She wanted me to keep a vigil.'

'Martha,' he said, keeping hold of the photo. 'Martha. God, Martha.'

He walked to the nearest sofa, collapsing onto it. 'What have I done?'

'Why did you do it Bryan?'

He sat with his legs apart, his elbows balanced on his knees, his head bent, staring down at the floor.

She sat down beside him.

'Are you happy?' he asked without looking at her.

'I don't know.'

'That means you're not.'

She thought about this. She'd often thought about it before, but now she had to give an answer because she wasn't asking it of herself. 'I'm happy with my life, I'm just not happy in it,' she said at last.

They sat there in silence for a while until Bryan said, 'D'you remember the fret – the day I disappeared?'

'I saw you disappear into it.'

He stood up again – standing limply in front of her, his arms hanging down. 'I was meant to meet Laura on the beach between here and Seaton Sluice, but then the fret came in and I just about made it to the rocks at St Mary's. The island was deserted because the tide was in. I pushed the kayak off the seaward side where the graves of the Russian sailors are, and waited for the tide to go in. When it was on the turn, I waded across the causeway and phoned Laura from the pay phone in the car park on the headland.

'When she eventually arrived, I got into the passenger seat and sat there, shaking. I couldn't stop. I turned to her and said, "Hold me," and she held me and I cried. The shock – of doing what we'd talked about.'

'Where did you go?'

'She drove me to the Haymarket and I got a bus up to Rothbury.'

'Why Rothbury?'

'D'you remember that place you used to camp when you and Laura were kids?'

Anna nodded.

'We often went there later. There was a hut in the woods. I lived there for a month or so. No CCTV; barely any roads; no mobile signal.' He paused. 'It was a long month. I thought a lot about meeting you that day – on the beach, the day I disappeared. I thought a lot about you. I thought –'

'What?'

'That you'd somehow know I hadn't really disappeared. That you'd come looking for me.' He walked over to the windows, watching the blades on the turbines turn. 'I couldn't believe it had actually worked – gone to plan. Laura was talking about the insurance money and selling the Marine Drive house; about moving to Uruguay – buying a house on the beach. She wouldn't stop talking, and I let her talk because I felt free, but I knew I wasn't going to do any of those things – I wasn't going to give up my freedom again.'

'Laura met you – in Uruguay.'

'It was meant to be a house hunting trip. I stayed on after she left.'

'Why Uruguay?'

'It's cheap. Sun. The sea –'

She stood up and crossed the room until she was standing beside him at the window. 'You've got the sea here.'

'Uruguay's a long way away.'

'From what?'

'Our old life. You.'

'I was never in your life.'

'Oh you were. Everything we've done – Laura and me – every decision we've made, we've made because of you.'

Ignoring this, Anna said, 'You travelled to Uruguay as Tom Bowen.'

'I liked being Tom Bowen. I was going to contact you, from Uruguay. I wanted you to join me in Punte del Este.'

'You wanted me to come to Uruguay?'

'Would you have come?'

When Anna didn't answer, he said, 'If you'd have come, I would have stayed. I wouldn't have come back here.'

'What about Martha?'

'We'd have found a way –'

Anna walked back into the middle of the room. 'Why are you still married? Normal people get divorced.'

'We talked about that. We talked about it a lot. The imminent divorce became a feature of our marriage.'

'I don't believe you. I don't believe any of this. Why now? It's been sixteen years, Bryan. You haven't contacted me in over sixteen years, and now – this. Whatever this is. I was pregnant when I left for university. I asked you what we were going to do and you told me – you were the one who told me – to get an abortion. So that's what I did, and I'm tired, Bryan. I'm tired of wondering what it would have been like, if I'd spent my life with you.'

She started to cry and he tried to take hold of her, but she wouldn't let him. 'What are you doing here?' she yelled. 'What the fuck are you doing here? You chose Laura.'

'I could give Laura the life she wanted. I didn't know where to start with you. I did it so that we'd have this – so that I could feel the way I felt that day, seeing you for the first time again after all these years, the way I still feel.

'You wanted to go. You didn't want to stay. I couldn't go with you. If you'd had the baby, you'd have stayed with me – you'd have ended up hating me and that would have destroyed me. I loved you too much to ask you to keep it.'

'You've got no idea what you asked me to give up.'

'You'd already left, Anna. You'd already left.'

'Well, I'm back now.'

They started to move towards each other.

Neither of them had seen Laura's car go past Roy, standing in the office doorway smoking again. They didn't see the car pull into the bay next to the yellow Capri, or Laura get out and look up at the apartment. They didn't hear her push open the front door, which Bryan hadn't thought to shut, and they were only dimly aware of footsteps on the stairs – of Laura herself in the room behind them taking in the scene she'd foretold would happen at some point in all their lives. Maybe not quite like this, but this was the scene that had haunted her all her married life.

A marriage she'd built from scratch, and it had been a grind from the beginning having Martha so young. She'd renounced romance for decades of life-threatening rows over spilt milk, and they'd survived – only to find Anna standing in the middle of their marriage now.

Laura had known the risks as soon as they started talking about faking Bryan's death. She'd known then that until he was pronounced officially dead, he was free . . . But the financial black hole they'd been in was threatening to swallow their marriage whole and the only way to hold onto to it was to give him up, but not to this – not to Anna.

'Don't touch him,' Laura said, automatically, staring from

one to the other. She was breathing heavily and shaking uncontrollably, but didn't care; no longer cared about anything. 'I want to see what she does –' Laura held onto the sofa, trying to get her breath back. 'I want to see what she does when she knows everything because I know you haven't told her everything.'

'Laura, he chose you. We were both pregnant at the same time.'

'I know – he told me. I got pregnant on purpose, and it worked, but only because he's a coward. He was terrified of what you'd think.'

Anna wasn't looking at Bryan any more, she was looking at Laura. 'About what?'

'Terrified that one day you'd find out.'

'About what?'

'Him killing Roger Laviolette.'

Anna carried on staring at her as Bryan took hold of Laura, pulling on her. She felt choked as she remembered finally who it was who'd let her out of the wash house that day – realised that she'd known all along, but somehow suppressed the memory.

It was Bryan who let her out. Jamie Deane locked her in that day – the day Roger Laviolette died – and Bryan let her out.

Then she remembered something else – that his left arm, stomach and some of his face had been covered in blood. The air in the wash house had been so full of blood she thought it was blood from the deer as he pushed past, but now – thinking about it pointedly, deliberately for the first time in years – she realised that Bryan had appeared in the doorway to the wash house already covered in blood, and that the reason he'd gone to the sink by the window was to wash it off.

'I thought he'd come to let me out, but he hadn't – he

didn't even see me. He was covered in blood – I forgot that,' she said, shivering.

The sky outside was becoming darker by the minute, but none of them made a move to switch on any lights.

Anna turned to Bryan. 'It was you. You killed him.'

'I knew,' Laura said, quietly. 'I've always known. I realised early on that romance depended on ignorance so I gave romance up. I loved him harder than anyone ever loved him in his life before. That's why he chose me; he chose me because I knew him. He loved you because you didn't. Life's not fair. If only, when you left, you'd given him up. I kept waiting to hear that you'd met someone, but you never did. You just kept waiting, and now he's chosen you and I can't live with that.'

Bryan was shaking her so hard that she could no longer talk.

'Stop it,' Anna shouted, attempting to pull them apart. 'Stop it!'

But they ignored her. Laura's eyes were fixed on Bryan – her body had gone slack. 'Finish it,' she said, 'just finish it now.'

Slamming her hands hard into Bryan's chest, Anna pushed him back until he hit the wall near the front door.

Laura stood motionless, watching them both as if they were no longer real. 'I phoned Laviolette. I told him you were alive. I told him you were here.'

Bryan stared at her. 'D'you realise what you've done? Do you realise everything that you've done?'

He turned, helpless, from Laura to Anna – who was staring out the window.

'Laviolette?'

She shook her head. 'Your brother – Jamie.'

The white transit van was parked at an angle across three bays.

*

Martha stood outside the school gates, jostled on all sides, looking for the now familiar white transit van. The road was chaotic – full of the usual coaches, cars, and streams of girls – but there was no sign of Jamie and his van. She didn't know what to do. He'd been there every day since September; he'd become habit – the drive home with him in the van something she relied on. She was his reason for getting up in the morning, that's what he told her; he said that getting out of bed when you had to was hard enough, but getting out when you didn't have to was even harder.

She crossed the road and sat down on the low brick wall circling the horse chestnut where she'd seen Bryan all those months ago, waiting. Today was a Thursday and on Thursdays they'd started going to the leisure pool at Whitley Bay because Martha was teaching Jamie to swim – or how not to drown, as she put it. They made a strange pair – the white sinewy, tattooed man with the shaved head, and the skinny, laughing girl – but the lifeguards had got used to them, looked out for them even, and made encouraging comments on Jamie's progress.

It had taken Martha a fortnight to get him to let go of the side, but now he was using a float with only one hand. They had a wave machine at the pool and a separate diving pool whose deep, narrow proportions and dark blue water terrified Jamie. The diving pool had an underwater window that Jamie stood shivering at as he watched Martha dive, waiting for her small body in its black school swim suit to cut through the liquid mass of blue. She would swim towards the window and put her hand against it – the flat palm an amphibious white against the glass, her face covered in goggles and an underwater smile that bubbles escaped from, the water around her full of her slow moving hair – until he banged on the glass, worried that she'd been under for too long. Then she would rise to the surface of the deep, narrow pool, breaking it with a spluttering laugh as she pushed her goggles up and swam to the steps.

She waited on the wall until half four then made her way slowly to the metro station.

The day felt suddenly all wrong – fathomless in the way it had the day her dad disappeared.

She got out at Whitley Bay and caught a bus going up the coastal road towards Blyth. It wasn't until she saw the line up of vast warehouses to her right that she realised she'd completely missed her stop. They were going past South Harbour on the outskirts of Blyth. She stayed on the bus as it made its way down Ridley Avenue, getting out on the edge of Ridley Park. She could walk to the Quayside from there – she hadn't seen Anna in a long time.


As Jamie shut the van door, he saw a man standing in the twelve-centimetre length of the wing mirror. The man was gaunt and had blond hair and looked nothing like he remembered his brother looking, and yet he knew – without a doubt – that the man was his younger brother, Bryan.

He stood momentarily inert with disbelief that the man in the mirror was a reflection of something real; half expecting, as he turned round – which he now did – to find the Quayside behind him empty.

It wasn't.

Bryan was still there – and he'd grown. He was no longer twelve centimetres tall, but well over six foot.

The two men were suspended somewhere between grief and panic.

In spite of everything, a brief joy – too instinctive to be suppressed – passed across both their faces. They were brothers, after all, and it had been a long time.

Then there were the memories; unbidden, but as impossible to suppress as the brief joy they'd both just experienced

– and so long forgotten they had no form as they fell shape-lessly between them on the Quayside where they stood.

Jamie remembered a silver stereo he used to have that he recorded songs on from the radio; a black and orange NCB jacket, which had only just been hung up on the back of the door and was swinging still . . . a pile of laundry on the bedroom floor and a woman's legs in tights and slippers standing beside it . . . sellotape covering the holes in the carpet . . . him grabbing a red tractor out of Bryan's hands, the tractor breaking and Bryan crying . . . a tea towel on top of a brown gas heater and the smell of the tea towel as it started to burn . . . a blue deck chair with a white rose motif on it, and their mother's perfume . . . not their mother, just her perfume, which was dusty and sweet smelling because it had been saved for too long, for a life that never happened, and gone off . . . she'd used it all up the day she died because she knew it was the last time she was ever going to wear it. The wash house – the washing out on the line in the garden; the garden itself – had been full of the smell of it. He'd smelt it in his dreams ever since, and it was the smell of depart-ure . . . unspeakable loss.

Jamie felt suddenly closer to this woman who was his mother than he ever had anybody. For the first time, he understood the creeping despair she must have felt when the one man capable of making her happy no longer had the time, energy or inclination to manufacture so much as a minute's worth of joy between them, forcing her to first wait then lose hope then go looking for it elsewhere.

She was a woman who loved to laugh; who felt that laughter was the best cure for the indignities life imposed. After the joy had gone out of the big things in life, she was happy to look for them in the little. It was after the joy went out of these as well that the despair set in. It was despair that sent her to Roger Laviolette, it had to be – that tight, airless man who was no match for his mother.

'I loved her too,' he said suddenly to Bryan, poised opposite him still – it was the first thing he'd said to him in twenty years.

Afterwards, he wasn't even sure he'd said the words out loud so he said them again. 'I loved her too.'

'Then why didn't you do it? I waited and waited for you to do something.' Bryan shifted position, distressed. 'It was an accident,' he finished helplessly. 'I just wanted to look at the house, that's all. I thought – I don't know – I wasn't even thinking about Roger Laviolette, I just wanted to see the place she'd gone to when she left us because part of me didn't believe it existed. I went round the back . . . then I saw him, the kitchen door was open. He was sitting at the table mending something. There was this patch of white skin at the back of his neck. It . . .' Bryan searched for the word; trying to articulate something not governed by reason, 'bothered me. A lot. D'you remember how things used to bother me? Like that time I went through your drawers and cut up all your T-shirts? Well, it was like that only much worse.

'There was a kid in a buggy beside him and I thought . . . I thought maybe it was his and her's. That's what I thought – without thinking. Of course it wasn't,' Bryan said – to himself – almost angry. 'But the things is, that man was whistling, Jamie. There he was, mending a radio, whistling and the sun was shining into the kitchen, and it was like nothing had happened; like none of it could ever have happened. I half thought that if I went home then, I'd find her there doing the same thing . . . whistling in the sunshine. But that wasn't true. So I picked up the radio and brought it down . . . on his head . . . hard. I kept on banging the radio on his head, and the kid was just staring at me.' Bryan

334

looked like he might laugh at this recollection. 'There was blood, and he was moaning, and the whole place smelt of white spirits. He'd been using it to clean the radio and I must have knocked it over because I remember him trying to right the empty bottle, but his hand wasn't working properly. I watched him stand up and go over to the cooker, and put the fucking kettle on or something and there was all this blood on his shoulders and running into his eyes and mouth. He'd stopped whistling by then, but he turned to me and said, 'Rachel's boy.'

Then the fire started on his hands and arms and he was screaming and by then the kid was screaming, and I tried to get the kid out the buggy but couldn't work the straps, so I just picked it up with him in it still and pushed it down the garden away from the house. I ran then. It was an accident – an accident, Jamie. I never would of done it if he hadn't been whistling . . .'

It was then that Jamie saw Laviolette, and called out instinctively – not his name, just a sound. He heard the sound fill the air, shocked.

They needed to run – Bryan and him – but Bryan was already running.

Jamie ran after him, trying to close the gap between them – and the gap was closing – yelling, 'Bryan!' as he swung his arm towards his brother's collar, hitting him on the side of the head and pulling him so forcefully towards him that Bryan lost balance and ended up trying to hold on.

Up close, Bryan saw the horrible brightness of Jamie's eyes – remembering now that they were blue – then they started to fall.

Jamie had the sensation of falling before they actually started to fall.

Holding onto each other as though they'd been wrestling like this for years, they carried on falling, anticipating a landing that never came as they fell over the edge of the Quayside into the sea.

Bryan, disorientated, couldn't hear anything any more – Jamie had hit him on the side of the head and he'd lost his hearing almost immediately then his leg got caught in the ropes belonging to one of the fishing trawlers and instead of landing, he carried on falling, hitting his head again on the side of the prow as he went down.

It was dark and cold, and he was bearing a great weight.

He'd heard his daughter's voice – he was sure – calling out, but not for him; for his brother. How did she know Jamie, and why was it that her calling his name out like that – which was enough to bring any man back to shore – left him, Bryan, with nothing? The love and intimacy of the past fifteen years – an intense, wrenching sort of love – became incoherent and meaningless.

He didn't think to struggle. He was no longer thinking at all . . . not even about Martha.

He was alone, and ceasing . . . he was nothing.

Just before hitting the water, Jamie heard voices – he thought he recognised Martha's – then the water closed over his head and he started to struggle to find a way out, quickly losing all sense of direction. He wanted, more than anything, to go up, but couldn't be sure where up was. There was no light and nothing to hold onto even though he had been holding onto something, he was sure, before falling. He pushed his arms through the water, but the only thing they came into contact with was more water.

Martha had seen her father and Jamie disappear over the edge. Without thinking, she'd thrown her bag to one side, yelling, 'He can't swim!'

336

'Martha!'

It was Anna's voice.

Turning round, she saw Anna running across the Quayside towards her. Her mother was there, just behind Anna, running as well, but not as fast – and Laviolette. Everybody was there. If only they would stop rushing about and stand still . . . they'd lost all sense of perspective, and with it their balance. They'd spent too long making happiness their goal when all they needed to do, was be. She'd tried showing them when she took the picture of Bryan in Cephalonia – that it didn't matter. It didn't matter that he was sad; it didn't have to mean anything. It was just sadness, for a moment – terrifying, beautiful, real and true. Why did it have to be anything more than that? Why couldn't they all just stop this rushing towards – what?

Turning her back on them and their shouting with relief, feeling suddenly calm and full, she jumped into the dark messy water. The sense of emptiness that had kept step with her all her life had gone. She loved everybody – Laviolette, Anna and her mother (even her mother) on the Quayside above, and Jamie and her father down here in the water.

When she broke the surface, the sea was washing noisily against the hulls of the trawlers moored there and the rigging on the masts sounded irate. She saw a head, briefly, about three metres away – then it disappeared beneath the surface. She swam instinctively towards it, hearing Anna's voice again, a long way away now.

Jamie flung out his arms, desperate to find something to hold onto, but there was nothing. After what felt like twenty years of falling, he wanted to land and come to a rest. Water was everywhere, rising above him, over him, entering him through every orifice it could find, filling him. His throat was burning and his eyes felt as though they were being pulled from their sockets. His insides were collapsing and he was still falling; it was like falling twice. If he didn't find something to hold onto, he'd carry on falling like this forever.

He had a short breathless memory of a girl in water, her hair moving around her and her costume black against white tiles. Tiles . . . the pool. His feet sought out the chipped edges of the pool's tiles and touched something . . . there was a girl in the water.

It was the hair – he thought it was Laura and tried to hold on. Then he remembered Laura had already tried to kill him once. Using her body to haul himself up and break the surface, he took in one last lungful of air before pulling her tightly to him and down with him this time.

Anna wrenched off her trainers – she took off her trousers as well, but left on her running top – as Laviolette, standing beside her, slipped awkwardly out of his coat and suit jacket.

Anna curled her toes over the edge of the Quayside. She could see what was happening and knew that if Martha managed to haul Jamie to the surface, he was going to struggle – uncontrollably – and probably drown her.

'Who are you going for?' Laviolette asked.

'Martha.'

Anna dived in at the same spot Martha had – it was a good spot – cleared the trawlers and their moorings, and surfaced, trying to swallow as little water as possible, which was difficult with waves this high. She saw them breaking now over the north harbour wall, crashing in from the open sea, then turned and swam back towards the trawlers, her arms already aching – as Jamie and Martha broke the surface, reaching them at the same time as Laviolette.

As Jamie pulled Martha back under, she found herself momentarily alone in the water with him.

'Get Martha away!' he yelled.

338

They went under.

Below the surface there was only panic and silent struggle – any sense of individuality was lost. All Anna could make out was a mass of limbs, darkly clothed, indistinct, constantly moving. It felt as though they weren't attached to anything; that there was nothing completely human in the water with her. In the end, it was Martha's hair she managed to get hold of as the current brought it billowing slowly towards her. She took hold of as much of it as she could, filling her hands and kicking hard, pulling Martha backwards through the water towards her.

She swam with her round the stern of a trawler – *Flora's Fancy*, that had volunteered its services on the police search for Bryan after he disappeared. She watched Martha haul herself up the ladder on the harbour wall and onto the Quayside where she knelt, vomiting and choking as Laviolette struggled to keep Jamie above the surface long enough for him to grasp onto the ship's ropes.

Then Anna turned and scanned the harbour's water, unsteady now with three-foot waves, but there was no sign of Bryan Deane.

Anna surfaced then dived, surfaced then dived, frustrated that the waves made it impossible to check near the trawlers themselves where he'd gone down. After a while she noticed the surface of the whole sea was creeping down the harbour wall. The tide was going out and the current had a strong pull – she could feel it now – Bryan could have been carried out to sea. The waves were cresting and hitting the north harbour wall with such force on the side facing the open sea, it made a mockery of the man-made defences she was now starting to swim towards.

The water felt thicker and greener near the harbour wall and it took her five attempts to haul herself up the ladder. She had to use her arms to protect her head as the waves pushed her up against the wall and they pulled her back with such force that she didn't have time to grasp the rungs properly and kept losing her grip. Twice, she managed to hold on, but the waves breaking over the harbour wall, filling the sky above with water, pushed her back under.

Eventually, somehow managing to time it, she climbed exhausted to the top of the ladder, clung on as another wave washed over the wall then pushed herself up, got to her feet and ran. She had three minutes before the next big wave crested to run the length of the wall to where the old coal staithes were.

She got to the wooden staithes as the final wave caught her, drenching her back, and lay along the wet moss-covered wood staring up at the wind turbines as the indifferent blades continued to turn.

Her ears still full of the sea, she turned and saw the group of tiny figures on the Quayside, human in their attitudes but barely recognisable across what seemed like a vast stretch of churning water. For a moment she couldn't remember who they were, and didn't care. She saw her yellow Capri and the white transit van and behind them the windows of her apartment – and half expected to see herself.

That's where she should have been – behind glass, looking out – not lying stretched and shivering along a sea defence. She'd been in the water too long, looking for somebody who was already drowned. Her attention was taken again by the wind turbines, white against the grey sky – as she attempted to guess the immense intentions of these immense machines who knew nothing about Bryan Deane or the last twenty years of all their lives.

# 20

It wasn't the sight of Mary herself that made Anna cry, it was the small plastic bracelet that had been clipped round her wrist on admittance, with the name written on a piece of paper: MARY FAUST. She sat now with her eyes shut, listening to Mary's breathing, and the machinery around her and, further away, like an undercurrent she knew she was going to have to face sooner or later, the rest of the world – shuffling, scuffling; waiting. After a while, she picked out a set of footsteps emerging from the undercurrent, approaching steadily with the light tread of hesitation. She knew who she wanted it to be.

It was him.

They smiled at each other.

'How's she doing?' he whispered.

'You don't have to whisper,' she said.

'I know,' he replied, whispering still.

They smiled at each other again then Anna turned and contemplated Mary. 'She was Bryan's alibi – that's what was on the tape you never played me.'

'The tape that's gone missing,' he pointed out.

'She told me – she told me it all, I just wasn't listening properly. She said – love hangs on strange threads.'

He nodded, looking from Mary to Anna then said, quietly, 'I want you to stay.'

'You're still whispering.'

Laviolette coughed, attempting to pitch his voice, and said again, 'I want you to stay.'

'Nobody's ever asked me to stay before.'

Even though they'd been talking for the past five minutes – it was as if the silence had suddenly broken.

# Acknowledgements

A heartfelt thank you, as always, to my agent Clare Alexander . . . and to my editor, Katie Espiner, *haute couture* tailors both.

I would also like to thank Sgt Kelly Martin of the Durham Constabulary for the patience she has shown in answering my many questions about policing.

This book would not have been possible without the faces, places and stories that peopled my childhood.